The Necklace of Goddess Athena

by

Effrosyni Moschoudi

© 2011 Effrosyni Moschoudi. All rights reserved

Effrosyni Moschoudi asserts the moral right to be identified as the author of this work.

Cover design: © 2013 Deborah Mansfield. All rights reserved.

This eBook is licensed for the personal enjoyment of the original purchaser only. This eBook may not be resold or given away to other people. If you would like to share this book with another person, please purchase an additional copy for each recipient. If you are reading this eBook and did not purchase it, or if it was not granted to you directly by the author for your use only, then please purchase your own copy. Thank you for respecting the hard work of this author.

This is a work of fiction. Names, characters, places, and incidents either are the products of the author's imagination or are used fictitiously, and any resemblance to locales, events, business establishments, or actual persons - living or dead - is entirely coincidental.

Effrosyni Moschoudi

To my parents, Fotis and Ioanna, and my sister, Antigone.

Prologue

Efimios stood at the edge of the precipice. Down below, the sea raged with tremendous force. A howling wind caused his long robes to billow like broken sails on a ship that's lost in a storm. He opened his hand and stared odiously at the necklace. The salty bite of the wind stung his eyes but funnily enough, that gave him comfort. He couldn't have chosen a better place for what he was about to do.

"Athena, almighty Pallada! Protectress of the city of Athens, hear me!" he cried out with all his might and yet, his voice was barely audible over the deafening crash of the waves on the rocks below. As he stretched out his hand, the sky erupted with lightning and loud crashes of thunder. The pendant was now hidden from view inside his fist, but its golden chain was swirling in the wind, whipping his hand. Undeterred and not in the slightest afraid, he looked up to the rumbling heavens, his teeth clenched, his eyes alight with fury.

"Here in my hand," he yelled, "I hold the necklace that you entrusted me with when I was only a child. For the services I have offered you devotedly for the protection of Athens, you have repaid me with cruelty! I could perhaps understand it if you were to punish only me but my son? What has Phevos ever done to you? He is just a boy! How could you do this to him?"

Efimios lowered his hand to take one last look at the necklace. It glowed brilliantly as lightning bolts ripped the sky but its beauty was lost upon him.

"Do you forget so easily?" he burst out, his face contorted with wild exasperation. "I have been at your command for so long! And this is how you thank me? Did you think that following your orders has been easy for me? Because of you, I belonged nowhere and to no one, having anything but a normal life... but since you chose to repay me in this manner, surely you cannot expect me to serve you any longer! Indeed, this is where it all ends! Your wretched cave in the Acropolis hill will never be used again! I have made sure of that! As for your precious necklace, this evil noose you had me wear around my neck, I have minded it for you long enough!"

With a forceful throw, the necklace of Goddess Athena disappeared in the vastness of the foamy sea. A myriad of thunderbolts flashed all around Efimios as he started to walk away from the precipice. He quickened his pace, and his face brightened with the promise of a smile. His heart felt lighter already. Without a shadow of a doubt, he knew one day his suffering would end.

Chapter 1

Eleven years later

First, there was this tremendous roar. Everything around them shook with force and then, a blinding light surrounded them as they were taken through a cyclone of ear-piercing sounds.

Phevos held the hand of his sister Daphne inside the forceful vortex of Time. Neither of them knew where they were headed as they swirled frightened beyond description, their bodies surrendered to the powerful whirlwind. Their eyes were tightly shut to the blinding flashes of light, and a sound that resembled a sweeping tornado tortured their ears. In the twenty years of his life, Phevos could never have imagined the intensity of the experience.

Although still captured in this unprecedented storm of light and sound, he managed to recall random pieces from his father's stories. Efimios, his father and teacher, had described to him hundreds of times his experience of the Passage through Time, but Phevos had never expected there would come a day when he would experience it himself and at that, in such a different way.

Gasping with panic, he realized his sister's hand had slipped away from his. He started calling out her name, but through the roar he couldn't even hear himself speak. All at once, there was darkness and a soothing silence and next thing he knew, he was lying on the ground.

A strong buzz still sounded in his ears. It took a few moments to fade as he opened his eyes and tried to gather his wits. His body felt numb at first, but he managed to sit up somehow and look around him. The ground felt wet under him and the air smelt of grass. The moon shone high above on a starry sky with a velvet light that was ample, allowing him to inspect his surroundings quite easily. He was in an orchard. There were trees, plants and bushes all around him. Panicking, he realized he was alone.

"Daphne!" Phevos looked around, his expression frantic. His sister was only nineteen. Up until a few minutes ago, she was living a secluded life within the safe walls of their rich estate house and its beautiful gardens. He knew well that adventure did not suit her disposition.

"Over here!" came a wavering voice from the bushes to his left. Fearing the worst, he sprang to his feet. His attire, a white shirt and jeans, although perfectly suitable for a young man his age, would have been baffling to anyone who might have known where he had just come from. Both garments were heavily stained with mud. He ignored a slight dizziness that hit his temples when he stood up and ran jumping over the bushes, his shoulder-length blond hair waving in the air like a lion's mane.

Sat by a lemon tree, Daphne was holding her head with one hand. When she looked up, her face betrayed her distress. Her eyes were huge, childlike. Her auburn hair fell on her shoulders in rich curls. Her skin was perfectly white; her facial features flawless and delicate. She looked like a fine porcelain doll despite wearing just a simple, rather unimaginative sleeveless dress in deep blue. However, the stunning jewels she wore on her ears and around her neck befitted perfectly her rare beauty.

"Almighty Zeus! What has happened? Are you all right?" asked Phevos breathlessly as he knelt before her. Willing himself to calm down, he used the cuff of his sleeve to wipe the blood from a minor wound on her temple. It was only a scratch, but Phevos felt guilty all the same. He had tried all he could to hold her hand through the Passage but he had somehow allowed it to slip away. What if he hadn't been able to find her at all? He shuddered at the very thought. Daphne grimaced when he pressed the fabric on her temple again, but then she smiled faintly.

"Don't worry," she said, "it is nothing... I just slipped and fell. I must have hit my head on a rock." As her voice trailed off, her face contorted with discomfort. Her temples were pounding with an increasingly strong headache.

"It'll be all right," he mumbled, not knowing what else to say. He was still quite confused. How had this happened? Why hadn't their father chosen to come along? Phevos did think the scratch was nothing to worry about but felt uneasy all the same to know he could no longer ensure his sister's safety in this unknown world. The thought overwhelmed him, and he made a silent plea to the Gods for protection.

"Come here sweet Sister, try to stand up!" he encouraged her, as he pulled her up gently. Cautiously, he attempted to let go of her, but she faltered on her feet and grabbed his waist to steady herself.

"I do not think I can walk Phevos... I feel rather dizzy," she said with regret. At that exact moment, they both heard frantic barking. When they turned to look, they saw a small-sized dog standing a few feet before them, making an incredibly loud noise for his size. Phevos and Daphne were stunned by this encounter but not frightened. The dog didn't look fierce. No doubt he just felt protective of his territory.

His fearless bark compared to his small size seemed rather comical to them, and they would have grinned, amused, had their situation not been grave. In all their misery, the last thing they needed was a yappy dog who could attract strangers to them, even trouble.

***

Ksenia sighed. Manos's room was messy as usual. As much as she loved her little brother and enjoyed taking care of him, she wished she could trade one of his many good points for his unprecedented disregard for tidiness.

At the age of twelve, the only things that interested him were computers and pc games. A few items of clothing were lying messily on the armchair, and Ksenia knew she'd have to lift them one by one if she were to ensure her washing wouldn't include any items that didn't belong there.

Today, the 'catch' was again rather rich: a mutated warrior, a T-Rex, and a half-eaten pack of biscuits. There were scattered magazines on the bed and underneath it, she could see two pairs of shoes and scattered socks lying messily on the floor turned inside out. She wrinkled her nose with disapproval and picked the socks up, adding them to the pile on her hands.

As she turned to go, she noticed the pc screen on the desk. A screensaver she hadn't seen before displayed a series of stunning underwater pictures. Intrigued, she abandoned the clothes on the armchair and approached the monitor to take a closer look. Although she didn't have her own pc, at the university where she studied Business Administration she had plenty of opportunity to use them. She was quite computer literate as you would expect from a nineteen-year-old, but her little brother was already a bit of an expert. She didn't mind that he spent hours staring at a screen at home, although she'd prefer that he spent less time indoors and more out on the street, playing with other children.

Manos had expressed a passion for computers from a very young age. Three years earlier, after harassing her unstoppably for weeks to buy him a specific one he wanted, he'd finally got his wish and had delved into pc use with the dexterity and dedication of a teenager. She supervised his Internet use of course and felt proud of him for not just using it for fun, but also to study for school. Ksenia gave the mouse a gentle nudge to reveal the program running on the pc. It looked like Manos was on the Internet again, downloading freeware games.

"What are you doing here?" came the abrupt interruption from the door. The dark-haired boy that stood there had his hands on his hips in an inquiring manner, but his face revealed no trace of irritation.

"Busted!" Ksenia giggled raising both hands. She picked up the messy heap of clothes from the armchair and turned to face him again. "Actually, I came in here to find you and instead, I found these." She put out her arms and pulled a face of mock indignation.

Manos rolled his eyes. "If you save me from this talk, I'm willing to forget you were spying in here! How's that?" he offered with a crooked smile.

"Sounds good to me!" Ksenia laughed as she walked past him. "And just to show you what a multi-talented spy I am, I'm going to go in there now and make you pasta for tonight, all right?" Smirking, she pointed to the kitchen across the hall.

"Great, I'm starving!" Manos rubbed his tummy, as he turned around to follow his sister. "Oh! I'd better feed Odysseus. He must be hungry too by now."

Ksenia rolled her eyes. "That's for sure! I wonder why he's not barking to remind us."

The kitchen felt warm. The big table that reminded Ksenia of happy dinners with her parents was set with a white tablecloth. On one corner, there were neat piles of freshly ironed clothes. Thick curtains of flowery patterns hid the view to the orchard from the window. Ksenia placed the dirty clothes in the wash and put away the ironing board while Manos opened a dog food can and went out the kitchen door to feed their pet.

The young girl looked at the round clock on the wall. The time was eight p.m. and this surprised her although she followed the same pattern every Saturday. On weekdays, having to attend classes at the university and then to help out Mrs. Sofia at the family guesthouse, she never had time to do house chores. Luckily she managed to do it all on Saturdays. She didn't mind that it took her all day to finish, as long as her Sundays remained her own to do as she pleased.

In the past eleven years since their parents' mysterious disappearance, Ksenia and Manos had no other family but each other. Sunday was their special day, which they always spent together having fun. If they chose to stay at home, they'd watch TV or play good old-fashioned board games. Sometimes they'd go out instead, but it never had to be anything fancy. After all, simple things often provide greater pleasure.

Every week they would decide together what they'd like to do for the coming Sunday. This was something that their parents used to practice and now the children carried on the family tradition. Ksenia had experienced countless Sunday pleasures in the company of her parents. Her memories were crystal clear despite the fact she couldn't have been older than eight years old at the time. She remembered for example having ice cream cones together in the summer. Under the scorching sun, they'd wind up giggling madly as they licked melted chocolate off their fingers.

Sometimes they would sit in a park feeding and petting the stray cats. Even today, the purr of a cat reminded Ksenia of her father. He was a bit of a cat-whisperer, in the sense that he could tame even the wildest creature, getting even the biggest males to lie belly up and purr loudly in response to his gentle petting. Yet, amongst all the simple Sunday pleasures that they often sought as a family, there were some that were quite exceptional. The fact that you had to wait for months on end for these, only made them even more special. Those were truly unique, unforgettable experiences.

There were nights in August for instance, when the view of the full moon from the top of the Acropolis hill or from a high terrace could steal your breath away. The moon would slide over the clouds like a seducing princess dressed in her finest, silvery silk. And the sky would be full of stars that trembled feebly, like servants that bowed before her. During those nights under the light of the August full moon, the city of Athens would become an enchanted kingdom that slept lazily under the sweet light of its ethereal mistress.

Those nights had the power to make you feel strong and weak at the same time, because the soul could then fly all the way to the moon. In those moments, you inevitably felt that if you were to whisper a wish, the stars would surely hear you. And that is what Ksenia as a child strongly believed on those special nights. These are beliefs that once entered in the soul of a child, can never be uprooted from it, no matter what blows life may have in store. And so, the power of faith was safely kept inside her chest, where her soul remained forever gazing at a starry sky with the scent of basil lingering in the air.

Ksenia smiled melancholically. She'd just returned to the kitchen after putting away the ironed clothes. She walked to the window to peer outside, but it was far too dark to make anything out. Her mind wandered again. Manos was only a baby when their parents disappeared, so he had no memories of them. Ksenia on the other hand, remembered so much... One Sunday, they had all returned home wet to the bone. A sudden rain had caught them by surprise, as they were walking lazily around the lanes of Plaka, the old quarter of Athens where Ksenia still lived. Despite being wet, they were laughing madly when they got home. Their spirits were high on the smell of the soil and the aroma of honeysuckle and jasmine coming from every front yard.

This particular memory often led Ksenia back to the same lanes. She often picked flowers during her walks there, like her mother used to. She'd put them in the vase that still stood on the windowsill in the kitchen and Ksenia now did that too. She felt it was her duty to pass on her memories to her brother and to keep them alive for their parents' sake.

Tenderly, her fingers caressed the heads of two pink carnations that stood rather lonesome inside the vase. Ksenia would never give up on her parents. She always hoped that one day they would return and explain everything. She knew in her heart they were alive, and that was enough to her as to keep believing.

She turned her back to the window and tried to focus her mind on happier thoughts. Her brother would walk in any moment, and she didn't want him to see the sorrow in her eyes. For the next morning, they had planned a walk to the Pillars of Olympian Zeus through the lanes of Plaka. Then, they'd visit a computer & games exhibition at the nearby Zappeion Hall. This would be Manos's main treat for Sunday morning.

Afterwards, her contribution to the plan for the day would take them to the adjoining National Garden for a leisurely stroll. This was her favorite place in the whole of Athens. She couldn't wait to sit on a bench before the duck pond. She could see the sunlight now, dancing with the thick foliage of the trees, fluttering above her. Soon, it would reach down to caress her face again. It would fuse with the children's laughter behind her closed eyelids, lifting her out of herself for a while.

The sound of the door opening startled her out of her reverie.

"Ksenia, Odysseus is not outside. I can't find him!" Manos looked ruddy-cheeked, and his facial features were pinched with anxiety.

Ksenia gave an exasperated sigh. "Not again! Hang on; I'll just get our jackets. Let's try to find him before he causes chaos for yet another time," she said, leaving the kitchen hurriedly. Five minutes later, they were outside in the cold, March night. Manos led the way holding a flashlight. Odysseus hadn't got his name by chance. He had been named after the leading character of the Odyssey for a reason. His roaming adventures every now and then had become legendary in their street and had caused them embarrassment with the neighbors more than once.

Somehow, Odysseus managed to find small openings in the wire fencing of the orchard despite their best efforts to mend them. During many of his getaways, he had trampled on the neighbors' vegetable patches. It had been mortifying to apologize to their annoyed neighbors who delivered him back, announcing in every detail the damage to their produce.

But Ksenia and Manos loved their pet despite all that. They had raised him from a tiny puppy, and he was now a sprightly three-year-old. To them, he was the most faithful friend and guard. They couldn't get enough of petting him while looking at his clever little eyes that gazed back at them with evident adoration. Whatever frustration his antics caused them to feel, it never lasted long. Of course, they were now livid with him once again. They both had their minds set on telling him off once they caught him, especially as they were out on this cold, miserable night because of him, roaming in the semidarkness while their stomachs grumbled with hunger.

The orchard was inaccessible in many parts, as nobody had tended to it for a good while. It was a stretch of almost two acres. Wire fencing on either side marked the boundaries between the property and neighboring gardens of fellow Plaka inhabitants. On the back, the land reached up to the foot of the Acropolis hill where a massive rock face stood vertically. Ksenia and Manos felt grateful for the border on this side of their property for two reasons: firstly, the Parthenon towered above their land offering them a stunning view to one of the greatest miracles of the ancient world. Secondly and more trivially, the rock face meant they had one less side to worry about when it came to their pet's Houdini-style escapes.

Tonight, the Parthenon stood proud as always despite its demise over the ages. The moonlight surrounded it with a misty, surreal light. Ksenia looked up for a few moments to marvel at it and then continued to follow Manos, treading carefully, her eyes glued to the rough ground. There were dips and bushes everywhere. Ksenia stubbed her toe on a rocky bump and let out a small cry. Her delicate leather shoes didn't offer much support for trekking in such inhospitable grounds in the dark. She assured her brother, who came to her rescue, that she was all right and then silently, scolded herself for her procrastination. She was forever putting off finding someone to tend to the orchard and to sort out this unacceptable mess.

And then they heard Odysseus. They exchanged wild glances and broke to a sprint, following the frantic noise that their pet made. It sounded like it was coming from the rock face. Little did they care now about the mud that splattered on their clothes, as they ran carelessly through murky pits of rainwater.

Chapter 2

"Don't worry Daphne!" said Phevos. His sister had grown distressed by the loud barking and her knees gave in again. Phevos set her down on the ground gently. Standing in front of her and facing the dog, he tried to think of the best way to silence him, without hurting him of course. Perhaps if he were to speak to him gently, he might calm down. Odysseus kept barking tirelessly without moving an inch from his spot. He obviously took himself seriously as a guard, and attempted to make as much noise as possible in order to raise the alarm for his masters.

"Odysseus! Where are you? Come here, Odysseus!" Ksenia and Manos kept calling out. When they first appeared from behind the trees, the dog turned to look at them only momentarily and then turned his stare back to the strangers. Triumphantly, he raised himself on his hind legs, now that his deed was done. His owners ran to him and petted him, and all this time he didn't stop staring at the strangers, growling and barking now even louder than before.

Phevos and Daphne became even more stunned by this new encounter, this time with people. Ksenia and Manos were quite alarmed to find the strangers on their land. They stood for a few moments there, speechless. Daphne raised her arms to her brother. He helped her up and she clung to him like her life depended on it. For a few seconds, they both felt the same instinctive urge to run away, but as he stood looking at the seemingly kind strangers, Phevos thought better of it and reconsidered.

Ksenia pulled her brother close to her placing a protective hand on his shoulder. Manos ordered the dog to stop, and it obeyed at once. Odysseus stood at Manos's feet staring silently at the strangers, but with his senses fully alert still. His dark eyes glinted with tension like two pieces of burning coal. Ksenia dared two steps in the direction of the others, leaving her brother behind. Although they had trespassed on their property, somehow she didn't feel threatened by them. There was this expression of distress on the girl's face that made her sympathize with her immediately.

"Hello, what are you doing here?" Ksenia's voice was calm.

Phevos extended one hand toward her, exposing the palm of his hand in a plea. "We do apologize, Miss! We mean no harm, I do assure you!" he said, guessing they were on private property. "We never meant to trespass on your land. We are travelers and we got lost. We will go now. Please forgive us for the disturbance..." he added, feeling embarrassed, yet trying to smile.

Ksenia was relieved by the apologetic manner of the stranger, but the whole thing puzzled her. She was sure there were no openings in the fencing and their front gate that led to the street was locked. She couldn't see how they could have ended up here by mistake. She moved closer to them, and the generous moonlight allowed her then to see Daphne's face better. She had noticed before that the girl kept placing her hand on the side of her head, and she had wondered why.

"Oh my God, you're hurt!" she exclaimed and approached them hurriedly to examine the girl's wound. Manos followed her with Odysseus, who was now wagging his tail. It was clear to everyone now that the trespassers presented no threat after all. What's more, they seemed to be in a difficult position.

"How are you feeling? Are you in pain?" Ksenia asked Daphne as she took a closer look at her temple. It was no longer bleeding, but the skin looked angry.

"My head hurts…. I feel dizzy…" said Daphne faintly. Her lips were trembling. This was all too much for her. On top of everything else, she had now started to shiver. Her dress befitted a warm summer's day, not a cold wintry night.

"How did you get hurt?' enquired Ksenia, her face the picture of sympathy.

"She slipped!" answered Phevos truthfully although that was only half the truth if any. Ksenia looked at Daphne and felt overwhelmed with sympathy for her. She noticed her beautiful long hair that was tangled and her dress that was covered in mud. However, there was this air of nobleness about her, something aristocratic, almost regal. Her moves seemed ethereal as she ran her delicate long fingers through her hair, in full awareness of her unruly state in public, clearly not a common experience for her.

"Please, come with me!" piped up Ksenia with a decidedness that surprised her. Phevos stared at her questioningly in response. In his arms, his sister looked ready to faint.

"Come!" Ksenia repeated. "Let me take care of that scratch properly at our home. She needs some rest. Do come," she encouraged them again, placing one arm around the girl.

Phevos faltered still, squeezing Daphne closer to him. She was still shivering and looked so frail, but he was afraid. He was afraid to let her get into this new world that wasn't familiar to them. The first step seemed to be the hardest.

"Please, let me help!" pleaded Ksenia. "Don't you see that she needs to be somewhere warm and comfortable?"

"I.... I don't know if it would be right Miss," he faltered, "perhaps if you were to lead us to your stables? We would be fine there. No need to enter your home..." he suggested, unbeknown to him in his distress that in this different time, what he had just proposed sounded rather odd.

Manos laughed impulsively, driven by the light-heartedness of his young age. "Stables? This is Plaka, the center of Athens! There are no stables here, man!" he piped up, laughing loudly at the ridiculous thought.

"Athens...." whispered Phevos exchanging a quick glance with his sister as the comforting word confirmed their hope and eased the angst inside them somewhat. Instinctively, they both looked up behind them then for the first time. The Parthenon Temple greeted them back in dignified silence.

Completely unaware of what was going on in their heads, Ksenia turned to glare at Manos, and he lowered his gaze, realizing his reaction had been inappropriate. The strangers seemed to be in a difficult situation of some kind, and the girl needed help. Perhaps it wasn't such a good idea to laugh at them. Of course, Ksenia had also thought that the young man's reference to a stable was odd, but she didn't show it. She imagined they were perhaps tourists from another part of the country. Maybe they lived in a rural area where farmers own horses or sheep, and perhaps it would be natural to them to assume that a stable might exist here by the orchard. As always, Ksenia gave everyone the benefit of the doubt. With a kindly look on her face, she turned to Phevos again.

"I'm afraid that we don't have a stable. But don't worry; there's no bother at all. Please follow us home. The young lady needs to rest. You'll both be warm and safe there, please come!" she encouraged them again, beckoning to them to follow.

Phevos heard the word 'safe' coming from her lips, and it soothed his troubled mind. Her eyes seemed gentle, and when she started walking away, motioning for him to follow, somehow he found himself eager to accept. He picked up Daphne in his arms and took that first step that now seemed easy.

A minute later, Ksenia opened the door and stepped aside to let Phevos get in the kitchen first. Daphne still shivered in his arms, but at least she hadn't fainted.

"Manos, please feed Odysseus," she asked her brother. The boy nodded and took the dog back out to eat from the plate he'd left by the door.

"Now please come with me," she said gently, motioning to the siblings, who had remained frozen at the threshold. Despite her dizziness, Daphne was marveling at everything around her. At the patterned curtains, the stainless steel appliances and pans, the ticking clock on the wall.

Everything stunned her. But most of all, she couldn't believe the strong, electric light that shone from the ceiling. Phevos was looking around equally dazzled. How miraculous seemed all the machines in this room, how extraordinary were the wooden cupboards and furniture!

Ksenia turned to find them both looking around in awe and thought again that this pair seemed rather strange indeed. But that didn't make her change her mind or falter in her intention. If anything, it reinforced her previous guess that perhaps they were farmers from a rural area and that their homes were rather minimal, if not primitive; although she couldn't imagine that kind of house existing anywhere in Greece these days.

"Please, this way!" she urged them and Phevos followed. Ksenia turned the light on in her parents' bedroom. It was only next-door to the kitchen, just a couple of steps down the tiny hallway that led to the front door. The room was no longer used, but Ksenia always kept it tidy in anticipation of her parents' return. This is why she wasn't even using this room for herself. In time, she had chosen to redecorate the room upstairs that her parents used to rent, and that now was her own space.

Phevos faltered at the door with Daphne in his arms, as they both gazed with admiration around the room. The double bed was made with white sheets and a thick monochrome blanket. Satin curtains hung from the rail above the window. Next to it, there was a dresser with a mirror where among other girlish things, miniature perfume bottles circled a crystal jewellery case. On the walls, there were framed paintings of mermaids, boats with open white sails, and fishing villages built on the surf. It was quite obvious that Ksenia's parents loved the sea. The glass bowl that brimmed with seashells of various shapes also bore witness to that. It stood on a small driftwood table by the door, safely storing treasured findings from leisurely strolls on the beach.

"Do come in," said Ksenia, beckoning to them to approach the bed. She went ahead of them to the armchair to pick up a bed throw. She spread it on top of the bedding hastily and didn't mind knowing it would be stained with the mud all over Daphne's dress. "There you go! Let her lie here and have some rest!" she urged Phevos.

He set his sister gently on the woolen throw, and Daphne shut her eyes with relief for a few moments. Her hair framed her beautiful face the way an expensive frame sets off a rare work of art. As her head sank into the pillow, she felt as if she were melting in the warmth of the room and the fragrance from the linen. The feeling was incredible. It brought to her weary mind the memory of springtime back home when the gardens were in full bloom. With a dreamy expression on her face, she opened her eyes again.

Ksenia was seated on her bedside now with one hand on Daphne's forehead. It felt really cold, but that was no surprise after seeing how the girl had been shivering out there all this time.

Phevos stood rather awkwardly close by, watching the kind-hearted stranger tend to his sister. He still felt lost, totally unable to grasp how all this madness could have happened so quickly. Less than an hour ago, he was still happy and carefree in his far away world that funnily enough, involved this very same city. He looked down at the clothes he was wearing. They felt so strange to him. Instinctively, his fingers traced the golden chain of the necklace through the fabric of his shirt. His father had put it around his neck only a few minutes ago. Daphne's sweet voice brought him back to the overwhelming present.

"Thank you," she said to Ksenia.

"You're welcome. I'll just bring what's necessary to tend to the wound. I'll be back in just a moment." Ksenia gave a little smile and moved to go.

"Miss, I am truly indebted to you," said Phevos approaching her. "My sister and I are most grateful...." he added and then faltered, unable to find the right words to express his appreciation.

"Not at all, I've done nothing really. I'm sure a bit of a lie down will do her good." Ksenia looked into his eyes. He seemed to her a lot taller all of a sudden, and she also noticed his eyes were deep blue, like the open seas depicted on the surrounding walls.

"I beg to differ! If it hadn't been for you Miss, I really don't know... I cannot imagine..." His voice trailed off and once again, he failed to find the suitable words. As if the shock of coming into this new world wasn't enough, he also had to strive to speak Modern Greek and it was hard.

His father had always insisted on him and Daphne speaking this strange and awkwardly simplified version of Greek over the years. Phevos often complained, as he couldn't understand the necessity of this, but now of course, it had finally made perfect sense to him. He had come to the conclusion that his father, somehow, had always known this would happen one day. Phevos felt gratitude for his father's shrewd wisdom and for the countless hours he'd spent teaching his children this strange version of Greek.

As he now spoke to this beautiful girl with the kind face, Phevos struggled to remember the right words. He also tried to conceal the fact that he didn't understand all that she was saying. He made a great effort to decipher the meaning of the odd word that was unknown to him by using the context where possible.

"Don't worry," said Ksenia placing a hand on his arm reassuringly. He looked quite distressed. "Your sister will be fine in a while, I'm sure. When she feels better I can call a taxi to take you to your hotel. Is it nearby? You mentioned you're travelers. You're tourists in our city, right?" she enquired amicably.

Phevos kept nodding as she was speaking, especially through the unknown words, trying to look calm and collected. He had no idea how to answer her questions, so he just nodded in a non-committal manner. He was afraid he might give the wrong answer and thus let her see he didn't understand her strange language. Most of all, he dreaded being exposed for what he truly was: an outcast, someone who didn't belong to her world.

"You're tourists then?" Ksenia insisted but not out of sheer curiosity. Concern was now growing fast inside her for both her unexpected guests.

"Yes, yes indeed Miss," he said, glancing at her quickly with a wrinkled brow before he returned his gaze to the thick carpet under his feet. "Thank you, Miss. No need to do anything else for us. We will be on our way soon..." he added, unsure if that was indeed a valid answer to all she had asked. He hoped she wouldn't think of him rude or ungrateful in any way. Ksenia patted his arm, causing him to look up. To his relief, she gave him a warm smile and left the room.

With a deep sigh, he turned on his heels and rushed to his sister's side. In response to his warm hand that tenderly caressed her hair, Daphne opened her eyes.

"Do not worry, sweet Sister! You rest now; it will be all right." He tried to soothe her, yet his eyes twinkled fervently, betraying his own distress.

"Phevos, these people are kind and their house is truly exquisite, but I wonder, what are we doing here? Should we not go?" she asked, although she was aware he knew no better than her how to act in this world and where to go next. The touch of his warm hand, as it rested on her forehead, felt like balsam in her weary mind.

"My dear Daphne, let us see how you feel first. Rest a while! Besides, you know well that since these kind people invited us in their home, we cannot possibly refuse them. Their invitation is an honor to Ksenios Zeus, patron of hospitality toward strangers. Do rest now and do not worry about anything else. When you feel better, we shall depart."

Daphne chewed her lower lip. "And where shall we go?" Her almond-shaped eyes seemed alight with worry.

"I trust that Goddess Athena will light the way for us to go forth. Like she has always done for Father when he used to fare across the centuries to protect our city."

"But how do you know Father sent us here on an errand for Athena?"

"I do not, Sister. I have no idea why he has sent us here. I am only assuming! What do *you* think just happened?"

Daphne shook her head. "I do not know! But Father does nothing without a reason. And he seemed to expect all this unlike us. He seemed sure and purposeful with his actions..."

"I agree. But whatever it is we are supposed to do, if Father thinks we can manage it, then we can!"

"But what does he want us to do? He never said anything!"

"He did say something Daphne, remember? He said to look out for the signs!"

"Oh, I do not know..." Daphne exhaled heavily.

"Do not worry, Sister! We need to keep our faith now. Think of this: would Father have sent us here had he been unsure in the slightest about our safety? Truly, the only thing that worries me is your condition. I blame myself! I should never have let go of your hand... you are hurt and it's my fault," he lamented.

"What nonsense is this, precious Brother? How could this be your doing? And besides, I feel better already!" she encouraged him with a smile. "I rather think the dizziness was due to my distress at the time, not because of this silly little wound. Do you not think so?" She cocked her eye at him and gave an easy smile.

Phevos touched the velvet skin by her wound and thought his sister did look better already after all. Her alabaster face was indeed tinted again by the rosy pink of her cheeks as she smiled.

Daphne's eyes widened as she guessed her brother agreed. "And how can I not feel better? This has to be the softest bed in the whole wide world!" The wide grin on her face made her look like a little girl.

"Oh, yes indeed!" he replied. "I have never seen a house as magnificent as this. It is exactly the way Father has always described them to be. He always said the Athenians of this age have all the commodities of the Gods!"

"Truly. How happy they must all be!"

"We do not know that, Daphne. Remember what Father always says? 'Happiness stems not from what you own but from what you are grateful that you own'!"

"Yes Phevos, that is what Father says, but—"

"So you agree it is possible to have wealth and commodities and still feel poor and unhappy? Others may be the richest and happiest people in the world having very little indeed!"

"Well Phevos, that may well be, but our young hostess has so much kindness! Surely that cannot go amiss where it comes to the pursuit of happiness!"

"You are so right, Daphne. She and the little boy must be truly blessed I imagine."

"Did you see how easily they trusted us and invited us in? What a virtue for modern Greeks, who do not even pay respects to Ksenios Zeus!"

"Careful, Sister," Phevos shushed her suddenly, "I believe the damsel is approaching!"

"Really, Brother," she teased in a whisper, "do try to remember to use the correct words instead of the ones from our time!"

"What did I say?"

"You said 'damsel' silly! The right word is—"

"I know, I know, it's 'girl'!" he interrupted her, and Daphne started to giggle. She was always better in Modern Greek than he was. She often teased him about it. At that moment, the warmth of the room combined with her feeling better, contributed to this mad giggle that threatened to make them look like idiots, if not impostors in the eyes of their kind hostess.

"Oh, stop it already you naughty little fox!" he teased her, putting his hand playfully over her mouth. He managed to withdraw it quickly enough, before Ksenia entered the room. The girl's face lit up when she found Daphne smiling as she lay on the bed, looking at her brother with an amused expression on her face.

"Goodness gracious! You're right as rain!" Ksenia smiled with relief and approached the bed, placing a bottle of iodine and a pack of cotton balls on the side table. In her hand, she held a cotton ball soaked with alcohol solution.

"Yes, I must admit I feel a lot better now, Miss! I still have a headache, but the dizziness seems to be gone now. I think it was your bed that made me better. It is so soft, it is unbelievable!"

"Oh, I'm so relieved the dizziness was nothing serious. You had us all worried a bit out there!"

"I know, I am sorry," Daphne said, shrugging with embarrassment.

"Oh, don't apologize," Ksenia gave a little dismissive wave. "Anyway, here is something to treat the wound. I normally stock up on a disinfectant for cuts and grazes, but I only seem to have clear alcohol at the moment."

"That is all right, Miss, thank you," replied Daphne.

"My name is Ksenia. What's yours?" she asked amicably as she sat on the bed, about to apply the cotton ball on the wound.

"It is Daphne. And my brother's name is Phev—" The girl stopped mid-sentence, and jerked her head away from Ksenia's hand, letting out a single shrill of pain. "Almighty Zeus, that burns!" she uttered in shock. The discomfort of the sensation had overcome her too suddenly to allow her to choose her words carefully the way she had managed so far.

Ksenia looked at her, bewildered. Had she heard right? Had the girl just mentioned Zeus? Standing just a step away from them, Phevos panicked and tried to think of something to say to make things right again. He had heard from his father about the alcohol solution that modern Greeks use. Efimios had described how it stung. Phevos thought perhaps his sister had forgotten this mention, or maybe the burn she'd felt had been too strong to bear all the same.

"Oh, come on Daphne!" he said, interrupting the stunned silence between the two young women while he tried to fake non-pretence as much as possible. Taking the cotton ball gently from Ksenia's hands, he tried to sound like the whole thing amused him. "Really now, Daphne! What harm could clear alcohol possibly do to you?"

His sister stared back at him numbly with a mortified expression on her face. Phevos patted the wound for just a moment with the cotton ball and then out of nowhere, got the notion that if he blew on it, it would be helpful. He couldn't tell where the idea had come from, but he felt grateful all the same when to his surprise, it turned out it had actually worked. The alcohol solution had stung her again but blowing on it afterwards had eased the expression of discomfort on her face.

"All right, all right now, thanks," Daphne whispered with impatience for a change of subject. She felt terribly embarrassed by her exaggerated reaction.

Ksenia remained speechless as she sat on the side of the bed. Her mind was now wandering to the young man's previous mention to stables. She thought of the girl's childish innocence that was evident in her manner like an almost visible aura. It was the manner of both, as a matter of fact, that had something odd about it. It wasn't so much the way they looked. It was rather their choice of words. They used many dated ones from the Katharevousa Greek that is an older version of the modern language. The Katharevousa Greek hosted a staggering amount of ancient Greek words and phrases. It started to fade away during the 1970's, gradually giving its place to Modern Greek across all fields of oral and written expression.

Ksenia determined it was indeed the dated words that they used in the odd sentence, which gave them this aristocratic, regal air. And now the mention of an Olympian God had completed the mystery that surrounded her two intriguing guests. Their eccentricity had provoked her curiosity. She wondered if there were still villages on the foot of mount Olympus perhaps, where people may still refer to Zeus in the local vernacular. Not believers of course; yet, maybe this was some kind of local idiom that had survived over the centuries. The notion amused her enormously and excited her vivid imagination further. Perhaps they did hail from some tiny, God-forsaken village perched on mount Olympus and that was their local dialect. Or perhaps they were referring to Zeus between themselves as a private joke. Could they just be strange characters from the outskirts of Attica with an odd sense of humor and nothing intriguing about them after all?

Despite her curiosity, Ksenia reacted tactfully again. Her upbringing did not permit her to ask any relevant questions. She took the bottle of iodine from the bedside table and inwardly hoped Daphne wouldn't react strangely again. She thought it best to prepare her somewhat this time, just to be sure.

"Right! Now the iodine and we're done. It will color your skin for a while, but it won't burn, I promise. And it will disinfect the wound perfectly. Is that okay?" asked Ksenia with a warm smile as she held the cotton ball ready for application.

"Yes, yes of course," replied Daphne in a whisper, still embarrassed from before. She knew Ksenia was only trying to help and felt relieved to discover she hadn't lied either. The iodine hadn't stung at all.

"Right, that's done! And now get some more rest, okay?" Ksenia stood up. She collected the items she had left at the bedside table and smiled at her guests amicably.

"Thank you," the two siblings replied in one voice.

"Not at all! You're most welcome to stay here overnight if you wish," she informed them impulsively without really thinking. "You can stay in this room. I'm sorry to say there's only this double bed for both of you though," she added regretfully, which was ridiculous seeing what she was proposing. Not many people would offer hospitality to total strangers. But there was honesty and kindness on their faces. She felt strongly she could trust them, that they could never mean any harm despite the awkward mystery that so intrigued her about them. She did hesitate for a bit as she stood by the door, but then she met Phevos's eyes again and her tiny doubts melted in the clarity of his eyes.

"Thank you a million times, Ksenia," he said, his voice thick with emotion, as he walked up to her by the door. He knew they had no choice but to accept her invitation. "How fortunate for us to stumble upon a hostess who bears the name of Ksenios Zeus! Truly a befitting name to someone as kind and hospitable as you, Ksenia!"

"Oh yes, Zeus! He's the patron of hospitality, right? You know, 'Ksenia' is short for 'Polyxeni' actually, but that's nice anyway, thanks," she said with a tittering laugh. She didn't care by now that Zeus was so widely used in their vocabulary. All caution had been thrown to the wind, along with her curiosity. All she saw now was the blue sea from her mother's paintings, raging in his eyes.

Phevos was completely unaware of the effect he had on her, although he was equally enchanted by her presence. "Well Ksenia, regardless of the origin of your name, to me you will always be the epitome of hospitality!" he said with an easy smile. "This room befits a king and a queen, let alone two common mortals like my sister and me. May God repay you for your kindness," he added, consciously omitting the word 'Zeus' from his wish in order to match her religious beliefs.

"Well, thank you," Ksenia replied with a giggle, feeling overwhelmed. How peculiar was the way he expressed himself verbally! His words conveyed the feeling that what he said, came straight from the heart. And he spoke so politely, like a prince. There was something regal in his manner too, in the solemn pauses between his sentences, and the gentle way that he gestured with his hands as he spoke. And how deeply religious he must be! People don't often mention God these days. God has become a taboo subject that you only refer to when heartache takes over your life. The rest of the time the idea of God lies dormant in people's minds, like a pack of medication in a dark drawer.

From the bed, Daphne watched amused. Trying to conceal her smile, she had placed one hand surreptitiously over her mouth. Her brother hardly ever spoke to young ladies. She had never seen him act like this around a girl before. She felt terribly pleased to have found one more thing to tease him about.

Ksenia looked away from Phevos to glimpse at her wristwatch. It was almost half past nine.

As if on cue, Manos appeared at the door. "Ksenia, when will we eat? I'm starving!"

"Of course, Manos!" she said, feeling a prick of guilt inside for neglecting her brother. Where had the time gone? "I'm so sorry, my sweetheart. I'll go make some quick sandwiches now for all of us. We should go to bed as early as possible. Our guests must be awfully tired," she said patting his head tenderly, and then turned her attention to Daphne and Phevos again. The more she looked at them, the more trust and sympathy they instilled in her.

Manos was taken aback. Why had his sister referred to these strangers as their guests? What on earth was she thinking? Had she gone mad? Didn't she watch the evening news? She had actually invited two total strangers to stay for the night? His face was now carrying an expression of surprise without the slightest effort to conceal it. Stunned, he stared at the strangers for a few seconds while his sister engaged into some kind of small talk with them again. The girl was lying down on his parents' bed, and he didn't like that at all. But truth be said, she had looked really bad out there in the cold, shivering like that, unable to stand. Perhaps she needed the rest. And she looked harmless enough. Manos darted his eyes at Phevos next, inspecting him thoroughly. He thought he looked like a tramp in those stained clothes, but he had a kind face, and he smiled a lot. Robbers and killers don't often go around with girls who bleed from their heads, do they? Perhaps he was harmless too after all. Manos turned on his heels and silently left the room.

"Well, I'd better go and prepare those sandwiches. You must be hungry," Ksenia said.

"To be honest, we are," Phevos admitted laughing comfortably. The warmth in her eyes had melted away all the worry inside him. He looked at his sister, who was nodding in agreement from the pillow. Ksenia made to go but hesitated again at the door. "Would you like to have a shower after your meal?" she asked Phevos.

His warm smile froze, and his eyes darted to the floor. He had no idea what she had just asked, and he started scratching his head awkwardly, trying to think, trying to guess what she could have possibly meant.

Being perceptive, Ksenia knew immediately what was going on. He couldn't possibly have understood what she asked and falter so much. If he didn't want a shower, he would simply have declined by now. Feeling sympathy growing in her heart for him all the more, she rushed to his rescue tactfully. "I think a shower would do you good. Nothing better than hot water and soap at the end of a tiring day, right?" she asked, nodding encouragingly.

Phevos looked up from the thick carpet and grinned at her with evident relief. "Thank you Ksenia! Indeed, that would be marvelous!"

"I still don't know your name," she smiled with the preposterous, sudden realization. Imagine inviting someone to use your shower whose name you don't even know.

"Of course, I do apologize! My name is Phevos. Delighted to make your acquaintance!" he said, offering his hand, relieved she hadn't felt estranged enough by their odd behavior to kick them out.

Twenty minutes later, Phevos and Manos were sitting at the table exchanging awkward glances, as Ksenia served the meal. It was a large bowl of salad, a smaller one brimming with chips and also, individual plates of omelet sandwiches with feta cheese and oregano. She invited them to start eating and then left them briefly to take to Daphne her dinner. She helped her sit up on the bed, then she plumped up the pillows on her back and placed a tray on her lap. Other than a sandwich, chips and salad, it contained also a warm glass of milk and a pill that she advised her to take afterwards for the headache.

Daphne smiled gratefully as she watched her leave the room to join the others for dinner. When she finished her meal, Ksenia returned there again to take away the tray and to say goodnight before she turned out the light. As Daphne lay in the dark waiting for her brother to come in after his shower, she watched as ghostly beams of moonlight crept through the half-closed window shutters. They toyed with the darkness of the room, reaching out to the opposite wall where they danced with the delicate shadow of the young olive tree that stood guard outside the window.

As she bore witness to this mesmerizing spectacle with the scent of flowers still emanating from the bed linen, Daphne wished again that her kind-hearted hosts would always be grateful for all the riches they had, for that would always guarantee them happiness according to her father. At the thought of Efimios, a single tear rolled down her cheek and then, ever so softly, she surrendered to sleep.

Phevos stood before the tall mirror in the bathroom. He had just enjoyed a hot shower and had found it easy to operate the strange taps. His father had described to him time and time again in graphic detail, everyday life in this modern world. This meant Phevos could identify many of the strange items he now saw around him, like the toothbrushes on the sink, the hairdryer that rested on the shelf, and the radiator by the door where towels were hung neatly. He looked around him some more and felt pleased with himself for remembering his father's stories so well as to be able to identify so much now. The recognition of everything he saw came so easily to him that it almost felt like he knew all this from before and he thanked his father silently again, for his endless storytelling.

His own eyes looked back at him from the mirror admiring the second set of strange clothes he'd been given to wear today. Ksenia had left them for him on the washing machine. They belonged to her father. Black cotton slacks, a brown sweater and woolen socks. They had all felt wonderfully soft when he put them on. A strange word was written across the front of the sweater, and he tilted his head as he tried to decipher it from the mirror image. The word was in Latin characters, but he didn't know what it meant despite him being proficient in Latin. The reason was that it wasn't a Latin word but an English one, the name of a British seaside town where Ksenia's parents had once spent a week's holiday.

Clueless, he pulled a face of dignified resignation and turned around. He picked up his dirty clothes and placed them in the washing machine as Ksenia had previously asked him. He had been mystified by her request, but once again she had helped him out by pointing to the machine. Phevos was well aware by now that she had realized he didn't understand everything she said, and he was grateful for her tactfulness to explain eagerly without asking further questions.

As soon as he entered the kitchen, Ksenia walked up to him with a smile. She was pleased to see the clothes had fitted him well, except for the sleeves of the sweater that seemed to be slightly too short on him. Before dinner, she had also given Daphne a nightdress of hers to sleep in. It had been a tad too long for her, but other than that, it had been fine.

Manos had already gone to bed, and Ksenia stifled a yawn as she switched off the kitchen light. When she said goodnight from the bottom of the staircase, Phevos thanked her one last time. He waited until she entered her bedroom upstairs, and then switched off the light in the hallway.

Aided by the moonbeams that still danced with the olive tree shadow on the wall, he found his way to the bed in the semidarkness. His sister slept soundly beside him, and he sighed with relief that at least for now, she was safe. Under the heavy duvet, his troubled mind surrendered to the warmth and to a restful sleep. Quite unexpectedly, on that same night, he was granted the first of many signs to come.

Chapter 3

The morning sunlight filtered through the satin curtains and bounced off the crystal lampshade on the bedside table. From there, iridescent beams reached the opposite wall, chasing each other like a bunch of joyful children dressed in all the colors of the rainbow. Phevos opened his eyes and panic kicked in as a first reaction to the odd surroundings. With a single jerk from his muscled body, he sat up in shock, sending the side of the duvet flying into the air. A split second later, realization hit him and he covered his face with his hands. When he looked up again to stare blankly at the iridescent colors on the opposite wall, an expression of worry wrinkled his face.

He had had an odd dream the previous night. It was about Goddess Athena. He had never dreamt of her before, so he thought this was obviously a sign. She had spoken to him with soothing words. He could not remember what they were, but he had a vivid recollection of the sweetness in her voice. She wasn't wearing a suit of armour, the way he would have expected her to. Instead, she had looked almost fragile, like a fairy tale princess, standing tall and proud in a long silky dress that accentuated her slender figure.

It was sunny in the dream and her dark, long hair flowed wildly in the breeze. She started to speak to him softly, but he couldn't understand what she was saying and then a storm broke out. There was thunder and lightning and a heavy rainfall and Phevos could no longer hear her voice. And then, through the storm, he finally heard her speak, and she said this: 'Remember my sister Artemis, the huntress! A good hunter knows where to seek refuge. I am going to find one. I command you to come and find me!' With those words she had disappeared and that was the end of the dream.

Daphne yawned lazily and sat up with a sleepy expression on her face. She placed her hand on her brother's arm, worried to find him lost in contemplation. Phevos turned to look at her and tried to smile, although his mind was still engaged in deep thought, trying to interpret the dream. He didn't know the reason why his father was no longer at Athena's command. Nonetheless, the young man worshipped her for the honor she had once offered his father to act as her servant and as the guardian of the city. This is what made him think Athena was perhaps the reason why he was there. He also hoped she would lead him to fulfill a certain purpose; just like she used to direct his father in the past during his secret assignments.

"Well, how did you sleep young lady? And more importantly, how are you feeling today?" he asked his sister with a concentrated effort to look amused. As he beamed at her then, although he did feel relieved he wasn't all alone in this unknown new world, he thought he would be feeling less afraid if she weren't here. If instead, she were safe with their father in the world where they belonged.

"Well, I slept wonderfully, thank you!" she replied with a grin that lit up her sleepy eyes. Her hair was tousled. Silky, auburn curls sprang untidily on her cheeks and shoulders, as she spoke enthusiastically. "I swear this bed could resurrect the dead. It is *that* miraculous!" she exaggerated, and they both laughed merrily for a few moments, forgetting everything else.

Phevos stopped laughing abruptly, when it occurred to him he had no idea what the time was. If it was very early, he hoped they hadn't woken their hosts. Guessing his thought, his sister pointed to the antique clock on his bedside table. They had both used clocks and watches many times in the past, as their father had brought home quite a few during his travels when he was still a young man. It was half past eight.

"I wonder if they are awake," he said, as he touched his sister's face gently, examining the wound. The red mark from the iodine was still there on her temple.

"Do not worry, dear Brother. It does not hurt. I am fine now."

"I am glad," he whispered with a solemn look on his face.

"What do we do now, Phevos? Where do we go today?" she asked, and the smile faded from her face too. Although she knew he had no answers for her this time, asking her older brother made her feel better all the same. Throughout her life, he had always made everything better for her. She trusted him blindly because of that.

"I do not know, precious Sister… but let us have faith. Father gave me his necklace for a reason. We just have to wait to find out what it is," he said, as he watched his sister get up and walk to the window.

She pulled the thin curtains to one side and immediately, bright sunlight warmed her face. "Oh what blessed light! And look at this gorgeous garden outside!" she said gratefully. As she peeked through the half-closed shutters, she continued recounting morning blessings, describing to Phevos all she could see past the young, olive tree outside.

"Here, let me do this for you!" said Phevos, approaching to open the windowpane. As soon as the shutters were open too, the morning light entered the room like a welcomed guest with happy news. They both stood at the open window, admiring the wild flowers and the herb bushes along the path on the side of the house. The fragrance of rosemary and mint entered the room wafted by the crisp morning air, and Daphne smiled again as she approached the dresser with the mirror. Phevos watched her as his mind wandered again to his dream about Athena.

"Divine Aphrodite, what mess is this!" she exclaimed before the mirror, lifting up comically in her fingertips a couple of her silky, auburn curls. "Look at me, just look at me!" she said to her brother, wrinkling her nose.

In response, he burst out laughing with her girlish vanity and the absurdity of it all. Regardless of everything else, that was all she had found to complain about.

"You girls! There! Take that and comb your hair if you like." Still laughing, he pointed at the big brush on the dresser.

"Do you really think I should? Won't our hosts mind?" she asked, picking up the brush reluctantly.

"They have done so much for us Daphne. I do not think they will mind you using their brush, honestly!"

"I guess you are right," she agreed happily and smiled to herself in the mirror as the comb started to slide through her long hair, the curls springing into life one by one.

When she finished, Phevos spoke to her about his dream, and she was delighted to hear about it. They both shared the same affection for the Goddess whom their father once served and so, they both found solace in the belief that she was protecting and directing them on this unexpected adventure. They couldn't understand what the message was though. What did she mean when she asked Phevos to find her at her refuge? Maybe that made no sense now, but they both knew it was a sign and so, they believed that soon enough, they would understand.

There was a faint knock at the door, and Daphne stood up to answer it. Her nightdress was too long for her and to avoid falling over, she lifted the hem as she walked.

Despite the comical scene, as he watched her, Phevos thought how ethereal she looked, and in his mind he saw her again like the little girl she once was, when they used to play in the gardens of their estate. He still remembered how her hair shone with the golden color of honey under the sun. It was flowing in the wind tied in ribbons as she ran, her laughter echoing like the tinkle of fine crystal, like the musical sound of the river that flows gently down the stream. During the time they had spent in their gardens as children, he'd promised himself countless times he'd always protect his beautiful, fragile little sister from harm. Once again, he made silently the same promise.

Ksenia smiled from the door. She was still dressed in her pajamas. Her dark, brown hair was short with a fringe that had grown too long and tickled her eyelashes. With a delicate movement from her fingers, she swept the long strands from her big blue eyes while making a mental note to visit the hairdresser's soon. Phevos stood up and smiled cheerfully as she approached.

"Good morning to you!" she said to her guests, beaming at Phevos for a few more moments than is customary before turning her attention to his sister. "How are you today, Daphne?" she asked breezily, resting a hand on the girl's shoulder.

"Good morning Ksenia. I am fine, thanks to your generous hospitality."

"Indeed, we are much obliged to you. If we could have our clothes back please, we should be ready to go now," said Phevos. Although he was grateful, he felt they had imposed on their kind hosts too much. He thought it best to leave as soon as possible, before the strange and growing fondness he felt toward Ksenia made it even harder. Besides, he and Daphne were on a mission. Sooner or later, they would have to leave.

"Please, no need to rush! Your clothes have been washed and hung to dry overnight on top of the radiator. By the time you've had some breakfast, they'll have been ironed and ready for you."

"Please Ksenia, there is no need to—" Phevos tried to protest.

"I'm not listening! Unless you want to tell me what you prefer to drink. Coffee or tea perhaps?" She gave an obliging smile.

"All right, a glass of milk please. This would be fine for my sister too, thank you," Phevos replied and Daphne nodded her assent with a smile.

"Milk it is then! Manos and I haven't had anything yet either, so if you'd like to come to the kitchen, we can all have breakfast together."

"Of course, let me come and help you," offered Daphne. When the girls left the room, Phevos walked up to the mirror and glanced at his reflection again in the beautiful clothes he'd been given. Outside the window, the ground was still damp after last night's rainfall. The small olive tree swayed rhythmically to the breeze, as if signaling a grateful good morning to the warming sun.

As Phevos walked back to his side of the bed, the thick carpet felt pleasantly soft under his bare feet. He put on the slippers that Ksenia had also provided for him and with a determined look on his face, paced out of the room feeling ready to experience his first full day in this modern world. Somehow, he felt prepared and unafraid to leave this house with his sister. His first priority would be to seek refuge just like Goddess Athena had urged him to do in the dream. Then in time, he'd follow the signs as his father had advised him. This had been the only thing he'd said before they parted, and Phevos was determined to keep his eyes and ears open, in order not to fail his father, in order to recognize all the signs as they come.

Phevos found everyone sat together in the kitchen. The little radio on the counter played a happy tune, and Manos was engaged in conversation with Daphne as he showed her the glossy pages of a magazine. Daphne browsed in amazement through the colorful display of pictures and thought how remarkable all the strange figures looked. It was a magazine that featured a wide range of PC games. Daphne tried to conceal the feeling of awe that consumed her as she turned each page. Until now, she'd never seen paper so smooth and colorful, and she marveled at the imagination of the artist who had created these images. They all seemed mind-blowing to her. Every now and then, she would utter an exclamation of surprise, or she'd nod happily as Manos described the basic storyline of his favorite games. Of course, she only pretended to understand, as she couldn't possibly fathom words like 'nuclear explosion', 'galactic journey' or 'zombie'.

Ksenia watched them in silence as she enjoyed a cup of filtered coffee and only spoke once to remind her brother that his cocoa drink was getting cold in his mug. Manos didn't talk in length with many people, and she was pleased this rare opportunity had arisen for him to come out of his shell for a bit, casting aside his shyness for once in order to share with someone his passion for games.

Phevos sat beside Ksenia. For the last minute, he'd also been watching Daphne and Manos in silence while sipping milk from his glass. Ksenia had placed a tray of warm mini-croissants on the table and she urged her guests to have another. Both of them obliged her eagerly, enjoying another of the tiny desserts that melted in the mouth softly, releasing the warm hazelnut filling, sweeter than honey, on the tongue.

Ksenia commented on the sunny weather as she watched her guests enjoy the confectionery with evident contentment. She sipped her coffee while feeling her curiosity about them grow even more inside her. Secretly, she was hoping to see them again after their departure. The strange feeling of familiarity she had felt toward them the previous night resurfaced as she looked at Daphne. It took her a few moments to place it and then, to her surprise, she realized that somehow, quite absurdly, the young girl reminded her of her mother.

Maybe it was the jewellery that Daphne was wearing, the heavy long earrings in particular. Ksenia had vivid memories of her parents getting ready to go out for the evening to the theatre or for a meal when she was still very little. Before leaving, her mother used to hold her and kiss her goodnight, and then she'd leave her in the trusted hands of her best friend Anna. During those goodbyes that Ksenia remembered so well, her mother had looked just like Daphne did now. Her face was gentle and full of joy, framed by sparkling jewellery on her ears and neck. And little Ksenia would cling to her tightly, inhaling her perfume as her mother held her close. It was a comforting scent; it was precious to her, almost holy. And when her mother kissed her and let her go, Ksenia would look up and she'd see nothing but the sparkle of gold and diamonds behind her teary eyes.

Ksenia had never liked to part with her mother. And now, this young girl had come unexpectedly into her life to bring back the feeling of being with her. It had been the only connection with her mother—albeit remote and unreasonable—that she'd experienced for so long, only to have to part with it again. Understandably, she felt unwilling even more so now to let Daphne go, to let both of them go as a matter of fact.

For totally different reasons, she was just as unwilling to accept the possibility she wouldn't see Phevos again either. The look in his eyes had stirred feelings in her she'd never known before. Someone who grows up while having to deal with such a loss, someone who is responsible for a small child without even being his mother, surely cannot have the luxury of romantic love. Or so she thought until now, until this funny beating started in her heart. This frantic rhythm that peaked every time his eyes rested on hers.

"Are you staying in our city for a few days? Is your hotel nearby?" Ksenia tried to sound casual as she placed her coffee cup on the saucer. She hoped that if only she could arrange to see them again, it would be easier for her when they left the house. Oh how she wished goodbyes didn't make her so miserable!

"Um.... actually, we are not staying anywhere in particular at the moment," answered Phevos. It didn't feel right to him to start producing lies. That wouldn't be honorable considering what Ksenia had done for them. Phevos looked at his sister, who had now finished her milk and was gazing back at him silently.

She smiled to her brother and decided to contribute to the conversation somewhat in order to take off him part of the burden that she saw in his eyes. "Indeed, as you know we are travelers. Tourists!" she smiled, uttering the strange word Ksenia had mentioned the previous night. "We arrived at the city last night. We had a little walk around and we lost our way. Then you found us on your land—"

"Oh! You arrived here at Monastiraki station? Was it a long journey from home if I may ask?" interrupted Ksenia surprising herself. Her eagerness to know more about her guests bordered on tactlessness, but it was irresistible to her.

Daphne bit her lip, and her eyes sought refuge to the colorful magazine that still lay before her on the table.

"Yes, we took the train from the port of Pireas... after a long boat journey," Phevos lied, "we intended to find a hotel for the night, but as my sister said, we got lost. Then she slipped and fell and well, you know the rest!" he added swallowing hard. Sweat prickled his forehead and pangs of guilt tortured him inside for repaying Ksenia's kindness with lies. How else were they to explain their situation though? And who would believe the truth?

"But, what about luggage?" enquired Ksenia.

"Luggage?" asked Phevos, frowning at the unknown word.

"You know! Suitcases, trolley bags, your belongings! You didn't have any with you?" Ksenia wasn't even attempting to conceal her curiosity. As she finally got to unravel the mystery about them, the excitement was becoming so intense that she had no regard for her manners any more and no idea of the discomfort that her protruding questions were causing them.

"Yes indeed... we did have one large suitcase between us but... it got stolen!" Phevos replied surrendering to the realization that lying was just inevitable. The truth was out of the question so this left them with no other choice. All he could do is try to lie as little as possible.

"Wow, that's terrible!" Manos interrupted enthusiastically. Until then, he'd been listening in silence without being particularly interested, but what he had just heard had excited his boyish imagination that yearned for adventure. As a rule, he wasn't interested in conversations among adults, and he hardly ever spoke unless spoken to. But somehow, the bout of bad luck that these two strangers seemed to attract upon them had made him interested enough as to engage in the conversation despite his usual shyness. When they all turned to look at him though, that shyness promptly returned forcing him to lower his gaze and to bite his lower lip in an instinctive retreat back to his comfortable shell of silence.

"Yes it is terrible," intervened Daphne with a sigh, giving her brother a fleeting look that conveyed to him, her own feelings of guilt. The knot in her throat made it hard for her to speak, but she didn't want her brother to have to lie on his own. "It was stolen on the train that we took from the port. It was crowded in there and we never noticed," she added. Thankfully, her father's detailed descriptions of all things of this age included the itinerary of the old surface railway line that still runs across central Athens, linking the port of Pireas to the city's northern suburbs. Neither Phevos nor Daphne could ever have imagined their father's stories would come in so useful one day and at that, for resorting to lies. But as they say, the cause justifies the means and telling the truth was not an option.

"Oh I'm so sorry!" said Ksenia sympathetically. And then, her eyes lit up with a wonderful idea. So wonderful actually, that she felt amazed she hadn't thought to ask them sooner. "You know, we have a family business of room rentals close by. It's on our street, literally just two steps away. It's a small, traditional guesthouse. Nothing fancy, but it's clean and hospitable. Would you like me to show it to you?

Perhaps you'd like to stay there?" she asked, looking at them eagerly.

Daphne's face lit up. She turned to look at Phevos, and her eyes begged him to accept. Ksenia's offer meant they wouldn't have to roam the city aimlessly. It seemed to her like a godsend, something they ought not to refuse.

"Ksenia, your offer is very tempting," said Phevos politely, "thank you, but we must decline."

"But why, Phevos?" piped up Daphne before Ksenia had time to express her own dismay. Daphne smiled to Ksenia and Manos awkwardly, hoping her brother hadn't caused them offence. She immediately noticed how Ksenia's face dropped, how serious she now looked, almost upset.

"Daphne," Phevos said as he turned to his sister, "do you forget that all our money was…inside the suitcase?" he asked her with a meaningful stare. Secretly, Phevos wished he could give a positive answer to Ksenia. But Athena had asked him in the dream to get out there and find her. Not to stay in one place idle, un-seeking. He would have to roam the city with Daphne looking for a sign that would explain the dream. It could be miles before they might find something that made sense. They had no time to lose. By sunset, they would need to have some cash for food and shelter. He wouldn't allow himself to subject his sister to an overnight stay outdoors, not even for one night.

"Excuse me…." faltered Ksenia as she treaded carefully with her words, "I hate to intervene in a discussion between you on a subject as sensitive as your financial state, but you see, fate has brought you on our doorstep and as fellow human beings, we have the obligation to help you out. Don't worry about payment in advance. None of our guests give us down payments anyway!"

"Don't they?" asked Phevos, surprised.

"Of course not!" answered Ksenia, hopeful now she could convince him. "They settle their bills upon departure. And I don't even need to see identification for you two. You both have honest faces, so there!" she joked with a huge grin.

"Oh, that's great Ksenia! Thank you for your trust," replied Daphne with relief, and then threw her brother a glance full of hope.

Phevos had bent his head in deep thought. When he looked up again, his eyes searched Ksenia's deeply.

"Are you sure? You don't mind?" he whispered. He was moved by her kindness once again, but he still felt they had to get out there in the city.

"Of course I'm sure Phevos! Some of our customers stay for long periods. Sometimes a whole month passes before they make any kind of payment. You and Daphne are welcome to stay for as long as you like. I'm sure your bank will help you if you provide them with some sort of identification. Or perhaps your family or friends could send you some cash until you sort this problem out. Or I can even help you with that, if you like. Please accept! We will worry about you if you leave without money or a change of clothes even. It's cold out there at nightfall. Daphne doesn't even have a coat! I'm guessing that was in your suitcase too, right? Think about it! Where will you go?" she asked as she gestured wildly. She had already decided she wouldn't allow them to do something stupid. She cared for them too much by now.

For the first time, after all the lies Phevos had uttered, he had finally lost his voice for good. He knew Ksenia was right. He looked at his sister and saw the silent plea in her eyes. They were both right. His sister's safety had to come first. Perhaps he could earn money somehow and start paying for the accommodation soon. They could still look for signs from Goddess Athena. Phevos looked from Ksenia to Daphne and back again determinedly. "You are absolutely right Ksenia. We accept with pleasure. And we are much indebted to you once again!" he finally said, and his face lit up with relief. The same feeling shot across to the faces of the two young girls, and Daphne sprang up from her chair to fall into his arms.

Ksenia smiled from ear to ear and Manos, who sat across from the others, seemed to share their enthusiasm as well. His sister didn't exactly have a multitude of friends, and so he thought it would be nice for her to have Daphne around for a few days. Phevos seemed all right to him too. He was the first young man that had ever been in his house and he didn't mind the novelty. On the contrary, he thought he could hang out with Phevos. He seemed nice enough although he wasn't too keen on the way he and Ksenia kept holding each other's gaze in an odd way. It was amusing to watch, but it felt a bit annoying too.

"Great!" said Ksenia as she stood up. "I'll just go and check on your clothes. They should be dry now. Give me about ten minutes and we should be ready to go!" She felt so elated as she walked away that she almost glided out of the room.

Phevos took the magazine from the table and started leafing through the pages while Daphne treated herself to the last croissant on the plate. She then stood to gather the cups and the cutlery and started to wash them in the sink. It was easy enough to work out how to use the washing up liquid and the sponge although she used too much and had to rinse the dishes quite well, filling the sink with rich soap suds as she did so.

Manos watched them both in silence and decided right there and then that he definitely liked them being around. He thought of his life alone in the house with his sister. Living without their parents, their social life had inevitably suffered. Ksenia studied in the university and then took care of things at the guesthouse in the afternoon while Manos went to school and then studied in his room or played on his pc for long hours. Inevitably he was a bit of a loner. Adults hardly ever surrounded him and he didn't exactly make friends with other kids easily either. Ksenia was all he had, and so he clung to her as if she were not only his sister but both his parents too. It was a mutually strong bond, but in a way, it had robbed them both from all other kinds of human relations. It had escaped them both for years that there's more to life out there. Friendship, companionship, even romantic love had eluded them as they clung strongly to each other, until now.

Just a quarter of an hour later, Phevos and Daphne were back in the kitchen dressed in their own clothes that had been washed and ironed. Ksenia was thoughtful enough to lend Daphne a woolen cardigan too, seeing that her dress was sleeveless and the cotton fabric too thin. The two siblings sat at the table again watching Ksenia. She was tidying up the kitchen now in her jeans and a sweater, putting the crockery and the pans away in the cupboards.

Manos didn't feel like escorting the others to the guesthouse, but he was itching for his day out to start as soon as Ksenia returned from there. He had grown quite impatient by now as he sat with the others. He was begrudgingly suffering the wait, indicating his frustration by drumming his fingers on the kitchen table every now and then in silent protest to his sister's slow pace.

"You mentioned the guesthouse is a family business. Do your parents live there if I may ask?" enquired Phevos casually.

"Yes, it's a family business but I'm afraid that Manos and I are the only members left in the family. Unfortunately we lost our parents eleven years ago..." she hesitated, lingering by the open cutlery drawer a bit longer before shutting it. She wasn't sure how to word this for it to sound right. Since last night, the pain of her parents' loss had been stirring in her soul, hurting her more than usual. She desperately didn't want to have to explain right now how they had been lost to her.

"I am very sorry for your loss," replied Phevos with an expression of deep sympathy on his face. He had inevitably misunderstood that they were dead rather than literally lost. He sensed her pain regardless and spoke no more about it.

"Thank you," she answered managing a faint smile before changing the subject. "Anyway, I think you'll like our guesthouse. It's an old neoclassic building that our father had inherited from his own father. When he was still very young, he decided to convert it to a guesthouse. The original stately home was refurbished and divided into a set of rooms, most of them with private facilities."

"I am sure it has been a very rewarding business venture for your father," commented Daphne.

"Oh yes! Thankfully our area is very popular among tourists."

"We are in Plaka, am I correct?" enquired Phevos, who remembered Manos mentioning this the night before. He still winced at the memory of his mistake, suggesting in the orchard that they should lead them to the stables.

"Yes! We're at the heart of the old quarter of Athens at the foothills of the Acropolis," answered Ksenia enthusiastically, sounding like a tourist guide. "Plaka is the perfect tourist spot with its picturesque lanes, neoclassic buildings, archaeological sites, antique and souvenir shops, busy tavernas and cafés. You know, tourists come here all year round in droves. We're very lucky to have our business here."

"You must have a steady influx of customers then," said Daphne.

"Yes, indeed we do. But I don't think it's only due to the location. You see we have a sign above the entrance. It's a painting really by an old friend of my father's. I think the tourists are greatly attracted by it!" she added laughing enigmatically and Manos promptly joined in.

"Why is that?" asked Daphne mystified.

"Would you believe they walk in specifically to ask what the painting is about? Once they've met Mrs. Sofia, and once they've had a laugh upon hearing the story behind the painting, they always wind up staying. I've no idea how many guests that painting has granted us. And over the years, Mrs. Sofia has learnt to relay the story to the tourists quite well, despite her limited English. I guess it involves more gesturing rather than talking, and she's good at that!"

"I don't understand. What could possibly be on that painting?" asked Phevos, perplexed.

"Well," Ksenia replied as she savored the moment, "the painting depicts Pallada—"

"Pallada?" Phevos exclaimed. He'd been sitting back on the chair in a relaxing manner, but the sound of the word had made him jump and spring forward, as if struck by electricity.

"Yes, Pallada. That is to say, Goddess Athena!" confirmed Ksenia. "Anyway, the painting depicts the moment that she's born as she springs out of the—"

"Out of the head of Zeus—" interrupted Daphne in a whisper that was barely audible.

"While shaking her spear!" said Phevos finishing the sentence. When he turned to look at his sister, his face had an expression of ecstasy. In silence, they shared in that moment the greatest, the most divine revelation.

"You know," Manos piped up for the first time, "I know a fact about this! Goddess Athena is called 'Pallada' because of the way she was born. The name comes from the word 'pallein' which means 'to shake'. Athena shook her spear, making a fearful noise as she burst forth from Zeus's forehead. My sister taught me that!" he added swelling with pride and Ksenia approached to pat him tenderly on the head.

Phevos and Daphne had barely heard Manos's contribution to the sign that had just hit them forcefully like a whirlwind. There was no missing and no mistaking such a sign. Manos turned his attention back to his magazine, and Ksenia hurried to store the last few items in the cupboards while Phevos held his sister's hand reassuringly under the table.

The moment was only theirs to savor alone as they stared silently into each other's eyes, trying to contain in silence the feeling of sheer joy that brewed in their hearts. In Phevos's mind, the words of Athena from his dream echoed as clearly as a church bell on a Sunday morning. *'A good hunter knows where to seek refuge. I am going to find one. I command you to come and find me!'*

And with this sign, solid hope had finally nestled in their hearts. Their father had taught them that the Gods respond to prayer by guiding people through signs. Their faith in that was strong, and it never failed them as they sought anything in life, no matter how big or small. Simply by looking, they always found signs of guidance whenever they needed them and so, they strongly believed from their experience that there is no such thing as coincidence. They both refused to take life as it is, without ever asking or seeking, knowing that this fatalistic approach never granted anyone any miracles. If anyone were to challenge Phevos and Daphne for their beliefs, they would argue that the world is miraculous, made with infinite wisdom and with an evident abundance in nature as to cater for every human need.

People are born into this world with the freedom of choice and surely, given the right mindset, this divinely endowed gift can grant them the power to acquire anything they desire. Efimios had passed on to his children the firm belief that indeed, they had this power. He taught them that the whole world shifts to guide you if you only believe it, and that miraculous things may happen during this shift that are only powered by one thing: one's own faith.

Chapter 4

Ksenia led Phevos and Daphne past the front yard and through the gate where a quaint, narrow street bustled with activity. All three stood for a while to take it in. An elderly man stood behind a large stall on the opposite side, inviting passers-by to browse through jewellery and wooden artifacts. Motorbikes and mopeds buzzed past, their riders honking the horns impatiently. Tourists walked leisurely even in the middle of the street, totally oblivious to traffic.

Loud bouzouki music echoed from the souvenir shop across the street, and tantalizing scents of roast meat and tomato sauce filled the air from the taverna next to it. Two young waiters were outside unloading beer crates from a delivery van. Behind them, the tables with the checkered tablecloths that stood forlorn under the overhead vine trellis would all be occupied by lunchtime. From then on, the taverna would stay busy till nighttime when the antique-style lanterns in the yard would be all lit up again, illuminating happy faces to the sounds of laughter and the perpetual chink of tableware.

Daphne turned around to look at Ksenia's house on the outside. It was a neoclassic building like all the others in the street. The façade was quite imposing with its marble steps leading up to an ornate front door made of iron and glass. There was a small balcony on the upper floor. On its black railing, the golden figure of a sphinx glinted in the sunlight. The tall window was open, and the curtains were blowing gently in the breeze. On the roof, mossy ceramic tiling added character to the gracefully aged structure. On the very top, the figure of a sprightly cockerel made of iron indicated mutely the direction of the wind.

Daphne drew her brother's attention to it all, and as they complimented Ksenia for the beauty of her house they moved on, reaching a fruit store next door. Ksenia raised an arm to greet its owner, Mr. Giorgis. He was standing outside at the time, under the green canvas awning that protected his produce from unfavorable weather all year round. He was engaged in conversation with a customer, miming one of the many politicians of this country, whose lack of intellect and ethics only begs for the sharp tongue of satire. The customer was still laughing uproariously as Mr. Giorgis raised his arm to greet Ksenia back, shouting 'good morning' with his deep, thunderous voice.

The tall and burly greengrocer had the towering looks to match his voice. However, what was on the inside matched nothing harsher-looking than a kitten. His heart was one of gold, full of kindness. He always laughed loudly, and when he spoke to you, he'd look at you straight in the eyes. He'd pat you on the back, touch your arm as he asked you how you are, and he'd squeeze your hand firmly when he shook it. The store was his pride, and joy and the love he'd put in it in the twenty years that he owned it, was evident in the well-maintained areas inside and out. His merchandise was always fresh, and the best one could find. He was famous all over Plaka for it.

Mr. Giorgis stepped out to the sidewalk to talk to Ksenia, and as she stopped to greet him, Phevos and Daphne marveled at the wide variety of colorful vegetables and sweet-smelling fruit on display. Some of them were totally unknown to them, and they hovered with interest before crates of common potatoes, tomatoes, lemons, and oranges.

Ksenia beckoned them closer in order to introduce them to Mr. Giorgis, and when they moved on again, Daphne jerked her hand, closing it into a fist and opening it again repeatedly. Mr. Giorgis's handshake had been particularly firm for her liking, and Ksenia timidly confessed she sometimes avoided shaking hands with him for the same reason.

Phevos gave a titter, and that's when Ksenia pointed at a beautiful edifice that stood before them, right next door to the fruit store. Above its marble-paneled entrance, the large sign drew attention from afar. Ksenia had been right. In the painting, Pallada stood tall in her helmet and shining armor. She looked beautiful with dark eyes and wavy hair that flew in thick strands against a cloudy sky. She stood on top of Zeus's head and his eyes were turned upwards in a rather comical way. The creator of the painting had obviously chosen to paint Zeus with a bit of humor, emphasizing by contrast the greatness of his daughter Athena, who had sprouted perfect and strong from his wisdom. Daphne smiled when she saw it, and Phevos felt so much awe that his knees almost gave in.

"You see what I mean?" Ksenia said with a grin. "The tourists just keep coming in to ask Mrs. Sofia about it. Do come in and meet her. You'll love her, everyone does!" With these words, she hopped up the steps and led the way through the wide-open front door.

As he crossed the threshold, Phevos thought longingly of his father. This street was full of beautiful, old houses and he wondered if he had ever been there; if he'd seen or visited these edifices in the past at any time throughout their long history. The very thought filled his heart with consolation. It made him feel a little like his father was there too.

The reception area was unattended. The sunlight that came in through the tall window to the left was still too weak to compete with the bright lights of the antique chandelier. It hung from the center of the ceiling opposite the entrance, adding character and a sense of old grandeur to the large room. Around lunchtime, this electric light would be redundant as the midday sun shone high in the sky, favoring this window at the peak of its strength and generosity. On the reception desk, a bunch of biro pens stood crammed up in a pencil holder. The sunlight filtered through the pens and projected beams of iridescent light on a block of lined A4 paper. There was silence in the room apart from the heavy ticking of a clock on the wall behind the counter.

Two big posters of Greek islands decorated the same wall, one on either side of the clock. The one on the left was a picture of a blue-domed church in Santorini, set against the deep blue of the sea and the sky. The volcano crater in the background foamed on its edges. It looked like a giant blackbird about to take flight over the vastness of the Aegean. On the other poster, an aerial picture of the historic square of Corfu town stood witness to the conquerors that had left their marks there through the centuries. The Venetian fortress stood on one side of the picture while the middle was a marvel of gardens and monuments including the open cricket field that was introduced by the British. On the right, the vaulted street of Liston, made by the French to the likeness of Rue Rivoli in Paris, stretched across from the cricket field, packed with wandering tourists. Ksenia had had to search high and low to find this specific poster. A lovely one of Zante used to be in its place, but Mrs. Sofia had kept insisting for a poster of Corfu. Finally, just a few months ago, Ksenia had managed to get hold of this one through a travel agent. Mrs. Sofia was a Corfiot, and she had a longing for her homeland that was beyond description. She often sat behind the desk during idle periods just looking at the poster of Corfu town, every now and then letting out a deep sigh.

Daphne and Phevos sat on the sofa at the right end of the room while Ksenia disappeared down a corridor to look for Mrs. Sofia. The sofa looked just as worn as the two armchairs on either side of it. Their style spoke volumes for the age that burdened their ornate, worn out legs. On the opposite wall by the window, a wooden bookcase held countless dog-eared paperbacks in various languages of the world. They were unwanted leftovers from the departure of customers over the years, which somehow had served their purpose many times again in the hands of later travelers.

The whole room had a timeless feel about it, and it felt strangely familiar. This peculiar feeling was perhaps due to the musty smell of old wood. It was the kind of smell that could take you back in time, like the smell of cotton candy, or homemade cookies, or the earth after the rain. It felt pleasant in the measure that one would care to revisit the resurfacing memories from a long, forgotten past.

Ksenia returned to the reception hall and stood at the bottom of the stairs.

"Good morning!" she said, breaking the silence, to address the old lady, who was coming down the stairs.

Mrs. Sofia was halfway down, returning from her chores on the first floor. In her wrinkled hands, she carried a bundle of linen. A heap of used sheets was lying untidily on the floor, at the arched entrance of the corridor that led to the back of the house. The old woman dropped the linen onto the heap and sighed deeply. With a reddish hand on her lower back, she took a deep breath and smiled genuinely at Ksenia, a smile that reflected in her aged, brown eyes.

"Good morning to you too, *kyra mou!*" she said as her melodic voice filled the room. "*Ore*, these two are new, aye my luck!" she lamented pointing at Phevos and Daphne on the sofa. "*Agie Spyridona*, it's still too early to let them in the room, *psyche mou*! I haven't even started the washing machine yet, and then I have to make all these beds, clean and sweep and tidy up! Can't you ask them to go for a walk or something and come back later? We've got some more coming at midday today, have you forgotten?"

Her singing perpetuated as she gestured frantically with her hands that conveyed her angst about the unexpected guests. Perhaps because of Phevos's light blond hair or maybe because Greeks hardly ever stayed there, she had thought they were foreigners, hence speaking to Ksenia and not to them. Ksenia didn't mind her outbursts when she talked in this frantic manner. On the contrary, she adored the melodic cadences of her speech that characterize the Corfiot vernacular. It sounded in her ears like a passionate Italian serenade to the sounds of mandolin.

Perhaps this is the reason she had let her speak on and on again, without explaining sooner that Phevos and Daphne were Greek, and that they were special guests of hers. Ksenia loved Mrs. Sofia beyond words and had known her all her life.

The old lady had left Corfu with her husband Spyros when they were in their forties. The couple was driven at the time by the desire to make a fresh start in life. Spyros could only find work sparsely on the island. It was the 70's and there was of course plenty of work in Corfu for waiters, barmen or people who could just sit behind a reception desk all day, but Spyros was a handyman. When he found a job through a friend as a worker at the Skaramangas shipyard in the western outskirts of Athens, he and his wife packed their bags for the city at once. They rented a tiny apartment in the suburbs where Mrs. Sofia raised their little daughter while Spyros worked six days a week. They were rather poor. Sometimes, Spyros would bring home scrap fabric pieces that the workers had at their disposal for cleaning their hands after the dirty work at the shipyard. With those scraps, Mrs. Sofia would make clothes for their little girl.

Once their son was born, it became even more difficult to make ends meet. Through an advertisement in the paper, Mrs. Sofia found a job as a cleaner in Pallada. Ksenia's father had just refurbished it. The rooms smelt all fresh then with new varnished furniture and light fixtures that glinted and sparkled. Ksenia's father was in his twenties then and full of dreams to make Pallada a profitable business. In Mrs. Sofia's kind eyes he saw someone who would put love into their work. Indeed, in time she proved to be the best asset Pallada ever had.

But her best years were behind her now. Her husband had died fifteen years ago, and she was almost eighty years old. Both her children lived far away. Her daughter was in England happily married, and she hadn't seen her in years. Her son was an engineer of the Greek Merchant Navy, who

The Necklace of Goddess Athena

was mostly at sea but visited for a few days at a time. Mrs. Sofia missed Corfu too but somehow, it was like she had grown roots over the years that kept her in Athens.

She loved working in Pallada, and of course she loved Ksenia and Manos. She was like a mother to them, having taken care of them for the last eleven years. Her room in Pallada had been her home for so long that she wouldn't trade it even for a palace. Her nights there were sometimes lonely in the solitary company of aged black and white pictures, and the framed painting of Dying Achilles on the wall. In a corner next to her bed, she often stood praying before the mounted icons of Virgin Mary and various saints. Among them, one icon held a prominent position. It was the icon of St Spyridon, the patron saint of Corfu. He was dressed in silver in a wooden frame with a glass cover where she had pressed her lips to seal thousands of prayers to his name over the years. They were prayers that involved care and protection for others, and somehow, they had granted multitudes of care and protection back to her.

Unlike the lonely nights in her room, throughout the day people always surrounded her: the customers, Ksenia and Manos, and the whole neighborhood as well. She was very sociable, caring, and attentive and everyone loved her for that. She worked in Pallada with the gusto and the attitude of an owner. As a result, the guests often assumed she was the proprietor. The odd guest would knock on her door even late at night if they felt unwell, or if they needed help. And she took care of everything.

She had a small cabinet where she kept all the paraphernalia necessary to treat cuts and grazes as well as medicine for headache, colds or tummy trouble. The neighbors benefited also from the mini pharmacy contained in that cabinet. She had given Mr. Giorgis headache tablets numerous times during the summer months when the excessive heat under the canvas awning became too much to bear. She took care of all the storekeepers in the street too, taking to them herbal teas that she prepared in her tiny kitchen. Chamomile for indigestion, sage for colds, thyme or marjoram for coughs and so on.

Once Mrs. Sofia finished her frantic speech, Ksenia did explain to her that the newcomers were Greek guests of hers who had no place to stay. When she heard about the stolen luggage and Daphne's accident, the old lady approached them with compassion in her eyes. She patted Daphne's hand gently and offered them magazines from the coffee table to read while they wait. She treated them to orange juice and swiftly returned to her chores upstairs accompanied by Ksenia. Twenty minutes later, Ksenia appeared at the top of the stairs and asked them to come up, then led them down the corridor. Mrs. Sofia was standing at the open door of one of the guest rooms. With a warm smile, she beckoned them inside.

The interior was bathed in sunlight thanks to the large window that had a lovely view of the tiled roofs of Plaka. In the background, the Lycabettus Hill dominated the skyline with the whitewashed church of St George on its top. According to legend, the hill was created when Athena accidentally dropped a massive rock while carrying a handful of them across the city in order to build a temple. Phevos smiled to himself at the thought of this myth, as he gazed at the hill. This city was indeed his eternal home and he felt truly welcome in this room.

The furniture was just as old as the ones at reception, but these were in much better condition. Lacy covers with intricate designs decorated the drawer cabinet, the mirror dresser, as well as the bedside table that stood amidst the two single beds. There were minor items of furniture too, like the pretty handmade stool by the window and the two thatched chairs that had beautiful engravings of flowers on their backs. Many knickknacks were also on the furniture as well as the walls, adding character to the room and giving it a warm, homey feel. Daphne smiled with appreciation albeit with a tint of wistfulness in her eyes. The warm glow in Phevos's eyes indicated he felt the same.

"We keep it for returning customers as a special treat." Ksenia piped up breaking the awkward silence with her enthusiasm. "It has a great view and ample sunlight throughout the day. My mother has bought most of this furniture from the Monastiraki flea market. Some of them are really old antiques like that miniature drawer cabinet in the corner. I thought this room might cheer you up after your unfortunate adventure yesterday."

"Thank you, indeed it is marvelous. We will pay for this the soonest possible," promised Daphne with a tremor in her voice.

"Don't worry about the cost Daphne! As I said, there is no rush."

"This is very kind of you, Ksenia," said Phevos, and then he gave his sister a solemn look that she returned to him with misty eyes. Ksenia and Mrs. Sofia left the room without further ado, closing the door behind them. In the first moments of silence that followed, emotion escaped from Daphne's heart in one big sob, and then her brother's arms closed in around her.

Softly, he whispered to her words of encouragement as she cried. Caressing her hair, he sang to her a lullaby they both knew from childhood. It was the one thing that had always calmed her when she cried, and over the years he had been singing it to her in times of happiness too when they played in their gardens. It was a song that had stayed with them at all times, like an old friend that you call on whether you're happy or sad, but mostly when you need comfort. It was a song their nanny used to sing to both of them when they were little. It spoke of sweet-smelling mountain herbs, of cool river waters and colorful singing birds.

The melody gradually eased the shudder on her shoulders as he wiped her tears away with his hands. Soon enough, her crying stopped, and she looked up with sorrowful eyes to meet his. And then in unison, as if responding to an invisible stimulus, they both turned their gaze to the same spot on the wall. There, above the drawer cabinet, a copperplate engraving of Goddess Athena was smiling down at them, as if to praise them for following the first of many signs on their way. Their eyes met again as they found new hope, and he swept the last tear away from her face.

Chapter 5

A month had passed. Phevos and Daphne had found a new life in that narrow street of Plaka. If you didn't know, you would think they'd lived there all their lives. That's how settled they were by now. During the first few days, they resorted to selling most of their jewellery for cash. Daphne's golden earrings and necklace went first, and then the expensive rings they both wore. They didn't mind this at all. The cash had allowed them to buy clothes, food, and some basic items.

As for the necklace that Phevos's father had given him, this still hung around his neck, for that was far too precious to part with. They had both grown very fond of their room and the whole guesthouse. As it was named after Athena, it felt right to stay there for good. They both managed to get jobs soon enough, and from the way it all happened so easily, they had acquired even more confidence that they were treading the right path. During the very first week, Ksenia mentioned to Daphne that she was looking to hire someone to help Mrs. Sofia with her duties. Daphne jumped at the chance and immediately asked her if she could have the job. Ksenia was very surprised at first as at the time she thought they were only going to be in Athens for a short while. When Daphne announced they had decided to stay, Ksenia was thrilled.

And so, Daphne became Mrs. Sofia's eager helper in Pallada, enjoying as such an even lower rate for her rented accommodation with her brother. It was the first time she had ever worked, and she relished the feeling of accomplishment at the end of the day, the knowledge that she'd been useful. Even on a slow day that didn't involve the upheaval of departures or arrivals, she'd find joy and purpose simply by directing the odd passer-by to one of the many landmarks in the area.

Daphne nurtured in her heart a feeling of debt toward humanity. She was driven by the urge to repay the kindness she'd known all her life. Fate had been kind to her. She wasn't a biological sister to Phevos. Efimios had found her in the street when she was only eight years old. Her parents were slaves and so was she. Her father used to be a citizen of Athens, who had lost his freedom due to debt and later had ended his own life driven by shame. Daphne and her mother had wound up as slaves in a mansion. When her mother got sick with high fever and skin lesions from an infectious disease, her masters mistook it for the plague. Fearing for their lives, they threw mother and daughter out in the street on an extremely cold night.

Efimios had found little Daphne early the next morning lying in the dirt next to her dead mother, sobbing inconsolably. He picked her up in his loving arms at once and took her home. As he had expected, his father did the right thing for her. Being a rich merchant and a prominent member of the Athenian society, he used his influential power to legally free Daphne from slavery, adopting her as his daughter. Although this in effect made Daphne Efimios's sister, because of the age difference, and as his parents died a few years later, inevitably their relationship evolved in time to one of father and daughter.

Phevos was only one year older than her. Daphne found in him a loving brother, and in Efimios, the father that she needed. And so, through their hearts, they became a family. As she grew up, Daphne never wanted for anything. She wore dresses and golden jewellery that would put a princess to shame. Situated at the foothills of the Acropolis, their rich estate provided her with a home and long stretches of land. She was particularly fond of their olive grove. She would often wander there as a child taking in the beauty and the heavy shadows of the trees. Their land contained orchards too, which provided fruit generously. Both she and her brother would rest in the cool there under the trees after running and playing in the summer heat. In the same place, their father would often sit with them for hours, teaching them Philosophy, Latin, Arithmetic, Geometry, and lots more.

Efimios was a great teacher. He taught young men and received generous rewards from their grateful parents, who saw in their children considerable changes in their reasoning, knowledge, and ethics. Since his father's death, Efimios had taken on his merchant business although with a lesser involvement. He had maintained relations with a couple of his father's main associates and by renting out to them his father's ships free of charge, he received part of the imported goods and a standard percentage of the overall sales profit.

But Efimios hadn't always been just a teacher and a merchant. In his youth, he had devoted his life to serve Goddess Athena and the city itself. This was a secret that he had initially shared only with his parents. Later of course, he also shared his experiences from his time travels with little Phevos and Daphne. They perceived his fanciful stories about life in Athens centuries later like a fairytale, but they had never doubted him.

Who else, other than a child could ever accept whole-heartedly strange stories about steel birds that can carry people, ships that sail underwater, or other contraptions that can shoot up beyond the end of the sky? Of course, they had honored the vow of secrecy they'd made to him in return for all the amazing stories they relished to hear. It's easier to trust a child than an adult with some secrets. And although it's easy with children, you cannot make adults believe absurd stories without proof.

Like Phevos, Daphne was also highly educated because of her father's thorough teachings. However, her acquired wisdom reflected mostly in her modesty and silence. She preferred to listen rather than to speak, for that was her way to learn more and to know people better. She tried to put herself in people's shoes and hearts, in effect earning more compassion and a greater understanding of the world.

Phevos had roamed the city in the first few days since their arrival, looking for a job but to no avail. Two weeks later, he was passing by Mr. Giorgis's shop one morning when he noticed a large image of Athena on the side of a delivery van that stopped and parked outside. Startled, he stopped dead in his tracks. A man came out of the vehicle and began to unload crates of produce onto the pavement by his feet.

Every single one had a depiction of Athena on it, helmet and all, stamped on the wood. He then turned to look at the fruit on display in the shop and was astounded to see that most of the crates had the same stamp on them too. Phevos couldn't believe he hadn't noticed this before. Mr. Giorgis then appeared from inside the store and wished him good morning. As he greeted him back, he noticed on the wall by the entrance a large sign that read 'Help Wanted'. Before he even got to comment on it, Mr. Giorgis pointed to the same sign and asked him if he'd be interested. And so, picking up yet another sign on his way, Phevos shook his hand with gladness and early the next morning, he was there to start work.

There are forces out there that conspire to bring you anything needed to serve a purpose and as they do, they sow signs on the way for you to follow. Others call these forces saints, others angels or many other things. Phevos on the other hand, saw only Athena behind all these signs because she used to guide his father in the same way. He firmly believed that for whatever purpose his father had sent him there—and he had a secret wish for what that might be—he had a protector watching over him. He felt it deep in his heart that something divine, more powerful than the world was leading the way. It wasn't a coincidence to him that they were living in a house called after Athena where his sister had also found a job. And now, he worked in a store where he could see an image of the same Goddess throughout the day.

The very city they lived in was a constant reminder of her. References to her could be found everywhere: on food labels, medicine packets, newspapers, magazines, shop signs, works of art etc. Phevos and Daphne felt safe in this city, even though it was extremely different to the one they used to live in. But it was still Athens, Athena's beloved godchild that she cared for and protected through the ages.

Phevos loved this modern city and felt far more comfortable here than his sister did. Of course, he had his moments of confusion when things he didn't really know, seemed like a déjà vu to him. He'd had those ever since he was a boy, and his father had always said it was because of the cloud in his head after the accident. All he knew is that something terrible had happened when he was nine years old, something that hurt his head to the point that he had no memory of his life before that, not even of his mother. He didn't even know her name as for some strange reason his father never spoke of her or of their lives together before the accident.

Although he didn't remember her, Phevos missed his mother with a longing that was beyond words. In the first year after the accident he was often tortured by agonizing dreams that brought on memory flashes of a previous life that didn't seem right to him and frightened him. His father never helped him understand those memories but on the contrary urged him to forget them and let them go. He advised him there was a reason why he couldn't remember his mother or his life before the accident. He told him it was the Gods that had taken them away and so, fighting the fading memories was like fighting the Gods, which was futile. He gave him hope that one day the wrong would be made right again. As he held him in his arms in the middle of the night, after every upsetting dream, he cried with his son the same tears of pain and undying hope.

Phevos hadn't had a déjà vu in years, but now that he was here, they'd come back and he had them all the time. It wasn't so much as a déjà vu, rather than a strange feeling of familiarity although his sensible mind told him he only knew about these things through his father's stories. For example, one day at work, a tourist had pointed a camera at him as Phevos was crossing the street to deliver vegetables to the taverna. When he saw him, Phevos stopped to pose, knowing immediately what the tourist wanted of him. What surprised him the most was that it felt natural to him although he knew he had never posed for a picture before in his life. One Sunday morning, he was walking around the National Garden with Daphne when a traffic helicopter flew overhead. Daphne was immediately terrified by the deafening noise it made, and she rushed to his side. Yet, Phevos remained calm and stood to watch it until it hid behind the trees, and the sound slowly faded away. He couldn't remember the name of that strange object in the sky, but he had identified it immediately, as if it were another fragment of his lost memories, behind the cloud in his head. Now that he was here, Phevos often wondered if his father had taken him along—and possibly also his mother—during one of his time travels to this age. If the accident had happened here, then perhaps his father felt guilty. That might explain why he didn't want to talk about the past. Phevos still couldn't understand why his father had chosen this silence, but he respected his wish all the same. As a result, he hadn't broached the subject again since childhood. He hadn't forgotten about the cloud in his head or his mother though, and still waited for the Gods to right the wrong as his father used to promise.

It was gloriously sunny that April morning and around midday, Daphne left Pallada to take a sandwich and a glass of juice to her brother. She brought to him food every day during her break with Mrs. Sofia, and when she returned from the shop, she and the old lady would have their quick lunch too. Each time she went to the store, Mr. Giorgis wouldn't let her leave unless she took two fruits with her back to Pallada.

As for Mr. Giorgis, his attentive wife always packed a lunch for him from the day before. He loved his family, and the wall behind the counter was always full of pictures that he often alternated so that most of them were relatively new. There would be his son riding his bike or kicking a ball, his daughter with their dog at home or with the rest of the family on the beach. But among all the recent pictures, there was a wooden frame where the picture remained unchanged and was as old as the frame itself. It was a black and white picture of his engagement day with his spouse.

That picture never changed any more than the expression on his face when he looked at it. He would proudly show the latest pictures of his children to his old customers and in the end, he would always touch the glass of that wooden frame as if to acknowledge its presence too, as if it had feelings he might offend if he didn't. He had no words when he tapped the glass, except that look on his face that said far more than words ever could.

That specific morning he was in a mood that was even chirpier than normal if that were ever possible. He gave Daphne two juicy oranges and then took a plastic tub of fresh strawberries from the counter. Smiling widely, he offered it to her.

"They've just arrived, straight from the farm. Enjoy!" he said to her with a wink.

"Thank you Mr. Giorgis, but I couldn't possibly take all that!" Daphne gave a little wave, refusing to take the strawberries too. He never let her pay for any of this.

"Nonsense! Take them to Mrs. Sofia! They are her favorites! Go on, that's a good girl!" he prompted her.

One minute later, Mrs. Sofia appeared at the entrance of Pallada.

"*Ore* Giorgis! Thanks a lot!" she yelled as her melodic voice echoed across the distance. "I promise you *ore matia*, on your wedding day I'll be carrying water for you with the wicker basket," she added, chewing on a strawberry. She liked to tease him and for some strange reason, whenever she used that Greek idiom in order to express her gratitude to him, the result was always an explosion of his amusement.

Today was no different and as soon as he heard her absurd promise of the wicker basket, his laughter echoed like thunder in the street. It lifted into the air, reaching up to the pointed roofs overhead where wild pigeons suddenly took flight with a single flap from their wings. Whole flocks of them would suddenly take to the sky in panic each time Mr. Giorgis filled the air with his uproarious laughter.

Chapter 6

It was mid April and the yard of the Economics University of Athens was bustling with the energy of youth. Students were sitting on concrete pavements or lying on the patches of grass, reveling in the midday sunshine or chatting whilst gesturing wildly. Laughter and the buzz of loud conversation made it impossible to be heard without shouting. It was Friday. Another week within the gloomy confines of the university's corridors and auditoriums had nearly ended.

"Ksenia!" Zoe called out to her friend as she rushed behind her. As she hurried down the marble steps, the red scarf that held her blond hair back in a ponytail came undone, falling to the floor. She stopped as soon as she realized, and a young man rushed to pick it up for her. She thanked him quickly and rushed on. Cursing the loud noise that didn't allow her friend to hear her, she ran faster now and finally caught up with her at the gate.

"Wait!" she said out of breath as she grabbed her elbow.

"Oh! You startled me, Zoe! What is it?" asked Ksenia with a dreamy look on her face.

"You've lost your mind, that's what it is!" she scolded her jokingly.

Ksenia knitted her brows. "What?"

"Here you are." Zoe handed her a leather wallet.

"Oh! Did I leave it behind?"

"Duh! You took it out to pay me for the coffee, remember? And then you left it at the auditorium. If it wasn't for me…" She shook her head with mock exasperation.

"Okay, then! Thanks," answered Ksenia rather impatiently. She was in a hurry to go.

Zoe rolled her eyes. "You're losing your mind over this guy. It must be love."

"Oh please, don't start again!"

"Why do you keep denying it? What's just happened is proof, isn't it? You left your wallet behind, and you had no idea! You're so forgetful recently, and forever daydreaming. Admit it girlfriend! You're in love!" She gave a suggestive nod.

"Oh Zoe, really! Stop it already!"

"All right, I'll stop but only for now." She raised both hands. "When I finally meet him tonight, I'll tell you my opinion in all honesty." She took a step back and gave her friend the once over, wrinkling her nose with mock distaste. "Really! How do you expect a man to notice you in jeans, for God's sake! I bet he hasn't even seen you in a skirt yet! But wait till he takes a look at you once I'm finished with you tonight. You're not coming out of your room unless I personally turn you into a goddess first!"

"All right, all right! But don't you dare make me look like an airhead! I've got a personality you know. We're not all like you!" Ksenia teased her back laughing.

Zoe gave her a gentle squeeze and finally let her go. Ksenia waved happily at her friend and promptly vanished into the crowd that was hurrying along the pavement.

That day was special to Ksenia. Not only was it her nineteenth birthday, but she was also planning to go out that night. She was very stressed about it because she had invited Phevos and Daphne to come along. She was rushing now, as she needed to take care of a few things in Pallada before she could go home. She knew her afternoon was going to be mad with Zoe around, helping her with her clothes and make up.

She never spent hours in front of the mirror trying different outfits and styling her hair, but she knew she was going to do all that later that day. Although she hadn't admitted it to anyone, the truth was she had grown really fond of Phevos and often thought perhaps she was in love with him. She couldn't be sure because she had never felt like this before. Her heart was telling her this must be it, since she thought of him day and night. She didn't see him often because of his work, but when she did see him, she felt so awkward because of her feelings that it became agony to her to act normally.

On the contrary, she saw Daphne every day when she returned from university to take care of things in Pallada. There were matters to discuss with her accountant, supplies to be ordered, and various issues to be addressed with guests. She had spent a lot of time with Daphne and loved her company, yet she was still quite a mystery to her. She knew by now not to ask any questions about her family or her life back home. The couple of times she'd done that, Daphne had become tongue-tied. It was quite clear she didn't wish to offer any information. Ksenia had surmised something terrible had happened to her family that had made her and her brother leave home.

Ksenia's mind was full of these thoughts as she ran to catch the bus. When she got on it, she found an empty seat and returned to her thoughts of Phevos, as blurry images of Athens city life fleeted past the window. Often she wished she weren't so tactful or shy every time she passed the fruit store. If Phevos or Mr. Giorgis weren't in sight, she'd simply rush on. As a result, she only spoke to Phevos on the rare occasions when he happened to be outside the store as she walked past. Sometimes, if he had no customers to attend to, he'd walk up to her, quickly enough for her blood pressure to fly off the mark, to ask how things were with her studies or how Manos was getting on with school.

If there was no immediate rush for him to go back in the store, she'd linger there a bit longer, and they would talk about the cool evenings of spring and how they both longed for the heat of the summer. Three days earlier, during one of those brief discussions, Ksenia asked him what he thought of the city. Phevos looked at her deeply in the eyes, as his smile slowly faded. He remained silent for a couple of seconds longer and then replied that perhaps Athens should be explored in the company of someone who knew it well.

Ksenia found herself volunteering for the task, and the huge smile he gave her then had been haunting her ever since. When she relayed this to Zoe, her friend had given her the idea of a night out on her upcoming birthday, inviting him and Daphne to come along. It was a wonderful idea, but unfortunately he wasn't in sight at the store when she passed in the last two days, and so she hadn't had the chance to invite him in person. Instead, Ksenia had asked Daphne for both of them to come but wasn't sure if her thankful response meant Phevos was coming for sure. Yet, she felt too nervous to push the point. It was also out of the question for her by now to barge into the store and invite him in person.

She had thought it out well and imagined that in case he declined the invitation she would become so disappointed that it would be impossible to hide it. She shuddered at the very thought and focused on a single wish, in the hope that fate would be kind to her, as if owing it to her because of her birthday. Her wish was that as she passed by the shop, he would be standing there.

Ksenia hopped off the bus and started to walk briskly along the busy avenue. She turned right onto a narrow street and from there, changed course confidently a few times through the Plaka lanes. She knew them like the back of her hand. A gentle breeze cooled her cheeks as she almost ran now with her head held high, her eyes looking straight ahead, lost in the thought of her secret birthday wish. The thought that it might be granted in the next few seconds made her heart beat erratically. It felt like a fluttering dove in her chest that strived to break free and fly away for the first time to faraway places described through the ages with bright colors, places she longed to see too with her own eyes. Her heart kept beating faster and faster, as she hurried along a narrow passage that led her to her street, straight opposite the fruit store. She approached slowly trying to catch her breath. Her birthday wish had just been granted. Phevos was standing on the pavement, saying goodbye to an elderly gentleman who was just leaving, laden with bags.

"Ksenia!" he cried when he saw her and with two long strides he was there, standing before her, wearing his brightest smile.

"Hello, Phevos," she replied rather breathlessly.

Phevos put out his hand. "Hi, Ksenia! Happy birthday to you."

Ksenia took his hand and willed her knees not to buckle with the excitement. "Thank you!" His touch felt warm and from the palm of her hand, it shot rays of glorious sunshine throughout her body. It was like a surreal dream standing so close to him, with his tall figure towering over her. The sunlight reflected in his eyes, and their blue became a warm sea again. She lost herself in its depths once more, in that timeless place where she felt safe and blissful. If it hadn't been for him to withdraw his hand first, she wouldn't have found the way back on her own, out of the nirvana depths of his gaze.

"Thank you for the invitation for tonight. My sister has told me and I never got the chance to thank you earlier. I'm sorry," he said.

"So, you're coming?" she asked as casually as she could while trying to control the wild beating in her heart.

"Of course we are!"

"Oh, that's great!"

"So, are we meeting in your house?"

"Yes! My friend Zoe from university is coming too. The restaurant is here in Plaka and we're going there in her car. Is eight p.m. all right with you?

"That's great! But are you sure about all of us getting there in the car? If there's not enough room I could walk perhaps—"

"No need for that! It's only going to be the five of us so there's room for us all. The restaurant may be within walking distance, but since we have the car at our disposal, it makes no sense to walk. Besides, a bit of luxury is always best I say!" She giggled, buoyant with joy.

At that moment, a couple of customers walked into the store. Ksenia couldn't thank her lucky stars enough for the perfect timing. Not only had her wish been granted, but also this perfect intervention meant he'd have to go now. Her heart was still pounding, and she'd started to feel uneasy. She felt she had to leave while she could still act relatively cool.

"I'm sorry, I have to go now," he said just as she had predicted.

"That's okay, see you tonight!" Smiling sweetly, she gave a wave and turned to go.

"See you!" He waved back, his bright smile reaching up to his eyes.

Ksenia walked away, feeling as if she were gliding rather than walking, as if she had flapping wings on her back. She went up the marble steps of Pallada and turned around at the entrance to take a last look at the fruit store. What she saw then brought her heart to its previous frantic state. Phevos was standing at the shop front under the awning, watching her. When he realized she'd seen him, he raised a hand to greet her. She did the same with a nervous giggle and entered the reception hall in a state of bliss. That's when she saw Mrs. Sofia coming from the corridor opposite. She was walking quickly, huffing angrily as she did so. Ksenia's dreamy smile faded and concern colored her face. "Hello, Mrs. Sofia! What's the matter?"

"*Psyche mou*! Let me wish you first," she said rushing to embrace her. "Happy birthday! May you reach a hundred years of age! Health and happiness and a good fortune to you with a good husband!"

"Thank you Mrs. Sofia! May you also have health and happiness! You and your children!" replied Ksenia, repaying Mrs. Sofia's wish with one of her own, as is customary in

Greece. "Where's Daphne?" she asked looking around, eager to see her friend.

"She's gone to get a few things from the supermarket. She won't be long."

Ksenia nodded and placed a gentle hand on Mrs Sofia's arm. A frown of concern creased her forehead. "So tell me now, what's the matter? When I walked in, you looked rather upset."

"Need you ask, *psyche mou*? It's that Scottish girl again in number seven upstairs! She's had another overnight guest! Another young lad, who didn't look any better than the rest of them, mind you! I caught him as he was going down the stairs!"

"Really?" Ksenia's worried expression relaxed into a smile as the melodic sounds of the Corfiot vernacular rang in her ears again like the opening chords of another mandolin song.

"Oh, yes indeed! I heard his stomping on the wooden floor and came out at once. I was cleaning the room next door at the time you see! I saw him go down those stairs like a baby goat, jumping about, oh what a sight! And I shout out to him, 'come here you rascal!' And when he caught sight of me, he jumped in surprise and tripped half way down the stairs like a mad thing! He nearly fell over his bony face, and then he was out the door like a bolt of lightning! He was a miserable looking thing, like a plucked out bird! Skinny, with spindly legs and his hair, oh his hair! It was short and spiky as if he had stuck his fingers in an electric socket! I bet you can find goblins walking around on New Year's Eve with more meat around their bones! *Agie mou Spyridona*!" She exhaled loudly and crossed herself with bulging eyes.

"And how do you know that he's spent the night here with the Scottish girl?" asked Ksenia as she covered her mouth surreptitiously with one hand, trying to hide the laughter that brewed inside her. Mrs. Sofia's selection of words when she was excited always amused her immensely, and she tried desperately not to laugh.

"Ah well! I may be old, but I'm not blind *ore kopela mou*!" she protested, shaking her finger in front of Ksenia's face. "She was standing at the bedroom door all right! She was in a t-shirt and her knickers seeing him off! Ah, the shame of it! And he was going down the stairs with sleepy eyes and bare feet, holding his shoes in his hand! Imagine that! He must have taken off his shoes to be quiet and yet, he was stomping on the wooden steps like a baby lamb on Easter day! He made enough noise to wake the dead, for God's sake!"

Ksenia doubled over and was now laughing uproariously. Mrs. Sofia had set the scene vividly before her eyes, as she gestured frantically with her hands, goggling at Ksenia and grimacing continuously to demonstrate her surprise when she saw the lad and his terror as he tumbled down the steps. Ksenia's eyes were alight with mirth when she finally caught her breath and looked at Mrs. Sofia again. "And what did the girl do?" she managed to ask before she started laughing again.

"*Ore* Ksenia, I'm talking seriously here, and you're laughing? Have you forgotten what trouble this girl has been already? He's the third one she brings in here in a week! *Agie Spyridona*, woe is me!"

"I'm sorry, Mrs. Sofia," she apologized, "but it sounds so funny!"

"Why don't you talk to her?" she asked with pleading eyes. "She's lucky I don't speak English, or I would have given her a sound piece of my mind as she stood there in her underwear, the little minx! I did say a thing or two mind you and from the look she gave me, I think she understood me all right!"

"What? Do Scottish girls speak Corfiot?" asked Ksenia giggling, still unable to conceal her amusement.

"Oh yes, I'm pretty sure she understood me! But I got really cross afterwards because she shut the door on my face. Fancy that, what a nerve!" Mrs. Sofia placed a hand on her forehead. She sighed heavily and when she looked up again, her eyes looked really tired. The black attire she always chose to dress in, amplified the effect.

"Calm down now Mrs. Sofia," said Ksenia in a soothing voice. The old lady had started to look distressed and this always worried her.

"Well, it'll take me a while to calm down, that's for sure! It's only just happened you know. It wasn't five minutes before you came in."

"What? They woke up at one p.m.?" asked Ksenia looking at her watch. "I would have thought she'd smuggle him out much earlier than that!"

"*Ore Ksenia*, you know what these Northerners are like! They drink and drink until they can't feel their toes or their fingers, and then they hibernate in their rooms for hours on end! Don't you remember them Scandinavians last month? For two weeks we hadn't seen the inside of the room! They barely opened that door to hand us the garbage and we handed them rolls of toilet paper, as if they were prisoners in there! Aye, I'm surprised we didn't find cockroach nests in that room by the end of the fortnight! Two weeks! No cleaning, no sweeping! All day they were asleep and all night they were out on the prowl for yet more drink!"

"Yes, yes I do remember!" Ksenia couldn't help giggling again.

"Go and talk to that little minx for me now, will you? There's a good girl!"

"Sure, I will do that," she said obligingly and started to climb the stairs.

"If she lies to you, tell her I saw them both with my own eyes! And tell her that if I catch her again, I'll throw her stuff out the window!" Mrs. Sofia's lower lip quivered as she spoke.

"Don't worry. If she does it again, she *will* go. I will make sure she understands that! Now please, calm down Mrs. Sofia. All this aggravation is not doing you any good." Ksenia's eyes were pleading. Mrs. Sofia sighed in response and nodded, but her eyes remained alive with anticipation as Ksenia continued to go up the stairs.

By the time she reached the landing, the girl's face was no longer amused. She now wore the professional expression required for the occasion. She was determined to uphold the regulations of her hotel. A few minutes later, she was half way down the staircase when Mrs. Sofia appeared hurriedly at the bottom holding a broom. She wore an unmistakable expression of impatience across her face.

"Okay, I've told her," said Ksenia when she came down the last step. "She apologized and promised me it won't happen again."

"Did you tell her I'll throw her stuff out the window if I catch her again?"

"Don't worry, she's fully aware we won't be giving her another chance. So let's forget this now, my dear Mrs. Sofia, shall we? If she does it again, I'll throw her out myself! All right?"

"Oh, all right!" Mrs. Sofia resigned with a huff and then hugged Ksenia to wish her a happy birthday again. The young girl held her close to her and thought what a joyous gift this little episode had been, this generous dosage of Mrs. Sofia's explosive temperament. Reserved as she was by nature, Ksenia admired Mrs. Sofia for her passion in everything she felt and did, which made her unique in many ways.

Chapter 7

"You're so pretty!" exclaimed Manos from the open door. His sister was standing before the tall mirror in her bedroom. She wore an elegant, blue dress that accentuated her slender figure and she was very happy with it. It was a new dress she'd bought earlier that week at a shop near the university. Zoe had convinced her to buy it and Ksenia felt really pleased she'd listened to her. The beautiful color and the velvety feel of the fabric made her feel wonderful, almost like a different person. She knew she could never feel this way in any of the dreary clothes contained in her wardrobe.

Indeed, Ksenia was a rare sight tonight. Hairpins with turquoise sequins sparkled on her gelled hair, and her face was made up to perfection in a way that set off her blue eyes and full lips. Zoe stood behind her smiling with glee, as their eyes met in the mirror. When Manos walked up to them, the girls turned around to take a better look at him. He looked dashing, dressed in a white cotton shirt, black jeans and dark leather shoes. To please his sister he had accepted gladly to wear these clothes she had bought for him, despite the fact that the new shoes felt rather uncomfortable and the white shirt was too flimsy for his liking. It offered infinitely lesser warmth than the sweaters he was used to wearing in cold weather.

"Hey handsome, come over here!" Zoe urged him taking the tube of hair gel from the bed where it lay among hair accessories, brushes and make up products. With quick and confident movements, she applied gel on his hair and then took a step back to admire the overall picture. "There you go! Models on photo shoots never look better than this!"

Manos smiled appreciatively at his reflection in the mirror. All three of them stood there now, admiring themselves, and only Zoe seemed unaffected by her own image. After all, it was the norm for her to dress up for a night out. Her French mother had passed on to her, her Parisian genes of fashion-consciousness and style. As she brought her up, she had fed her vanity by offering her a standard supply of fashionable clothes and accessories. Zoe was the type of girl who never passed unnoticed, and that evening was no different.

She looked alluring in a purple silk shirt and a long, black skirt made of satin. A delicate belt embraced her thin waist, and her blond hair fell loosely on her shoulders. On one side, it was held back from her face with a large, studded hairpin that caught the electric light and sparkled, making her look extra glamorous. Both girls wore high heels and again, this was a novelty only for Ksenia. Zoe had prompted her to buy this pair of blue shoes to match her new dress, and when Ksenia refused to risk the discomfort of the high heels, Zoe went behind her back to buy them for her as a birthday gift, knowing that this way she'd have to wear them to please her.

Zoe had ways to convince people, but she never did it for her own benefit. She wanted everything to be perfect for her friend, and as she admired the result of her efforts, Ksenia's happy smile confirmed to her she had done well to persist. Single-handedly, she had transformed her into a catwalk model, albeit a novice one, seeing that she had to walk the length of her room up and down for quite some time in order to get used to the high heels. Ksenia had got reasonably comfortable with them by now, and no longer feared she would fall. Zoe had assured her that by the end of the evening, she'd have Phevos's arm to lean on. It had been a clever trick on her part, for it had worked miracles on Ksenia. She was excited beyond words by now at the prospect.

Her image in the mirror kept smiling back at her confidently. She looked so different... Even the stars that twinkled in her eyes seemed to be there to fulfill one wish only: that this night Phevos would become hers somehow.

No aspiring Cinderella could ever find a better fairy godmother than Zoe, who stood behind her now beaming with contentment.

"The doorbell!" yelled Manos running down the staircase, and the two girls stared at each other shrieking with excitement. They fell silent as soon as they heard the front door open. The cheerful voices of Phevos and Daphne echoed from the hall, and Ksenia's enormous eyes met Zoe's again. Without a word, they hurried to take a peek from the top of the stairs. All they saw was their shoes, but that didn't stop Ksenia's heart from skipping a beat. Zoe giggled and grabbed Ksenia's arm as they hurried back to the bedroom to get their coats.

The visitors stood in the hall. Phevos was in black jeans and leather shoes in the same color. Only the blue shirt that showed under his jacket broke the dark monotony of his formal appearance. When he heard the footsteps on the staircase before him he raised his eyes, eager for Ksenia to appear. Daphne stood next to him in a brown dress under a dark coat. She wore brown shoes with tiny studs that sparkled, and she held rather awkwardly in front of her a clutch bag in the same color. As always, she was a picture of beauty.

The two girls came down the stairs slowly. When Phevos saw Ksenia he found it hard to take his eyes off her, hardly noticing Zoe behind her. The girls wore long coats and delicate, black bags. They looked like princesses as they descended elegantly, dressed in their finest. When Ksenia made the necessary introductions, Zoe shot a look of approval at her for Phevos's dashing looks. The birthday girl received kisses on both cheeks from Daphne and then to her excitement, from Phevos too.

When they went out into the cold spring night, Zoe asked everyone to follow. The sky was clear but the wind was cold and so they hurried to her car that was parked nearby.

"Manos my darling, come sit next to me in the front. Tonight you're my date!" said Zoe in an attempt to give Ksenia a chance to sit next to Phevos in the back. Manos obliged her joyfully. Daphne entered in the back first and then Phevos motioned to Ksenia to follow before he got in last. The car set off for the short ride to the restaurant, and on the way they discussed enthusiastically the location of the venue and the food on offer. Phevos didn't care much about any of that, as he silently watched Ksenia. As for her, she kept blathering on unstoppably, too nervous to be silent as she sat next to him.

A couple of minutes later, they arrived at their destination. A pleasant feeling of warmth embraced them as they entered the restaurant hall. An obliging waiter led them to their table by the fireplace at the far end. Chunks of olive wood burnt in bright flames. The fire crackled every now and then, breaking the monotony of murmuring voices and tinkling glassware. Antique paintings hung on the surrounding walls. The marble floors were decked with burgundy carpets. Zoe took the initiative to arrange people around the table and managed it so that Ksenia and Phevos sat side by side.

The waiter took their order answering every question politely and shortly later, their meals started arriving at the table. They were meat and pasta dishes as well as a variety of delicious appetizers that tickled their noses with heavenly smells. As they drank barrel wine from crystal jugs, the merriment increased and soon enough, even the nervous among them managed to relax and enjoy themselves fully. After dinner, a surprise little cake with one lit candle was brought to the table thanks to Zoe's prior secret arrangement. She completed her plans for the evening by producing her digital camera from her bag. She got them all to huddle together to be photographed with the cake, and Phevos changed places with her so that she can be photographed too with her friend. Before putting her camera back in her bag, Zoe made sure to get a picture of just Ksenia and Phevos, and even urged them to embrace each other for the shot, something which they both obliged to willingly with awkward smiles.

Later, as they ate the cake, Daphne took a little packet out of her bag and offered it to Ksenia as a present from both her and Phevos. It was a make up set of eye shadows and lip-gloss and Ksenia thanked her gratefully. She turned to him to thank him as well, and he smiled at her with a nod. A few moments later, while everyone else was engaged in cheerful conversation, he leaned toward her. "You have one more gift and this one is only from me," he whispered deliciously in her ear.

Surprised, Ksenia turned to look at him and he smiled at her sweetly. "Ksenia, when we leave, would you like to walk with me to your house while the others ride in the car?"

"Yes, I would love to," she whispered as her eyes lit up with renewed enthusiasm.

When they all went outside, they stood by the car while Zoe searched her bag for the car keys. That's when Phevos took Ksenia's hand in his, and the fluttering dove inside Ksenia's chest finally took flight.

"Listen, Phevos and I will walk home! You go ahead!" she announced breathlessly, as she felt the warmth from his hand shoot arrows of bliss all the way to her heart.

Manos made noises about joining his sister, but of course Zoe was not going to let this happen. "You're my date tonight young man, remember? What if there's danger on the way? Daphne and I will need a man to protect us. You can't leave us!"

"Oh, okay," replied Manos readily. He flashed Zoe a proud grin, and sat happily on the passenger seat in the role of man-protector. Zoe had it all in control as always and even remembered to take the house keys from Ksenia, as they were bound to return home first in the car.

As soon as the others were gone, Ksenia and Phevos began to saunter hand in hand. It was quite cold and when she commented on that in order to break the awkward silence, he let go of her hand in order to put his arm protectively around her. When they reached a small square, he took her hand again and led her to a wooden bench.

They sat there in the quiet, holding hands. The only sound they could hear was the rustling of leaves coming from the vine that draped over the wall behind them. When Ksenia shivered, Phevos rubbed her back. She giggled nervously in response, and this time, he put his arm around her to hold her closely beside him. Silently still, he took a little jewellery box from his jacket pocket and offered it to her. It was blue and tied with a golden string. "It's as if I knew," he said at last. "It has the same color as your dress."

"And your shirt!" she replied and they both laughed. Ksenia thanked him and slowly untied the string. As he watched her, Phevos caressed a strand of her hair with his free hand. Under his fingertips, it felt like the most precious silk.

"It's so beautiful! Thank you Phevos," she said. Her present was a silver chain with a delicate pendant; a silver heart that was studded with tiny, amethyst stones. They sparkled under the light of the nearby lamppost, and when she turned to look at him she felt her heart melt. "Will you help me put it on?" she asked, and when he obliged her she touched the pendant gently with trembling fingers. She thought at that moment how magical this night was, and how it felt like a dream. The best dream she'd ever had. Her eyes were half-closed when she felt his warm breath in her ear.

"Ksenia..." he whispered and then the velvet of his lips came to seal hers with a silent vow of love in a tender kiss that was the first one for both of them. When they looked at each other's eyes afterwards, they felt like time had suddenly stopped, like they had just found each other in a distant dreamland of bright colors where time didn't matter and was eternal. They must have spent another half hour in reality sat on that lonely bench having no words at all to describe what their eyes far more eloquently managed to say.

Although shrouded by the coldness of the night, they kept warm with the raging fire in their hearts, and when he kissed her hand and said 'I love you' she didn't think at all before repeating the same words to him. To the young, love comes easily. The young heart, like a courageous ship, drops anchor with certainty when it finds love, and it doesn't easily set sail again. On the other hand, an old heart looks for love like a damaged ship that's seen better days, scarred, tired, untrusting. An old ship is unsure of the waters it casts its anchor in. But not the young ship! This one drops anchor blindly into the deepest ocean, without a single reservation.

Phevos looked at his watch. It was gone midnight and the cold had become intense. They didn't want to go yet but knew the others would be waiting for their return. Reluctantly, they left the bench behind them and walked the rest of the way to Ksenia's house. They kissed one last time outside and then Ksenia rang the doorbell. Zoe appeared at the entrance at once, and Daphne got out in her coat. The two girls got very enthusiastic as they looked at the couple that stood at the door with exultant faces. Only Manos didn't seem to understand, and he complained to his sister that she was late.

After Phevos and Daphne left, the two girls retired upstairs, but unlike Manos, who fell asleep at once, Ksenia and Zoe stayed up for hours in the bedroom discussing what had happened. Zoe made Ksenia tell her every single detail of her return home with Phevos. In the end, they fell asleep on top of the beddings with their clothes on. Just before dawn, they woke up freezing to the bone. They put on their pajamas quickly and hid under the duvet to resume their sleep.

In Pallada, it took Phevos and Daphne a lot of time too to fall asleep, as Daphne also wanted to know everything that had happened between him and Ksenia. She was very happy for her brother but also felt worried. She wondered how his feelings for Ksenia could affect the unknown purpose for which they had arrived there. They were there only for a while. They didn't belong to Ksenia's world. In the end, she couldn't contain herself and asked him how he felt about that. When Athena's obscure plan was complete, and it was time to return to their world, would he want to stay to be with her?

Phevos didn't have an answer to that. All he could tell her was that he felt that fate had brought them there. Athena hadn't sent them any more signs in a month. But they had found shelter there, work and even love. A life that makes you feel good under your skin surely has to be an indication that you're treading the right path. And they both felt happy and secure. This was all Phevos had to say to his sister as a means of answering her questions.

Once again, he was right. The next sign would come quite soon, within less than twenty-four hours to be precise. They were lucky because things don't always happen so quickly. Often, the plans that the Gods make are revealed after long periods of wait. This is because the Gods are not bound to the cruel confines of Time like we are. What we may conceive as a year's wait for example, might seem like only a breath away to the Gods because for the soul, there is no concept of Time. One thing is for sure: once things have come full circle, they finally make sense. This golden rule has exceptions but only for people who choose to ignore the signs and to go their own way. Thankfully, Phevos and Daphne knew better to trust the signs, and they were determined to run the course in this fashion. Phevos hoped their purpose involved finding his mother again, for that was the burning desire he'd had in his heart ever since he could first remember the world. He couldn't help thinking by now that perhaps she had been trapped in this world and that's how they had been separated. The pain of her absence was unbearable to him still, although he was no longer a child as to allow it to show as evidently as before. Children suffer when separated from loving parents and absolutely no one has the right to do that. Soon enough, the Gods would intervene to put things right.

Chapter 8

The sun shone faintly the next morning as it emerged from behind white cotton clouds, rising over the tiled rooftops of the old Plaka neighborhood. Plump magpies walked on spindly legs on stone cold pavements pecking at the odd scrap of food. Others perched in line on the overhanging telephone cables and the reclining rooftops. They looked around them with tall necks and proud chests, ruffling their feathers busily like hurried troops getting ready for inspection. The world below them was slowly starting to stir into life.

Mr. Giorgis had opened his store early as usual. A bunch of tiny sparrows were pecking busily at the breadcrumbs he had just thrown for them on the shop front. The shrill sound of a bell echoed in Ksenia's bedroom. It had come from a rusty bicycle outside. Its rider had just swerved skillfully around two sleepy-looking tourists.

Ksenia opened her eyes and immediately smiled happily to herself. She yawned and stretched lazily as she got out of bed, then walked to the tall window. When she opened the blinds, the morning light rushed in like a cheerful friend coming to share in her joy. She breathed in deeply the humid spring air, smiling still, relishing the warmth of the sun behind her closed eyelids. Zoe stirred under the duvet and then sat up looking at Ksenia with drowsy eyes and a puzzled expression on her face.

"What time is it? I feel like I haven't slept at all!" she said with a croaky voice, wrinkling her nose. Instead of giving her an answer, Ksenia broke out laughing.

"What is it?" Zoe asked surprised. Unbeknown to her, her eye make up had smeared all around her eyes. Her sparkling hairpin that had made her look alluring the night before now hung on its end from a strand of her tousled hair, as if holding on for dear life.

"You look like a scarecrow!" she teased as she approached her. Zoe responded by throwing a pillow at her, and they both started laughing.

In Pallada, brother and sister had awoken too. Phevos had already shaved in the small basin but was still in his pajamas. Daphne was in her nightie, and they were sitting on their beds watching TV absentmindedly. They still had a bit of time before having to get ready for work. Phevos felt elated still about the events of the previous night, but there was a shadow too that lingered in his eyes.

"What is it Phevos?' Daphne asked him, concerned when she noticed.

"I feel guilty Daphne," he confessed, a single line creasing his forehead.

"But why?"

"I've told Ksenia so many lies!" He sighed and raised both hands to his head, tormented.

"No you haven't!"

"Yes I have!" he insisted. "By not telling her who I really am, I'm hiding the truth from her. In effect this is a lie, isn't it?"

"Oh, I blame myself," Daphne replied, frowning with concern. "This is all my fault. Please forgive me! I shouldn't have said these things yesterday! I should never have put such ideas and dilemmas in your head. Just enjoy the love you share with Ksenia and don't worry about anything else for now. You said it yourself that the Gods are auspicious. Surely they wouldn't be in our favor if we are less than true with others!"

"I can't, I just can't help feeling like this!" He sprung up from the bed and turned to look at her with sadness in his eyes. "How can I love her and not be able to tell her who I really am?"

"My dear brother, when the time is right, I'm sure you'll be able to do that."

"And how am I ever going to leave her behind when we have to go back? I can't even bear the thought of it!" he said, pacing aimlessly up and down the room in anguish.

"Phevos, when we complete our purpose here, I'm sure you'll have to make a choice. Just trust that when the time comes, you'll have the freedom to make it. But for now, we don't even know how we are to go back to Father and our world. It's not right to make hasty decisions about the future at this point, when we don't even know where Athena's will is to take us."

"Athena's will!" He scoffed, his face alight with despair. "What if her will is for me to lose Ksenia? To tell you the truth, right now I feel that if I have to choose between Ksenia and my loyalty to Athena, I won't be able to resist disrespect to the Gods! For Ksenia, I could denounce the whole world, and all the wealth that's in it! Look at this!" he said as he produced from under his pajama top the necklace that he always wore close to his heart. "For Ksenia I could denounce even this sacred necklace that belongs to Athena herself which our father entrusted to me!" he added sitting heavily on his bed, distraught.

"My dear brother, please calm down!" said Daphne rushing to him to place her arms around him. "Don't speak disrespectfully about Athena for you know her spear can be cruel and cold! It crushes down the will of people who oppose to her wishes. Please don't let your lips utter such words of blasphemy!"

"I'm sorry Daphne, forgive me." Phevos shook his head. "I guess you've never loved someone like this yet, and you don't know... but for *your* sake, I won't speak of this any more. I promise I'll try to let it lie quietly in my heart until indeed, it is time to make decisions."

Spent, he let his sister caress his hair and said nothing else. As she hugged him tenderly in the ensuing silence, Daphne wished that somehow her brother would never have to come to such a difficult choice.

***

Manos's room was dark. Ksenia walked in hurriedly and opened the shutters to let the sunlight in.

"Hey, wake up sleepy head!" she said pulling down the duvet to see his face. He stirred when she tousled his hair, and he opened one eye only, making grunting noises.

"Oh let me be! It's early still!" he complained.

"No, it's not! It's ten! Come on, time for breakfast!"

"It's not ten! You're lying!" he said sitting up. He yawned, then scratched his head and stretched like a cat.

"Of course it's ten! Zoe and I have been up since eight. It was a late night yesterday, so I let you lie in a while longer."

Manos grinned. "Good girl! That's what I call service."

"Come now, off you go young man! Breakfast's on the table," she urged him and he stood barefoot on the carpet, grunting as he looked around for his slippers. Ksenia walked to the open window where a pleasant breeze brought in sweet smells from her pots outside: carnations, roses, as well as spearmint, marjoram, rosemary, and lemongrass. The trees were in bloom. Little birds rested on the branches singing gratefully for the coming of the spring. Under a lemon tree, Odysseus was lying on the ground chewing on a muddy bone he had probably just unearthed.

***

A tall man in his thirties sprinted effortlessly up the steps and rushed through the entrance of Pallada to find no one there. He was dressed casually in a white t-shirt and blue jeans. His hair was dark and short. His brown eyes scanned the reception hall, alight with enthusiasm. With a lithe movement from his strong shoulders, he dropped on the floor the heavy backpack he'd been carrying. He took a few steps forward and cried out confidently. "Hello! Is anybody here?"

Daphne was in the laundry room downstairs when she heard him. She hurried to reception and when she got there, she still had a hand on her unkempt hair, trying to pull an unruly curl back from her face. She looked up and when she saw the man, she froze on her spot for a few seconds. She tucked the unruly strand of hair behind her ear and smiled rather nervously, as she wished him good morning.

The man's eyes lit up when he saw her. He expected to see Mrs. Sofia instead for this was not the first time he was visiting. He greeted her back with a pleasant smile and lifted the backpack over his shoulder again. Daphne had already taken her place behind the reception desk, and he followed her there. He placed his hands confidently over the counter, looking rather expectant and also mildly amused.

"How can I help you?" she asked chirpily. Her gentle voice sounded an octave higher than it normally did.

"You must be new!" he replied with a confident smile.

"I'm guessing you've been here before, sir!" she replied.

He chuckled. "Oh yes! Quite a few times actually!"

"Well, in that case, welcome back, sir! Is it a single room you're after?"

"Not quite!"

"Are you traveling with others?" she asked looking toward the entrance, scanning the street for any companions of his.

"No, it's just me," he replied. He knew he was being naughty, confusing her like that; yet, he didn't want this exchange to finish just yet. He gazed back at her without offering further explanations, magnetized by the sudden flush on her cheeks and her brilliant green eyes.

"Well, what do we normally interest you in?" she asked totally perplexed.

"For starters, what normally happens when I arrive, is I get to meet Mrs. Sofia. Is it possible to see her please?"

"Certainly, I'll go get her for you!" Daphne felt dumbfounded, but also quite relieved to finally have a sensible request from this very odd customer. He moved toward her as she passed by him, and she turned to face him, once again flustered by his strange behavior. As they stood facing each other then, he looked even taller and Daphne looked more delicate and more microscopic than ever before.

"I'm sorry Miss, how rude of me! Please let me introduce myself. I'm Aris, Mrs. Sofia's son," he said offering his hand.

Daphne's eyes turned huge, then she gave an easy smile. "Oh! "How silly of me, I should have guessed really!" she said as they shook hands.

"How could you possibly have guessed?" he asked, bewildered.

"Well, she has described you many times and also I've seen old photos of you on her wall among her icons. I should have recognized you."

"Oh yes of course! But don't beat yourself too much young lady. These pictures are quite old. I believe my face is covered in pimples and I clutch schoolbags on most of them!" he said and they both laughed.

"You work on the ships, am I correct? It must be exciting, traveling the world like that."

"It has its good sides I guess. Like everything, one takes the rough with the smooth. It can get pretty tedious after a while. It's not all fun and games as one might think!" He smiled pleasantly. "And I can tell you that the sea has its bad moods too. I shudder to think of a fragile-looking creature like you traveling at sea on a bad day. I wouldn't recommend it."

"I'll bear it in mind," she said with a giggle. "Well, I'd better get your mother. I'll only be a moment," she added and made to leave.

"Wait! You haven't told me your name yet."

"It's Daphne," she answered with an awkward smile, and then she disappeared down the corridor. Seconds later, Mrs. Sofia came out of a room on the far end, rushing down the hallway on her aged legs like a schoolgirl on a field trip. When she appeared before him, Aris dropped his bag and opened his arms wide. She rushed to him then, beside herself with joy, nestling in his embrace like a chick that basks in the warmth of his mother's wings.

"Oh my son, my pride and joy! *Panagia mou*, every time I see you, you seem taller than before! *Psyche mou,* I shall go mad with the joy of it! How sudden was this! Why didn't you tell me you were coming? I could have made something nice for lunch. Goodness me, we spoke on the phone recently. You never said anything, you naughty boy! Oh you must be tired! When did you get here? Did you have good weather at sea?"

Aris kept laughing and holding her tight, placing kisses on her cheeks, and she kissed him all over his face, caressing his hair while bombarding him continuously with questions. Daphne stood nearby happy for both of them but mostly for Mrs. Sofia. She knew she hadn't seen him in two months and was looking forward to his next visit.

At the guesthouse, Daphne often witnessed reunions among loved ones after long periods of separation. Her favorites were by far those between mothers and children. She knew there was no other love like it that filled both reunited parties with unsurpassed comfort. Every time she witnessed such a scene, she couldn't help remembering her own mother. As she stood watching children of any age cradled in their mother's arms, somehow it made her happy too, and it numbed for a while her longing for her own.

"Come on my son, let's go and get you settled. You must be tired but let's put some food in you first," said Mrs. Sofia. Aris lifted his bag once again to follow her but not before he cast another look at Daphne with a happy smile on his face.

"Don't worry about the rooms, Mrs. Sofia! I'll finish up everything on my own today," said Daphne as they started to walk away, in order to allow the old lady to devote all her time to her son. She guessed she would want to give him a cooked meal for lunch and she'd also have to make up the foldable bed that leans against a corner of her room, forever awaiting his return. Mrs. Sofia accepted her offer thankfully, and mother and son walked down the hallway to her room. Her voice echoed in high octaves as they went. She was now reciting out loud her list of things to do, prioritizing among putting the pan on the stove, letting him have his shower while she found him fresh clothes, unpacking his bag to do his laundry and making his bed for a kip after lunch.

Just over an hour later, Mrs. Sofia had managed everything that needed to be done, and she was now making the table. When Aris came out of the shower she sent him to reception to invite Daphne to eat with them. He was pleased to hear that and rushed there to fetch her. Daphne was unsure at first about her answer as she felt that on the day of his arrival, Aris should be able to speak in privacy with his mother while they shared their news.

Every day she had a quick lunch with Mrs. Sofia that the old lady prepared in her tiny kitchenette. Most often it was sandwiches that Phevos also benefited from at the fruit store. But sometimes, Mrs. Sofia invited them both to her room to treat them to cooked meals in the evenings. Daphne knew what an excellent cook she was and when Aris announced that the invitation involved his mother's secret tomato sauce with spaghetti, her stomach grumbled on cue. They laughed light-heartedly with the apt, embarrassing sound and Daphne followed him gladly down the hallway.

***

It was around midday. Phevos stood at the shop front basking in the sunshine. He had just enjoyed a plate of pasta that had come as a wonderful surprise instead of the usual sandwich. His sister had brought it to him steaming on the plate, topped with lashings of grated Parmesan. The tantalizing smell of the Corfiot spice mix in the sauce tortured his sense of smell for five whole minutes until all lingering customers left the shop allowing him to finally devour his meal.

Phevos heard a rough, whirring sound and when he turned to look he saw Manos and three other boys. They were cruising down the road on their skateboards at high speed with Manos in the lead. He seemed quite skilful. It was the first time Phevos saw him do that, so he stood to watch. He hadn't seen those boys before either. Actually, in the short time that he was there, Phevos hadn't seen Manos play in the street before, either on his own or with other children. They were halfway down the street now and Phevos thought that if they were racing, Manos was going to win. Phevos got excited for him and was about to cheer him on when an elderly lady approached him. She needed help with weighing some greens and so, he followed her dutifully inside the store. A couple of minutes later he was back out at the front, eager to watch Manos some more, but what he saw was not what he expected.

The boy was sitting on the ground, on the other side of the street. His head was bent down and he sat still, holding his skateboard in both hands. Phevos knew immediately something was wrong and he rushed to him.

"What's the matter, Manos?" he asked placing a hand on his shoulder. The boy looked up. His eyes were full of tears. The skateboard had a bad crack halfway across its middle, and a small piece was missing on one side. Manos wiped his tears with the back of his hand and Phevos helped him up.

"Tell me Manos, what happened? Did you fall?"

"No, I didn't...."

"So, how did it break? Why are you crying?"

"He broke it..."

"Who? One of the boys that were here before?"

Manos nodded.

"Why?"

"Long story..." he whispered and started to walk away in the direction of his house.

"Manos, wait!" Phevos took a few steps toward him.

"I'll be ok, thanks...." replied Manos without turning around, still walking away.

"I'm here if you need to talk anytime Manos! We're friends, right?"

"Yes, I know. Thanks Phevos..." he replied, finally stopping to glance at him. He even managed a faint smile before turning to go again.

"Maybe we can fix it! Let me see it at least!"

"Some other time...." Manos hurried to his front gate, clutching the skateboard to his chest like a wounded friend, but in reality it was his own wound inside his heart that he was nursing. Manos hid his pain well from the world. Perhaps that was his way to deal with it. To try to forget the cruelty in others that hurt him.

Running now, he opened the garden gate and rushed through his front door. He walked along the hallway and was relieved when he heard his sister and Zoe chatting in the bedroom upstairs. He didn't want anyone to see him like this. He didn't want to upset his sister again with his usual problems. He entered his room and placed the skateboard gently on the floor, hiding it from view in a corner on the side of his wardrobe. He then walked slowly to the window as fresh tears escaped from his eyes, but he wiped them away swiftly.

He had become better at this by now and was able to keep strong. From the window, he noticed Odysseus out in the back yard. He was lying on the warm soil on a clearing among the trees. His eyes were shut and his legs stretched out. Every now and then he flicked his ears as if he was trying to ward off flies. He was such an amusing sight that Manos laughed, forgetting for an instant the sorrow that weighed down on his heart. His eyes darkened again at the thought that he had no other friends except his dog. None of the boys at school really cared to call him a friend. All they ever did was call him names. Children may be pure at heart, but they can also be very cruel with the weak. And their cruelty is what Manos had been suffering since his first day at school. The other children had initially asked insistent questions about his missing parents, imagining various scenarios about their vanishing that they felt obliged to relay to him over and over again. Later on they started to tease and bully him, sensing his inability to stand up for himself.

Even in class, whenever the teacher would refer to parents, someone would point at Manos and say things like, 'you don't need to listen to this, it doesn't refer to you' or they'd whisper to each other stifling their giggles with their hands. They taunted him endlessly, especially around Christmas. 'Santa won't bring you anything!' they'd say. 'He doesn't care for orphan children!' And Manos would listen to them without talking back although he knew they were wrong. He knew for a fact that Saint Vassilios remembered him every year. As Mrs. Sofia and Ksenia had taught him, every Christmas Eve little Manos would leave a saucer of milk and some grass outside his windowsill. He always remembered unprompted to leave this treat for the reindeer that waited outside in the orchard while Santa placed large parcels for everyone under the Christmas tree.

Every Christmas morning, his face would be the picture of joy to see all the parcels that Santa had brought and also to find that the reindeer had once again enjoyed his humble offering. When he opened his presents, whatever they were, he was always happy in the knowledge that he hadn't been forgotten after all. It was some kind of confirmation to him. If the children were wrong about Santa forgetting him, then they were also wrong about everything else. This meant that he deserved to have parents like everyone else and to have friends too.

But sadly, the other children still didn't seem to think so. Often he would come back from school in tears and Ksenia would try again and again to console him, to make him feel loved and accepted, despite the cruelty of others. And the children persisted pointing out to him how he was different to them all. Instead of protecting him, they ganged up against him to gain pleasure from his weakness to stand his ground. When he was a lot younger, they would often reduce him to tears, but he knew better by now not to let that happen. He had gained strength in him that allowed him to act as if he was unaffected by it all. That seemed to work along the way and the teasing was not as bad as before.

In the schoolyard or in the case of the odd birthday party, he would be invited to play with them as if he were fully accepted as one of them. But sooner or later, just when he thought he had made friends, they'd betray him again, treating him like an outcast. Just like today. These boys had got annoyed because he had proved to be faster than them on the skateboard and the oldest boy among them had accused him of cheating. He had pushed him to the ground and had snatched the skateboard from his hands. His words still rang in his ears: "You jumped the gun! That's why you finished first, admit it or lose this!" he had threatened him as he shook the skateboard violently in his hands.

Manos had sprung up on his feet and tried desperately to take it from his hands while the other boys laughed. But the bully was a lot taller and stronger than him and he had lifted it over his head, beyond Manos's reach.

"Give it to me now!" Manos had demanded, overwhelmed by the sense of injustice. He had tried desperately to reach up but hadn't managed to retrieve it from his grasp. As the other boys kept laughing, Manos had felt a surge of anger consume him. That had eventually made him drop his hands to his sides, scowl at the bully and stare into his eyes with determination. "I never cheated! You're a liar! Give it to me now or else!"

"Or else what? What will you do, Orphan? Will you beat me up? I doubt it! Or will you get Daddy to do it for you? You don't have one, remember?" he had said laughing at his face. That was it. Six whole years of suffering quietly had just reached boiling point.

Manos raised his arm and punched the boy right on the nose with strength and courage that he didn't know he possessed. He'd never hit anyone before. The demeaning laughter of the other boys that had been ringing in his ears until that moment suddenly ceased, and the bully let out a loud yelp. The skateboard dropped from his hands, as he brought them instinctively to his face. Manos bent down to pick it up, but the bully got there first somehow. He pushed Manos angrily to the ground and started to pound the skateboard repeatedly against the cement wall behind them. By the time Manos got back on his feet and over there, the damage had already been done. The bully threw it on the pavement and ran away with the others, all of them clutching their skateboards in their hands.

Before disappearing around the corner, the bully had stopped and said: "This should teach you to call me a liar! Let's see how you'll cheat again without a skateboard. Serves you right, Orphan Boy!"

That's what they'd always called him: 'Orphan'. But Manos didn't feel like one because he had a sister who loved him. Because Mrs. Sofia had been a substitute mother to him too. He had the refuge of his home whenever the world hurt him and most of all he still had hope and the certainty that his parents would come back one day. Plus he knew that wherever they were, they loved him as always. He had these beliefs thanks to his sister, and they'd been etched so deeply in his psyche that no amount of cruelty could ever draw them out.

Manos turned his gaze to the orchard again drawn by an instinctive need to focus his mind on something he loved because only such a thing can help someone overcome sorrow. A sense of comfort stirred in his heart as he watched Odysseus napping still in the clearing, the invisible flies still making his ears twitch unstoppably. And as if by magic, Odysseus then lifted his head and sat up, looking back at him with sleepy eyes. Manos smiled and Odysseus let out one loud bark wagging his tail frantically. The boy rushed to the kitchen and through the back door and ran to his friend.

When you're young, not only in years but also at heart, it's easy to find comfort even in the adoring eyes of a canine. A warm snout can say so much with a lick on your neck or your face, making you smile again, offering unexpected comfort just when you thought you were alone.

Chapter 9

Ksenia saw Zoe off after their morning together and then walked up to the fruit store to say a quick hi to Phevos. In half an hour he would leave work and they'd go out on their first date just as they had planned the night before.

"Phevos!" she called out to him from the pavement. His face lit up when he saw her. He jumped down the steps and rushed to her, lifting her in his arms. She shrieked with joy, and he put her down again to kiss her.

"I missed you so much since yesterday!" he said caressing her face with the back of his hand.

"Me too! Zoe just left. I'll come and pick you up when you finish work, okay?"

"Yes my love, not long now," he said, looking at his watch for the hundredth time that day.

When Mr. Giorgis came out to the front, Ksenia greeted him with a genuine smile. She was still in Phevos's arms but found she didn't care if the whole world knew about them. That was so unlike her. She had always kept up appearances and a low profile in her community. But love had come into her life now. Like a mighty wind it had swept through her being, taking away her reserve, her shyness and her pretences. She had nothing to hide any more. She felt strong in his arms, ready to take on the world if she had to. Mr. Giorgis hardly presented in her eyes a potential threat anyway and to prove it, he was now smiling widely at them both.

"You lucky rascal," he said with a chortle. "You've won the lottery of love from the looks, haven't you? You'd better take care of our Ksenia or you'll have to deal with me, you hear?" he teased shaking his finger at Phevos. The young couple started laughing, and he let out another uproarious laugh as he turned around to go.

"I've something to tell you. It's about Manos," Phevos said as soon as Mr. Giorgis had gone back in his shop.

"What about Manos?" she asked, the smile freezing on her face. She knew her brother had gone out to play with some other boys on their skateboards. It didn't happen often, and she had been glad to hear it, but now, she felt uneasy.

"Well, he had a fight right there with some other boys just a few minutes ago," he replied pointing vaguely to the street.

"A fight? Did he get hurt?" she asked, her faze ablaze with alarm.

"No, not physically anyway. But he got upset. They smashed his skateboard. I don't think it's reparable—"

Ksenia tipped her chin and rolled her eyes. "Oh, why can't they leave him alone? Damn them all, damn them all to hell and back!" she said gritting her teeth.

"Has he had this kind of trouble before, Ksenia?"

"Try forever…"

"But why?"

"Because he's different! Because he hasn't got any parents! They've been bullying him for years in school. You don't know what he has been through…."

"But it's so unfair! He's such a kind and clever boy. He doesn't deserve this. Surely he has friends at school too, who accept him for who he is?"

"He has no friends, Phevos! Not one! He has been low on self-confidence for years because of all this!" she answered with a quivering voice, the upset rising in her chest.

"Don't be upset, my Ksenia! It will be all right! As he grows up, he'll eventually feel strong in himself. Life works miracles for good people. You will see," he said as his arms closed around her again.

"I hope you're right, Phevos," she replied taking a deep breath to calm herself. She wouldn't allow herself to break into tears. She looked at Phevos lovingly and comforted herself with the thought that she had him in her life now to share everything with. She wasn't alone any more.

"Would you like me to speak to him?"

"Thank you but it would be better not to. He's not very good with talking about his problems. I'd better go home and check on him." She turned to go.

"Don't worry Ksenia. He'll be fine. Children are incredibly strong and resilient. Before you know it, he'll be a confident teenager surrounded by girlfriends," he joked, trying to amuse her.

"Thank you my love," she replied, forcing a smile. "Indeed, he's very strong. Every time they try to hurt him, he doesn't dwell on it for too long. He gets over it soon enough."

"That's encouraging surely," he said with a wink, smiling still.

"Yes I guess so. See you soon, my Phevos!" With her good spirits partly restored, she left a grateful peck on his lips and hurried to her house.

Ksenia went from room to room but didn't find her brother. In the end, she went out to the back yard and was relieved to find him in the orchard, playing with Odysseus. He greeted her with such a joyous smile that had Phevos not said anything, she would have been none the wiser. That made her wonder how many times he'd come home from school looking like like this, unwilling to share with her any similar incidents.

Her heart went to him as she watched him play. His laughter filled the air as he ran with the dog among the trees. Their branches swayed lightly in the breeze full of blossom as if cheering them on. Manos kept throwing a tennis ball, and the dog would run frantically after it. He would grab it in his mouth and fetch it to Manos while chewing it relentlessly. He'd then growl if the boy tried to take it from his mouth but would eventually allow him to. Manos would throw the ball again and the whole thing would start from the beginning. Over and over again, the tennis ball would be chewed mercilessly. Each time Manos took it in his hands to throw it, it looked a bit sorrier for itself than before. A tad more bitten and wet, a tad less round than earlier. Ksenia watched them and laughed until her gut hurt.

When Manos got enough, he turned on his heels and took out his old bicycle that had been rusting away in a corner. Odysseus lost his interest in the ball immediately and let it drop from his mouth. He followed Manos and lay on the ground near him watching him inflate the tires with a hand pump. He hadn't used his bike since last summer when he got his skateboard. As he inflated the tires, he told Ksenia how he'd missed it and how he thought it would be a nice change from the skateboard. Ksenia chose to respect his obvious intention not to tell her what had happened. He was obviously trying to make do with what he had right now, in terms of playing outdoors. It was enough to her to see that he still sought to play outside and not only with his pc. After all, he had better chances to make friends one day if he played outside in the real world rather than pc games with virtual characters. Mostly, Ksenia was relieved to see that her brother had demonstrated the same determination once again to take remedial action, to seek an alternative means rather than allow his heart to sink in the sorrow of his loss.

Ksenia remembered Phevos's advice. He was right. Her brother would be fine. He had first found consolation in his four-legged friend and now in his old bike. She sighed with relief, as she watched her brother ride his bicycle in the back yard with Odysseus barking away behind him. She thought how easy it is to replace an irreparable skateboard. A strong heart makes sure that's done easily, the way her brother had just shown her so well. The only thing that would be hard to replace, would be a weak mind that is stuck in defeat and self-pity. And from what she could see, her brother wasn't in any danger of that.

***

Daphne came out of the bathroom dressed in her nightie. It had been a long day and it was now half past ten. She yawned when she sat on the stool in front of the dresser in order to comb her hair. Phevos was lying in his bed with a grin on his face. He was staring at the ceiling lost in happy thoughts.

"So, it was nice on the Lycabettus Hill, was it?" she asked him.

"Oh yes! I must take you there, Daphne! You can see the whole of Athens from up there!" he replied, still enthused about his afternoon visit there with Ksenia.

"That would be nice!" she said pleasantly yawning again on her way to her bed.

"So! This guy Aris...." piped up Phevos with a playful glint in his eyes.

"What about him?" she asked slipping between the sheets.

He arched an eyebrow at her. "Well, he could take you there instead of me, couldn't he?"

"What? Don't be ridiculous, Phevos! I hardly know the man!" She huffed with a shocked expression on her face, amusing her brother enough to push the point.

"I don't think so, Sister! Ever since I came back today all I've heard from you is Aris this and Aris that. You seem to know him pretty well."

"That's preposterous!" she protested sitting up on her bed. "I just thought it'd be nice to tell you all about Mrs. Sofia's son, that's all."

"Okay," he said holding up his hands. "I'm sorry! Looks like I got the wrong impression there! Thought you liked him or something," he said with a smirk.

"Apology accepted," she replied, looking mildly offended.

"So, how long is he here for then?"

"I don't know. But Mrs. Sofia has said in the past that he never stays for long periods. Just a few days I guess."

"Oh yeah? And what does he do with his time here? Does he have any friends in the city?"

"From what I know, he spends a lot of time in Pallada with his mom. He has a few colleagues in Athens, but they seldom meet because they don't often have time off simultaneously."

"Oh! If that's the case, why don't you ask him to take you to Lycabettus Hill?" he asked letting out an uproarious laugh. Daphne shot a disapproving look at him and switched off the light in a huff. She hid under the covers as her brother's amused laughter lingered in the darkened room.

"Oh come on, Daphne, admit it!" his voice echoed in the gloom. "Your face is radiant when you speak about him. I've never seen you like this before. You like him!"

"Good night, Phevos!" she replied firmly feeling thankful for the darkness that hid the crimson color of her cheeks.

"All right, Daphne. I will let you off for now," he teased. With a last chuckle he rolled on his back and let his mind wander to his Ksenia again. Soon enough, his eyes got used to the darkness, and he started to make out shadows from all the surrounding objects. Beams of light from the other buildings crept through the shutters and huddled on the ceiling like reunited friends.

His eyelids grew heavier and heavier as he thought of his new life with Ksenia and soon enough, he surrendered to a peaceful sleep. That night, his soul regained its wings for another special journey in time and space, to one of these places where the Gods weave their will to produce the fabric of destiny.

In spirit as he slept, he found himself on a sandy beach that stretched out as far as the eye could see. Phevos stood there and looked around him. There were beautiful dunes of fine sand that shone like gold dust as well as a hill that towered over the beach at a great height. He could see a magnificent temple on its top. Its marble and gold decorations glinted in the sunlight. Before him, the sea was deep blue and fairly calm with small waves that lapped gently on the shore.

Phevos welcomed the cool caress of the sea breeze on his cheeks and felt safe there, protected and happy. But suddenly, his heart was overpowered by an unfathomable feeling of awe. Something or someone was approaching and the feeling it gave off as it did so, indicated that the entity was supernatural. His eyes filled with inexplicable tears that felt salty and stung his eyes. He looked around him frantically but then all at once, he got the feeling he had nothing to fear. Phevos didn't know how he could guess all that, but he just knew it was so.

His heart was beating fast now and he thought then that the entity he could sense was perhaps Athena. All at once, a gigantic wave rose from the sea. It rocketed sky high hiding the sun as it foamed with an exploding sound. Foam and clouds became one against the dark blue of the sea and Phevos fell on his knees, terrified, with his eyes tightly shut. He felt the wet sand under him for a few moments only and then a mass of cold seawater took him in an instant, carrying him to a crystal blue abyss.

He was on the seabed now for he could see colorful corals, black urchins with long, glistening spikes and fish with iridescent colors. And then, as suddenly as he had been taken there, he was somehow returned back to the shore. He was kneeling on the sand again, but somehow he wasn't wet at all. Phevos was shocked to the core at this realization and then instinctively looked up.

Towering above him stood a majestic-looking stranger with an incredible air of grandeur. He was unnaturally tall and heavily built. He had a long, red beard on his harsh-looking face and looked resplendent in his robes of blue silk and crimson velvet. They were adorned with gold thread and buttons made of pearls. In one hand, he held a long metal staff that shone in the sunlight in a blinding way. Phevos could only glimpse at it with great effort but he managed to notice a forked shape on its top. In his other hand, the stranger held a much smaller object that Phevos could see clearly. It was a wand made of crystal. Countless shards of seashells in various colors swam in a transparent liquid inside, along with grains of fine golden sand. The wand gave off an eerie light that made its contents sparkle like stars on a summer's night sky.

The sight of this magical object overwhelmed him, and he bowed before the tall stranger, who smiled in response. His eyes were kind, and they filled Phevos's heart with an inexplicable feeling of reverence and awe.

"Don't be afraid, Phevos! I am here to help you!" said the stranger. His voice sounded like thunder. It echoed across the beach like the roar of a thousand horns.

"You know my name?"

"Of course I know your name! And I know your father's too. It is Efimios!"

"You know my father? Who are you, good Sir?"

"It does not matter at the moment who I am! What matters now, is this!" he bellowed stretching out his hand to give the wand to Phevos. He took it from his incredibly large hand and as he brought it close to his chest to examine it better, it suddenly gave off a blinding light and then, an image of his father appeared in its midst. He was smiling through the light reassuringly, as if he was giving him comfort. He smiled and smiled and Phevos stood mesmerized until his father's face faded away, and the iridescence of mother-of-pearl took his place as the shards of shells floated in a golden sea of sand and light.

Phevos shuddered and nearly dropped the wand but managed to tighten his grip in time. Astonished, he looked up again gazing at the stranger for a few moments with unbelieving eyes.

"What...what is all this? I don't understand! My father...." he stammered when he finally managed to speak.

"Your father is safe! And soon enough, you and Daphne will be reunited with him. But first, you must trust me!"

"Your Lordship, I don't know who you are, but if you know my father I will do as you ask!"

"First of all, there are a few things to explain. What you saw in the wand is not reality, but a glimpse of what will happen if you take the right steps."

"What do you mean, my lord?"

"I mean that with every decision you make, you take a new step along the path of your life. There are millions of alternative paths that you will never walk as a result of your choices. The right path for you is the one that is favorable by the Gods and you are fortunate for I can tell you that you are treading the right path right now! In your endeavors to reunite with your father as well as with your lost mother, you will have plenty of divine protection. But beware; you will succeed in your purpose only if you take *all* the right steps! Wrong choices along the way will lead you to alternative paths, but only the right one will take you to your purpose. So take extra caution not to stray from the one path that has been prepared for you to take you there!"

"Sir, I think I can understand what you mean but it sounds terrifying! How do I know what choices to make when the time comes?"

"Do not worry, Phevos. That is why I have appeared here before you. I can help you but you must trust me first!"

"I trust you, Your Lordship! Tell me what to do!"

"The wand in your hand is indispensable for your journey. But to let you have it, I must take something from you in return."

"Of course! Just name it, sir. What is it?"

"It is the necklace that you wear around your neck."

"My necklace? How do you even know about that?" Perplexed, he took it out from under his shirt. The moonstone in its center sparkled in unison with the tiny quartz crystals all around it. On either side of the moonstone, two shapes were engraved: a spear and a battle helmet. Phevos shook his head, unwilling to part with the sacred object that Athena once gave his father in return for his services to her.

Phevos jutted out his chin. "This belongs to my father. It is not mine to give, kind sir."

"You will only need to lend it to me. That is why I told you to trust me. I promise that once you have walked the path, I will return Athena's necklace to you."

"How do you even know this is Athena's? How do you know so much?" he asked and then the wand in his hand shone with a brilliant light again. Phevos was startled and his uneasiness turned to rage. "What trickery is this? Who are you and who sent you to deceive me?" Phevos threw the wand away, and the tall stranger caught it in mid air in his massive hand, his face darkening like a stormy sky.

The wand gave off a blinding light inside his palm and he raised his head, letting out a thunderous cry that sounded like a stampede of wild horses. He raised the long staff in his other hand and started to shake it with terrible force. The white clouds turned murky and started to move. Lightning bolts ripped the sky and the deafening noise of thunder filled the air. Huge waves rose from the sea, threatening to swallow the beach in a single gulp while whole flocks of seabirds took to the skies and flew in manic patterns inland. The whole beach shook with a powerful earthquake.

Overcome by it all, Phevos fell on his knees and shut his eyes against the salty wind that carried sand and hurt him like a whip. Although his eyes were shut now, for some strange reason he could still see the tall stranger. His height had increased three fold. His face was angry against the backdrop of a dark sky strewn with flashing lightning bolts. The gigantic waves still threatened to swallow him up. Yet, in a miraculous way, they seemed to be held back by an invisible force. They were not moving but rather hovering over the surface of the sea, foaming and roaring.

"Did you think that I have a reason to deceive you? Do I look like I need anything from you?" echoed the stranger's voice through the raging storm. "You fool! I can command these waves to crush you in an instant! There is nothing in the sea that I do not command! Enormous creatures of the deep, mighty storms and powerful sea currents are mere servants of mine! Large, magnificent ships laden with mythical treasures have perished underwater in the hour of my wrath and you dare think that I require your permission to take your meager necklace from you? Nothing could stop me from taking it from you right now! How foolish you are! Don't you see that it has no value to me, unless you part with it willingly?"

And then, everything fell silent. Phevos opened his eyes to see the stranger back to his original height looking at him with his head tilted to the side, his expression calm.

"Do you see now?" he asked, his eyes kind.

"I... I think I do my lord..." stammered Phevos, still in shock.

"That is better, my good lad!" He smiled. "I am sorry if I scared you a bit back there. I do find it hard to control my rage sometimes. But you challenged me!" he added with a wink.

"I am sorry too, Your Lordship. I didn't mean any offence. Let it be as you wish," he said, feeling awestruck by what he had just experienced. He lifted the necklace in his hands, about to take it off but the stranger motioned to him to stop.

"Not here! Not now!" he commanded with authority. "I will trade it with you later. In the meantime, get yourself a good shovel. It is time to make use of your gardening skills!"

Before Phevos could manage an answer, the stranger disappeared into thin air and then somehow, the sea engulfed Phevos in an instant. He was back on the seabed. A school of tiny, silvery fish swam by him and then he was enveloped in a void of darkness.

The next thing he remembered, he was awake in his bed clutching his father's necklace in his hand as it hung around his neck. He could still remember every single detail of the dream, and as soon as Daphne awoke moments later, he told her all about it. His sister agreed with him that such a vivid dream could not be overlooked as it might contain signs.

It was Sunday morning and they didn't have much time to analyze it in detail, as they were invited at Ksenia's and

Manos's house for lunch, but they agreed to try to decipher the dream together when they got back home in the evening.

Ksenia and Manos were looking forward to spending that Sunday at home with their special guests. For the first time, they had felt the need to include other people too in their family tradition of leisurely, treat-filled Sundays. It had all been planned ahead among the four. They were going to have lunch together at home, and in the morning Manos was going to show them around the orchard. He often wandered in it with Odysseus and knew all its beautiful nooks and crannies. He knew for example where the largest anthills were or where to find jade green lizards basking in the sunlight on the rocks among the bushes.

Phevos stood shaving before the bathroom mirror and thought of Manos's excitement whenever he spoke of the orchard. As he rinsed his face, the words of the stranger from his dream echoed in his mind: *"In the meantime, get yourself a good shovel. It is time to make use of your gardening skills!"*

Chapter 10

"Good morning! Come in through to the sitting room. I'm making filter coffee," announced Ksenia in between kissing Phevos and Daphne, who had just arrived. As they followed her down the hallway, Manos came rushing to them from the other end. He was still in his pajamas and held a handful of dog food in dry pellets.

"Hi! You're here!" He greeted them with a huge grin.

"Hey, how are you, my friend?" replied Phevos patting him on the back. Daphne gave the boy a hug and kissed him on the cheek.

"I'm fine, thanks. I was just going to give Odysseus his morning snack."

"And then go and get dressed, okay?" his sister urged him.

"Duh! Of course Ksenia!" he replied with a smirk as if she had suggested something preposterous. "I'm hardly going to show you around the orchard in my pajamas, am I now?"

"Off you go now, you cheeky devil!" she said and he was off with a tee-hee. She turned to face Phevos and that's when they both realized Daphne was no longer standing there with them.

They entered the sitting room to find her peering through the glass at the contents of a china cabinet. It stood in a corner of the small room, looking tired with age, laden with intricate, carved designs of flowers in the dark wood. Daphne's delicate nose was stuck on the glass, as she marveled at the miniature knickknacks inside. They stood among fine porcelain tea sets with pink and blue flower designs and golden rims. Most knickknacks were in the shape of animals, such as Mr. and Mrs. Rabbit, who held hands dressed in rustic clothes. There was also a hen hatching eggs inside a basket, a kitten that stared with beady eyes climbing out of a beautiful purse with a golden chain as well as some mice that inhabited a boot with a door, a window and a chimney.

Daphne stared at them with admiration, enthusing over them with short gasps and numerous other exclamatory sounds. She looked adorable in her girly innocence, and Ksenia stood with Phevos chuckling away as they watched her.

"They're so beautiful!" she said, turning to face them.

Ksenia approached her to slide the front glass window to the side so that she could take a closer look. Daphne stood there intrigued, resuming her exclamatory praise.

"You must excuse my sister, Ksenia. She just can't resist marveling at pretty little things. She goes gooey in the presence of beauty. Come to think of it, this one runs in our family!" he said, squeezing Ksenia in his arms and laughing.

That Sunday morning was rather cloudy, but by eleven a.m. it was warm enough for them to go out into the orchard without their jackets on. As soon as they emerged, Odysseus ran up to them with cheerful barks, wagging his tail. Manos led the way in order to give the others the long awaited tour. The sun peeked through the fleeting clouds every now and then as they sauntered along, Odysseus never leaving Manos's side. His clever eyes shone in the sunlight, his mouth gaping open, and his tongue hanging out in a goofy smile. Manos kept bending down to pet him and Odysseus responded with playful moans and yelps of adoration as he wagged his tail non-stop.

"You're very fond of dogs, aren't you?" Daphne asked Manos.

"Well, I'm fond of my Odysseus, that's for sure. He's my best friend!" he replied patting the dog on the head.

"That's nice," said Phevos. "It's nice to have friends. Daphne and I are your friends too, right?" he asked and Ksenia squeezed his hand in hers with gratitude.

"Of course we're friends!" replied Manos with a smile.

"Oh, how lovely it is here!" said Daphne. "This orchard reminds me of our own back home," she added with a hint of melancholy in her voice.

"Yes, it's indeed beautiful in the spring, isn't it?" commented Ksenia. "Especially with the blossom on the trees and everything. Although it needs a lot of work... We used to have the assistance of a neighbor, but last year he retired and moved back to his hometown in the Peloponese. I keep telling myself we should hire someone to tend to it. We have to... Manos and I don't know anything about gardening."

"Gardening, you said?" interrupted Daphne. She gave a meaningful stare to her brother, and he returned her gaze with equal enthusiasm. A light had just come on inside his head at the sound of Ksenia's last word. He knew it was a sign in connection to his strange dream. He was looking out for it and now it was here. The word 'coincidence' did not exist in his world.

"Well, I could help you out! I'm a very keen gardener back home, you know!" he piped up.

"Really? You never told me," she replied.

"Yes, it's true. Father is also a very good gardener and tends our gardens himself back home. He's taught Phevos all he knows," interrupted Daphne.

"That's great," answered Ksenia. "But are you sure? Look at the state of it all!" Cringing, she pointed at the weeds and the thorny shrubs that threatened to suck the life out of all the herbs and flowers on either side of the rocky path.

Phevos gave a dismissive wave. "Don't worry about that. Weeding is easy! There are proper tools for everything. I can get rid of all that, even the rocks and the pits. I can shovel dirt in the right places to create smooth paths for us to walk on. I can make vegetable patches and tend to the trees too," he said with confidence as if he were doing a job interview and trying to impress.

"I don't know, Phevos. It'll be a lot of trouble for you. What about your job? I can't ask you to do all that after leaving the shop, you'd never rest!"

"Ksenia, don't worry about it. I love gardening so it won't be any trouble. On the contrary, it'll be the perfect way for me to relax after work. And it won't take a lot of time. First, I'll do a bit of weeding and tidying up, then will clear up the paths. I could sow vegetables and some basil to keep the insects away... And I could make some flowerbeds... I'll have to prune and fertilize as well, of course..." Phevos kept talking, reciting tasks while Ksenia nodded, her expression exuberant. When he turned to look at her, she laced her hands around his neck.

"Thank you, Phevos! It all sounds wonderful. I can't wait!"

"Yeah!" Manos cheered on.

"I could help out, if you like. I know a few things too," offered Daphne.

"I don't know anything, but I'd be glad to help too, if I can," said Ksenia.

"Of course, that'll be great," answered Phevos to both of them.

"Yeah! And I'll carry the tools for you, Phevos!" chimed in Manos.

"You have tools?" asked Daphne surprised.

"Oh yes! They're in the back yard. They've always been there. Although I don't think my parents had green fingers either. They must have hired help too." Ksenia giggled. She was so happy that day that not even the memory of her parents could dampen her spirits.

"Do you have a shovel?" asked Phevos.

"Sure! A big and heavy one!" answered Manos, wide-eyed.

"I bet it's a good shovel, too," murmured Phevos squeezing Ksenia in his arms, happy to have received a clear answer to his mystifying dream. He tried to stifle in his heart the feeling of guilt for hiding all this from her. But he knew he had no choice for the time being and hoped that one day he would be able to tell her everything, and that she'd understand.

Manos's tour had brought them to the far end of the orchard. There was no fencing there to mark the end of their property, only the rocky foot of the Acropolis hill that towered over it. The Greek flag overhead rippled in the breeze. The Parthenon temple looked magnificent. Behind it, cotton clouds fleeted past like saluting troops on parade.

Phevos and Manos stood for a while admiring the temple while Ksenia picked wild flowers for her mother's vase. Daphne lingered nearby on her own looking around mystified and all at once, she had one of those déjà vu feelings that cloud your mind for a few moments. There was something familiar about her surroundings, but she couldn't decide what it was. She approached her brother and looked up to see the Parthenon too. She still couldn't believe its demise through the centuries. It was even more devastating to her, because she had seen it in its glory days. And then, realization hit her. It wasn't only that the orchard reminded her so much of her own back home. There was something else too that brought on this strong sense of familiarity and at last, she knew. This very spot was where she and her brother had first arrived into this modern world. She had raised her eyes to the top of the Acropolis that night, and she remembered seeing the flagpole with the Parthenon from the same angle. She also remembered the cluster of lemon trees to her right and the two cypress trees that stood tall side by side. This was the exact spot where they had arrived that night. She wondered why they had to wind up here of all places. Why not anywhere else?

When Ksenia called on her to give her some of the wild flowers she had picked, Daphne rushed to her, putting aside these nagging thoughts. It was time for lunch and Ksenia prompted everyone to follow her home. She had cooked roast lamb with oregano and rosemary. The fresh air had made everyone hungry so they followed her without further ado. Odysseus ran up and down among them on their way back, and they all laughed at his antiques as Manos chased after him.

After the delicious lunch, they retired to the sitting room for coffee, tea and cake. Manos switched on the TV and sat in an armchair to watch a family movie that was on. Every now and then, he turned his head to chip into the conversation of the other three, who sat together on the sofa.

"So your house is old, is it?" asked Daphne.

"Yes! My great-grandfather bought the land and also helped in building the house. He was a rich merchant from Asia Minor. He loved good, honest work and was a man of decency and honor. That is how my dad spoke of him always. It was also my great-grandfather who acquired Pallada later on. It was a stately home at the time. He believed in the value of land, and I'm glad he felt that way as all his property was passed on to us through the generations. If it weren't for Pallada, we would have no source of income today."

"When was it converted to a hotel?" asked Daphne.

"My father did that many years ago," said Manos and then turned back to his film.

"I know you mentioned your parents are no longer with you Ksenia, but are your grandparents alive?" enquired Phevos. He had an arm around her and with the other he toyed with a strand of her hair between his fingers.

"No, we don't have any surviving grandparents."

"What a pity! You must miss them," said Daphne. Although she never knew her own biological grandparents, she had known Efimios's parents and they were as loving to her as any grandparent could ever be. She knew well how it felt to miss them.

"Yes it's true, although we have Mrs. Sofia. She's so caring and protective that she might as well be our granny," Ksenia replied.

Phevos gave an easy laugh. "I know what you mean. A few days ago I got first hand experience of that! You see, I had a stomach cramp and when she heard she brought a plate of soup in the shop for me at lunchtime! She returned again in half an hour just to make sure I'd eaten it all. And before she took the empty plate, she told me off for not being too careful with what I eat. What's more, for days later she kept prompting me to list for her everything I ate! It was hilarious, bless her!"

"She's the same with me," replied Manos, who was listening in again at that time. "She keeps reminding me to dress warm, not to stand in draughts and not to drink ice cold water!" He giggled and the others joined him as his words had struck a familiar chord.

Mrs. Sofia had a particular distaste for draughts. Often, she'd rush around Pallada shutting windows and doors when a wind picked up outside, eager to protect herself and others from getting a stiff neck or back. She was forever warning everyone not to stand in draughts in order to avoid the 'freeze' as she called it. Mrs. Sofia always uttered this word goggle-eyed, in dreaded remembrance of her painful experiences trying to treat it with warm compresses and heat-inducing ointments.

"See? We all have a granny after all!" piped up Ksenia and everyone giggled. "And what about you? Do you have grandparents back home? And what about your parents? Do they live far from here?" she asked with a serious expression on her face. She wasn't so much curious any more, but now she cared about them too much. She also felt she knew them well enough by now as to dare these personal questions without worrying she's causing embarrassment or offence. Ksenia was wrong though because despite the growing familiarity between them, Daphne became tongue-tied again. However, Phevos felt he had to reply and what's more, he didn't want to lie to Ksenia any more. He bridged his hands before him as if in silent prayer, focusing his thoughts, choosing his words with caution.

"Our grandparents are dead too. My father raised us. His name is Efimios."

"And we miss him terribly," added Daphne with a slight tremor in her voice. She also felt relieved she could say something to her new friends about her past that wasn't a lie.

"That's a very beautiful and rare name! I don't think I've heard it before," commented Ksenia.

"Wait a minute!" said Manos. "So your father's name is Efimios Efimiou? How odd!"

"Yes… it is!" replied Phevos. He couldn't confess that his father had no surname, and that he was just Efimios. 'Efimiou' only meant 'of Efimios'. It was a surname that Phevos had come up with along the way as everyone in modern Greece were asked to quote their full name sooner or later. So he had chosen this surname, as to state who he was: Phevos of Efimios.

"And your mother?" asked Ksenia interrupting his thoughts.

"I'm afraid I have no memory of her. I was still very young when she lived with us…" His voice trailed off, and he took a deep breath before speaking again. "It's a mystery. She's somehow disappeared from our lives. That's all I know. My father never explained what happened."

"She disappeared?" asked Manos astounded, turning to meet his sister's gaze.

"You don't remember anything about your mother?" asked Ksenia, knitting her brows.

"I know it sounds strange. I know I should be able to remember her but I don't. Father said I had an accident around the time that she vanished, and that this explains the strange amnesia I suffer from."

"Amnesia? Did you hurt your head?" asked Manos thrilled.

"I don't even know what happened to me or to her. All I know is that we lost touch with her eleven years ago. I was nine at the time." His voice was laden with emotion. Ksenia and Manos turned to stare at each other in stunned silence. In their world, coincidence was just coincidence but somehow, Phevos's words had managed to stir wonder in their hearts.

"It all sounds very strange, I know," Phevos sighed, "but Father promised one day I will know everything and that Mother will come back to our lives again." His voice wavered toward the end of his sentence.

Ksenia took his hand and squeezed it in hers to give him comfort. "I'm very sorry to hear about this, my love! My heart goes to both of you. I'm sure you realize Manos and I are going through something similar," she said, her brow creased as she glanced at Phevos and Daphne.

"I don't remember my parents either you know," said Manos. Chewing his lower lip, he left the armchair to come and sit on the sofa near Phevos.

"So how did you lose your parents? When did they die?" asked Daphne moving to sit closer to Ksenia.

"No, our parents aren't dead! Or at least, there's no evidence of that. From what we know they just vanished overnight," answered Ksenia.

"I thought you said you lost them eleven years ago!" said Phevos.

"Yes we 'lost' them! As in they can't be found. I meant it literally... Oh! I guess I can tell now why you got the wrong impression. I'm so sorry!" replied Ksenia feeling silly for the misunderstanding she'd caused.

"Well I guess that's better in a way, isn't it? It means there's always hope if you keep the faith, right?" asked Daphne. Ksenia nodded in agreement.

"So your parents disappeared out of the blue just like my mother did? Eleven years ago? That is really odd!" commented Phevos.

"Yes, it's an amazing coincidence, isn't it?" replied Ksenia. "I was only eight when my parents disappeared. Manos was only one. Of course, he doesn't remember them at all, but I have quite a few memories of them. We have no idea how it happened, where they may be now and why."

"But don't you think it's very odd that both you and I lost loved ones eleven years ago under mysterious circumstances?" queried Phevos, his mind stuck on the notion this could not be a coincidence. His fingers caressed Ksenia's cheek, and he felt a shudder from her shoulders. A tear rolled down from her eyes, and he caught it in his fingertips, wiping it away. Ksenia squeezed his hand in hers once again, this time to draw comfort from him.

"Don't cry, Ksenia!" said Daphne. "There's always hope! Phevos always hopes to reunite with his mother one day." Ksenia looked at her puzzled then, and Daphne felt compelled to explain. "I know, I haven't clarified this earlier. Phevos's mother is not my own. I've never even met her. Efimios's father adopted me when I was only eight. Both my parents had already died by then. It was eleven years ago too.... I guess that period changed everything for all of us, huh!"

"This is so tragic!" whispered Ksenia after a few moments of silence. "It's incredible how much in common we have! Right now, I feel both of you as family. That's how close you feel to me," she said with a quivering voice.

"Yes it's incredible indeed, my love! Although I will try to forget what you said about us being related if you don't mind! It would be rather illegal to hug you like this if I were your brother you know," he teased winking at her, trying to lift her spirits. Ksenia responded with a big smile relaxing in his arms, her sorrow somewhat alleviated.

"Can I ask another question if you don't mind? Did Mrs. Sofia raise you as soon as your parents were gone or did any relatives look after you for a while first?" asked Daphne.

Ksenia shook her head. "We have no other family. But we had Mrs. Anna in the house at the time. She took care of us during the first few weeks before Mrs. Sofia took over in raising us."

"Who is Mrs. Anna?" asked Phevos.

"A very kind lady who used to live upstairs," answered Manos. Over the years, he had learnt from his sister all the sparse details that she remembered from those days.

"Yes, she was indeed a lovely lady, who used to rent the upstairs rooms at the time."

"What? Your bedroom upstairs you mean?" asked Daphne.

"Well, there was another room also to her avail which is now a storeroom. And there's also a small bathroom up there," Ksenia explained.

"And she lived on her own there?" asked Phevos.

"Well, she used to live up there with her husband at some point. According to Mrs. Sofia they were close friends with my parents. I don't recall any of that, but I do remember her after she was widowed."

"Her husband died?" asked Phevos.

"Yes. Poor Mrs. Anna! She had such an aura of sadness about her! She didn't smile often, but her heart was full of love. I still remember how she held me in her arms to comfort me as I cried when our parents were gone. She had such a good heart! I don't remember her husband, but I have the impression she loved him dearly. She seemed just lost without him. I think the short time she spent taking care of Manos and me was good for her. It helped her put aside her own loss for a while. When Mrs. Sofia moved here in our home to take care of us, Mrs. Anna went away to make a new life for herself. That's what Mrs. Sofia explained to us in time about her. She said she needed to move on and leave the pain behind. She had lost her husband recently at the time and all these tragic incidents in our house had become too much for her to bear.

"Oh how terrible! Imagine fostering two children while mourning for your husband and worrying over two friends as well!" commented Daphne.

"She sounds like a wonderful person. Where does she live now?" asked Phevos.

"All I know is that she moved out of Athens. I haven't seen her ever since she left," replied Ksenia.

"It's so strange about your parents! Just like my mother I guess... How do people disappear like that? Did your parents vanish without a trace? Didn't Mrs. Anna or Mrs. Sofia know anything to tell you?"

"Yes, exactly. They did vanish without a trace... Neither of the women who took care of us ever passed on to us any information. Mrs. Sofia wasn't even here at the time. She was at her sister's in Corfu, who was terminally ill back then. I expect that if Mrs. Anna knew anything about their disappearance she would have said. On the contrary, she never spoke about it. It must have been too painful for her."

Their high spirits had dampened because of the last topic of discussion, and Ksenia took the liberty to try to shift the mood. She got a board game out, one of Manos's favorites, and they all jumped at the chance to have some fun. Soon enough, the sitting room filled with shrieks of joy and playful banter. When they tired from the game, Phevos and Ksenia engaged in excited conversation about the work required at the orchard.

Manos was leaning on Daphne now, who had a tender arm wrapped around him. They were seated on the sofa too, leafing through a photo album that Manos produced from a drawer at the bottom of the china cabinet. They were photos of Ksenia and Manos as well as Mrs. Sofia from the recent years when they were under her care.

And then, when she turned another page, Daphne gasped, causing the others to whip their heads around. Her eyes were open wide at the sight of a single photo. She turned her head and looked at Phevos. She looked ashen, as if she'd seen a ghost.

"What is it, Daphne? Are you all right?" he asked putting his arms around her. Her eyes were burning like fire in the pale desert of her face. She looked so frail, as if she were about to faint. Ksenia got just as alarmed while Manos was standing frozen near them now, unsure about what he had done to cause such upheaval. Ksenia stood before Daphne and picked up the photo album from her lap. She had noticed Daphne kept glimpsing with bewilderment at a specific photo and that she kept looking from there to Phevos and back, unable to word her evident anguish.

"Daphne, what is it? Talk to me!" Phevos demanded as he sat next to her. Daphne gave him another helpless look.

"Is it this photo?" Ksenia asked her as she pointed to it. It was a picture of a couple in their thirties. Ksenia's eyes were full of hope as she waited for Daphne's response.

"Yes..." Daphne whispered. "Who.... who are they?"

"I don't understand, Daphne! Who are you talking about? Please, let me see, Ksenia!" Phevos asked and she obliged by letting him take the photo album in his hands.

"This is an old picture of my parents!" Ksenia announced full of hope. "Have you seen them? Please tell me if you have!" she begged placing her hands on Daphne's trembling hands. Phevos's eyes rose from the page and met Daphne's with a look that now resembled hers. When they turned to look at Ksenia together, their intense stare told her that the answer to her question was yes. Yet, judging from the tormented look in their eyes, her instinctive reaction was to worry that the news wasn't good.

Manos clung to her and they both towered over them now, two siblings staring at the other two, who sat there sharing the same shocking realization and the same feeling of utter inadequacy to word it. Phevos's mind was deep in thought now, trying to make sense of this. Daphne had already guessed the truth, and she gave him a faint smile as if trying to speed up his tormented thinking. This divine intervention had come to them without warning. It looked like it was high time for Ksenia and Manos to hear the truth.

"Phevos, please talk to me! This is about our parents for God's sake!" Ksenia exclaimed as Manos clung to her, absorbing into his heart her own distress. Phevos reached out and held her hand, urging her to come sit next to him with Manos. They all sat on the sofa again, clinging to each other like worry beads in the playful hands of destiny.

"Calm down now..." Phevos patted them both on their backs. "I think it's all good news. I just don't know how to start, that's all... Goodness knows how you'll receive what I'm about to tell you, but unless I speak the whole truth, Daphne and I will never know what to do from here any more than you will in your own quest to reunite with your parents."

"Destiny plays impossible games with people sometimes," Daphne interrupted, "but in the end, it always turns out it's all been engineered with infinite wisdom. I don't believe in coincidences. It's not coincidence that brought us here in your home!"

"Please tell us what you know! Don't leave us guessing any longer. I'm fearing the worst!" Ksenia begged while Manos clung to her, as if for dear life. His eyes had grown enormous. Daphne looked at him with compassion.

"Don't worry, it will all be all right," she promised.

"Do you know my parents?" Manos dared ask her and Daphne gave a reassuring nod.

"Are they alive? Are they okay?" asked Ksenia.

"Yes, they are!" said Phevos.

"Oh thank God! But where are they? Why don't they come home to us?" she asked, her voice trembling.

Daphne shook her head, compassion coloring her face. "It's not that simple."

And then, Phevos started to speak. He held his sister's hand and put an arm around Ksenia and Manos too as he shared with them the feeling of mystification that had just set his faith free to grow bigger than ever before. He commenced by telling them first the total truth of his reality.

This revelation left Ksenia and Manos dumbfounded. How could they believe that Phevos and Daphne were time travelers from ancient Greece? How was it possible their parents, Kimon and Eleni had been living in antiquity with them and their father Efimios? How did they get there? How is it even possible to travel in time? But why would Phevos and Daphne lie?

Ksenia and Manos listened carefully, but their rational mind kept rejecting everything they heard including the absurd story about Efimios traveling back and forth in time to serve Goddess Athena and her city, by using a secret cave in the Acropolis hill. They stared back in bewilderment at both Phevos and Daphne, but before they could voice their angered response for the absurd and unfeeling lies, undisputable proof ensued.

Both Phevos and Daphne spoke to them then with details about their parents. Details they couldn't have just come up with in random. Of course, it would be easy to find out their parents' names and to quote them back to them. But how could they know about Eleni's love to sing all day or to draw seascapes depicting quaint fishing villages, boats with white sails and mermaids with long wavy hair? They spoke about Kimon, who loved his carpentry tools and was a keen handyman, jumping at the chance to mend anything that broke around the house. They even knew about his affinity for animals that led him to save strays from the streets, nurturing them with extreme care and tenderness until he found them a safe home.

But the most astonishing proof came when Daphne, sensing the strong resistance of their doubts, stood up, paced to the middle of the room and broke into song. It was a beautiful lullaby that echoed in the room as Daphne's tears rolled down her face. It was the same song that Phevos had sung to her on their first day in Pallada, and it was also the very same song that Ksenia knew well from her mother. Eleni had sung this song to all four of them when they were still small in their beds. It was her own favorite lullaby that her grandmother had brought with her along with her family heirlooms when she had fled from her homeland in Asia

Minor back in the 1920's. Daphne had guessed Ksenia and Manos would also know it and she was right. The tears that rolled down Ksenia's face signaled to her that all doubt had finally vanished from her mind. And indeed, Ksenia rushed to Daphne and hugged her, breaking into uncontrollable sobs.

Manos and Phevos approached them and they all huddled together, their hearts united as one heart that ached at the sound of that forlorn melody. It took them a long while to bring themselves round and once they did, they spent hours discussing their two worlds, trying to make sense about everything. That day, the truth about what had happened to Kimon and Eleni was still a shattered puzzle that lay at their feet in a messy heap, still missing quite a few pieces. But from that day forward, their attempt to solve the puzzle was going to be simply a matter of time. They could tell by now that their destinies were somehow entwined. In their united efforts to solve the mystery behind Kimon and Eleni, they were going to make progress with finding Phevos's mother too.

Chapter 11

Two weeks had passed since that fateful Sunday afternoon. All four of them met as often as they could now, trying to make sense of things, consoling each other that the truth was just around the corner. Phevos and Daphne were still perplexed about it all. How could Kimon and Eleni be Ksenia and Manos's parents? How had they wound up far back in time with them? It was obvious their father Efimios knew where they truly belonged. Why had none of them spoken about it? And why hadn't Father helped them come back? How was this connected to his separation from Phevos's mother the same year? Did she belong to this world too? And if they all had to go back in time with Father's help, why did she choose to stay behind?

These questions tortured Phevos more than all the others because he had this cloud in his head where his childhood memories once were. Thinking of Kimon and Eleni now, he realized how they must have suffered in silence all these years, separated from their children and the world they belonged in.

Ksenia and Manos had their own unanswered questions. Had their parents chosen to be separated from them? They couldn't accept this possibility so they focused on the thought they were made to leave. That something terrible had forced them to go. But even so, why had they remained silent about it, why did they live in antiquity without even mentioning their children to anyone? After the initial shock of the revelation about their parents' inconceivable whereabouts, hope had nestled in their hearts that somehow, they could bring them back.

Phevos had shown them the precious necklace he hid under his shirt. According to him, it once allowed his father to travel back and forth in time, but this was not possible any more. Somehow, Phevos and Daphne had come here but not through Athena's cave and so, Phevos had no idea how to use the necklace to go back. He didn't even know where the cave was and from what he knew, Efimios had seen to it that it couldn't be used for time travel again.

Although he had told his children many stories about his travels, he had never disclosed the exact location of the cave or the reason why he had destroyed it eleven years earler. All four of them had the burning desire to solve this big mystery and after a lot of thought, decided to follow the one evident lead that they had. Mrs. Anna was the only adult in the house when Kimon and Eleni vanished. Perhaps she remembered vital details that could give them a clue. Perhaps she knew more than she had admitted to back then. They had nothing to lose and so, they tried to find any old contacts of hers that may be lying around the house. Ksenia searched all drawers and cabinets and found nothing, but then she remembered Mrs. Sofia was in contact with Mrs. Anna for a while after she had left.

She didn't want to ask her in case she raised suspicion, so she searched behind the reception desk in Pallada and rummaged through all the old address and phone books that Mrs. Sofia kept year after year with names of old acquaintances and guests. In one of these books, Ksenia found an entry with the name 'Anna' on it. There was no surname, but next to it, the word 'Sounio' had been handwritten and then crossed out. On top of it, Mrs. Sofia had added with her scrawly handwriting the word 'Anavisos' and had also replaced the old telephone number with a new one.

Ksenia put the book in her shoulder bag and left Pallada, rushing home to make the phone call there in privacy. As soon as she saw that entry, she had remembered Mrs. Sofia had once mentioned to her that Mrs. Anna had moved to Sounio. On her way home, she made a short stop to tell Phevos what she had found, assuring him this had to be the right Anna they were after.

But alas! To her dismay, it proved to be a wrong number. The person who answered said no one called Anna lived there. Now, they had no more leads to find her. They didn't know her last name and after all these years, she could be living anywhere.

Ksenia suggested to the others not to ask Mrs. Sofia any questions about Anna or about their parents' disappearance and everyone agreed. The old lady had a weak heart since an episode after her husband's death years ago, and so, they didn't want to distress her by forcing her to remember the sadness of that period. In effect, they had to give up on locating Mrs. Anna.

Ksenia surrendered to the defeat with a sense of deep sadness. But Phevos didn't let her or the others lose hope. He reminded them they still had another lead that rested on the end of his shovel as he worked hard in the orchard evening after evening. There was something hidden inside the earth there. He knew it by now with certainty. As he focused on his effort to plant new life, to level the rough paths and to tend to the trees, as their branches billowed full of blossom in the spring air, Phevos awaited the disclosure of the next sign.

He was besotted by now with the memory of the stranger in his dream, who had asked him to trade his necklace for that magic wand. The stranger had urged him to find a shovel and when the day dawned after that dream, he was offered the chance to tend to the orchard. Only a fool would have taken this prophecy as a mere coincidence.

On the 1st of May, the orchard was ready to host a festive lunch that they had decided to enjoy together in their garden, surrounded by sweet-smelling flowerbeds and trellises draped with fleshy leaves and tiny, bright-colored flowers. Phevos had indeed worked very hard. For weeks he had been planting and trimming, digging and watering. As promised, Manos had helped, handing him tools and pots and helping him cut open the sacks of earth and fertilizer.

Both the girls had assisted too, watering and planting flowers. When the day came to sit around their garden table on the grass, they all had a feeling of satisfaction for the evident result of their efforts. Mrs. Sofia had been invited to join them too and she had assisted Ksenia in the preparation of delightful dishes. As soon as everyone sat around the table, Ksenia surprised them all when she produced some flowers out of a bag. She handed out two flimsy daisy chains to Mrs. Sofia and to Daphne and then placed a third one around her neck. She had threaded the flowers with a needle. Making these was a ritual she followed on May 1st every year, as it was something her mother used to do for her when she was little. To include Phevos and Manos too somehow, she had picked carnations for them, and she stood up to pin them on their shirts before announcing the commencement of their little feast.

A couple of days later, Phevos visited the orchard again in the afternoon after work. He was walking along the main path he had smoothed out, which led to the back end of the property. He was walking absentmindedly, whistling a tune that had stuck in his head for hours after listening to it on the radio that morning. It had been a warm and sunny day. It was Saturday. The children in the neighborhood had been playing in the streets all day. As the sun lowered itself onto the golden cradle of the horizon, the echo of their happy voices began to fade in the fragrant air.

Manos had been one of those happy children today. He had been passing by the fruit store all day, up and down the street, on his brand new skateboard that Phevos and Daphne had given him a couple of weeks earlier as an Easter present. They all loved to see Manos on a skateboard again. Of course he still enjoyed his pc games too but somehow, he now played in the streets more often than he did indoors. Ksenia was very proud of him these days as he had recently made new friends, who had made a big difference in his life.

Phevos reached the end of the orchard. The clearing of grass and wildflowers before him reached up to the rocky border of the imposing Acropolis hill. As Daphne had concluded, this is where they had first found themselves when they had entered this new world. For that reason, there was something about this spot that attracted Phevos more than any other in the orchard. He spent a lot of time there on his own, examining every blade of grass on the ground in silent contemplation, wondering if it had any secrets to confess.

Perhaps this is why his attention was immediately drawn to what he found there that day. It had seemed to be so out of place, so peculiar, worthy of closer inspection. His find was a kite, which lay shattered on the ground. It had bright orange and blue colors, and he recognized it at once. He had first seen it that very morning hovering over the rooftops across from the shop, and he had found the figures on it peculiar. Mr. Giorgis had been most helpful when he explained they were Phevos and Athena, the mascots of the Athens Olympics 2004.

Phevos had seemed impressed and Mr. Giorgis had teased him then, commenting that Phevos on the kite was far better looking than him, even though he was wearing a skirt. Mr. Giorgis had also said he knew the teenage boy who flew this kite. He had it all these years since the Olympics and seldom flew it these days, as it was one of his favorites; a precious souvenir from his early childhood. Mr. Giorgis had explained the boy had a large collection of kites that he made himself and that he loved to fly them as a hobby.

His kite had been the only one in the sky but that had come as no surprise. As a rule, the majority of Greek children fly kites only once a year: on Lent Monday. Phevos felt sorry as he looked down at the shattered kite, thinking how sad that boy must feel. He also wondered what it had been that had driven him to choose to fly his precious, favorite kite today. Despite feeling sorry for the boy's loss, there was a glimmer of hope in his heart as well, as he knelt down to examine his finding closely. It was too much of a coincidence to hear of the Olympics mascots in the morning and to find them again at his feet later the same day. The sprightly figures of Phevos and Athena returned a cheerful gaze at him that looked quite out of place considering the kite's predicament. Just as he was about to take the kite in his hands, he noticed a strong glint in the dirt under the broken, wooden frame. He picked up the kite and the messy tangles of string, setting them aside, in order to inspect closely the spot on the dirt that now sparkled in the faint afternoon sunlight.

With his fingers, he brushed the soil and decided that what he was looking at was a shiny yellow plaque or stone. Phevos rushed to his wheelbarrow where he kept minor tools and hurried back with a small spade. He started to dig with caution, trying to uncover the full surface of the stone without damaging it. His heart started to race when he realized what he was unearthing was manmade. Its shape was a perfect rectangle and what's more, another similar stone began from its edge, buried vertically into the ground. With a bit more effort, he concluded he was looking at steps of yellow marble, and he kept working with even more fervor now, wondering all the while where this set of stairs could be leading to.

Half an hour later, he heard Ksenia call his name. She had been looking for him everywhere with a glass of orange juice in her hand.

"Phevos! There you are! Here, I thought you might be thirsty," she said as she approached him.

"Ksenia! My Ksenia!" he said jolting upright. His eyes were wide with enthusiasm when he opened his arms to embrace her. Ksenia tried to salvage the drink as she laughed in his arms. He was now planting kisses all over her face.

"Yes! I love you too, you lunatic! Careful now! Your drink!" she protested but to no avail. "What's the matter with you? I knew you shouldn't be spending so much time in the sun!"

Phevos stopped to gaze at her, his eyes alight with the thrill of his discovery. He took the glass from her hand and downed the drink in one go. Then, without a word, he led her to see his finding. Two steps were fully visible.

"Oh my God! What's this?" she exclaimed, bringing her hands to her mouth in astonishment. The marble steps shone in the faint sunlight. Kneeling before them, she caressed them with two gentle fingertips. They felt cold after their longwinded slumber in the dark confines of the soil.

"Do you see Ksenia? My dream was true! This must be the sign we've been waiting for! This is it!"

"Wait a minute Phevos... I remember this place!" Ksenia looked around her with distant eyes, as she tried to recall a faint childhood memory. And then her face lit up. "Of course!" She stood up and looked around her again. "Of course! The gardener's storeroom!"

"What storeroom?"

"It used to be right there," she said, pointing vaguely to the massive rock face that stood before them. "It was used by Mrs. Anna's deceased husband, Mr. Thimios. He helped my parents with the gardening and he had a storeroom here. There was this beautiful garden also that he always tended to... Oh, how could I have forgotten all that?" Astonished, she brought a hand to her head.

"A garden? Right here?"

"Yes! It had beautiful flowers... there were roses, carnations, chrysanthemums... How could I have forgotten about it? The steps to the gardener's storeroom were made of yellow marble. It must be these right here! But why are they buried now? I don't understand," she said resting her bewildered eyes on Phevos.

"Are you sure? There was a storeroom here? Is that all?" he said, somewhat deflated.

"Yes. It was used for the gardener's tools. My parents told me so. Although, I never went in it, come to think of it. Its entrance was right there in the rock."

"In the rock? Are you sure?"

"Yes. And the door had a figure on it... I think it was a bird... yes... an owl! My goodness, it's all coming back to me now!" Ksenia shook her head with disbelief. Normally, she was able to recount her childhood memories with ease. But the ones surrounding the gardener's storeroom seemed to resist resurfacing from the dark confines of her memory with unprecedented persistence.

"An owl, you said?" Phevos was intrigued. The owl was one of Athena's symbols. He didn't fail to make the connection.

"Yes. I'm sure of it! It was an owl without a doubt."

"And where is the door? You said it was in the rock. I don't see it."

"It must be buried too. It must all be buried!"

"But why, Ksenia? Who buried it and why? Please try to remember!"

"I don't know, Phevos! I don't know anything about it! I was very little when the gardener used it, and I never went inside. Its door was always closed. I do remember wandering in the beautiful garden that was right here though... but it's all changed now. Everything about this place is different."

"In what way?"

"Well, there's no flower garden here any more to start with! And also, as you walked through the garden toward the door in the rock, the path used to have a rather steep downward slope. But now it's all level from here to the rock. It's like it's all been buried deep down, garden and all!"

"But why? Who would do that?"

Ksenia shook her head.

"Shall we ask, Mrs. Sofia?"

Ksenia's eyes grew huge. "What? No!"

"But surely you can see we have no other choice! We have to find out why the door was buried. And I'm intrigued this storeroom was in the rock, aren't you?"

"Of course I am, my love. But I don't want us to upset her!"

"Why would we upset her?"

"Phevos, anything that has to do with all the losses of the past might hurt her. When her husband died and she had that major heart attack, she nearly died too!"

"I think she's much stronger than you think. Let's just ask her about the steps and nothing else. We don't have to explain why we want to know. And we can try, if we can, not to mention Mrs. Anna or her husband or your parents or anyone else whose memory might upset her."

"You promise?"

"Of course, Ksenia! Come on, let's go ask her now."

"Now? Are you sure?"

"Are you serious? I can't wait another second to find out what's under there! Can you?"

"You're so right! I can't either," she admitted rushing down the path with him.

"Ksenia, the answer is down there, buried in the dirt," he said reaching out for her hand.

"Yes," she replied as their hands locked together, "and that answer will lead us to my parents and your father. And your mother too!" she added as they strode among the trees.

"I can't agree with you more, Ksenia. This is it! The very fact that the door to this storeroom has been buried is an indication that something was hidden down there on purpose!"

"But how can Mr. Thimios be connected to all this? Do you think he buried it at some point before his death?"

"I don't know, Ksenia! If my father knew your parents then maybe he knew Anna and her husband too from his travels in this age. Maybe my father had given Mr. Thimios something to hide in there for him. Something that my father or Athena expects me to find. Who knows?"

"I'm sure the truth will be revealed to us sooner or later!"

They came out on the street and holding hands, rushed to Pallada determined to find the answers.

Chapter 12

"Phevos! Ksenia!" cried Manos, and they both turned around. He was coming down the road on his skateboard. He swerved around a can of soda and came to a stop in front of them with incredible ease grinning from ear to ear.

"Well, that's impressive!" said Phevos patting him on the shoulder.

"Thanks!" chirped Manos smiling.

"You're aware of the cars, right?" asked Ksenia, protective as always.

"Oh, don't worry! There are hardly any in this street! Besides, I'm off to the square to skate with my friends. No vehicles are allowed up there so you can relax!" he replied with a cheeky grin.

"Ok Manos, I'm going to Pallada for a little while, and then I'll return home to make dinner. See you around eight?"

"No worries, Sis! See you," he replied with a wave and he was off. Within seconds he had already disappeared around the corner but the whirring sound of the tiny wheels on the hard concrete lingered in the air a while longer.

"My goodness, I get so nervous when I see him down the street on that skateboard!" she said, clutching her chest. She couldn't help feeling overprotective toward the only family she had left.

"Yes, but surely you can see how good it is that he's out there now and not indoors on his own any more?" replied Phevos as they resumed walking to Pallada hand in hand.

"Of course! He seems so happy now, doesn't he?"

"Yes! And did you hear what he said? Off to the square to skate with his friends?"

"Yes, I've seen them. They look like good kids. He started hanging out with them during the Easter break."

"This is wonderful, Ksenia!"

"Yes! Have you seen how different he is? How happy and confident in his manner? But I owe it also to you. Not just to those kids—"

Phevos scoffed. "Me? I can't take any credit for that."

"I disagree. You're the very first friend he ever made. You've helped him come out of his shell, so that he could get out there and seek companionship that makes him feel good for a change."

"I haven't done anything, Ksenia. It was just the right time for him, that's all. And he's such a nice young man that you can't help but like him anyway. As for those horrid bullies, I'm glad they let him be in the end. I don't see them around here any more... How are things in school nowadays?"

"Well, Manos seems so happy all the time now so I guess things are fine! Perhaps he just broke away from the vicious circle. They used to sense his weakness and hurt him. And the more they did, the weaker he got and so on. But once he found strength and confidence in himself, they left him alone, just like that."

"It makes sense Ksenia... I do believe it's the way you see yourself that determines the type of people you will attract in life. Be it friends or anything else.

"Yes... and he has made quite a shift in his short life. From being the timid and miserable six-year-old who was cornered in the schoolyard, he has somehow turned into this strapping twelve-year-old on wheels! And he's got so tall, bless him!"

"Yeah, and I bet he charms all the girls with that big smile of his too!" Phevos replied, and they both laughed as they went up the marble steps of Pallada.

Daphne was standing behind the reception desk smiling at a young American couple. In the two months that she'd been working there, Daphne had found it quite easy to learn Basic English, and her solid knowledge of Latin had helped her a lot along the way.

Mrs. Sofia was at reception too, dusting the bookcase shelves. The afternoon had been quiet in Pallada. Ksenia had helped in the morning with preparing the rooms for new arrivals. These days, the two young girls took care of all the hard work, leaving to Mrs. Sofia the easier tasks, such as dusting and reception duty. Any kind of exertion caused the old woman to pant on her spindly legs these days. Osteoporosis had chiseled her frail body to a stance that seemed like an eternal bow to the relentless passage of time.

"Mrs. Sofia!" Ksenia and Phevos said in unison when they saw her.

"Hello my darlings!" she replied, turning around.

"We have something to ask you," Ksenia said.

"Anything your little hearts desire. Just let me sit down for a bit if you don't mind. Come sit here with me," she beckoned from the old sofa.

"Mrs. Sofia, I found some marble steps as I dug around the orchard," said Phevos when he and Ksenia sat on either side of her.

"Steps? What steps, *psyche mou*?" she replied, startled.

"I remember those steps," interrupted Ksenia, "they're made of yellow marble. I think they belong to the old gardener's storeroom," she said, feeling uneasy. Mrs. Sofia's face had darkened somehow, and her eyes were staring into the distance.

"Ksenia remembers that there used to be a storeroom in the rock at the far end of the property... that's right, isn't it?" Phevos tried to sound nonchalant. The old lady's growing distress was evident, but he knew he couldn't afford to falter in the least.

"Yes... that's right," Mrs. Sofia said in a trembling voice. "But the man who used it was very odd!" she added with a deep sigh. "He didn't let anyone enter that damned hole of Satan, God forgive me! The door was always shut!"

"Do you mean Mr Thimios? Mrs Anna's husband?" asked Ksenia.

"Yes."

"I do remember that the door was always shut. But why would you speak that way about him?"

"*Psyche mou*, don't ask. Just forget about it! No one should remember this wretched place! Now you go and do the right thing and bury those steps again, you hear? They don't deserve the light of day. That place is cursed!" she shrieked shaking a wrinkly finger in front of their faces. Her bottom lip was quivering now, and Ksenia panicked to see her that way.

"What's the matter?" asked Daphne as she approached them. The guests had just left, and she was concerned to find them all looking so distressed.

"Come here my girl and talk to them please!" Mrs. Sofia pleaded. "You're a sensible girl, they'll listen to you! Please tell them to bury those steps before another disaster occurs!"

Daphne was understandably bewildered. Phevos and Ksenia explained to her what they had found and the young girl responded with a look of enthusiasm behind Mrs. Sofia's back. She managed with great difficulty to contain herself in order not to scream with excitement. All three of them were certain by now that Mrs. Sofia knew a lot, and they were mystified by what they had heard already. Their main concern for now however, was to calm her down.

She was clutching her chest with one hand, trembling with distress. Ksenia put her arms around her making soothing sounds while Daphne rushed to the back, returning moments later with a glass of water for her.

"Come on now, *yaya*, it's okay," Phevos said trying to soothe her by rubbing her back as she drank from the glass.

"Don't worry now... I just wanted to know if I remembered correctly about the storeroom, that's all!" said Ksenia.

"That's right, we were just curious," said Phevos shrugging his shoulders.

Mrs Sofia gave a heavy sigh. "My children, please try to understand! People perished because of that damned storeroom! I never went in there but I know it in my soul that it's evil! I wasn't even here when it happened. I was in Corfu then, visiting my dying sister."

"Are you referring to the disappearance of my parents?" Ksenia asked flabbergasted.

"Yes of course, *psyche mou*! This is what I'm talking about." Somehow, the worst had passed and she looked a lot calmer now, perhaps thanks to their deliberate casual manner that hid their real purpose.

"Are you saying the storeroom had something to do with their vanishing?" asked Phevos.

"All I know is that poor Anna believed that! She couldn't bear to see it after they were gone. She had confessed to me she thought it was cursed. Even though the police went in there to search and found nothing, she still believed it had something to do with the vanishing. This is why in the end she decided to bury its entrance in the rock, to make it disappear from the face of the earth. To stop this from happening again."

"Mrs. Anna buried it?" Ksenia asked incredulous.

"Yes, my love! She brought some workers, who came with trucks full of soil."

"So is this why it's now level over there? Ksenia said there used to be a downward slope toward the rock face."

"Yes, Phevos. They leveled it all out. She wanted it to be perfectly hidden and deprived from the light of day. It wasn't enough to her to just bolt the door shut forever. She said she didn't want any chances of it being visited again. Even the flower garden got buried under tons and tons of soil."

"I remember the garden," piped up Ksenia. "I used to wander around there a lot when I was little. I can't believe I had forgotten all about that until today... Mom always put me to bed after lunch in the summer, but I used to escape to visit that garden while she had her midday siesta. I remember hopping from one flowerbed to another pretending I had wings and that I was a fairy—"

"I remember that too well!" Mrs. Sofia chortled and sat back on the sofa, her face brightening up somewhat. "You were one fanciful little girl! You used to beg your mother to dress you in a flimsy nylon nightdress of hers. It was light blue with velvety little bows on the front. Do you remember it?"

"Yes," replied Ksenia in a whisper. She had just redeemed that memory without effort, and yet it felt surreal as if she had claimed it from the misty fragments of a distant dream. "It felt so light and soft on my skin," she continued, "and I pretended it was my fairy dress made of pure silk. Mom used to tie the fabric up in knots on top of my shoulders to make the nightdress fit better around my arms, but it still was too long and I had to lift the hem as I walked. Such a vivid memory! I can't believe I just recollected that! I loved that garden! Mr. Thimios must have been quite the gardener," she said, amazed.

"Oh my sweetheart, you remember well. Your mother always knew where to find you in the afternoon after her siesta. You were always there wandering barefoot, sniffing the flowers and sitting on the grass pretending to have long conversations with butterflies and ants! What a cute little fairy you were too!" Mrs. Sofia gave a little laugh and pinched Ksenia's cheek. "Although there's one thing where your memory doesn't serve you well, if I may say so!"

"Really? What's that?" she asked with a grin, still amused by the recollection of her childhood frivolity.

"Well, his name wasn't Thimios and that's for sure!"

Ksenia knitted her brows. "It wasn't?"

"What was it?" enquired Daphne and Phevos in unison.

"Oh, in the name of St Spyridon! I can't remember what I had for breakfast! Surely you don't expect me to remember that man's name, do you now?" she replied.

"Well, it doesn't matter anyway. I was too little back then, perhaps I confused his name with someone else's or something. He must have been a good man though. Mrs. Anna loved him very much, I'm sure."

"I guess he was all right... albeit odd," answered Mrs. Sofia, "and indeed, he was a good gardener."

"Fancy the storeroom being in the rock though!" interrupted Phevos.

"Well, Ksenia's parents let him use it for storing his tools. That room in the rock has always been used for storage from what I know. Ever since the time of your great-grandfather, my Ksenia!"

"Mrs. Sofia, please don't get upset again, but I just think this is very strange," said Daphne, who had been silent in contemplation all this time.

"What is strange, my sweet?"

"Well, if this storeroom has been used for so many years, how come it only caused one disaster and not more? How did it even come about that it was cursed as you said? That it was even related to the disappearance of Ksenia's parents?"

"As I said, all I know is that Anna believed it. You are still young. You have no children yet and you don't know. A mother's instinct is infallible!"

"What do you mean 'a mother's instinct'?" Ksenia asked, confused.

Mrs Sofia gave the girl a puzzled look. "Don't you remember her little boy?"

"What little boy?"

"Her son of course, Ksenia! He was only nine when he vanished that night with your parents. Poor soul!"

"A nine-year-old vanished on the same night with Ksenia's parents?" asked Phevos incredulous with a voice that sounded more like a faint whisper. He sprang to his feet as he said this and couldn't help pacing up and down in front of them shaking his head to himself, unable to grasp what he had just heard. Daphne followed him with her eyes that now glinted with emotion. Yet, she bit her lower lip to stop herself from speaking just yet.

As for Ksenia, she had frozen where she sat. Her mind was overwhelmed by a torrent of thoughts. Phevos stopped pacing and was now staring into the distance. He thought this could explain why so much in this modern world seemed so familiar to him. Eleven years ago he could have been that nine-year-old! But if this was the case, his mother was... no, it couldn't be so easy! His mother was Anna? But how could it be? What about her deceased husband Thimios? Who was he then?

Across from him, once again, Daphne had already concluded her thoughts having the benefit of a clear and objective mind whereas emotion in the case of the others had clouded their thinking into overload. She calmed herself for their sake and took her time to word her questions, but before she could speak, Ksenia beat her to it.

"Mrs. Sofia, are you sure Mrs. Anna had a nine-year-old boy, who vanished with my parents? I don't even remember her having a son!"

"Of course she did, Ksenia! She, her boy and her husband lived upstairs in your house where your bedroom now is. That poor woman lost everything overnight. Both her son and husband at the same time!"

"What?" exclaimed Phevos rushing back to the sofa to sit by her side. "Her husband did not die?"

"No! He vanished just like the rest of them!" she replied.

"But I thought he had died! She always wore black! I thought she was a widow!" intervened Ksenia.

"She did wear black and it was the right thing to do too! Maybe she didn't see them dead but they were lost to her, *kyra mou*! So she mourned them all the same!"

"Oh my God!" replied Ksenia turning to meet Phevos's eyes that were glazed over, as he tried to process in his mind what he had just heard. "All these years and I didn't know!"

Ksenia said and her heart went to Phevos. He looked like he had turned to stone.

"Mrs. Sofia..." Daphne spoke when she thought the timing was just right. "Please try again and remember the name of Mrs. Anna's husband."

The old woman shook her head. "It doesn't matter, does it? What you should only worry about now, is burying those damn steps again!"

All three claimed they intended to do that soon. They didn't mind lying in order to reassure her. Their cause was too sacred, justifying all means.

"Wait a minute, I remember now," Ksenia lied. It was an assumption of course. "Was his name Efimios perhaps?"

"Efimios!" exclaimed the old lady, and her face lit up. "Of course! I thought he had a rare name! It's so funny you remembered him as Thimios instead!" She rambled on, unaware of the bombshell of an answer she had just delivered.

"And the boy's name?" asked Daphne, "Do you remember that too?"

Phevos was still unable to speak and could only just about manage to listen.

"Oh, that's easy! He had the same name as you, *psyche mou*!" The old lady gave a wistful smile and patted Phevos's hand that rested on his lap. "His name was Phevos. What a tragedy! He would have grown into a strapping young lad just like you I'm sure, poor soul!"

Ksenia and Daphne watched speechless as Phevos stood up, his demeanour calm.

"Right! I'm running late with my gardening duties. Shall we, Ksenia? Daphne, would you like to join us too?" he asked. Both the girls started at him aghast, unable to believe how collected he seemed, considering what had just happened.

Ksenia took his hand and they made to go. Daphne couldn't bear to contain her joy any longer and what's more, she wanted to see their finding too with her own eyes. Soon it would be dark and she couldn't wait till the next day, so she excused herself to Mrs. Sofia and rushed to join them.

As soon as they passed Mr. Giorgis's shop, the three of them finally unleashed their excitement by letting out howls of laughter and mad shrieks of joy. They kept hopping up and down, hugging each other, and making quite a spectacle of themselves. Of course, they couldn't have cared less about the strange looks that passers-by gave them, and they rushed to the front gate of the house with entwined arms and exuberant faces.

***

When the next day dawned, all four of them couldn't wait to get out of bed. They had made plans earlier that week for that day, as it was a Sunday. However, after the previous day's developments, their planned excursion to the seaside for a taverna meal had to be cancelled. Instead, they had an early breakfast and headed straight to the back of the orchard, laden with supplies in order to spend the whole day there, without interruptions.

Manos was walking ahead with Odysseus for he was the only one who hadn't seen the unearthed steps yet and he couldn't wait. He carried a spade from the back yard and a small trowel. Behind him, Phevos was holding a large shovel while the girls were laden with bags containing drinks, snacks and sandwiches as well as a blanket to sit on.

As they strode to the back end, Phevos and Ksenia walked side by side. Their faces were beaming with elation, for now they knew they were no strangers whose paths recently happened to cross. Far from it, they had known each other forever because they used to live in the same house when they were children. Although Phevos was aware of the 'cloud' in his head that had robbed him of his childhood memories, Ksenia had reasons to feel perplexed about the fact that she couldn't remember him living with them back then.

Thanks to Mrs. Sofia, that piece of the mystery puzzle had

just been redeemed, but they knew they had to withhold the truth from her. Sometimes it's inevitable to lie in order to protect someone you care for. How could they explain to her that Phevos and his father as well as Kimon and Eleni had all gone back in time somehow? How could Phevos present himself to her today with his true identity? And how could they confess that far from burying those steps, their burning desire was to enter that mysterious storeroom in the rock?

When they walked past a cluster of orange trees in blossom, Phevos found the scene so beautiful, the sense of belonging so great, that tears welled up in his eyes, and he wished his parents could be there too. Now he knew his mother was Anna, and he wondered where she was, if she was well and most of all, if she even wanted to be found.

The previous evening, Ksenia had shown him an old photo album that contained pictures of two young couples. Kimon and Eleni, Efimios and Anna. They looked so carefree and joyful in these pictures. They had been taken during the first years of their friendship when they had no children yet. His mother was very beautiful in these pictures with kind laughing eyes and wavy brown hair. His father held her in his arms, and they looked happy together. Phevos felt devastated that his parents were destined to part, but the pictures had made him sure they did so against their will.

When they reached the clearing at the end of the orchard, Manos ran ahead and knelt to examine closely the unearthed marble steps. With Phevos taking the lead, everyone got to work immediately and throughout that day, they all contributed to making progress. By sunset, they had unearthed seven more steps. As daylight gradually diminished, they reluctantly picked up their things to go. Their bodies ached from the exertion, but their faces were bright with excitement as they took the path home. The last rays of light caressed their hair before vanishing behind neighboring rooftops, coloring the ceramic tiles gold. All around them, gossiping wild pigeons chattered in the thick foliage of the trees.

Later that evening, when Phevos and Daphne returned to Pallada to retire for the night, Phevos faltered at the gate once he made a sudden realization. Above it, the painting of Athena emerging from Zeus's head now held a special sentimental value for him. Just a couple of weeks earlier, Ksenia had mentioned that her father's old friend who had painted that sign was none other than Anna's husband, Mr. Thimios. But as it had turned out, his name was Efimios after all.

Phevos stared at it now with a wistful look in his eyes. His father had sent him off with the advice to look out for the signs. And now Phevos knew with certainty he had sown at least one sign along the way for him as to make sure he would wind up here, of all places.

Chapter 13

Another three weeks passed, and it was now mid June. Phevos had taken full advantage of the warm weather in order to make great progress in unearthing the door of the storeroom in the rock. Only the previous evening, he had managed just before sunset to reveal the heavy, metallic door. It looked like it wasn't going to be easy to force it open and as darkness started to fall, he had left reluctantly while promising himself to come back the next day straight after work.

He was at the shop now, restocking the display outside with fresh produce, and he was thinking of all the work he had done until now. At some point, he had to hire some workmen in order to make progress faster. They came with a truck and managed to carry away a great amount of soil, exposing the rest of the steps to the welcoming light of day. The workmen dug to a depth of about seven feet as they progressed toward the rock until they revealed the first signs of the door.

To their questions, Phevos answered that the old gardener's storeroom that was in the rock had been buried after a tremendous storm many decades ago, a storm that had brought down from the hill tons of soil, burying it overnight. To their insistent curiosity, he then claimed that financial trouble had not allowed the owners to seek hired help earlier in order to reveal it. Once they located the door, Phevos made an excuse that he'd run out of cash for further work, dismissing them. This ensured that once the door was fully revealed, he wouldn't have them hanging about, curious to try to open the door to have a look inside.

Phevos would never have risked that. He knew by then that if his father lived there once, then what the rock hid was not a mere storeroom but the cave of Athena that he had been using for his time travels. This was the only logical explanation he could find for the mysterious room in the rock with its locked door.

It was midday, a Saturday. Phevos felt thankful the shop was full of customers that kept him very busy as otherwise he knew he could have gone mad with anticipation for closing time. He was having a delicious sandwich Daphne had just brought him for lunch. As he ate, he let his thoughts wander to his father again. He kept thinking about him a lot that day. He had asked him to follow the signs and as it had turned out, he had known all along that one day he'd send him to this specific place to find Ksenia and Manos and to make sense of it all in order to bring his family and Ksenia's together again.

His rational mind couldn't think of another possible purpose. Inside his shirt, hidden from view, he wore as always the necklace that his father gave him the day they had parted. Phevos hadn't seen it before until that day, but he had known about it all his life. Efimios had spoken to him extensively about his service to Goddess Athena, and had also shared with him many times the famous story of how the necklace was given to him by her in person. That story was by far, the most remarkable of all the ones his father had ever told him.

***

When Efimios was a boy, he and his friends used to play in a small forest near the estate where he lived with his parents. The forest stretched as far as the foot of the Acropolis hill, and the boys had a secret location in it where they hid various toys in the hollow of a large tree trunk. Among them, wooden swords and spears, slings, spinning tops, bows and arrows that came in handy when they rushed there, straight from the longwinded daily tuition, in order to play and to run carefree.

Their favorite game was a warrior version of hide and seek. Efimios excelled in this. The goal was to defeat the person who was looking for you and to sneak up on them as they did so. Efimios was nine years old at the time, and he was faster and stronger than all the others, including the ones who were older than him. He would jump out and wrestle anyone who wandered near his hiding place, or he'd wait for them up in a tree and jump down just as they passed, in order to grab them from behind.

And when they surrendered, he'd run to the starting point to claim his victory, getting there faster than anyone else could. The other boys knew they stood no chance in competition when they saw him run on the mossy ground, his long blond hair flowing in the wind like the silky mane of a fine horse.

That afternoon, he had enjoyed many hours of play with his friends. They had just parted for another day, and Efimios was treading on the narrow path he knew well that would take him out of the woodland. From there, home was just a breath away. His tummy grumbled, and he thought how hungry he was when he heard a strange sound.

It sounded like repeated strikes of some sort, and he thought it was peculiar because there were no homes or workshops close by. The sound didn't stop but kept echoing in regular intervals, exciting his innate curiosity. Without thinking twice, he ignored his hunger and left the path in order to investigate.

He wandered through the tall trees, stepping with caution over rough boulders and dense, thorny bushes, focused on following the sound. From a closer range it sounded metallic, like the sound iron makes when the blacksmith strikes it on the anvil. As he continued to approach the source, the sound got louder and louder until he had to put his hands over his ears to protect them but even then, he didn't turn and go.

He didn't give up either when the ground under his leather sandals got rougher and rougher and thorny thistles scraped at his feet. He was wincing from the pain and the piercing volume when he reached a small clearing. The sun shone on it and in its midst stood crouched an old lady dressed in black.

She wore a black scarf on her head, and she had her eyes fixed on him, as if she knew he was coming. She had deeply wrinkled skin and a hump on her back. In her hands she held a walking stick made of wood that looked as old as her, and she was banging it on the grass.

Efimios stood awestruck, unable to process in his mind what he could see. The wooden stick was hitting the ground, creating the shrill metallic sound that had him covering his ears for protection, yet his rational mind knew this was physically impossible. Then, the old woman stopped what she was doing. Relieved, Efimios put his hands down.

"Good morning, young man!" she said with a smile that revealed rotting teeth. Efimios was startled once again. Her voice didn't match her looks. It sounded young and brisk and what's more, it had sounded strong too, like the roar of a lion, so much that the moment her words echoed in the air, a flock of wild pigeons took to the skies from the nearby trees.

For the first time since he had first heard the metallic sound, his curiosity seemed to yield to a sense of uneasiness. He turned to go without a word, forgetting even his manners, but then the old woman stopped him by calling out his name.

"Stay, Efimios!" she burst out in a voice that was full of authority.

"How... how do you know my name?" he stammered as he turned around again.

"I have been watching you play with your friends. You are the strongest, the fastest and the most intelligent of them all," she said, taking a few steps toward him. "I have something to show you that I am sure will interest you."

Efimios stood and listened as she shuffled toward him. Appearances seemed very deceptive with her, and he continued to feel quite uneasy in her presence. Neither her voice nor her manner suited her looks, and he was also still bewildered about the mystery sound of her walking stick as it hit the ground. He tried to think of an excuse to give her as to turn and run without further ado to the safety of his house, away from her.

He was rich and he wanted for nothing. He couldn't imagine what this shabby-clothed old woman would have to offer him that would indeed be of interest or use to him. He thought she probably had something to sell him in order to buy a scrap of food, and he gave her credit for trying to win him over by complimenting him like that.

Now that he thought it through, there was nothing mysterious about her after all. He was just hungry and tired, and his mind was playing tricks on him. As for her knowing his name, if indeed she had been watching him play with his friends, there was no question as to how she had got to hear it.

"Thank you kind lady, but I do not need anything," he replied, trying not to sound rude. After all, he had been brought up with manners that dictated respect to elders, no matter how strange they might seem.

"I have nothing to sell to you if that is what you presume!" she spat at him. She stopped walking toward him then and just stood a few paces away looking offended.

"I do apologize, kind lady, I meant no offence," he said extending the palm of one hand to express sincerity.

"As I said, Efimios, I have something to show you. But I do not need your money! I only require your services," she assured him as she spoke with the type of regal pride that would only suit a queen.

The young boy thought then that it was quite possible a frail old lady like her would need help from someone fitter. Perhaps she had a sack that needed carrying, or maybe she wanted him to run an errand for her in the city. After all, she did refer to him being strong, fast and intelligent. Maybe she just needed help and that made sense.

This made him relax around her as for the first time something made sense of this old woman. His father had taught him to care for the weak and needy in the community, and now he felt ashamed for his rudeness toward her earlier. With eagerness, he walked up to her, an easy smile on his face.

"I am sorry about before. I would be delighted to help you, kind lady!"

"Well, my home is close by," she answered, a sweet smile curling the corners of her lips. "I need some help there. Please follow me, I will not keep you long."

Efimios obliged her—albeit with apprehension—and she led him through the woodland along a beaten path he had never walked before. Soon, they came to a cluster of wild chestnut trees. Their mighty boughs formed a thick canopy that didn't allow the sunlight to reach the ground underneath. Mushrooms of different kinds, both big and small, had sprouted on the dewy grass there in the semi-darkness.

Despite the enchanting beauty of his surroundings, Efimios felt uneasy again, but to his relief, the path then led them to a clearing covered with snow-white lilies. On the far end, stood the foot of the Acropolis hill, and the boy exhaled with relief to see it. For a while, he had started to fear he'd never find his way home again. But the Acropolis hill was his point of reference and as long as his eyes rested upon it, he knew home was near.

The old woman beckoned to him when she saw he had stopped walking, and he followed her up ahead, until they reached a massive rock face that was covered in moss. Among many cypress trees that stood there like faithful guards, the branches of a tall willow scraped in the breeze against the rock, making shrill noises. They sounded like ghosts dragging their chains in turmoil. Phevos shivered when the old woman halted in that eerie spot. Right there, a big boulder was wedged in an opening inside the rock.

The old woman put out both hands, her face glowing with pride. "Here we are!"

"You live in there?" he asked, incredulous. He didn't expect she lived in a cave in the wilderness.

"Yes, Efimios. This is my home but as you can see, the entrance is blocked, and I cannot get inside. I ask for your assistance to let me in." Her voice still sounded young, unbefitting. This made his uneasiness grow again, but he had set his mind on helping her, and he wasn't going to let her down no matter how surreal this experience had proven to be so far.

"This rock seems far too heavy for me. I can try but I cannot promise you anything."

"I have faith in you, Efimios! Move the rock aside for me, and I promise to give you something very valuable in return for your trouble." Although she was asking him for assistance, the tone of her voice was demanding. Her manner indicated a person who wasn't used to not getting their way, someone who didn't acknowledge refusal or weakness.

"Come on now Efimios! Go on! Do your best!" she urged him. Her voice sounded intoxicating in his head now, like a drug that numbed his defenses and his logic. It made him want to prove himself strong for her all of a sudden. It also made him curious to see the mysterious object she had in mind to give him.

Efimios took two confident steps forward. Placing his small palms on the left side of the rock, he started to push with all his might. The shape of the rock was an almost perfect sphere, so he aimed to try to roll it sideways. His sandals scrunched up the cool grass he stepped on, as the muscles of his upper body tightened and trembled with the exertion. He stopped just for a few seconds to catch his breath and then resumed the same position clenching his teeth, grunting as he exhaled from one deep intake of air after another.

He wasn't one to give up, and the old lady knew that. She had chosen well, and she smiled smugly as she watched now, rubbing her wrinkled hands together with satisfaction. Beads of sweat formed on the boy's face as he continued to push the cold rock, his palms red hot now, his face contorted with tension.

A big spider sprang out from behind the rock scurrying to the ground to find new cover, and then the boulder finally moved. Once it started rolling, Efimios found it easier.

When the opening was revealed, Efimios doubled over placing his hands on his knees trying to catch his breath. Sweat dripped like morning dew from his face as he bowed down. His hands hurt like they were on fire. The old lady approached him then, placing a gnarled hand on his crouched back.

He felt a shiver and then, something magical happened that took from his body all signs of pain and exertion. The sweat dried up on his skin, the feeling of heat in his hands dissipated as well as the burning sensation in the muscles of his upper body. He was no longer panting but now found himself breathing normally again. He stood, feeling rejuvenated, so rested as if he'd just awoken from long hours of sleep. Even the feeling of hunger and thirst which had started to bother him, was now gone. Stunned to silence, he turned to look at her and guessing his thoughts, she smiled to reassure him.

"Don't worry, Efimios! There is nothing for you to fear! As you can see, by touching you, I can only benefit you. Am I right?" She winked at him.

"Who are you, kind lady?"

"Come to my home and I will show you! In there lies your reward too. Let us not forget. A promise is a promise!" she said putting an arm around him as they walked in.

The cave was a single space, about fifteen paces in length but much narrower in width. Lit torches hung from the walls. There was no bed or even bedding on the ground that would suggest this was indeed someone's dwelling. There was no furniture either. The only objects Efimios could identify with certainty, were some large ceramic vases standing in a corner.

The woman noticed him looking at them and said she stored olive oil in those, adding that there is no light in the world without it. He thought that sounded rather poetic, and this made him relax around her somewhat again. There were other noticeable things in there, which however, didn't suit her story that this was her house. These things made the cave look more like a place of gathering for obscure ceremonies, and he wondered if far from being rewarded, he was to become an offering on the stone altar that stood in the midst of the twilit space.

His knees trembled somewhat at the thought, but after all, she was only small and fragile-looking. If he had to, he could push her away and run. His eyes darted to the strange candles atop their golden stands and he cringed. Their light was dim and eerie, promoting a haunting atmosphere.

Slowly, he started to walk away from the altar and toward the exit, hoping for a quick escape, just in case. This is when he noticed there were two thrones carved in the rock on either side of the cave. Just as he was about to comment on them in order to look nonchalant as he distanced himself from her, the old woman beckoned to him to return close to her.

She was standing in front of the altar and he swallowed hard, afraid to oblige. But then she looked at him in a way that made her look fragile and once again, he felt ashamed for letting his wild imagination get the better of him. She gave an amicable smile and he walked up to her.

Unafraid now, he followed her eyes that moved from the gentle light of the candles to the very center of the altar. There, he saw a necklace of untold beauty. Its pendant was placed in a round recess carved inside the stone leaving its long, golden chain free. In the middle of the pendant, there was a large moonstone, and tiny quartz crystals dotted all around it. Efimios had seen plenty of gems in his short life being the son of a rich merchant, but this necklace was quite impressive, more than any other he had ever seen.

The figures of a spear and a battle helmet were embossed on the pendant on the left and on the right of the moonstone respectively. Efimios hoped this was what the old lady had in mind to give him. Breathless, he watched as she reached out, taking it into her hand. The chain sparkled and slithered in mid-air and like a subdued snake, entwined with a faint rustling sound onto the palm of her hand.

"As you know, I made you a promise to repay you for your good deed. I will do so but first I will answer your question regarding my identity," she said with a smirk.

Efimios watched silently as she took three steps back from him and placed the necklace on her heart. With her other hand, she started striking her stick on the ground again and like before, it made that unnatural, metallic sound.

All at once, a blinding white light surrounded her, and the ground shook with force, and a tremendous roar. Blinded by the light and paralyzed with fear, the little boy fell to the ground with his eyes tightly shut. A few seconds later, it all stopped.

Stunned, he opened his eyes to see that semi-darkness had returned. He stood and what he saw before him then, left him lost for words. The old lady had vanished, and a young maiden of incredible beauty stood before him now. She was unnaturally tall. Her body was lithe and athletic. She was dressed in a flimsy robe underneath a suit of armour. She had long black hair under her helmet that shone like a halo, crowning her head in glory. She had a tall forehead, arched eyebrows, and her eyes twinkled like distant stars. Holding the necklace to her heart still, she gave a confident smile that exposed perfect, pearly teeth.

Efimios noticed then that she was holding a long spear in her other hand, the real source behind the unnatural sound of the old lady's walking stick. At that specific moment, he knew she had lured him there for a reason. He could also tell that unless the old lady was a witch who had fooled his mind with trickery, he was in the company of a goddess without a doubt.

"Efimios, come to me!" she commanded. Her look was proud, yet kind. Despite his fear, he made two steps forward and knelt before her, overcome with awe.

The woman placed a gentle hand on his back. "Stand up! You have nothing to fear, brave one!"

Efimios obeyed and rested his eyes on hers only for a split second, before bowing his head again. And then, she took his hand and led him to sit on one of the two thrones that were carved in the walls. She sat on the other and then revealed to him that she was Goddess Athena, the Goddess of wisdom and beloved daughter of Zeus.

That same day, she asked him to help her protect Athens, the city she had taken under her wing since the day she was announced on the Acropolis the appointed patron deity. Efimios was excited by the prospect and didn't falter even when she mentioned his services to her would involve repetitive transportation through Time.

Even then, humbled by the fact that she had chosen him, and driven by his innate bravery and courage, Efimios had found in himself no qualms about accepting. And so, that day he went home with her sacred necklace around his neck with a promise to come back to the cave the next day and the next after that, until all her biddings were done.

***

Under the awning, Phevos sighed at the thought of his father, who had accepted without fear, the honor to serve Athena. He had become an unseen hero to the city of Athens, but like all heroes in Greece, he had paid dearly for both his bravery and excellence. Phevos scrunched up the sandwich wrapper and threw it in the bin. On his way back in the store to resume work, his hand touched the necklace through the cotton fabric of his shirt. It had many stories to tell, and Phevos wished to know all its secrets. From his father, it had been passed on to him. Phevos hoped that when he finally opened that sealed door in the back of the orchard later that day, he would become enlightened somewhat as to the reason why.

Chapter 14

It was late afternoon. In two hours, Phevos would be free to leave the store. By now, he was bursting at the seams with anticipation.

Next door in Pallada, his sister was upstairs. She'd been thinking of Aris all day as she went from room to room, cleaning, sweeping and making beds. She'd just finished her chores and was about to return downstairs when she heard Aris's voice echoing from reception below. She wasn't startled because she already knew he was in Pallada again these days, visiting his mother. But that didn't stop her heart from skipping a beat again at the sound of his deep yet tender voice.

This was his second visit since Daphne's arrival, but she still felt shy around him despite having spent a bit of time with him already, mainly in Mrs. Sofia's presence. Every day, Aris greeted her with his earnest smile, but each time Daphne found herself feeling more and more awkward in his presence and quite tongue-tied, even for small talk. She knew by now she was in love with him but felt quite pessimistic about it.

In her eyes, Aris was a man of the world. She thought he could have any woman he wanted and that he'd never notice a church mouse like her. Her heart jumped again at the sound of his laughter when she reached the staircase. She came down the steps in a hurry, despite knowing that once she saw him, she would be tongue-tied again. She hadn't seen him since early morning. The color of gold in his eyes had become the sweetest drug to her by now. She knew she had to have her fix one more time before bedtime.

Reaching the bottom of the stairs, she found him standing before his mother near the exit. Soft rays of sunlight were coming in through the door, bathing the entrance in a golden hue, and embracing mother and son in an aura that made them look radiant. The effect created a scene that was almost religious. It was like a painting by one of the Renaissance masters of the past.

As her son stood before her, the old lady smoothed down the collar of his shirt. Her wrinkled hands caressed the fabric while his tender gaze rested on her face. She was smiling, looking back at him with pride. Mrs. Sofia let out a sigh. She looked at her son and her old heart swelled at that very moment with a longing for the time that he was little.

She wished she could sweep him into her arms again, hold him tight against her breasts and hide him there forever from the dangers of the world. In reality of course, as her body aged and weakened over the years, his was being sculpted to perfection in terms of vigor. By now, things had come full circle. Now, she was the fragile one and Aris was the protector.

To him, his mother embodied the absolute goodness in this world and he felt fortunate. As she always said, every mother raises an angel or a demon for the world with her love or her indifference. This is why it is the mothers that have the greatest power in the world. They can nurture life, but they can also destroy it completely.

A single son who has known no love becomes a demon for the world, bringing pain and devastation, sometimes to millions of people, like a malevolent force that holds no respect for life. Of course, Aris was not one of those sons. Mrs. Sofia had created an angel for the world. As she smoothed down his collar for far longer than was necessary, she felt herself swell inside again with pride for her feat.

When Aris noticed Daphne and turned to look at her, his face lit up. Once again, she seemed ethereal in his eyes, detached somehow from this mundane world. Perhaps he had heard too many stories about fairies from his grandmother when he was small, but sometimes he amused himself with the thought that Daphne was a fairy too, and that she had escaped her world to visit our own. She looked so foreign to this world, far too innocent. He thought her beauty was so perfect that she might as well have fairy-like wings on her back. He wished that it were true because all he'd have to do then is steal her handkerchief, and then she'd be forever his, according to the fairy tales he'd known as a boy.

He offered her an easy smile as he entertained that thought again, in the safe haven of his infatuated mind. It wasn't the first time he felt like that about a girl. He'd had his fair share of relationships by now but somehow, Daphne looked different to all the others. She was mysterious and elusive. So much that he found himself careful around her as not to scare her away, as if she were a timid singing bird that you wish to keep close to you so that you can hear their sweet song forever.

Daphne smiled back at him as she stood before him. Their eyes locked for a few seconds in an awkward silence before he engaged her in conversation. In his most polite voice, he asked her how her day had been so far.

Mrs. Sofia took her broom from the corner and stood at a distance, a crooked smile playing on her lips as she watched them. From her son's previous visit, she had noticed a change in the manner of both the young girl and her son. They seemed to be the same as always at any other time except when they were in each other's presence. The old lady loved Daphne. The prospect of what she could see at play before her gave her immense pleasure. They were talking about the weather now, but the mundane topic of their discussion did not fool her.

When two young people engage in small talk while losing themselves in each other's eyes like that, they can perhaps fool each other but not the elderly, who may be watching them. Old people can see far more clearly because they know a secret: the mouth moves but it can lie. It is only the eyes that tell the truth at all times. So when the youngsters speak, they only hear what the other says and that takes their focus from what the eyes say which is the most important. The old people know that well and so, they ignore the talking and just focus on the eyes. It saves time and it's infallible.

Of course, Mrs. Sofia didn't intend to let either of them know what she could see. She was never one to interfere in the matter of other people's hearts, and besides, it is no fun when you spoil it. There's nothing more beautiful than watching two people at the prime of their youth, searching blindly each other's heart, looking for love.

***

Ksenia was sitting behind the reception desk filing some paperwork after completing her chores upstairs. In a few minutes she'd pick Phevos up from work. From there, they were going to go straight to the back of the orchard, determined to open the sealed door at last.

"Ksenia, hi!" chirped Zoe as she entered Pallada, startling her friend.

Ksenia rushed to her with open arms. "Zoe! What a lovely surprise! What are you doing here?"

"Well, I was in Ermou Street shopping, so I thought I'd drop by and see you. I missed you!"

"I missed you too, Zoe!" she replied squeezing her in her arms. They hardly ever saw each other during the summer break although they phoned each other a lot.

"Phew, let me put those bags down, they're heavy!"

"So, what did you get this time, you Parisian coquette?" teased Ksenia as she watched Zoe place on the floor five large shopping bags from various designer outlets.

"Clothes and shoes!" The girls laughed as they said these words in unison. This was the standard reply that Zoe gave to this question.

Zoe rolled her eyes and let out a giggle. "What else?"

"My goodness, it's so good to see you! I missed you a lot!"

"Well, I keep asking you to visit me at home for coffee—"

"I know, I know! But it's been hectic in Pallada. I promise to come next week." Of course, Ksenia's real reason wasn't only the increased influx of customers, but she couldn't tell Zoe about her busy afternoons with Phevos at the back of the orchard.

"Say, is Daphne here? Haven't seen her since your birthday."

"She's not here but I'm sure she won't be long." As if on cue, Daphne came in then through the front door but she wasn't alone.

Aris was there with her. During their conversation earlier, he had proposed to her to have a coffee together, and she had been pleased to accept. They wound up walking a lot around the lanes first, just wandering and taking in the bustle of Plaka. When they came across a quaint cafe by the Aerides monument, they felt drawn by its shady umbrellas and the discreet, background music. They spent a good hour there finding it easy to talk to each other about so much.

They had returned to Pallada looking exuberant as they talked, relaxed with each other, as if they had been friends forever. Ksenia was surprised for she had never seen Daphne looking so carefree before.

Daphne was pleased to meet Zoe again, but when she introduced her to Aris, the smile on her face faded to watch Zoe bat her eyelids at him while shaking his hand. In Daphne's eyes, she looked gorgeous, all pearly teeth and high cheekbones. As she watched them talk, something unpleasant stirred inside her gut that made her wince with discomfort.

Zoe was a woman she couldn't compete with. She looked like a fashion model. Her mannerisms, her voice, her poise, they all spoke volumes for her self-confidence.

Daphne chewed her lips as she watched Aris engage in a friendly conversation with the two other girls. Zoe was the center of attention, larger than life as always. Ksenia was teasing her and informing Aris about her frequent shopping sprees that were dictated by her Parisian genes. Daphne's heart sank as Zoe's laughter rose up in the air in high, carefree crescendos.

Chapter 15

Ksenia and Phevos looked at each other. Their eyes were enormous with enthusiasm. It was peaceful in the twilight. The rock wall before them felt warm from the generous sunlight it had absorbed all day.

The sky was cloudless, a clear blue canvas that was darkening by the second as the moon shimmered through, as always punctual in its appointment to take over from the sun for the approaching night.

The trees were quiet, their leaves unmoving. There was no wind for them to rustle. Even the usually chatty wild pigeons had silenced themselves. It was almost like nature itself was holding its breath for the upcoming discovery.

The metallic door gleamed in the twilight as if it were caressed by it. At long last, it was free from the tons of moist earth that had sentenced it to oblivion for years. There was rust on it in some parts, and its green color had been chipped away in many others. Despite its demise, in its midst, the large figure of a golden owl showed no signs of decay.

The door had no handle and no lock on it. Phevos held a crow bar in his hand, and as he tried to force the door open, Ksenia stood behind him, cheering him on. Unfortunately, his efforts were to no avail. After several attempts, Phevos threw the crow bar to the ground and together with Ksenia they began to run their fingers over the edges of the door and its metallic frame on the rock.

They looked for a lever or anything else unusual that might be a secret means to open it but found nothing of the sort. Ksenia's hands were now feeling the embossed owl in the center. It looked like the emblem on the Greek one Euro coin that in its turn, had been modeled after the ancient four Drachma coin.

There was only one difference. The bird on the coin was standing while the one on the door was perched on an olive tree branch. Ksenia thought how beautiful the branch was, with its small delicate figures of olives and leaves. She examined it carefully and gasped when she spotted a figure among them that seemed out of place. It was a crescent moon shape that was barely distinguishable in the thick foliage. Ksenia guessed it was not meant to be a leaf.

When he heard her gasp, Phevos knelt beside her. She pointed out her finding, and when he ran his fingertips over it, his eyes lit up. He jolted upright and took the necklace out from under his shirt.

"What are you doing?"

"The necklace! The necklace is the key!"

"What are you talking about?"

"Of course! Why didn't I think of it earlier? Father always had it on him! Only the necklace could be the key to this door!"

"Phevos, what made you reach this conclusion? I don't see how—"

"Here!" He knelt beside her again. "Look on the back of the pendant!"

Ksenia watched as he turned it over. Its back was bare except for the engraved figure of a crescent moon. She hadn't noticed that before, as she had only seen the necklace once or twice. As for Phevos, he knew this mark was there but he had never questioned it. The necklace was a wondrous article in itself. Until now, he hadn't thought to look for clues on it and thus had never wondered about this particular shape before.

"Oh my God!"

Phevos brought the necklace close to the owl for them to compare the two shapes. The engraved crescent on the pendant had a smooth surface but on one edge, there was a tiny hole. The embossed crescent that hid in the foliage under the owl's feet had the same size and was its exact mirror image. On one of its edges, there was a tiny tongue of gold, and Phevos was certain now that if he was to bring the two crescents in contact, the two unusual marks on the edge of each crescent would lock on each other like long lost friends.

"Try to put one crescent on the other, Phevos," said Ksenia in a breathless voice. "Gingerly!" she added, praying inside that it worked.

Without a word and ever so carefully, Phevos obliged, trying to lock one figure on the other with small circular movements. When they heard a faint click, they both gasped looking at each other with eyes full of wonder and hope.

"What now?" His voice came out in a faint whisper. He still held the pendant against the door at the exact position where the crescents had locked on each other. He tried to push the door but it didn't give.

"Try to turn it around instead of pushing it in."

Phevos's eyes lit up. "Like a key?"

"Yes! Like you would turn a key in a keyhole!"

"Good idea!" Phevos turned the pendant clockwise. He pushed again but to no avail. Ksenia placed a hand on his shoulder, and when he turned to look at her, he saw determination in her eyes. Reading her mind, and as it was the only thing left to do anyway before they ran out of ideas, he then turned the pendant anticlockwise hoping for a miracle.

Like the answer to a prayer for two, they both heard a faint click. Phevos didn't even have to try the door this time. As they both gasped in astonishment, the door opened on its own, creaking in a haunting manner and at last, it was now a gaping doorway to a humid darkness.

They stood up with glazed eyes and took a single step inside as the heavy, musty air from within hit their nostrils. For years on end it had been trapped in there, a lonely guardian of terrible secrets. Ksenia shivered as she stared into the gloom, and Phevos picked up their flashlights from the ground. He turned them on and handed her one as he embraced her. In her smile, he saw her determination again and knew they were both ready. He entered first and she followed, fearless now and just as daring as him. The light beams shone on the mossy wall behind the door and from there, they wandered around the full stretch of the cave.

"Just as I imagined. This is the secret cave of Athena!" exclaimed Phevos as he walked further in with caution, looking around with wonder.

"You're right... There! The two thrones of stone against the walls, opposite each other. Just like you said!"

Phevos chuckled. "I bet you're sorry now that you didn't let Manos come along."

"No, not really. I'm still glad I never told him we were doing this today as he would have wanted to come along, and I wasn't going to put him in danger. We didn't know what lay behind the door."

"Well, I agree. Sending him off to play with his friends at the square was the best thing to do. I'd have done the same if I were you, Ksenia."

"I just hope he won't be too mad at me tonight when I tell him the truth," she said biting her lip.

"I'm sure he'll be fine once he hears all about it—"

"Look! There's the altar, Phevos!"

"Yes!" he said as they both approached it. "This is where my father first saw this very necklace." His voice wavered as his fingers pressed against the pendant. He still held it in his hand like a precious security pass that granted him unhindered passage in there.

"He was only nine years old that day, wasn't he?"

"Yes... That was the day Athena recruited him. And it all happened here, by this altar." He approached the imposing centerpiece of the cave, his face ecstatic.

"This is amazing..." Ksenia followed, just as awe-struck. "How can this magical place be in my orchard all these years, hidden from view? Although, this explains why your father chose to live in my house of all places."

"Yes, this is incredible, but I'm sure that in time we'll find out the whole truth behind all the mystery."

They used their flashlights to explore the walls all around them. Their stunned eyes took in all the details Phevos knew from his father's stories, including the torches that hung from the walls and the large ceramic vases in one corner. They stood in a neat line, set deep in the dirt against the wall, unharmed by time, with intricate designs and delicate handles. He knew that Athena once stored olive oil in those. As he looked at the ancient vases now, he wondered if they were still full from those days or if his father had kept them there as a tribute to her, empty vessels of former glory that once stored the most precious gift she'd ever thought to offer to this magnificent and brave city.

"It *must* have been Athena who tore our families apart. There can't be another explanation, Ksenia. And the destruction of the cave by my father has to be his resentful reaction to that."

"I think you're right... I wonder what happened... But most of all, I wonder why your father opted to destroy the cave instead of using it to bring you all back."

"Perhaps he couldn't. In any case, I expect we'll find out in the end. My father must have been determined to destroy this place. From what he told me, not only did he obliterate the interior, but he also sealed the entrance with large rocks just to make sure that no one would ever discover it, not even by chance."

"But I don't understand, Phevos. If he destroyed it in the past then how come it's here now, unharmed?"

Phevos shrugged his shoulders. "I don't know. Father was forever speaking about the relation between cause and effect. Any change in the past, will affect the future. Therefore, if indeed he destroyed the cave in the past, it should not exist today unscathed."

"And yet it does!"

"Yes, indeed it does. Perhaps a divine intervention has made this possible. Perhaps it was the will of a God, powerful enough to break the time continuum if you like, causing an upset in the all powerful law of cause and effect."

"But who would do that? Athena?"

"I don't know Ksenia, any more than you do. Father never spoke of an association with another God and never explained anything to me. I don't even know why he destroyed the cave, or why he stopped serving Athena." He shook his head forlornly. "As you know, he never even told me anything about my mother or our separation from her..."

"How could he not tell you anything about your mother, Phevos? It doesn't make sense!"

"My father never mentioned her. And don't forget that neither did your parents, who lived with me back there all these years. There has to be a reason behind their silence. It's like they were somehow sworn to secrecy."

"Athena has to be behind all this. My parents, your father and you, you all left overnight. She must have taken you all away against your will! You would never have left your mother behind and neither would my parents have chosen to leave Manos and me!"

"This is the only logical explanation I can accept too. And yet, I can't understand why my father taught me to honor Athena as he raised me. Why not voice his anger instead? Why all this secrecy? And why would he even mention that he destroyed the cave if he was unwilling to disclose the reason? Thinking back now, it's like he tried to sow a doubt in my head. Like he was trying to tell me there was something wrong, that she was not to be revered after all."

"I'm sure there's a reason for everything. As you said, we'll find out in the end." Ksenia gave Phevos a slow, encouraging smile and opened her arms to embrace him. When she moved away again, her eyes rested on the necklace in his hands.

"If only we knew why your father didn't use this necklace to bring you all back!" She gave an exasperated sigh. "I just can't figure out why instead of holding on to it for dear life, he let it wind up in the sea somehow. Did he lose it? Did Athena take it from him? Do you even know how the necklace wound up in the sea?"

"No, I don't."

"And yet it made its appearance in your life in the most unexpected manner."

Phevos nodded, his expression wistful.

"And next thing you knew, you and Daphne wound up here."

"That's right. For Daphne and me, it all happened in a different way to my father's stories. We never used the cave to travel in Time like he used to."

"You said that the necklace itself acted to make this happen."

"Yes. Somehow, it got activated once we got in the fountain."

"Why don't you tell me again the story of how you found the necklace?"

"Now? Here?" Phevos spread out his arms as he stood in the middle of the dark room, surprised with her sense of timing. They were both standing before the altar. He had just noticed something was out of place there but before he could voice his thoughts, Ksenia interrupted him again. She felt strongly about this.

"Why not? If indeed this is the secret sanctum of Athena, perhaps this is the most apt place for you to try to remember every single detail. Maybe I'm clutching at straws here, but even if you manage to recall from memory one tiny new detail, it could make a difference. It might give us yet another clue to complete the surreal jigsaw puzzle that you landed on me as you waltzed into my life!" Ksenia winked and smiled at him.

Phevos mirrored her expression, despite the eerie darkness that engulfed them. He turned his back on the altar and leant against it. What he had noticed there could wait.

He tried to gather his thoughts now in order to reminisce in the most effective way, that unbelievable experience again. He let his hands drop to his side and the flashlight shone down to the dirt by his feet. He half-closed his eyes in the semidarkness, and Ksenia entwined her arms around his waist gazing at his serene face.

Phevos took a deep breath and willed himself to relax as to recapture the memories from his twentieth birthday. The first image that sprang up in his head was pleasant. His father was happy and smiling from ear to ear as he stood in the kitchen, directing the servants as the seafood supplies came in. He was hosting a large banquet that evening to celebrate Phevos's birthday in the company of extended family and friends.

"It was around midday." Phevos sighed and opened his eyes, resting them on the far, mossy wall. "Father had ordered a generous amount of fish for that day's dinner. It was to be supplied by a good friend of his, who was a captain of a large fishing boat. He'd had a remarkable catch that day. He was a fearless fisherman in the sense that he took his boat to open waters with plenty of fish but also powerful sea currents that other fishermen with smaller boats steered clear from. One of these spots was located just off the coast of Sounio that's famous for the temple of God Poseidon, the protector of the sea and of all who fares on and in it. The captain had caught a large amount of fish that day including sea bass, sardine, mackerel and red mullet. However, one large fish wound up also in his net that nearly broke it in its attempt to break free. It wriggled out of it in the end but not before the brave captain hit it with his spear, injuring it fatally, then loading it with effort with the assistance of his faithful crew.

Everyone had marveled at it when it landed on the deck with a deafening thud, its skin glistening in the sunlight, its sharp teeth sparkling like pearls. It was a medium sized dogfish. It caused a big uproar in the kitchen among the staff when the men brought it in, still in one piece. By the time they started gutting it with a large knife, the whole household had gathered around to admire it. As they started clearing its insides, the incredible happened. Something was sparkling in its stomach.

We all moved closer, drawn by the irresistible shine that came from its core as the strong rays of the midday sun graced the kitchen through the large windows. The cook dipped his hand inside the bloody mess and when he opened it, we all gasped at the beautiful golden necklace with the long chain that lay in his palm. We all froze at the sight, except for Father of course, who lunged forward, snatching it from the cook's hand. He hurried to a tub of water and cleaned it from the blood that stained it.

When he raised his hand to see it in the light more clearly, his hand was shaking, and the beautiful pendant with the mesmerizing moonstone in its midst sparkled like nothing we had ever seen before. Both Daphne and I recognized it, of course. Father had described Athena's necklace countless times to us. He had never disclosed its whereabouts to us, and we'd never seen it before, not until that day. It came as a shock to us, of course, for we thought it was still in father's possession.

The servants were also stunned although they didn't know what it was, but its beauty was so great that they found no words among them to describe it, not even to speak about it. And as we all stood speechless, just watching Father holding it with trembling hands, he then started commanding the servants to leave the room. They were taken aback, for it was so unexpected and out of character for him to act like this, but they obeyed all the same.

As soon as they all cleared the room, Father mumbled something to himself in an inaudible whisper, and then he came to me and rested one hand on my shoulder. I remember his eyes.... they were huge and burning like fire, boring holes of desperate angst into my mind. I knew then that something terrible had happened or was about to happen, and I could tell that my life would never be the same again. Father put the necklace in my hand and ordered me to wait.

He hurried to his private quarters and came back with some clothes and a pair of shoes. This is what I was wearing when you first met me Ksenia. So you see, Father knew this was going to happen one day and he was prepared! He ordered me to go to my quarters at once, to change into these clothes and to return with haste. His eyes burnt still and his voice carried such an urgency that left me with no opportunity to argue or to question. So I obeyed and when I returned to the kitchen, I found Daphne in tears. She was hysterical, frightened and was begging him to explain what was going on, but Father had no words for her. He just held her in his arms, soothing her, asking her to calm down.

As soon as I returned to them, he left me alone with Daphne in the middle of the room and rushed to a counter where we stored olives, herbs and condiments. Daphne and I watched him perplexed as he rummaged through vases and pots, looking for something. I looked around me then and noticed Kimon and Eleni were still there. At the far end of the adjoining sitting area, they were perched at the end of a large bench holding each other and watching Father in silence, just like we did..."

"My parents were there?" asked Ksenia, astounded. Until that time, she was leaning against him with her eyes shut, holding him close as he took her on a mental journey into his old world, but this detail had caused her to jolt upright and snap back into the present.

"Funny, isn't it? I just remembered that." Phevos reached out to hold her again, his face lit up, pleased he had managed to recall this new detail.

"Last time you said everyone had left when your father ordered them to go. You said you and Daphne were alone with him by that time—"

"I know! But I remember clearly now. Your parents were watching from that bench as they sat there holding each other. They were crying Ksenia.... they were crying but their faces were happy! I remember now how this was baffling to me at the time. I couldn't fathom then why they looked pleased at this funny turn of events and my father's strange attitude. But now I realize why they felt so happy, happy enough to burst into tears!"

"They knew, Phevos! They knew what was happening!"

"Yes Ksenia. They knew! Just like Father knew what all that meant and what was going to happen next. Their hearts must have been full of hope at that time."

"My poor, poor parents! How they must have suffered...." lamented Ksenia and hot tears escaped from her eyes, yet she felt stronger now. Stronger than before, full of renewed hope. She wiped the tears from her face and tried to smile. "Carry on Phevos... what happened next? Tell me again."

"Well, we watched Father for a while as he kept rummaging through all kinds of containers. We were both numb by then and I held my sister in my arms as she sobbed. Her eyes were begging for me to keep her close. It was like she knew I was to go away, and she didn't want to let me go. Then, Father found a pot full of coarse sea salt, and it seemed to be what he was looking for. He took a big handful and rushed to me. I still had the necklace, and he took it from me then, putting it in his hand with the salt. He grabbed my arm next, urging me to hurry with him outside. He asked Daphne to stay behind but she wouldn't have it. Wailing, she rushed behind us holding on to my shirt or his robes as Father dragged me by the arm outside our estate. From our gate, we hurried along the short, tree-lined path that led to a small, public square just on the edge of the forest where I used to play when I was small. A fountain stood in the middle of the square that was quiet at the time. To my surprise, Father dragged me into the fountain and of course Daphne followed suit. We were in the pool all the way up to our knees, and the sound of cold water was heightened now as it rushed through the golden taps, crystal drops sparkling in the sun like precious diamonds. We stood under the spray and Father ordered Daphne to get out of the fountain. He was no longer pleading with her. He was demanding it now but to my surprise, Daphne stood her ground. Not that she shouted back at him of course, no. But she refused to let go of me and cried as she begged him in a heart-wrenching way that he couldn't ignore. I watched as Father's expression turned from exasperation to despair and finally into love and tenderness for her. He took Daphne's hand and put it in mine and then placed the necklace around my neck, careful not to lose the sea salt that was in his hand still. He said something to me then, and it was the only thing he said before we parted. He said, 'follow the signs!' I was too numb to speak, so I never asked him to explain what he meant. His whole body was shaking now, and my heart went to him for he looked deeply tormented. I had no idea what was going on, but my instinct was telling me to obey whatever he had in his mind to do with us next. He kissed us on our foreheads whispering a goodbye in a broken voice and then stepped out of the fountain. Daphne and I stood in the water holding each other's hand, shivering. Through the spray that still fell upon us like sparkling gems impairing our vision, we then saw Father swing his arm and throw the sea salt in the water. He said something then, but we couldn't hear it for the jet was powerful from the taps, even louder than before now. Father looked exhausted, drawn, and his eyes were full of tears. Then, the water started to shimmer and glint like gold, more and more, and we looked around us panicked and stunned by the sight. Everything was now so bright that we became almost blinded. A murmur rose up from the water, and within seconds it had grown to a mighty roar that was now deafening in our ears while the whole world around us started to shake. Through the golden haze that still blinded us, we then saw Father still standing there, looking at us. I could swear I saw a faint smile on his face then, despite his tears. It was a glimmer of hope beyond the grief that consumed him. And then, we were through the Passage to this world. The rest you know...."

"Didn't he say anything else to you? Anything at all?"

"Nothing, I'm sure. His only advice was to look for the signs."

"Well, that proved to be sound advice. You've found quite a few on your way. And here we are!" Ksenia said spreading out her arms as a hopeful smile lit up her face.

"Yes Ksenia. Indeed, here we are!" Phevos mirrored her smile and turned around to inspect the ancient altar again. They huddled together before it, using the flashlights to examine it more closely. It wasn't a mere block of stone. It had been decked with Pentelic marble around its base and its sides. Efimios had decorated it in honor to Athena and had also introduced to the cave numerous tapestries that depicted scenes from the Iliad and the Odyssey with the use of golden thread and faded organic colors.

Many of them were famous scenes that Athena had featured in according to legend. The tapestries decorated the surrounding walls, and smaller ones had been draped on the two thrones. Phevos took some time also to admire the torches on the walls. Unlike normal ones that are made of wood, these were solid quartz crystals of perfect clarity. They were quite large and pyramid-shaped. Supported by golden cradles, they hung on the walls, their perfect points sharp like needles.

Phevos returned his gaze to the altar, back to what had puzzled him earlier. He laid his finger on the round recess carved in the very center where the pendant fits. Further out on the circular top surface of the altar, there were three more round recesses carved on the stone. They were placed equally apart, forming an equilateral triangle.

According to his father's stories, three golden candleholders used to stand there playing an integral part in the procedure that caused the Passage through Time. However, all three candleholders were missing now and what's more, in one of the round recesses, a different object to what he was expecting stood in place. It was a long and smooth object that resembled a single candle.

Phevos leant in closer shining his flashlight on it. It wasn't a candle after all. Its surface was made of crystal. He gasped as the shock of realization pierced him through, making him jolt upright as if hit by electricity.

Chapter 16

"Ksenia, look! This looks like the wand that I saw in my dream!"

"But how can it be? You said the wand was shining in your dream. This one's dark."

"I know that but... wait a minute," he said leaning over the altar to study it closer. Ksenia was crouched next to him in a heartbeat with both their flashlights illuminating the object. They fell speechless when they noticed it contained grains of golden sand that sparkled as they floated in a transparent liquid. Tiny shards of pink and blue shells floated in there too with the iridescence of mother-of-pearl. Now, they were both certain this was the wand in Phevos's dream. It had finally manifested in their lives. He grapsed it in one hand, then tried to pick it up gently. It didn't budge so he attempted a bit more forcefully this time, but again, to no effect.

Ksenia frowned. "That's strange! Can I try?"

Phevos gestured for her to give it a go, but her attempt was to no avail either. "There must be a way to detach it. We just have to work it out," he said. They inspected the wand again and the recess it stood on, looking for clues but there was nothing.

Phevos turned around and leant against the altar, trying to detach himself from the perplexing object long enough in order to refocus. His gaze fell upon the torches around the walls, and he thought then that some source of light must exist in this place. Something had to illuminate these torches that returned a dark, crystal stare back to him, unwilling to unravel their secret. For sure, the right action would set them alight. He thought then that the wand on the altar might also illuminate like the one in his dream, under the correct handling.

His father had mentioned three candleholders on the altar that held crystal candles, which played an integral part for the Passage through Time. And yet, these were missing now. What else could illuminate this space now that these candles were no longer present? What could he use instead of that dark wand that stood lifeless there? Instinctively, the tips of his fingers touched the necklace around his neck and then he knew. Phevos spun around, his eyes open wide.

"What is it? What are you going to do?" she asked perplexed as she watched him clutch the necklace in his hand with renewed determination.

"This cave must have a light source. I think the necklace may be it! I say we put it on the altar."

Her face lit up with alarm. "What? Are you sure? What if it sets the Passage in motion?"

"I don't think it will. Don't worry Ksenia. The cave is destroyed back in time, right? I don't think the Passage can be initiated here any more. And you know what? I think I'm meant to place the necklace on the altar. Remember the dream? The tall stranger said that we should exchange the necklace for the wand. I think this is it! This is the only way we can take it off the altar!"

"All right, let's try it!" replied Ksenia, convinced. His answer had sounded logical enough in her sensible mind despite the fact that the whole situation was nothing but surreal. She smiled despite herself then as she thought of her mundane life before Phevos walked into it, sweeping away from it with the force of a powerful whirlwind, everything that she once held as true or possible.

Phevos grasped the necklace and was about to place it on the center of the altar when Ksenia clutched his shirt sleeve.

"Wait! What if this is a mistake?"

"What now?" Phevos furrowed his brow, mildly exasperated. He needed all the focus he could get and didn't need her doubts now.

"What if you can't get it back once you put it there?"

For a few seconds, he shared her panic at that thought as the necklace hovered over the altar. But then, the tall stranger's words echoed in his mind and his worry subsided. "Don't worry Ksenia! The stranger said this was only a loan. We're not parting with it forever."

Phevos put the necklace in place. There was a faint click as it lay down in its cradle and then, with a buzzing sound, the cave was bathed in light as the torches on the walls magically lit up. Enthused, Phevos exchanged glances with Ksenia. They laughed as they dropped their flashlights on the ground and hugged each other, cheering.

"And now, the moment of truth," Phevos announced as they turned to face the altar again. The crystal wand was still dark. He had hoped it would illuminate when the necklace was placed on the altar. Still, that didn't discourage him. He was sure his other guess would definitely be right. And indeed, as soon as he pulled the wand ever so lightly this time, he managed to detach it.

"You made it!"

"Yes, for the love of the Gods! Indeed, *we* made it!" he corrected her, and they hugged again. "Do you realize what this means, Ksenia? The stranger is real! We have a God-protector on our side!"

"You think so?"

"Of course I do! Father never spoke of him but I'm guessing he knows his identity. He never said anything about a wand inside this cave either. And I'm sure that even more things will follow that Father never mentioned."

"You think your father hid these things from you on purpose?"

"Yes. As I said, perhaps Athena or this mysterious stranger had sworn him to secrecy. You see, the Gods often enjoy pulling strings on people's lives."

"Pulling strings? This sounds cruel."

"No, not really, Ksenia. I don't mean the Gods are capricious or cruel. I refer to their infinite capacity to invent plans in order to answer the prayers of the faithful. There's no religion on earth that doesn't speak volumes for the Gods' inventive ways, as they weave people's destinies. Someone may mistake the answer to their prayers as a bad joke at first but give it time and it'll prove a blessing that brings the best results in the end."

"Is this about 'God's mysterious ways' and all that?"

"Yes, that's it Ksenia. The Divine loves to work in mysterious ways, and this is how it may bring the best results, if we only let it. Faith and patience are required and as for the frustration and the pain involved in the process, these are what shape characters, and it's all to be embraced."

"That reminds me of this teacher I had when I was little!" Ksenia said laughing with a snort.

"Oh yeah? Why's that?"

"He would often preach that life is hard. To make his point he'd say, 'if life were easy, it would be a cookie with sugar on top'!"

Phevos broke into uproarious laughter and Ksenia joined him. There was something about the intensity of their discovery that made anything mildly amusing sound hysterical.

"I must have heard it from his lips a thousand times!" Ksenia rolled her eyes. "I think about him whenever I encounter difficulty in life. And it always makes me smile."

"How original is that! He must have been a great teacher," commented Phevos shaking his head as they made their way out of the cave.

When they came out into the stillness of the night, the lights in the cave turned out as if by magic. Phevos held the wand against his chest like a trophy. The golden sand and the shards of shells floated softly in the clear liquid as the young couple hurried back to the house.

Chapter 17

It was ten p.m. Dinner had been served and everyone was in the living room watching TV. Manos was sitting on the rug as he watched, with Odysseus curled up next to him snoring. A mediocre series was playing on TV, one of those pointless ones that only serve to help you fall asleep faster. Manos seemed to be the only one to rather enjoy it while the other three watched absentmindedly. During the lengthy advert breaks they resumed their excited conversation about the day's amazing events.

Daphne knew about the impending discovery and had chosen to stay away in order to give Phevos and Ksenia their privacy. As for Manos, when he found out that evening, he got upset at first that his sister had left him out of it. In the end, as Phevos and Ksenia explained they wouldn't have risked his safety, his enthusiasm for their find finally overcame his disappointment.

Daphne and Manos kept asking the same questions, demanding to know every single detail about the cave. They couldn't wait for the next day so that they could see it for themselves. Everyone had had a chance by now to inspect the wand in their hands and in the end, it had been handed back to Phevos. He was its rightful owner and keeper since it had been his dream that had brought on the latest earth-shattering events.

Phevos felt strange that he wasn't wearing the necklace any more, yet he knew he had left it in a safe place. Even in the unlikely event that a trespasser was to enter the cave, Phevos knew he could never steal the necklace. Before he left, he had made sure it couldn't be detached from the altar, no matter how hard he pulled. Not that his integrity would have allowed him to take it away even if he could have. He had made a pact with the stranger in his dream and could only honor it.

However, his mind was now put at rest to know the necklace was safe on the altar in case of intruders. As for the entrance to the cave, he had placed a heavy boulder in front of the door to make sure it wouldn't lock shut from a strong gust of wind. They would be lost for sure if the heavy door was to close shut. Without the necklace they could never open it again.

The wand remained dark in his hands. As he glanced at it every now and then, his mind brimmed with thoughts and possibilities. His main concern was his mother now, Anna. Now he knew her name. Yet, he still didn't know why she had vanished from his life. A myriad of questions swam in his head. Was she alive and well? Had she remarried? Had she had more children? Did she think of him and his father at all?

He was now twirling the wand in his hands, and as he watched the gold and the pearl of its contents reflect the silver light from the TV, he became even more mesmerized by its beauty. Hypnotized by the iridescence inside the clear liquid, his mind wandered to his mother again with the softness of rainbow colors and the fluidity of water. His mind was set to find her, and he hoped she knew about this wand so that she could answer the mountains of questions he had.

"Hey, a penny for your thoughts!" said Daphne, who sat next to him on the sofa. Ksenia was seated on his other side, and she turned to look at him too and so did Manos, who was still on the rug. Yet Phevos was so lost in thought that he never heard them at all. He was still gazing into the contents of the wand that rested on his lap. His mind was wandering, and his head was bent. His slouched shoulders seemed to bear the burdens of the world.

"Oh my darling, please don't worry! Patience! It'll all be revealed to us in the end!" said Daphne with a pat on his back. Ksenia reached out and gave him a hug in quiet agreement.

"Sorry. I was just thinking of my mother..." he said when he raised his head to give them both a thankful but sorrowful look. "I'm guessing she knows about this wand... we just have to find her!" he added with urgency.

"Yes, Brother! Indeed we will!" replied Daphne caressing his hair. Her tender touch brought on a painful tightness in his gut that stirred his soul. The feeling made him feel nine years old again, when he cried in his father's arms at night, asking for his mother.

A wave of pain rose in his chest, and hot tears welled up in his eyes, rolling down his cheeks and shaming him, yet delivering him from the pain inside. He sprang to his feet and strode to the door. With his back to the others, he felt lucky for the semidarkness in the room that spared his dignity. He wiped the tears away with a single sweep from the back of one hand while still holding the wand in the other. The wondrous object was still dark and as long as it remained so, it kept his eyes hostage to the same gloom.

"I'll just go and have a glass of water, won't be long." Without expecting an answer, he disappeared down the hallway. Manos turned his attention to the TV screen, unaware and unaffected. But when the two girls met each other's gaze in silence, it was evident that they both knew.

Still, they could only imagine what it felt like, this vague and yet excruciating feeling of loss, this chilling cloud of darkness in Phevos's mind that robbed him of his early childhood memories.

***

The next morning, Phevos and Daphne returned to the house early from Pallada. It was Sunday and once again, they had planned to spend it with Ksenia and Manos starting from breakfast. As soon as Ksenia opened the door, Phevos gave a cheer and swept her up in his arms. Ksenia was taken aback. When they parted late the previous night, he looked distraught. And yet now, behind the closed door, she watched as he produced the wand out of his shirt, a wide smile across his face. It had remained on his pillow all night. He hadn't wanted to part with it even during sleep in case it gleamed even faintly. He was hoping to wake up if it were to do that, even before his closed eyelids, so he kept it close to his face just in case. The wand remained dark overnight, but Phevos was happy that morning for another reason.

"I've had another dream!" he announced as Ksenia led the way to the kitchen. She'd just put the kettle on. Manos was in his room getting dressed.

Daphne opened the cupboard to take the crockery out and judging from the look on her face, Ksenia guessed Phevos had already told her about his dream. She looked just as thrilled as he was.

"It must be quite a dream! Tell me all about it!"

"Let's wait for Manos," replied Daphne and as if on cue, the boy entered the room with a cheerful face.

"Oh, my goodness! Everyone's bright and breezy this morning!" said Manos when he saw the line of animated faces before the kitchen sink.

"There's a reason for that. Phevos has good news to share," said Ksenia.

"Oh no! I want to go first! I've got something very important to say!" Manos replied taking everyone by surprise. He looked frustrated all of a sudden, and there was a seriousness in his manner too that wasn't customary. Ksenia, who knew him best, was puzzled and quite curious as well to hear what he had to share.

Phevos and Daphne were also quite happy to oblige him. After all, Phevos's latest dream would need to be analyzed and discussed, so it made sense to leave this subject for last. All three of them expected Manos had something trivial to share, like the release of a new computer game or an upcoming event that he wanted to attend.

Adults often make the mistake to take the words of children lightly until they get to hear what it is, only to be amazed. In the same manner, Manos was about to amaze all three of them that morning. When they all agreed he could speak first, he sat in silence at the table waiting for them to join him. The look in his eyes was one of sheer excited anticipation, and his lips were pursed with a hint of a smile. He seemed about to burst with enthusiasm, yet he kept silent, unlike his usual self that would be blabbering nonstop at this time of day.

This puzzled his sister more as she watched him while bringing with Daphne to the table hot drinks, toast, butter and honey. Phevos sat across from him astonished as well, watching his strange behavior as he stirred sugar in his coffee.

"Hey you, looking like the cat that got the cream!" Ksenia teased the boy shoving him playfully with her elbow when she sat next to him. Manos chuckled in response but offered no comment. He wasn't ready to start yet because he needed everyone's full attention plus he knew the suspense would be worth it.

Daphne joined the table last. She opened the jar of honey and spread a generous amount on her pieces of toast while Ksenia and Phevos seemed to have lost their appetite. They were looking intently at Manos, eager for him to start. Daphne sipped from her cup and then joined the others, turning to face Manos with an expectant look.

By that time, all three adults knew the boy wasn't being his normal self. They were no longer chuckling and teasing him, but instead they were waiting in all seriousness. A dead silence fell upon the room for the first time ever during breakfast.

Before speaking, Manos savored the moment and looked across the table at everyone first, with an unbefitting solemnity on his young face.

"I couldn't sleep last night so I surfed the Internet. I wound up reading about time travel theories," he finally announced.

"And?" replied the others in unison egging him to continue, but Manos responded in silence with a cunning smile.

"Manos, tell us already!" demanded his sister, and he broke out laughing then, his childish ways fully restored. He so relished the attention he was getting and it felt great. He wasn't being conceited, but he had enjoyed the feeling that he had something important to say. Now, he couldn't wait any longer.

"Well, it seems there are many theories about the possibility of time travel," he continued. "I couldn't believe how much information there is out there. Not only in literature but also from people who actually claim it is possible. And what's more, it seems crystals seem to play a part in the process, especially quartz crystal. For example, there's a theory about this cave in a secret location in Europe that's a natural quartz crystal mine. People have allegedly disappeared only to reappear later there and it's believed they were transported to a different time for a while. Apparently, crystals of the same kind react to each other forming an energy field that can allow humans to travel in Time at will, given the right equipment and environment."

"So, it sounds like our cave is not one of a kind after all," said Ksenia mystified.

"They speak of the same things you see. It's all about crystals," continued Manos.

"Oh, we can see the similarities of course," interrupted Ksenia patting her brother's hand. She was careful not to offend her brother. He had seemed to think this was too important, and she didn't want to shun his confidence. "Have you read anything else to share with us, anything that could give us any clues?"

"But I've already told you! Have you missed it?" asked Manos looking across the table to the others. All three of them responded to him with a blank stare. They had no idea what he was talking about.

"Phevos, what do you think that is?" Manos asked as he pointed to the object that Phevos still cradled in his hands ever since he had produced it out of his shirt earlier on.

"It's a wand. And it looks just like the one in my dream." Phevos humored him, still unable to understand.

"But would you say that this is a crystal too?" Manos enquired.

"I think it is, yes," said Phevos, raising the wand in his hand for everyone to see. "Although this one is hollow inside. It contains this transparent liquid that could be water. It also has sand and shards of shells floating in it."

"Well, let's assume it's a crystal then," said Manos.

The other three nodded in unison. By now, they were all leaning forward in their chairs, their drinks getting cold by the minute. Even Daphne had lost her appetite for her toast with honey, her favorite delicacy of the day.

"Well, imagine there's metal in there mixed with the sand or even shards of tiny crystals perhaps. Who knows? Maybe this liquid or water or whatever you want to call it, acts like a conductor of some produced energy that through the surrounding crystal could react on another of the same kind. Have you ever thought of that?"

The other three stared mutely back at him so Manos exhaled and carried on. "What other objects in the cave do we know that have crystals on them?" he asked looking at the others. All at once, there was animation in their eyes instead of that silent, blank stare.

"There are crystal torches on the walls!" offered Daphne first.

"The necklace I left there also has crystals on it. When I placed it on the altar, I was able to take the wand," said Phevos.

"And what's more, when the necklace was placed on the altar, the torches on the walls lit up. They reacted to it, like you said crystals react to each other!" Ksenia added, turning to her brother.

Phevos shook his head. "It just... it just feels strange that the tiny crystals on the necklace could light up the torches on the walls. These crystals are massive! I wonder how it's even possible."

"Exactly!" answered Manos. "You see, this is not about size! As we've seen, it's possible for a tiny quartz crystal to cause a reaction on another one of the same kind that is much bigger. So this is about *the type of crystal*, not its size. It has to be the same kind for them to react on each other. For a light to come on or even for time travel to be made possible, they have to be the same. That is the key!" Manos added. "And as for that wand in your hand, you said that in your dream it was illuminated, right?"

"Yes, it was! But in reality it does not do that," Phevos added with a frown.

"Can you think why that is so?" asked Manos.

"Because there's no other of its own kind to react to it?" answered Phevos without even thinking.

"Another just like it?" interrupted Daphne. She turned a glazed look at Phevos, her mouth gaping open with enthusiasm. "Phevos, your dream!"

"What dream?" asked Manos.

"This is what I was going to say earlier, and you said you wanted to go first. But I'm glad you did, Manos! This is amazing!" said Phevos.

"You had a dream about the wand?" asked Ksenia, her blue eyes huge.

"Yes I have Ksenia... but please let me think this over for a minute..." Thinking aloud, Phevos turned to Manos again. "My father spoke of three candleholders that used to be on the altar. They had crystal candles on them. To create the Passage through Time, he had to place the necklace in the center of the altar. The light on the crystal candles would come on and then he'd be transported through Time at the will of Athena. He could always remove the necklace afterwards, and he would go about his business wearing it until his work was done. Then he would place the necklace back on the altar. Then through the same process, he would go back in time again. Yet today, it's all different! The three candleholders with the crystal candles are gone, and there was only this single wand on the altar. Plus, I had to leave the necklace there in order to get it. There has to be a reason for all this! Perhaps, a divine intervention has made all this possible, and my father, for his own reasons, never said. But why?"

"Do you want to know what I think?" asked Manos.

"Go on!" answered Ksenia.

"I think someone has left the wand on the altar and has taken the three candleholders away as a clue! Just as there used to be three candleholders on the altar, there are three wands, not just one! There are two more out there, Phevos, both looking the same like the one in your hands. And what's more, I do believe that like those three candleholders, the three wands are just as capable to create the Passage!" answered Manos, raising both arms in a triumphant gesture when he was done.

"Two more wands just like this one... reacting on each other to illuminate... all three together causing a Passage through Time?" mumbled Phevos.

"I think you should tell them about your dream now. It makes so much sense all of a sudden!" prompted Daphne.

"Ok! So, about my dream," said Phevos as the others egged him on, impatient to hear all about it. "It wasn't about Athena or the tall stranger this time. There was only I standing in front of a tall mirror holding the wand. Each time I looked at it through the mirror it would illuminate, but if I looked at it directly it would go dark again. I did it in my dream over and over and it was always the same. Only through the mirror it would light up. It had the same brilliant light just like in the earlier dream with the stranger."

"Amazing! It's a symbolism, right? This is what Manos has just suggested, isn't it? It needs its equal to light up!" said Ksenia while Daphne nodded in silence, her eyes still full of excitement.

This last dream had served as an undisputed confirmation of the theory they had just shaped together with Manos in the lead.

"When I woke up and told Daphne, we didn't know what to think. Believe me, I even went to the mirror to try it. I was *that* desperate for a clue but of course, the wand didn't light up in reality when I looked at it through the mirror. I knew the answer wouldn't be something so obvious and pointless. I knew the mirror was a symbolism of some sort and thanks to our brilliant Manos here, it now all makes perfect sense!" said Phevos and everyone joined in, congratulating the boy for working all this out on his own.

No one was more proud of him than Ksenia though. She had always known he had it in him to excel. Her prayers that one day he would find the confidence to do so had finally been answered. Gone was the introvert boy who shied away from conversation. Far from it, he was now amazing them all with his contribution to it.

They continued talking about their theory while sipping cold coffee and tea, but they didn't even mind. Mystified anew, they questioned how they could find the other two wands and wondered how they could bring their loved ones back to their lives. Phevos's mind wandered to the amazing way in which he and his sister had been transported there in the first place. They had never used Athena's cave, but instead, their father had made them stand in a fountain of water where he had tossed a handful of salt. Phevos made the connections with the contents of the wand and with his dream on the shore. He produced the same conclusion again but still felt he shouldn't yet share his thoughts with the others about the identity of the stranger in the dream. The answer seemed so evident, it was staring him right in the face. It seemed too simple to be true. But if he was right, then what would Athena's involvement be in this case? Regardless of the answer, Phevos chose to speculate in silence.

Suddenly, he snapped out of this state of deep thinking and became aware of the conversation that took place around him. The others were saying something about his mother. Ksenia had mentioned Anavisos, the place that Anna had once moved to according to the address book that Mrs. Sofia kept in Pallada. And what was that sudden glint before his eyes? Was it his imagination or had the wand just illuminated for a split second?

"What did you just say Ksenia?" he asked.

"What did I say?" she responded, taken aback.

"Please sweetheart, can you please repeat what you just said, word for word?"

"Word for word?" she asked, wondering why he had turned so pale.

"Please humor me!" he insisted, never leaving his eyes from the wand.

"Ugh, I don't remember exactly. What was it now?" she said trying to think while Daphne and Manos attempted to assist her.

"Try to repeat it verbatim please!" Phevos insisted with his eyes still glued to the wand.

"Right, I think I said... 'Who knows if she's still in Anavisos? We'll end up looking in Sounio too, no doubt'!"

And there it was again, that sudden flash of light inside the wand. And this time, everyone saw it because they were all looking. They had noticed how Phevos had hunched over the wand in his hands, staring at it in a puzzling way as he waited for Ksenia to repeat her sentence.

Everyone's eyes stayed on the wand for a few seconds more. One could only hear the soft sound of their breath as they stared incredulous. The heavy silence that fell in the room, made the ticking of the clock on the wall echo like the thud of heavy footsteps. When they finally took their eyes from the wondrous object, they looked at each other seeking confirmation that what they had just witnessed was true. A single glimpse was enough for their joy to erupt with loud cheers.

"Whoaaa!" went Manos.

"I can't believe it!" exclaimed Daphne. "What made it do that?"

"How is it even possible?" wondered Ksenia.

"Why not? It *is* possible if we believe this wand is not of this world!" answered Phevos.

"Did it react to a certain word?" asked Manos.

"This is what I believe...." whispered Phevos.

"Which word did it react to then?" said Daphne.

"Anavisos!" tried Ksenia, leaning toward the wand in case distance mattered in order to get its reaction. Yet, the wand didn't respond.

"Sounio!" piped up Phevos, and an obliging glow from the wand confirmed his gut feeling. The two girls goggled their eyes in astonishment, but somehow Manos didn't look surprised in the least when he locked eyes with Phevos. On the contrary, his smirk suggested he had worked out more than he'd let on.

"Tell me Manos, did your Internet search refer to Poseidon's temple at all? Did it mention anything about time travel in Sounio?" Phevos asked, not expecting a positive answer. However, he could see Manos was dying to reveal his thoughts so he threw the bait.

"Not really," answered Manos not looking surprised in the least. "But I *do* believe Poseidon couldn't resist getting even with a certain, naughty godmother!" he added with a cunning smile on his cheerful face.

"A godmother you said?" asked Phevos, grinning with amusement as the girls stared now, puzzled.

"Yep!" replied Manos. "And it looks like he'll finally get his chance to give her a taste of her own medicine!" he added chuckling.

It didn't take long for Ksenia and Daphne to realize about whom they were talking, as they watched Manos laughing. He had referred to Poseidon's defeat during the contest for patronship of Athens. Athena had prevailed and thus had won the honor to name the city after her. But Poseidon believed she had beaten him with deceit and perhaps did wait for a chance through the millenniums to scheme against her for the sake of divine justice.

The girls were now joking with Manos, impressed by his witty humor while Phevos looked at him from across the table with new eyes. It seemed the boy had matured quickly, driven by his yearning for his missing parents in order to rise to the challenge. This was the time for him too to claim his loved ones.

Chapter 18

It was the last Sunday of June, two weeks after that morning at breakfast when the wand responded to the word 'Sounio'.

Everyone except Phevos suggested visiting Poseidon's Temple there, but Phevos put forward that it made sense to try to find his mother first. In the old address book that Ksenia had found in Pallada, the word 'Sounio' was scribbled out and replaced by 'Anavisos' to indicate she had moved there at some point.

It had proved difficult for Phevos to convince the others to plan a visit to Anavisos instead, but his arguments won them over in the end. If Poseidon was indeed their God-Protector, he felt his temple in Sounio should be their last point of visit, with his mother present as well.

Furuthermore, Phevos believed they should only go there after a sign that would suggest the right time had come. To him, the glow in the wand in response to the word 'Sounio' was not a sign from Poseidon that they should go there, but simply a confirmation that he was their God-protector along the way.

By now, everyone looked up to Phevos, trusting his infallible instinct and unwavering faith. He was the one who had worn the necklace of goddess Athena and now was the keeper of Poseidon's sacred wand. He had powers of prophecy through dreams and incredible insight. No one could have picked a better leader for any type of quest.

And so, they were all now headed to Anavisos, standing in a crammed bus that they had taken early that Sunday morning from Syntagma Square. Their trip had been delayed for a week due to a large number of guests in Pallada the Sunday before. It happened sometimes in high season. Both the girls had spent that day helping out Mrs. Sofia, cleaning rooms and checking-in new arrivals.

But this delay had only meant they were now even more excited in the bus, despite being squashed against strangers, feeling hotter by the minute in the shimmering heat. None of them had ever been to Anavisos before. Ksenia had studied a map and calculated it would take at least an hour for them to get anywhere near their destination. They were still in the eastern suburbs of Athens, by the coast.

The bus cruised along the busy Poseidon Avenue passing by residential buildings, department stores and nightclubs. When they finally left the suburbs behind, they marveled at the quaint coastal landscapes of outer, eastern Attica along a much quieter, windy road. As they enjoyed generous sea views of deep blue under a cloudless summer sky, the bus carried on up and down the windy road, its engine often making grunting noises, as if complaining for the fierce heat that made the effort harder.

Since leaving the outskirts of Athens behind, the vast majority of travelers had alighted, and all four of them were now seated across one row. Phevos was sitting with Ksenia on the left side and Daphne with Manos opposite. Daphne had opened her window fully as the windy road had made her queasy. The sun warmed her face, and the sea breeze caused wavy strands of her auburn hair to do a mesmerizing dance before her half-closed eyes.

That is what a young lad saw, as he stood nearby unable to take his eyes off her. As usual, Daphne didn't notice. She was still completely unaware of the effect that her beauty had on men. On the contrary, she remained insecure and shy where it came to men, as always. She acted the same around Aris still even though she had got to be desperately in love with him by then.

Since the day that they walked together and then sat at that café in Plaka, instead of feeling happy and hopeful, she had been tortured by jealousy and worry at the thought of Zoe's encounter with Aris that same day. Of course, Zoe was quite attractive and could charm men with her Parisian finesse and fashion magazine attire. Aris would have had to be blind not to notice her.

However, what Daphne didn't know was that no matter how dazzled a man may be by the beauty of a woman, a true man's heart remains always in the hands of the woman he loves. Aris was secretly in love with Daphne too and knew he had his hands full with this particular woman because he could sense she was different to all the others.

Aris had spent countless hours on the deck of his ship gazing out to the ocean. He had wished a million times in those moments that the sea would freeze over like a crystal carpet so that he could run all the way to her. Although his ship had braved the waves of all the oceans in the world, his heart and thoughts remained safely anchored in the waves of her auburn hair.

Nothing could get her off his mind. Not the voluptuous, dark-skinned women of the exotic islands in the Caribbean. Not the tall, confident women of Scandinavia with the icy blue eyes. Not even the mysterious, seductive women of the Far East. When Aris looked out to sea from the deck, the sea would often change color to match the emerald of Daphne's eyes.

None of these things did Daphne know about him as she sat in the bus now, as the sea breeze kept whispering his name in her ear over and over again. If anything, she felt uneasy, fearing he'd forgotten all about her as it had been weeks since he left. She hoped he would come back again soon and also that Zoe would not visit again while he was there. She felt she stood no chance if she were to compete with her for his heart.

An elderly lady with kind eyes was seated in front of Ksenia and Phevos. They had already asked her if she could notify them to get off in Anavisos, and she had told them she was going there too. When a long stretch of a beautiful sandy beach came into view on their right, she urged Phevos to press the button for the stop.

On his way to the door, he picked up her trolley bag from the gangway before she had the chance to do it. He got off first, offering her a hand to assist her down the steps, and she complimented him for his gallant gesture.

She made to go then, but Phevos insisted on carrying the trolley bag to her house for her. He deemed it improper to let her drag it along by herself, but she refused politely. Thanking him again, and waving everyone goodbye, she went on her way.

Once the bus set off again with a complaining sound from its exhaust pipe, they all hovered for a bit at the roadside in order to take in their surroundings. The beach stretched into the distance alongside the main road. People were lying on towels and mats or sitting under umbrellas or shady trees. Countless others were swimming in the water as far as the eye could see. Children played in the shallows and on the beach, splashing around or playing with buckets and spades on the wet sand.

The sounds that were carried in the salty air was a symphony of happy shrieks and splashing noises that reached their ears like a seductive, siren song calling them in. But the magic was broken when Manos brought everyone's attention to what was happening inland, on the other side of the road. Everyone turned around to see a vast wasteland there.

It was mainly covered with dense bushes, but a large part of it at the edge of the road was barren. It seemed to be a popular meeting point for hobbyists. They were aero-modelers judging from the yellow, acrobatic airplane that was buzzing high above people's heads at the time, causing them to follow it with their eyes.

It took to the sky with amazing speed, performing a series of impressive acrobatic stunts under the capable hands of its owner. They spotted him easily as he was holding the controls in his hands and kept turning around to face the model at all times. Like most of the other men there, he wore a baseball hat and sunglasses for protection against the glare of the sun. The model ascended the sky vertically, only to nose-dive next at a tremendous speed. Then, it broke into a series of loops and rolls that caused the bystanders to gasp and yell with admiration, asking its pilot to do it again.

And he obliged with a smirk, sending the model high again, then making it nose-dive with its engine shut down this time in a seemingly fatal fall. But then, quite near off the ground, the model bounced up to the sky again as the engine revved with a loud growl, saving it from total destruction. It was now zooming past, high above the spectators once more, with its engine shrieking loudly, announcing its victory after an imaginary dogfight with a deadly enemy.

"Cool! That's awesome!" shrieked Manos. When he turned to Ksenia, his face was animated with excitement. "Please, can we go see?" he pleaded, his eyes ablaze. Needless to say, none of the others had any objection to that.

And so, they all crossed the main road and entered the wasteland. The hobbyists had parked their cars in a line, the trunks all open in the back. The men jabbered, the spirit of camaraderie strong. They helped out each other with technical problems, sharing tools, accessories and even fuel. The wives had all come together a bit further away with the children, sitting in foldable chairs under the shade of beach umbrellas. They expected their men to stay hours there, so they had planned to make the wait as pleasant as possible until it was time to hit the beach.

They had packed thermos flasks with ice coffee and cold water, snacks, and wrapped up sandwiches. Three of them had even catered for entertainment, as they sat under an umbrella playing cards. Occasionally, a man would join his family to get a drink or a snack and then, he would return to his friends for some more mingling. Also, most of the sons tended to stay close to their dads, their own thirst for models a passion that ran in the family.

Manos was bursting at the seams to watch the scene. With the others, he approached a few men who were huddled together, watching a man change the propeller on an impressive WWII model. They greeted the men and received a warm welcome. Seconds later, one of the women came up to them and offered them biscuits and fruit juice in plastic cups. All the modelers proved to be quite eager to chat, but one in particular, a moustached, elderly man, seemed very open to Manos's questions, and the boy took full advantage of that.

In the next half hour, while his three companions sat under the beach umbrellas with the wives, watching the action from afar, Manos was at the heart of it, standing by that kind modeler who had offered to show him the ropes as he flew his own model.

Ksenia watched them and felt relieved that the kind man didn't seem to mind her brother wanting to know everything in one sitting. At some point, he even gave him the controls for a few moments, something that made her gasp, but then she laughed when she saw her brother's face as he handed the controls back to the man. His expression of sheer delight made her think he would probably be asking for a model this Christmas. No doubt, he had already asked the man about the whereabouts of the model shops in Athens and the average costs.

She smiled to herself then, realizing how well she knew him, and how adorable he was. She thought how her parents would love him for his zest when they came back, for his passion for life and fun-seeking attitude. Phevos came to sit next to her then and said something that made her laugh. He had just had a chat with one of the men and had asked where he could buy a model for Manos for Christmas. Ksenia opened her arms wide and cuddled him then, giggling, and causing Phevos to give her a puzzled look.

After another ten minutes, Phevos approached Manos and asked him to get ready to leave. The boy was watching the same modeler refuel his plane at the time, but he didn't object. He was just as eager as everyone else to try to find Anna that day because he knew that by finding Phevos's mother, they would be getting closer to finding his parents too.

With a wide grin, Manos thanked the man for teaching him so much, and after everyone had said their thanks and goodbyes, they strolled back to the main road.

Within seconds, they stood at the crossroads where the coastal road intersected another that carried on uphill into the sparse woodlands of the mountains. On the other side of the intersection, the same road carried on just a few yards, leading to the beach. Everyone looked to Phevos then, as always expecting him to lead; an honor he didn't always handle with confidence, and this was one of those moments.

He felt lost now. In a desperate attempt to find a sign there and then, he took the wand out of his backpack. The sunlight made its aquatic contents shine, but other than that, there was no flash of light. It rather returned the stare unaffected by their need and non-committal. All four of them felt at a loss.

"Right! I suggest we walk down the road a bit!" piped up Phevos, more for the sake of saying something to encourage them, and less because he thought it might benefit them in the slightest.

"In which direction?" asked Manos.

"Well, if I had to choose, I'd say toward Sounio rather than Athens," replied Phevos.

"And why are we only considering the coastal road? Why not try *this* one?" said Daphne pointing to both sides of the street running vertically to the coastal road. Her suggestion took them all by surprise for some reason.

"You want us to go to the beach? This may be Poseidon's kingdom, but I doubt anything will come of it if we were to bathe the wand in there!" said Manos. He knew well that Daphne hadn't meant to go to the beach, but he could sense that everyone's spirits had gone low and felt it was time to share some of his perpetual cheerfulness.

"Of course not! I mean to go in the opposite direction," answered Daphne pointing to the street that went past the side of the wasteland and then uphill through a residential area, toward the imposing mountains in the distance.

"You want us to go toward the mountain?" asked Ksenia exasperated. She wished they would go anywhere, as long as they moved on and did something, rather than stand in the blistering heat, waiting for a miracle.

"Yes. It makes sense to try the residential area. After all, we *are* looking for Anna's house, or am I mistaken?" asked Daphne.

"Good choice," answered Ksenia. "There should be less houses along the main road".

"You're right," answered Phevos, "the main road is just shops and tavernas. Look over there," he said, pointing toward the establishments that stood side by side in the busy street, not a single private dwelling in sight.

"Let's go then!" said Manos and they set off, following his hurried steps. Looking determined, yet somewhat uncomfortable in the heat, they walked past the wasteland leaving the beach and the carefree swimmers behind. Some of the recent friends they had made noticed them and waved to them. All four returned the gesture, but Phevos was also careful not to let them see the wand.

He now held it in his right hand that was out of sight. At the first opportunity, he got a newspaper out of his backpack and rolled it around the wand to hide it from view. He didn't want to put it back in the bag in case it flashed but at the same time didn't want to risk raising suspicion among any strangers who might see it. So, he walked on while glancing at the wand inside the newspaper as often as he could.

They passed by impressive houses with high balconies and quaint villas with inviting gardens of freshly mown lawn. These beautiful dwellings were quite a contrast to the shabby weekend homes interspersed among them. Some of them looked old and neglected with chipped wood on the walls and discolored ceramic pots in the weedy, front yards. Their overhead trellises were overgrown, laden with bougainvillea and ivy that begged for the sight of a sharp pair of shears.

The heat had got unbearable as they continued to walk uphill. Phevos was desperate by now for a response from the wand in his hands, and the girls started to complain that they were thirsty. Only Manos seemed chirpy still. When they reached a church with a whitewashed yard, they all had the same notion. Without saying a word, they walked up to the large plane tree that stood there, drawn by the generous shade of its dense foliage and the serenity of the setting.

It was a very quiet neighborhood, and as they sat on the cool concrete bench under the tree, the only thing that broke the silence was the loud singing from the crickets in the branches. There was a mini market across the road, and Manos volunteered to buy water for everyone. When he returned, he handed the first bottle to his sister. She patted his head, but there was a tired expression on her face, nothing more than a shadow and so, noone really noticed as they quenched their thirst.

They all sat on the bench, fiddling with the empty bottles in their hands, enjoying the cool shade in the stillness, and just looking around. These moments allowed some of them to pray in silence. The tiny church stood right there before them with its wide open door in invitation, like a beacon of hope made of brick, mortar and marble.

Phevos looked at the wand again. Still no reaction. What now? Where would they go next? Phevos scolded himself silently. He felt guilty for bringing everyone there, for encouraging them, only to disappoint them like this. He hadn't chosen to be their leader. He had tried the best he could. He turned to look at them one by one as they stared out into space and felt responsible for the evident frustration on their faces. Ksenia looked so upset, about to burst into tears.

He reached out and put an arm around her shoulder. She didn't lift her head but kept it bent down in deep contemplation, and the guilt pricked him inside one more time. He opened his mouth but closed it again finding nothing of use to say. What did he expect? Did he really believe Anna would appear before them just like that? Or perhaps she was about to waltz out of that church right there, holding the other two wands like trophies. No. This time Phevos scolded himself for the bitter sarcasm, a quality he didn't possess and wouldn't allow himself to acquire now.

"Precious Brother, don't lose faith!" said Daphne. She had always had this gift of guessing his thoughts just by looking at him.

"Oh Daphne," he replied as his frustration burst out of his lips, "look at the wand! Nothing! What was I thinking?" he said and laughed bitterly, shaking his head.

"But we have Poseidon on our side! *You* said so!" Daphne reasoned. "I'm sure he has a plan for us. The signs are out there for us to find. Remember what Father said. Don't you forget!"

"The signs..." whispered Phevos. The thought that they were out there waiting to be found brought with it a glimmer of hope. Yes, he shouldn't forget his father's advice. Determined, he lifted his head again. His eyes were now bright with intention.

"Of course, Phevos! The signs!" exclaimed Ksenia jolting upright like a coiled spring. The others were startled, as they watched her walk away from them in long strides. For a moment they thought she was going into the church, but then she stopped and turned around. She stared at them with fury in her eyes, as she started to stride toward them again, gesticulating frantically. Her eyes softened somewhat as she approached them. They looked sorrowful now, which made the smile on her face confusing.

"How could you ever forget about the signs, Phevos?" she cried, "God forbid if we did anything sane these days instead of looking for immaculately disguised, artfully concealed, God-awful signs!" she spat out trembling all over with emotion. Her eyes were enormous now, and her arms were spread out when she stopped short before Phevos. "And you! Yes, I'm talking to *you*!" she continued gesturing wildly and pointing at him every now and then with a shaky finger. "You've traveled through the centuries to come here! You've made sense of strange dreams! You've dug up my garden to discover a wand that responds to words! And yet, *you* lose your courage? *You* doubt where we are going? If *you*, the strongest, the most gifted of us all, forget about the signs, then what are *we* going to do, I ask you? What?" she yelled and then let her arms fall limply to her sides.

She bent her head down and sighed. The others still sat before her looking stunned, but by the time she looked up again with tears in her eyes, Phevos was already there to take her into his arms and comfort her. He knew his Ksenia was one of those rivers that seem serene on the surface, allowing no one to see the currents that run in the depths, the currents of sorrow, of frustration, and pain.

His Ksenia had had to keep up appearances all her life in order to be strong for the weak, to take the place of the missing ones, and to do a job well done at the end of the day, regardless of what lay beneath. And because Phevos understood all that, he knew she was already feeling sorry for her sudden outburst when she sat back down on the bench crying like a child in his arms, letting it all out.

And that was a lot, seeing that nothing had been let out for nearly eleven years. Having to be a surrogate mother *and* a sister to Manos, she had never allowed herself to feel weak even when she was alone. And as he held her, wiping the tears from her face and kissing her hair as she leant against him, his eyes fell on the lamppost next to the church's entrance like an arrow that hits the bull's-eye.

His look had wandered in that direction earlier on, when deep in thought, he had been contemplating the next step forward. He had noticed the intricate designs of the metal work on the lamppost but not the poster on it. He couldn't read the writing because of the distance, but the title was in large print and his strong eyesight allowed him to read it now. The word resounded in his head like angel music and yet, it was an aquatic song for the word was 'Poseidon'.

Startled by his sudden cry of enthusiasm, they all rushed behind him as he walked up to it. The full title read 'Poseidon Grill Restaurant', and it was an announcement for its opening that evening. They all agreed it had to be a sign, especially because the day of the opening coincided with their visit to the town. According to the poster, the restaurant was situated on the coastal road, and they all agreed to go there at once. By the time they picked up their bags from the bench, their spirits had fully lifted.

Ksenia was still embarrassed and kept apologizing for her outburst on their way back, but by the time they returned to the main coastal road, her face had turned into a land of perpetual sunshine again, without a trace of the thundering cloud that had just fleeted past it.

They found the restaurant two hundred yards or so along the road to Sounio after asking two locals, who both knew where it was. They recognized it with ease from the photos on the poster. It was situated on the side of the beach and had a rather humble, pale yellow façade.

A plain restaurant sign was mounted above the entrance while a white banner hung across the wall announcing the opening that night. There was a trellis by the door with a vine laden with grapes. On either side of the entrance, large pots full of yellow, red and pink geraniums added to the scene splashes of vibrant color. There were no tables on the pavement outside, but that was no surprise. On their way there, just before turning the last corner along the windy road, they had seen the restaurant from afar. On its other side that looked out to sea, it had a large balcony that extended over the water. That was the restaurant's external sitting area, and it had looked extremely inviting. It was as if it was sailing on the sea, a ship deck of antique-style lanterns, festive garlands and pot plants.

As they stood outside the entrance, they hesitated for a while, feeling unsure about what to say once they were inside. Their plan had been simple. They were going to go in and ask to see the menu while Phevos had a look around for any clues or better yet, perhaps Anna would be there and Ksenia would hopefully recognize her. All she would then have to do is look at Phevos and he'd know. He could read her face like an open book by now. She wouldn't even have to nod or give him a meaningful stare.

As they hovered outside trying to work up the courage, Phevos looked up and noticed the terrace on the upper floor was full of pots with herbs, flowers, and even vegetables. There seemed to be a private dwelling up there. Old vines had crept up the front wall over the years, framing the entrance with dark fruit and delicate leaves that rustled in the sea breeze.

Phevos's affinity for gardening made him stare for a while at the pretty picture while the others were now discussing who should do the talking. Of course, they had all elected Phevos. Just as they were about to get his attention, a cheerful voice echoed from behind them.

"I don't believe it! Hello there!"

When they turned around, the elderly lady from the bus was still smiling. "We're opening tonight. Are you coming?"

"Oh! Is this your restaurant?" asked Ksenia, her heart sinking somewhat.

"No, my darling! I'm just the cook. Not permanent staff, that is; I'm only helping for tonight. We're expecting a lot of people."

"Oh that's nice," said Ksenia. For some reason, everyone else found nothing to say at that moment so her chatty nature had come in handy once again.

"Why don't you come inside? Let me treat you to some cold juice! The owner is a friend of mine. I'm sure she'll be thrilled to meet you." Phevos's kind manners had impressed her earlier, and she was pleased to meet them all again.

"That's very kind, thank you. To be honest, we intended to go inside anyway just to see what it looks like," answered Phevos, feeling hopeful. He thought it was peculiar they had met on the bus someone connected to this place. And what timing to meet outside!

"Yes, we'll just have a quick look and then we'll be on our way. I'm sure the lady who owns the restaurant will be very busy this morning," interrupted Ksenia, feeling awkward about the possibility of being a nuisance on a busy day. She knew how it was in Pallada when she ran headless with a million things to do. She didn't need any interruptions or unexpected arrivals on those days.

"Nonsense!" replied the elderly lady. "What are you talking about? She'll be thrilled to meet you! She appreciates good manners as much as I do, you see. When you work with people you tend to see a lot, and Anna and I have seen it all! Believe me, not all youngsters are like you. There's rudeness, there's yelling.... some make such a spectacle of themselves..."

The kind lady kept speaking but now, none of the others could hear her any more. They were all looking at each other but mostly at Phevos. He was looking up ahead now, his eyes distant, his body rigid, the hands balled into fists. All four of them had been astonished to hear the name 'Anna' from her lips. Was she the owner? Was that really the Anna they were looking for?

When the lady stopped talking, Phevos snapped out of his trance and gave her a confident smile, his fingertips fiddling with the straps of his backpack. The wand was safely hidden in there, and he wondered if it had glowed at all at the mention of that name. Surprising all the others with his relaxed manner, he motioned to the elderly lady to enter the restaurant first and then watched as the others followed before going in last.

The interior felt cool. A pleasant sea breeze was coming through the large, glass door that led to the balcony outside. Strings of fairy lights hung across the glass partition that separated the two spaces. There were many tables indoors too, covered with plain, white linen. On the wall to the left, a stone archway led to the kitchen and on the far corner, an old-style fireplace was also decked in stone.

Framed seascapes, mainly of large ships from various historical periods, decorated the walls all around. On the wall to the right, a large copperplate depicted another seascape that had in its midst, none other but Poseidon. He was standing on water holding his trident. His long, rich beard was blowing in the wind. Among foamy waves under his feet, there were dolphins and whales, fish and octopus, and even a small fishing boat with open nets on its side that looked like spider webs.

"How lovely it is in here!" said Daphne, and the others agreed with her, although their enthusiasm was far better concealed. Phevos was lost in his thoughts while Manos and Ksenia were so worried about meeting the owner that they were unable to manage more than one word at a time. They desperately wanted it to be her.

The elderly lady led them through the glass door to the balcony where the sea breeze welcomed them, awakening their senses after the torturing heat they had to endure outside. Manos went to the railing and called them all to see the school of fish that swam in the water underneath. The kind lady laughed, and informed Manos they were going to stay there until he threw them something to eat.

Apparently, the fish had grown accustomed to humans and expected to have food thrown in the water all day long.

Manos took a pack of crackers from his backpack in order to try out the lady's theory, and indeed, the fish devoured in seconds the pieces that he threw in. Thrilled, Manos threw into the water some more. The tops of the fishes' heads bobbed out of the water every now and then, as they gnawed at the food in a race against each other, making daisy-like formations around each piece as they circled it, carrying it along the surface of the water until it vanished altogether.

"Wow, they're like piranhas!" exclaimed Manos and they all laughed. The pack had only two crackers left. The boy handed one to Daphne to have a go while Phevos and Ksenia watched. Excusing herself, the elderly lady then went to the kitchen to get the refreshments. Thanks to the greedy school of glistening black fish, their spirits were higher now. Their worry had gone and pure hope had nestled in their hearts by the time the lady returned with another woman in tow. They were all sitting around a table by the railing at the time. When they saw the women coming, they all stood up.

The elderly woman put a tray down on the table. It contained tumblers and a large jug of orange juice with ice cubes. She then introduced them to the smiling woman next to her. She didn't know any of their names of course, so she only made a vague introduction of four youths with remarkable manners.

The woman was in her sixties and when she smiled, her face lit up in a pleasant, hospitable manner. She shook Daphne's hand first as she stood closer to her at the time, then she greeted Manos next to her in the same way. She kept smiling widely as she welcomed them to her restaurant, and when she turned to Phevos, who had his back to the sun, she had to shade her eyes with one hand. She smiled at him and then felt strange. His hand felt warm in hers and all at once, it was as if the temperature had risen considerably, the way it does when you approach a roaring fire.

She noticed his stare was intense, his brilliant blue eyes capturing hers somewhat intently. It felt to her like there was a deep meaning in that stare, a meaning that evaded her of course. She thought perhaps she was imagining things. She had been on her feet since dawn making preparations in a blistering hot kitchen. The sunlight that blinded her now didn't help. Feeling increasingly dizzy, she decided it would be best to take some rest for a while before the evening. After all, she had her friend now to help her.

Although the strange feeling had started as soon as she shook the young man's hand, when she drew her hand from his, she found herself feeling reluctant to, and she wondered why. By the time she reached out to Ksenia next, the sense of warmth had already dissipated, but there was another sense growing inside her now as she held the young girl's hand.

There was something about her face. She looked very familiar, but she didn't remember her visiting before. And yet, she had that strange feeling she was supposed to recognize her from somewhere. It made her hold her hand longer than is customary, trying to grasp what it was that she was missing.

"Hey Anna, let the girl sit down!" piped up her friend. "She must be exhausted after being so long out in the heat. You must all be thirsty kids! Go on, sit and have some orange juice!"

Anna beckoned them to do that too, feeling embarrassed about the whole thing. She sat down first, eager to get some rest. She wondered again if her mind was playing tricks on her, what with the stress of it all and the exhaustion from the preparations in the past few days.

Ksenia took a seat next to Anna and chewed her lower lip as she did so. It was hard for her to stop herself from telling her who she was and how she had missed her. She may have been only nine when she had last seen her, yet she had recognized her immediately. Of course, she had gray hair now and her face had aged visibly, but her smile and gentle eyes were still the same.

Phevos sat on the other side of Anna still feeling electrified by her touch. Of course, he had no memories of her like Ksenia did. Therefore he couldn't claim he had recognized her in the same sense, unless one can say the soul is able to recognize another beyond the common means of perception based on the five senses. And why not? This woman, who sat next to him, was the one who had brought him into the world. She had nursed him and cradled him in her arms countless times. Surely, her aura had fused with his in those moments, creating a vague memory inside his soul, so that he could identify her anywhere, anytime.

He had noticed Ksenia's meaningful look earlier that signified she had recognized her, but he hadn't needed it at all. He had already found inside of him all the confirmation he needed. In the private confines of his mind, he was now overwhelmed. His heart overflowed with happiness while he struggled to stop himself from hugging Anna and telling her who he was. He knew he shouldn't startle her like that.

They had to reveal themselves to her gently. While they shook hands earlier, he had noticed she felt it too, that overpowering feeling of familiarity. But he saw on her face and in her eyes especially, how she had reasoned with herself, how she had strived to remain collected. Of course, she couldn't guess who they were, but Phevos hoped what he kept inside his backpack would explain things to her better than he ever could, when he finally plucked up the courage to reveal his identity.

Chapter 19

The jug was now empty. The elderly lady of the bus had left the table long ago to help out in the kitchen but Anna lingered on. The more she looked at Phevos and Ksenia, who sat on either side of her, the more the feeling of familiarity grew inside her. She knew there was still plenty of work waiting for her in the kitchen despite her friend and also her resident cook being in there already. But she just couldn't leave them. She had enjoyed hearing their impressions about Anavisos so far and especially Manos's experience with the aero-modelers.

Phevos felt more anxious now that the other woman had left the table. While she was there, he knew he had to wait. Now that the setting was perfect in order to make a move, he started to feel uneasy again. He wasn't afraid but worried about Anna's reaction. He didn't want to shock her. What if she had health problems? Who knew how she would react in this case if she were to experience strong emotions? But then he thought Poseidon wouldn't have led him this far only to hurt his mother.

He looked up again and turned to Anna. In the last half hour, he had heard so much about her. She had spoken to them about the major renovation work she recently did in the restaurant. She moved to Anavisos ten years ago. Initially, she was renting the tiny apartment upstairs from a local who used to own the restaurant at the time. A couple of years ago, he moved to his hometown in the Cyclades putting the whole building up for sale. Anna jumped at the chance to buy it from him, as she always loved the idea of running a restaurant and loved cooking for people. She kept the same cook as they had formed a friendship already. She was none other than the elderly lady of the bus. Her name was Mrs. Gregoria.

Phevos kept watching Anna, his eyes insatiable to absorb every detail of her face as she carried on talking. She was now speaking about her friend again. Apparently, Mrs. Gregoria was incapacitated by arthritis in her legs the previous winter. It had kept her in bed for a long while.

During the months that her friend recuperated, Anna worked in the kitchen with a temporary cook while trying to convince her friend to listen to her children who urged her to quit work for good. When Mrs Gregoria accepted this, Anna hired Mr. Fanis. It was hard for the two friends to not see each other as often as before, but somehow their friendship grew stronger ever since.

Mrs. Gregoria moved to Athens to stay with her children but now that she was better, she visited Anavisos often for the odd swim and of course, to spend time with Anna. She had insisted on helping Anna with the opening, hence arriving in town that morning for a couple of days. In the summer, the discomfort in her legs diminished; the swims in the sea proved miraculous for her condition.

"Excuse me Mrs. Anna..." interrupted Phevos politely, "have you always lived in this area?" he asked, in his best attempt to try to broach the subject of the past.

"No, I used to live in central Athens, but I left the city eleven years ago." Her agreeable smile never reached her eyes. There was a frown on her face suggesting that perhaps, this wasn't a favorite subject for her.

"Pardon me for asking, but earlier you said you've lived in Anavisos for *ten* years..." Phevos insisted. It had to be done.

"Yes," she replied with a soft sigh. She didn't find it easy to talk about that specific period of her life. And yet, she couldn't understand why she felt willing to explain this time. "Indeed, I've been living here for ten years, but I lived in Sounio for one year before that."

"So, it's been eleven years on the whole since you left Athens," Phevos said staring deeply into her eyes.

"Yes, that's what I said earlier," she replied in a small voice. There was something about the young man's stare that made her feel strange again. It was like his eyes were boring holes into her soul. It felt intrusive, but at the same time liberating too, as if she had been begging for that intrusion for a long time, without realizing it until now.

"What made you move to Sounio if I may ask?" interrupted Ksenia. She felt she had to help out Phevos. He seemed determined enough, but she could sense Anna was tensing up somehow. They didn't want her to get the wrong impression, thinking them rude. If she got defensive enough, she would probably excuse herself and hurry back to the kitchen without them getting their chance to talk to her.

"I rented a holiday apartment there. It had a lovely view to Poseidon's temple," said Anna, without answering the question.

"Sounds very nice. And you stayed only for a year there? I imagine it wasn't easy to part with such a splendid view. What a joy it must have been!" said Phevos trying to smile nonchalantly.

"Indeed, it was lovely there. But I had my reasons to move here. And besides, that was a difficult year for me... I didn't spend much time enjoying myself..." Anna faltered, surprising herself. She never spoke about her past to anyone. Who were these strangers who had this effect on her, who made her want to split her heart open and talk about her most secret heartache?

She looked up and saw deep compassion in Phevos's eyes. Then she turned to Ksenia to find that she looked even more familiar than before. The young girl was no longer smiling. Instead, her huge blue eyes were brimming with sadness. Anna knew the feeling well. To see it coloring the girl's face so vividly made her want to tell them more. She didn't mind the young man's deep stare either. There was no intrusion any more, only that liberating feeling she had longed for.

Their mute gaze made her feel strong now. They encouraged her to keep on talking.

"I'm afraid I wasn't myself that year in Sounio. I mean, there was a lot of sorrow. I suffered a huge loss you see.... I lost my husband and my child plus my two best friends... a tragedy! I needed to be alone; away from it all..." She wavered and then realized tears were rolling down her face. How had this happened? She never spoke about this to anyone, and now she offered the information to strangers on a platter? Bewildered, she turned to them all, examining their faces. The fact that her face was wet with tears didn't bother her in the least. It didn't feel humiliating. It felt right somehow. When she turned to Phevos, he reached out his hand to cover hers tenderly while he stared at her with a faint smile.

"No more tears Mrs. Anna. We've come here with happy news," said Ksenia with a compassionate smile, as she rested a gentle hand on Anna's shoulder.

"Who are you, my girl?" asked Anna perplexed.

"It's been eleven years, Mrs. Anna... I've grown up and so has my brother." Ksenia pointed to Manos, who looked at them in silence. "Do I remind you of anyone at all?" She asked, hopeful.

Anna looked at Manos, who gave a sheepish look back at her. She made a quick calculation in her head, as she guessed his age but this proved unnecessary. By the time she turned back to Ksenia, she already knew. She saw her face and wondered how she could ever forget those sorrowful eyes of hers. That little girl had known so much pain and Anna knew it well.

"Ksenia, my Ksenia, it's you!" she exclaimed and the girl fell into her embrace. They stood now, crying in each other's arms. Anna then hugged and kissed Manos, who smiled happily at her and didn't mind her squeezing his cheeks. She stood before Daphne and Phevos rather awkwardly now, noticing Ksenia didn't offer any introductions about them, not even now.

She returned to her chair and sat next to Phevos again, feeling overwhelmed now, full of indescribable hope. Could it be possible? Phevos had closed his hands into fists under the table as he tried to contain himself. His fingernails hurt his flesh but he refused to embrace her. He had to stay collected now.

"Mrs. Anna, there's something we have brought for you..." he said and saw the confusion in her eyes. She had expected he would be introducing himself by now, as opposed to talking about material things. There was nothing material that she needed. All she wanted was for him to be the one she desperately longed for.

"Mrs. Anna," interrupted Ksenia sensing her disappointment, "what he means is that we bring wonderful news for you... really good news!" she added, patting her on the arm to give her courage.

"I know you too, don't I, young man?" asked Anna without taking her eyes off Phevos for a moment. He seemed to be the perfect age for the miracle she hoped for. The notion had formed a huge lump in her throat.

Phevos flashed a smile at her before biting his lips again. He couldn't say it any more than she could. They kept looking at each other now, their lips trembling, finding it impossible to say anything at all. Silently still, he reached for his backpack that he had left on the floor by his chair. Without taking his eyes from Anna, he opened the bag and took the wand out. The others watched breathlessly as he placed it on her lap.

Anna had lowered her gaze and watched amazed as Phevos produced the wand from the bag. She had followed it mutely from there to her lap with her eyes, the way you follow a sacred relic that passes you by in a religious procession, as you pray for a miracle.

Once the wand rested on her lap, with a sigh from her chest, a single tear rolled down her cheek. It dropped onto the wand where a faint glow acknowledged it in solemn greeting.

Unbelieving, she blinked only once and then looked up to meet her son's eyes for the first time in years. He was smiling now.

"My boy!" she yelled out with a sob that could have melted a stone. Phevos fell into her open arms, hot tears already streaming down his face. In the first few seconds that followed, there was a mixture of emotions. They cried and laughed at the same time. The sobs tore at their insides, but the tears brought deliverance to mother and son. They hugged and kissed each other unstoppably, as the others watched, sharing in the eruption of heartfelt emotions.

The excited yelling echoed indoors, alarming Mrs. Gregoria. Unsettled, she rushed to the balcony to find everyone wiping tears from their faces. She asked what was going on and when Anna explained who the youngsters were, she was overjoyed. She didn't even mind Anna had hidden from her that she had a son, whom she hadn't seen in years. A true friend can forgive secret patches in the other one's heart for they can understand that sometimes pain is too unbearable to reveal.

Yet, Anna had now shed all of her pain in her son's arms and what's more, she had found out she had a daughter too. She welcomed Daphne into her embrace, delighted at the thought she had lost one child but found two.

When Mrs. Gregoria returned to the kitchen seconds later, they all sat down again. That's when Anna started to ask questions, wanting to know everything about them. Phevos was still too moved to speak as he held his mother's hand, so Ksenia took over to inform Anna how she had met Phevos and Daphne, and also to assure her Mrs. Sofia was well in Pallada.

The moment she heard her old friend was well, Anna became overjoyed for she loved her fondly. However, she felt guilty too and started to apologize for leaving the house eleven years earlier. Ksenia tried to convince her not to feel guilty about that. After all she and her brother had been safe all along thanks to Mrs. Sofia.

Shortly after that, everyone except Phevos and Anna went to the kitchen to join Mrs. Gregoria. They felt it was the tactful thing to do, to allow mother and son some time alone, plus they thought Mrs. Gregoria and the cook could use the extra help. They had suggested this to Anna and she had thanked them for their kind offer.

She would have normally refused to indispose them of course, and she would have gone straight into the kitchen to carry on with her duties, but the day had proven anything but ordinary. By then she felt nothing like the broken woman who had awoken in her bed at dawn.

Within minutes, Mrs. Gregoria brought out some ouzo and a plate of meze with fresh bread as it was past mealtime. Anna and her son hadn't realized how hungry they were until they took the first bite and tinkled their glasses to seal the joy of their reunion. In the quiet of the early afternoon, they sat together on that balcony.

Phevos spoke to his mother about his life in ancient Athens with his father, Kimon and Eleni. He mentioned how he couldn't remember anything from his earlier life in this world and specifically, that he couldn't remember her at all.

Upon hearing that, Anna's face contorted as she expressed her hate for Athena. Phevos didn't understand and took his turn to pose a million questions. Why did she hate Athena? What had caused Father to stop serving her? Why had everyone gone back in time except Anna? Why didn't his father offer any information all these years? How had Athena's necklace appeared in the gut of a fish? What did Anna know of Poseidon's intentions? What could they expect from the precious wand that lay on the table before them?

And if Athena had caused their separation, what stopped her now from doing it again?

Anna watched Phevos as he spoke and when he stopped, she smiled to him promising to answer at once all the questions she knew the answers to, for there were still a lot among them that remained unanswered even to her. She handed him the wand and then led him out of the restaurant where they took the stairs to her home above it.

The entrance of the small apartment was almost hidden behind lush greenery. The air carried herbal fragrances from the pot plants that were mixed with the salty breeze. The inside of the house looked just as small. Behind the door, there was an open space that had a kitchenette to the left and a basic sitting area to the right. Across the middle, there was a corridor that led to a single bedroom and a tiny bathroom.

Anna explained that the owner used to live there when he was still single, so he had built it small to serve the needs of a lone bachelor. Later when he got married, he had built a large house nearby, and it was then that he had advertised in order to rent it out. It was at that time also that he renamed his restaurant 'Poseidon'. Anna lived in Sounio back then but looking to move because the owner of the house she rented was retiring and wanted to occupy it himself, eager to move out of Athens. Anna used to do gardening work for permanent residents in Sounio and in the surrounding areas, including Anavisos.

When her landlord had asked her to move out, she had felt lost, as she had no clue where to go. But that feeling hadn't lasted long because Anna had been advised by Efimios to look for signs from Poseidon, and these had just kept coming around that time. Whenever she visited Anavisos, there would be reminders of Poseidon here and there such as garden fountains with his statue in their midst, or tridents and dolphins decorating the fences of villas that she passed by.

And there was also that pick-up van. Many times, as she entered the town in her car, she would notice it parked outside the supermarket. Its driver had often indicated to drive away right in front of her, so that when she slowed down to let him do so, she could see that sign on its rear. It depicted the famous statue of Poseidon that's exhibited in the Athens Archaeological Museum.

As the van preceded her, for those few moments when it still indicated with its flashing amber lights, it had felt almost like Poseidon was beckoning to her, willing her to get a hint. It was as if he was making his presence known in the town, inviting her to it.

One day, as if by mathematical precision, the van had done the same thing again, and this time Anna had noticed to her left a large banner outside a restaurant. She had seen that establishment many times before but on that day, it seemed to have a brand new name: 'Poseidon Grill Restaurant'.

Anna had thought it was uncanny. Feeling compelled to have a closer look, she had stopped the car and crossed the street to read the announcement outside. It was an invitation to its opening a couple of days later. There was a smaller sign on the wall by the door too. According to it, the apartment upstairs was being put up for rent. Anna had thought that was uncanny too. Her landlord had asked her to move out the night before. These stange 'coincidences' had helped her make sense of things, and she had immediately known what she was supposed to do.

And so, she had rented the apartment upstairs and in time, when the owner of the restaurant put the whole property up for sale, it had felt right to buy it. And now, as she looked at her son behind her closed door, she knew she had been right all along. The same restaurant that had brought her there had just reunited her with her son, under Poseidon's all seeing, protective gaze.

The interior was dark. Anna had left the shutters closed in order to shield her home from the fierce heat of the day. She turned on the light and prompted Phevos to sit on the couch. She then excused herself and went to her bedroom promising to come back in a minute.

During her short absence, Phevos had a look around. The sitting area contained only a few pieces of furniture of basic practicality. A low TV table was nestled in a corner next to a bookshelf full of dog-eared paperbacks and large, hardcover volumes.

Other than the sofa, there was also an armchair across from the TV. Its old fabric was covered with a throw. A paperback had been left on the low coffee table before it. Phevos guessed the armchair was his mother's favorite seat during solitary evenings, and he swallowed the lump that formed in his throat at that thought.

Next, he turned his gaze toward the kitchenette where a small round table with two chairs confirmed the maximum size of her culinary parties these days. The lump in his throat returned, as he remembered the happy dinners he'd had with Ksenia and the others in the past months while his mother lived there all alone. Sadness overcame him, but when he heard footsteps echoing from the corridor, he strived to look happy for her as he turned around.

Once he did however, the surprise was too great to allow any other expression on his face other than one of sheer astonishment. Anna was walking along the twilit corridor holding something that gave off a faint glow. He still held the wand in his hand and didn't even need to look at it again to know the one in his mother's hand was identical. The more she advanced toward the ample light in the sitting room, the glow from her wand increased. Phevos froze by the sight, mesmerized and incredulous. This was all he had hoped for and yet, it still seemed surreal to him somehow.

When Anna stopped before him she couldn't stop smirking, blissful in the knowledge she had just brought him the happiest possible news. Phevos was bewildered as he stared at the dazzling glow coming from his mother's hands. Why hadn't his wand ever done that? As if guessing his thoughts, Anna motioned to him to look at the wand he was holding. He looked down and gasped. The magical object in his hand was now glowing just as radiant for the very first time.

"Unbelievable!" he whispered.

"Son, these wands belong to each other. Their glow is their bliss for being together. Just like you and me...."

"Oh, Mother! How right you are..." he said, choking at his last words. He had just realized that for the very first time, as far as he could remember anyway, he had uttered the word 'mother' and that shook his world. He had prayed a million times for the day when he would finally be able to say it.

"My son, if only you knew how I'd been aching to hear that word from your lips again!" she replied with that dignified smile that had served her so well for the past eleven years. Only now, her joy was sincere. She no longer had to pretend she could still smile. She reached to him and hugged him, then pulled him gently to sit together with her on her old sofa.

"Where did you find this wand, Mother? I found mine in the cave but I had to unearth it first. Was the cave buried when we lived together in Ksenia's house?" he asked, mesmerized still at the sight of the wands. Their glow hadn't faded in the least yet, as they rested on their laps.

"Patience, Phevos. I will tell you everything about that wretched cave!" she promised, placing a hand on his shoulder as she held him. "But first, I want to make sure you understand the origin and the purpose of these wands. They are tied to us, Son. But they have no value, no effect, and no relation to each other without us!"

"What do you mean, Mother?"

"Here! Take my wand and hold them together in your hands," she urged him. As soon as she let go off hers, they both became dark in his hands.

Phevos gasped. "What? How is it possible?" He darted his eyes at his mother, his brow deeply furrowed. "If they belong to each other like you said, then what's changed? They are *still* together! Why did they go dark?"

"Give me one back, Phevos. Better yet, give me yours! Just to show you it doesn't matter which one I'm holding." As soon as Phevos handed her his wand, they both glowed again. His jaw dropped as she continued to explain.

"My son, these wands are the answers to our prayers. It doesn't matter which one we each hold. They're all the same like *we* are all the same. There are three of these, my son! One for you, one for me and—"

"One for Father!"

"Yes! And when all three of us manage to hold one each at the same time, these three wands will be given the power to unite us again as one family," she said with tears of longing in her eyes.

Phevos was stunned, to say the least. For a few moments, he tried to process what he had just heard as his mother watched him. He thought his father must have known about all this. The reappearance of the necklace in the gut of that fish had been a sign to him. It told him the time had come to send Phevos in this modern world in order to find his mother and these wands. He had sent him off with a handful of salt. Phevos had long guessed that Poseidon was somehow related to all this. How could it have been anyone else?

The restaurant's name had become the last sign to lead him there. It had been a homing beacon all along, first for his mother and now for him. It had been a lighthouse at the edge of the shore, ready to guide the wandering ships that sought safe haven. But they couldn't get them all home yet. There was still one thing missing.

"Mother, where is the third wand?"

"All I know is that it's in the sea somewhere—"

"In the sea? Where?"

"I don't know.... but I trust that as these two wands have been given to us, so will the third one when the time comes. We need to keep our faith, Son!" Anna placed a reassuring hand on his shoulder.

"And to look out for the signs…" he said with glazed eyes.

"That's right…"

"And Athena? How does she fit in all this?"

"Athena…" said Anna, her eyes narrowing with detestation. "My boy, now is the time for me to tell you everything that I know," she added patting his hand. She was about to tell him a very disturbing story, so she took his hand in both of hers. It was the story of a nine-year-old boy that an old woman came to claim one night, snatching him from his house and from his mother's arms. She didn't want to tell him this fearful story but felt obliged to. To make it up to him, she would then tell him the story that had followed. That one would bring hope into his heart just like it had done for her.

Chapter 20
Eleven years earlier

"Eleni! Where are you off to so early?" asked Anna from her first-floor balcony. It was a lazy Sunday morning. Nine-year-old Phevos was sitting at the balcony table having a hot cocoa drink and sliced *choriatiko* bread with hazelnut paste. Anna was still in her long nightdress and robe. She hadn't combed her unruly long hair yet but didn't care if anyone saw her like this. She had never been vain, not even as a young girl.

Besides, it was only eight a.m. still. She knew well her street didn't normally wake on Sundays until much later. That's why it had been so easy to spot her girlfriend as soon as she came out into the street from the garden below. There was only Eleni down there now, although in the distance she could also see a municipal worker sweeping the pavement.

Eleni looked up and beamed at Anna. They had been friends for a few years now. To Eleni and Kimon, the tenants who occupied the upper floor of their house had become close friends, who felt like family. The feeling was mutual for Efimios and his beloved wife, Anna.

"Where am I going? Need you ask?"

"Not Pallada! Last minute bookings again?" guessed Anna, feeling sorry for her friend. Running a guesthouse meant she could never plan ahead. As hard as Eleni tried to manage bookings efficiently, and even when she hired temporary staff to fill in so that she could take one day off per week, she still had to work sometimes on Sundays too, limiting her family's prearranged plans for the day to much narrower timeframes.

"You guessed right! One of the agencies just called and asked if I can sign-in a young couple. They rejected the accommodation they were taken to."

"Do you want me to go downstairs to help with the kids? Do you need anything at all?" Anna often minded her friend's children. It was no bother at all and besides, Phevos and Ksenia enjoyed each other's company. They could play board games for hours while little Manos either slept or played in his pen.

"Thanks but there's no need, Anna. Kimon is up and preparing Ksenia's breakfast. The baby's still asleep. I'll see you soon! Is ten a.m. still all right with you and Efimios?"

"Sure, but will you be finished by then?"

"Of course! I won't be long at all. I have a room ready for them and they're coming soon. Olga could sign them in of course, but I need to see her this morning anyway. She got inundated with complaints from a funny customer yesterday. I have to talk to him about it. Sounds like he gave her a hard time."

"Really?"

"Would you believe he expected a cooked breakfast? He also demanded access to a bathtub instead of a shower although no one promised him these things. He even shouted expletives at her!"

"Oh, poor thing! She's so meek and mild! Shame Mrs. Sofia isn't here. She would have given him one of her infamous rants!" Anna rolled her eyes and they both laughed.

"You bet! Ah well, better go, Olga's waiting. She had to promise him that I, being the owner, would go and see him this morning. I intend to serve him a good piece of my mind for breakfast!" said Eleni with a grin, and both women laughed again.

"See you soon for our taverna meal by the sea then!" said Anna waving from the balcony.

"Can't wait! And look at the blue sky! Not a cloud in sight!"

"Yes! Isn't it gorgeous? It's March after all. The spring is upon us! Time for sea and sun!" She gave a bright smile, and her friend nodded in response.

"Right, bye for now! See you soon, girlfriend!" Eleni gave a hurried wave and turned to go.

"Give him a good one!" shouted out Anna, and in response her friend giggled again as she strode off along the pavement. Anna's smile was radiant now with the happy thought of their plans for the day.

Somehow their Sundays were planned around the seashore a lot more recently, but of course none of them, except perhaps Efimios, were conscious of that fact yet.

Anna watched her friend until she strode through the entrance of Pallada. She then tipped her head back with half-closed eyes and gave a smile to the heavens. As if in immediate response to her feeling of gratitude, a cool breeze picked up, caressing her face. Thankful, she turned her face to the sun, closing her eyes, the blessed warmth filling her heart with comfort and joy. How she loved her street, her home, and her life!

She had been blissfully married to Efimios for the past ten years. The child had come along quickly. Despite the crammed spaces, they felt comfortable and happy in the apartment. Besides, they had been close friends with the landlord and his wife for quite some time.

When Efimios was single, he used to rent the same apartment from Kimon's family, and they had been friends from back then. Then Kimon had got engaged to Eleni and shortly after, Anna had come into Efimios's life too. The friendship among the four had been strong and had lasted from the carefree years of their youth through to their more mature years as married couples.

In time, they had all happily adopted Eleni's delightful habit that involved fun plans for Sundays. They would spend them together, sometimes with whole days out to the mountains or the seashore, and other times with a short visit to a park or a café. There were also times of course, when money was too tight or spirits were too low because life can be like that. As you stay home sometimes to avoid adverse weather, you stay home too in order to sit out the difficulties of life. But even then, having each other's company made it special even indoors while the hail and sleet of life beat on their roof.

Anna opened her eyes again and turned around to check on Phevos. He had finished his breakfast and was now reading yet another book by Jules Vern. Since he was a toddler, he loved leafing through picture books. Once he started school, he had begun to read bedtime stories and then longer children's books with incredible avidity. The more he read, the more he asked for. The stories excited his imagination so much that sometimes his mother feared he would confuse reality with fantasy, as she watched him talk about the highly imaginative stories that he read.

His nose was forever stuck in a book for the best part of his waking hours, but unlike Anna, Efimios was not concerned. He tried to reassure her their son knew well how to differentiate reality from fantasy. He was certain Phevos could only benefit from his love for books because only through the imagination can the mind open so that knowledge can be planted like a seed in a child's mind. Before placing a seed in the earth, you make sure to water first. Should the seed fall onto dry land, it'll go wasted.

With these very words, Efimios had finally convinced his wife to stop worrying, and by now, she was able to watch her son read without feelings of worry churning up in her gut. Anna trusted her husband blindly because she knew she hadn't married the man from next door. It was different at first of course! When they had started to date, there were so many odd things about him. The way his obscure work as a salesman took him so often away from the city, the strange coins that she had once noticed as he'd opened his wallet to pay for a meal. Instead of letting her see them as she had asked, he had hidden them in his pocket saying they were foreign currency.

But one incident had stood out from the rest because it was then that her frustration had peaked and she had erupted. One day, she had visited him without notice. When he opened the door, he had rushed to hide away some strange-looking robes and sandals on his chair. To her insistent questions, he had given more excuses, just as he had every time she had seen an odd item in his possession.

He had claimed he was going to a fancy dress party that evening, but Anna didn't believe it. She'd almost convinced herself by then that he was a member of an obscure cult, or a thief of museum artifacts. She'd have believed anything, except that he was an ordinary salesman because her instinct told her otherwise. She had resorted to shouting then, threatening to break up with him and to her surprise, he had then finally offered her the truth. To prove what he was saying, he had taken her downstairs to the back of the orchard where he used the odd-looking necklace he always wore, to open the door in the rockface. Once inside, she had fallen silent to see the cave and believed him at last.

Anna smiled to herself as she remembered her sheer astonishment that day. She stood a while longer leaning on the balcony rail, showered by the morning sun, watching her son read.

As if on cue, Phevos looked up then and his mother laughed, walking up to him. She took his napkin and wiped his mouth clean, removing the traces of hazelnut paste.

"Leave it, Mom! I can clean it up myself you know!" Phevos licked his lips as he rubbed his tummy in mock satisfaction. "How do I look now?" He gave a smirk, and she bent over to kiss him on the top of his head.

"Come inside now and get dressed, my darling."

"Oh, let me stay here and read a bit more, Mommy! Please?"

"Okay. Just a bit more," she replied and went inside.

Efimios was sitting on the bed, reading his paper. Anna approached him and planted a kiss on his lips. He kissed her back tenderly, but when she looked at him then, there was something unaccountable on his face.

Anna frowned. "What's the matter, my love? Something upsetting in the paper?"

"Um, I don't know..." he replied absentmindedly. He knew then he should have blamed it on the paper, leaving it at that, but then again he wasn't good at lying. Not to her anyway.

"What is it then?" she asked, worried now. She sat on his bedside and fixed on him that examining look that had always caused him to stop what he was doing and spurt it all out.

"Oh Anna..." he whispered with an awkward half-smile. Fully aware he was cornered, he folded his paper and placed it on his lap rather nervously.

"Come on now, out with it! I'm not having my husband looking glum on a fine Sunday morning!" she said, hoping it was nothing. Maybe it was a case of low spirits she could easily fix with humor. "I'm listening!" she insisted with an encouraging smile as she placed her hand on his.

"It's nothing, my Anna! Just a dream, that's all!" Giving a faint smile, he reached out and caressed her long brown hair. She relished the gesture as always, but the look in her eyes darkened somewhat.

"A dream? You mean one of *those* dreams?"

"Yes, but not to worry. It's only a dream, it's nothing," he said, still caressing her hair, but then she pulled away and sprang to her feet.

"It's nothing? Ten years we've been married and Athena hasn't stopped yet giving you those dreams! And you tell me not to worry? What does she want from us? Can't she leave us alone?" she said as calmly as she could, trying not to yell. She didn't want to alarm her child outside. Yet, that didn't stop her from pacing up and down the rug, gesticulating fiercely.

"Don't worry sweetheart..."

"How can you tell me not to worry? She'll *never* give up! She'll always be breathing down our necks!"

Efimios looked at her and his heart sank. He hated the way his past affected Anna, how it upset and worried her. For ten years, Athena had been haunting his dreams, sometimes mildly, other times with terrible threats and anger. Efimios had never regretted his choice to tell Anna all about her. However, he had grown deeply concerned in the last few months. Athena's words in the dreams had become ominous and he had started to fear for his family. To protect his wife's peace of mind he had stopped mentioning the dreams to her, but the one of the night before had been particularly frightening and he had been unable to hide his distress.

He felt guilty now to see her so upset. He loved her more than anything. Meeting her had shaken his world from its foundations. Until then, it had never occurred to him to disregard Athena's call for duty in order to lead a normal life. But Anna had taken over his heart and mind, leaving no space for Athena. And so, although he had dated her while carrying on with his time travels for a while, his heart had been no longer in it. Instead, he had yearned to settle down with Anna in this modern world and to grow old with her without cheating Time any more.

Man is not made to live without the bondage of Time. The Gods had made it so in their infinite wisdom for good reason. Athena may have broken the rule out of love for her city, but Efimios was a common mortal. It was all very unfair to him.

To succeed in his missions of the past, Efimios had had to follow Athena's commands to the letter. Being a Goddess, she had her eye on events and people throughout the centuries. She could foresee how a single event could affect the future. All she had to do is make the moonstone on her necklace glow, something that caused a tingling on Efimios's chest as he wore it and then, he would rush to the cave where she would appear before him to give him instructions.

He roamed the same city back and forth from world to world and yet, he belonged nowhere. In the very same street where he lived in now, the same buildings had stood for centuries. Each time Efimios had visited this place in a different era, the inhabitants had always been different. Thus he knew no one, with the exception of the people in one house of course.

Through time, he had managed to meet everyone who had so far inhabited the house he lived in. As soon as Kimon's grandfather built it, Efimios had arrived to offer his services as a worker and gardener for the land, which stretched as far as the Acropolis hill. Athena had instructed him to do this in order to ensure the cave remained well hidden. Kimon's grandfather had installed wire fencing around his land with the assistance of Efimios, but he never knew the cave even existed.

Athena had protected it always from unauthorized access. Jagged rocks and thorny bushes totally sealed its entrance when not in use, but each time Efimios approached to enter, they would magically yield to the sight of the necklace.

During other travels, Efimios had met Kimon's father too but had never formed any relations with him. As for Kimon, he had met him once when he was still a little boy. He remembered clearly patting his head with affection a couple of times in the street where he played. Somehow, among the men in that house, only Kimon had become a friend to him. There was something about Anna, Kimon and Eleni that had felt like family, enough to make him want to stay in their lives forever. Before meeting them, Efimios had been a devoted servant to Athena traveling back and forth through Time, as she desired.

He had been in Athens in the 40's for example, a difficult era for the city that was under German occupation at the time. Athena often sent him to Athens then, to protect the city and the courageous men of the Resistance. His actions had been particularly heroic although they had never involved him toting a gun like an action hero. He did save lots of lives though, sometimes hundreds at a time. His actions had often been simple, involving a conversation to change someone's mind, or a seemingly chance meeting to warn someone or to lead him to shelter.

Once he had blocked a road with a van thus causing delay to an enemy vehicle. As a result, he had allowed others extra time to run away, saving their lives. And there was another time that was one of his favorite interventions in the city. One night, he had visited an underground taverna and had sung a few patriotic songs with two young lads, who had barely looked old enough to shave. But their time together had inspired them overnight to join the Resistance. In time, they became the masterminds of various major operations, leading dozens of foreign officers to safety in Egypt on board boats and submarines.

Another of his favorite missions had taken place on the very top of the Acropolis in the 1820's during the Greek war of independence against Turkish rule. At the time, the Turkish army had taken over the Acropolis, and they were under siege by the Greeks led by Odysseus Androutsos. The enemy had run out of ammunition and they had started to tear down the pillars of the Parthenon temple, gouging out the lead inside them in order to melt it and cast bullets. The Greeks had found out and the terrible news had spread like wildfire among the troops.

One of the few things that the average Greek has always been very sensitive about is the protection of the Parthenon from further harm. Led by this sensitivity, the Greeks had delivered to the Turks a load of lead with the famous phrase: 'Here are your bullets, don't touch the pillars'. Efimios had been there, having carried part of the load himself after raising the alarm among the men. As Athena had guessed, the Greeks had responded in the only way possible. They had virtually redeemed the pillars from the enemy with their blood seeing that the delivered lead was meant for their own chests.

This blind valor that borders on madness is the very reason why the Gods never forsake this nation. Its people have a favorite saying: 'God loves the Greeks'. Often, just when all hope seems lost, a handful of Greeks will come together and perform a small miracle. And in such times, although the rest of the world may watch in incredulity, the average Greek will deem it entirely normal because of the specific conviction that is etched inside his soul.

Efimios wasn't only needed during times of war though. After the 40's and the liberation of Athens, the city started to grow and flourish in times of peace, but Athena didn't think her work was done even then. This is because despite the city's financial and physical growth, there was something in the psyche of its men that started to fade and falter. Morale plummeted as the city grew bigger hurriedly without proper planning, as people flooded in and concrete blocks replaced lush gardens and playgrounds.

Efimios kept visiting back and forth from the 50's to the 80's as Athena commanded. She watched, as the people grew fearful of strangers, indifferent of their neighbors, uninspired to live, unwilling to dream, unable even to laugh out loud. She was particularly concerned to see the children gradually removed from the streets and the parks, to be isolated in apartments. She watched as their guardians handed them electronic equipment to play with in solitude instead of offering them the most precious soul pleaser: the company of others, starting from their own.

Efimios was called upon to fix these things in various ways, mainly to inspire and to help people come together, funnily enough, sometimes through tragedy, for there is no greater bonding material for people.

It was in the late 80's that Efimios had met Anna, Kimon and Eleni. From that time onwards, although he had carried on with his missions, he'd seemed to linger in that period a lot, following their lives as closely as possible. As for Athena, she had let this happen without seeing harm in it.

He had expressed a great interest in this era of great advancement for the city, and she couldn't have predicted his affection for Anna would make him disobey her in the end. This is because Man has the freedom of choice especially when it comes to his feelings. It's his birthright that not even the Gods can deprive him of. Athena couldn't have guessed his love for Anna would grow to be so strong because the choice had only been *his* to make.

Chapter 21

After the early morning upset because of Efimios's dream of Athena, the remainder of the day proved to be a lot more carefree. It was now early afternoon. The four friends were still seated around a table at the beach taverna where they had earlier enjoyed a lovely meal. Phevos and Ksenia were playing on the seashore close by, running up to the water and back and laughing every time a wave caught up with them and wet their shoes.

Their proud mothers were watching, sharing in their joy, judging from their faces. Manos was just under a year old then, and he was sleeping in Eleni's arms. Efimios and Kimon were deep in conversation, suggesting island destinations to each other for their next summer holiday. Every year, they would decide on a couple of Greek islands that were conveniently linked by boat, making them ideal for island hopping. They used to relish the element of mystery that came with visiting a new place.

They had always taken their summer holidays together during the latter part of August, as it was the only period when the shoe factory where Efimios worked in production would shut down each year.

"A penny for your thoughts!" said Eleni, startling Anna out of her reverie. She had been staring into the distance for the last couple of minutes.

"Oh sorry, I was miles away!" Anna looked embarrassed, but she didn't offer a smile. Eleni looked into her eyes, and the disquiet she found there alarmed her. She insisted to know what was troubling her, and almost whispering now so that the men couldn't hear, Anna opened her heart to her, telling her Athena had troubled her husband's sleep once again.

Eleni knew all about Athena and so did Kimon. A few days after telling Anna the whole truth about himself, Efimios had brought Kimon and Eleni to the cave as well for the same purpose. They had been friends for years by then, and a tremendous burden had lifted off his chest when he had finally told them everything.

His revelation had bonded the four of them since then even more, but it had also strengthened Athena's resolve to punish him for revealing her secret, as well as for settling down with Anna in an era where—according to her—he didn't belong.

Anna was striving to fight back tears as she kept confessing in whispers her deepest fears to her best friend. Eleni listened patting Anna's hand, telling her it would be all right, although she wasn't sure she believed it herself. However, Eleni was a Christian just like Anna, and they shared a strong faith in God. She urged her to pray just like she had already started to do in her heart. Sometimes a prayer does not need words. It's a single sigh that emerges from the core of your very soul. It's a few moments that you take feeling grateful for whatever you have in life that you love.

And so, praying in unison, the two women turned to look at their husbands, who were still discussing island destinations in high spirits. From there, they turned their gaze to their children, whose shoes were drenched by then, and who continued to giggle, making a musical sound that would put angelic music to shame. That very sound marked the end of their prayer in a loud crescendo. It made a tear roll down Anna's cheek, prompting Eleni to squeeze her friend's hand with compassion.

***

After the taverna meal, the two families made their way slowly back to the city with a bus ride that was interrupted along the way for a stop at a café. It was on Poseidon Avenue in the eastern suburbs of Athens, and it had a fabulous view to a marina. The spirits of the women were now fully restored, aided by the cheerfulness of their men and children. By the time they took another bus home, the early morning disruption seemed like a distant past. In the evening, the men refused to let the women cook seeing that it had been a fine but tiring day for everyone, so they had a home delivery of souvlaki and chips that they enjoyed in the sitting room in front of the TV.

The adults were laughing uproariously now as they sat on the sofa, watching a funny Greek movie from the 60's. Eleni kept checking on little Manos every now and then. He slept in his cot in her bedroom next door. Phevos and Ksenia were in her room at the end of the hall playing Monopoly. They had started playing in the sitting room after their dinner, but the loud noise from the TV had bothered them. Ksenia had suggested moving to her bedroom thinking she'd have plenty of moral support from her dolls there.

Phevos had laid the board on the floor, and Ksenia had sat opposite him holding a doll with curly blond hair. From the moment they resumed playing, Ksenia had kept pretending every now and then to listen to her doll, acting as if she were telling her which property to buy and which to turn down.

"Come on Ksenia! Leave that doll alone and answer already!" complained Phevos.

"What did you say?" Ksenia asked her doll, ignoring Phevos's indignation. She hesitated for a moment and then put out her hand, leaving with the poise of a duchess before his feet a handful of colorful notes. "We'll take it!" she announced regally.

"Thank you!" Phevos responded pulling a face of mock exasperation while processing the transaction, acting as the banker. He opened his mouth to tease her for pretending dolls could speak, but then he heard a strange sound that made his lips freeze into a perfect 'o' shape.

"Go on, Phevos! It's your turn!"

"Did you hear that?"

"Hear what?"

"It sounded like someone was knocking at the kitchen door. But it sounded metallic. That's strange!"

"I didn't hear anything. Play already!" Ksenia huffed and placed the dice in his hand. Thanks to her doll's sound advice so far, it looked like she might win and she couldn't wait.

"There it is again!" said Phevos springing to his feet. "No way! I have to go see. This is really strange," he added, determined to investigate. His immense curiosity would never have had it otherwise.

"Don't open the door on your own! Call the grownups to do that, you hear?" she shouted as he left the room.

Ksenia had been a sensible child, always playing it safe. On the other hand, Phevos had been very adventurous as a little boy, but even at that age, he was already fully aware of the dangers of the world. The classic bedtime stories, which are available to all children, see adequately to that. Through the use of symbolisms they speak cautiously to their sensitive psyche. For instance, Phevos knew about the big bad wolf, the cruel stepmother, the bad giant, and the wicked witch. Of course, he would never open the door to total strangers, especially at night.

But the sound was too strange and he only intended to investigate further without opening the door. As he walked to the kitchen across the hallway from Ksenia's room, he had already decided that the metallic sound couldn't have possibly come from the door that was made of wood. Besides, there was a doorbell outside. Why would anyone knock instead? And who would come around the back to knock when there was a front door just off the street?

The kitchen seemed asleep in the semidarkness while the rest of the house felt alive with bright lights and activity. Phevos could hear the grownups laughing still. From Ksenia's bedroom, the vibrant colors from the walls and the furniture seemed to pulsate with energy. Yet in the kitchen, Phevos felt enveloped in an uncomfortable sense of stillness.

It was as if something was lurking in the dark, and he felt a shiver on the back of his neck.

He stood at the door, listening intently. He heard the mewing of a cat in the back yard and some distant sounds from the street: a bell from a bicycle and the footsteps of passers-by. Moments later, the street noises died down and all he could hear was the sound of the TV. The door to the back yard was opposite him. All he'd have to do is walk across the kitchen to get there but somehow, he felt reluctant. It wasn't like him to fear the darkness, and he wondered what was wrong with him.

Determined not to falter, he put out his hand to turn on the light. He flicked the switch but nothing happened. He tried again and again but to no avail. Perhaps the bulb had blown. It was not important, and he saw no reason why he should tell the grownups about that. Still, it meant he had to give up just this once. He was about to turn on his heels and head back to his Monopoly game when he heard the sound again.

It had been barely audible this time, but it had shocked him because it hadn't come from the wooden door, but from somewhere inside the room, very near him. He had gasped when he heard it, and for the first time had considered calling his mother. But then, his adventurous instinct kicked in again, and he decided he needed no help to investigate.

Since he was very small, he'd been fighting against the sense of fear as if it were a mortal enemy. At the playground, he'd choose the highest slide. When the doctor held the syringe, he'd be the only child who didn't look away or cry. At home, his mother, who slept very lightly and woke up at the slightest sound, often found him wandering in the dark on his way to the lavatory or to the tap for some water.

His mother had placed a nightlight in his room but he kept switching it off. When she asked him one day why he insisted on doing that, his answer had left her dumbfounded. He had reasoned that since God allowed darkness in the world, it was to be accepted and explored too just like we did with light.

Anna had found a lot of wisdom in his belief, and Efimios had agreed with her when she had told him. Of course, they had both felt very proud of their son for the way his mind worked, although it had increased their worry somewhat too as it is more difficult to protect a fearless child.

Phevos heard the sound again. It was metallic, no doubt about that. It sounded like it was coming from behind the door again. With a shudder, he started to walk slowly toward it. He blinked a few times on his way there, willing himself to wake up in case he was dreaming. The whole experience felt surreal to him by then. In another attempt to decipher if this was a dream or not, he stopped half way and looked behind him. He could still hear the TV playing, and he could see Ksenia on the carpet combing her doll's hair as she waited for him to return.

Drawing courage from the knowledge that his loved ones were in close proximity, he carried on walking toward the door, but now his body was fully alert, pumped with adrenaline. His legs tingled with the purpose to run to the safety of his mother's arms, if needed. When he reached the door, he placed his ear carefully on its cold surface to listen and then gasped as with the corner of his eye he caught a faint movement in the darkness across the room.

Some light entered the kitchen from Ksenia's bedroom, but the wall opposite him was shaded by the tall form of the fridge and the overhead cupboards in a way that the space underneath seemed ominous in his eyes. The movement he had detected had come from that dark spot, and he watched intently now, sinking his eyes into that threatening wall, waiting.

There it was again, that lurking jet-black shadow that moved within the gloominess. His heart jumped in his chest and his shoulders did the same. What was that? And then, through that dark corner, a crouched figure seemed to detach itself from the wall. His legs trembled from the adrenaline rush and with a single jerk backward, his body stuck against the door. The figure walked two paces forward emerging into the faint light that came in from Ksenia's room.

An elderly woman stood there now, smiling at him. She looked harmless except for her eyes that stared at him in a hypnotizing way. Without breaking her stare for an instant, she took two more steps forward and then stopped again. Phevos relaxed somewhat. Although she was a stranger, and he didn't know how she had come in and why, he found nothing threatening about her. She looked quite frail, if anything. Her back was bent and had a huge hump. She was all dressed in black. In her wrinkled hands, she held a wooden cane. Thick leggings covered her spindly legs from the hem of her dress to her leather slippers. Her all-black appearance was completed with a headscarf. From under it, tufts of snow-white hair fell like thick cotton threads on her wrinkly forehead.

"Have no fear, my child! I will not hurt you..." she whispered hoarsely, putting out a hand with the palm exposed, to offer him reassurance. Her arm, as it got revealed more from under her sleeve looked skeletal.

"I know, *yaya*," said Phevos feeling more at ease now. Taking heart, he took a step toward her. As soon as he did that, the elderly woman approached him with hurried steps stopping right in front of him by the door. Once again, the boy grew distressed. The reason was that as he watched her come toward him, he'd seen her wooden cane hit the carpet but instead of the soft thud that he'd expected, it produced a clear metallic sound. "Who... who are you? How did you get in here?"

"How did I get here?" she gave a smirk. "With my key of course! I live here too you know," she said producing a little golden key from her dress pocket. She let him glimpse at it for only a second and then put it back in there. Smirking still, she fixed him with a confident stare that made him feel uncomfortable until her eyes started to cloud his thoughts.

He became rigid or rather frozen, unable to move, even to think any more. He stared back at her then, hypnotized by those eyes. He tried to think inside his head again but there was nothing now. His mind had drawn blank.

It felt empty like an abandoned house that had been robbed even of its echoes.

Trying to think, he felt as if he was trying to talk to himself through a thick glass. He could no longer get any answers in his mind or hear the sound of his own reason. All he could do is stare at the thick glass. That's how her eyes felt on him, weighing him down heavily. It numbed his mind all the more by the second.

"Shush now and do not worry!" she commanded with authority. "I have a treat for you! And all you need to do, is accompany me to my house in the back of the orchard."

"The orchard? But no one lives there...." whispered Phevos through the thick fog of his stupor.

"Ah, little one! Your father has never told you about me but not to worry, there is still time," she replied in a croaky voice, caressing the top of his head with a gnarled hand. Her touch made him numb all over filling his head with a sense of warmth that stunned him. It felt welcoming yet he knew deep down he had to resist it, except he couldn't.

With half-closed eyes, he tried to look at the woman but his vision was blurred now and in his head, he couldn't even feel the thick glass any longer. All there was now, was the warmth from her touch. It filled his head with swirling, psychedelic colors. His body fell numb in her embrace as she held him against her with incredible ease. His head was now leaning limply against her chest.

The old woman felt contented. He was hers at last. Her lips pulled back to reveal rotten teeth in a smile of pure arrogance, but at that very moment, the voice of a little girl made her face contort again with malice.

"Phevos, are you here?" asked Ksenia peering into the darkness. She had just tried flicking the light switch a few times but to no avail. She stood at the kitchen entrance holding the same doll in her arms. She'd come in from her brightly lit room and so she couldn't make out the crouched shape that stood before the door across from her.

Hidden in the darkness, the elderly woman became vexed by the intrusion in her moment of triumph. With incredible strength, she shifted the weight of the boy onto one arm only and reached out the other toward Ksenia, eager to get rid of her as soon as possible. Although her words echoed loudly in the room, she never allowed Ksenia to listen. Her curse fell heavily upon the little girl, without her ever hearing as much as a whisper.

"I command you to go now!" the malevolent woman spat out with fury. "You have enjoyed long enough what is mine. It *is* mine because *I* allowed you to have it! But no more! Tonight I am taking your little friend away and if his father wants him, he will have to follow too. As for you, you will now forget everything you ever knew about this boy! I know you are very fond of him but fear not, it will be like he never existed. Likewise, this boy right here will soon not remember you or anyone else in this place! He and his father do not belong with you. *I* gave them to you and they are mine to take away!"

Ksenia, blissful in her ignorance, never saw or heard anything. And then, as if led by an invisible hand, she turned on her heel and went back to her room with a blank expression on her face and her mind muddled, in a state of semi-consciousness.

With the intruder gone, the wicked woman opened the door and stole Phevos away, into the cold night. The only sound that could be heard was his soft breath when she came out to the orchard under the silver moonlight, holding him tight against her chest.

***

"Mom? Where's Phevos?" asked Ksenia placing her little hands on Eleni's lap. Her mother was still watching the movie with the others. It had only been five minutes since Phevos was taken. The little girl, hypnotized by the spiteful woman, had suddenly realized he was missing as she combed her doll's hair on her bedroom floor, in total ignorance of the past few minutes.

The last thing she remembered was Phevos going to the kitchen to investigate that strange sound. She still remembered him because it was only recent, but the woman's curse was sure to take effect on her in time, inevitably causing her to forget he had ever existed.

"What do you mean, my darling? Haven't you been together in your room all this time?" replied her mother.

Anna sprang to her feet and stormed out of the room, calling her son and searching for him around the house.

Efimios, equally alarmed, hurried upstairs to check their appartment.

Kimon and Eleni knelt before their little girl trying to find out what had happened.

Having searched all the rooms downstairs, Anna returned to the sitting room in a state of panic. When she heard from Ksenia that Phevos had gone to the kitchen to investigate a strange metallic sound, her horror became fully validated. She started to wail, causing Efimios to rush back down the stairs and into her arms. Anna then told him what Ksenia had said about the sound.

Efimios thought of the day he had met Athena, the old lady with the wooden cane that made that odd metallic sound... he was nine years old at the time, just like his son was now. His heart started to race, and an icy dread washed over him. When he shared his thought, everyone panicked.

What followed was pandemonium as everyone rushed to the kitchen door. They were now certain that no human could have taken Phevos away. The door was still locked with the key on the inside. The front door was locked too. In a panic rush, they all went out to the orchard except for Eleni, who yelled behind them that she was coming in a minute.

A mother's instinct is stronger than anything else. She wasn't going to leave her children uncared for especially as she didn't know what she was going to encounter out there, and how deadly it was going to be. Eleni took her little girl in her arms, who was still crying after witnessing Anna's wailing and the panic that had spread amongst the adults like wildfire. She had thought it was all her fault and she was inconsolable.

Eleni rushed to her bedroom and placed Ksenia on the bed next to Manos's cot. She hushed her and told her not to cry because it wasn't her fault. She promised her it was all going to be all right and showed her the phone on the bedside table, reminding her to call Pallada if needed. Ksenia knew the number well because her mother had made her memorize it in case of an emergency.

Eleni wished Mrs. Sofia was there, but she was in Corfu looking after her bed-ridden sister. However, she knew Olga would rush to help her children if needed. She bent over the cot to caress Manos's head as he slept soundly and tucked Ksenia in the bed next to him, asking her to take care of him until she returned.

She kissed her on the forehead one last time and then rushed out of the room and through the kitchen door. She locked it to keep her children safe inside and put the key in her pocket. She started to run, knowing well where to go. No one amongst the adults had mentioned it, but they all knew where Phevos had been taken to, and they had to get there fast. Efimios had just searched upstairs, and his necklace was missing.

Chapter 22

Athena hurried down the marble steps to the entrance of the cave. She had run all the way there, carrying Phevos in her arms with the vigor of an athlete despite the fact she was still bearing the form of a frail, old woman. With a confident move, she shifted the boy's weight and held him with one hand against the rock face by the metallic door.

Chuckling with satisfaction, she waved her hand before his closed eyes, and they opened obediently.

Phevos regained his consciousness, but his mind remained numb, and his body felt limp. With great difficulty, he turned to look at her and saw she had taken the little key out of her pocket again. It was studded with gems and sparkled eerily in the moonlight.

Slowly, he started to take in his surroundings. He was able to think again now through the thinning fog in his head. He realized he was at the back of the orchard before the entrance of the gardening storeroom, as his parents called it. He recognized it from the metallic door. He'd never been inside. How had he got here? Had he fainted? Had the old woman carried him here? Where had she found the strength? Was he standing, or was *she* holding him up? His legs were too weak and he couldn't tell.

He turned to her to voice his anguish, but a sudden glow from the key in her hand caught him by surprise. When the radiance subsided, what he saw in her hand astonished him. He'd seen it only once or twice before in his life. He didn't know anything about it, except that it was priceless and unique in the world.

"Where did you get that? This necklace belongs to my father!" he shouted at her as she pinned him against the wall.

"You are wrong!" she replied hoarsely, bursting into a wicked laugh.

"No, I'm right! It is my father's I tell you! Let me go! Dad! Dad!" he yelled as he fought to break free from her grasp of steel.

"You will do well not to antagonize me, Boy!" she said, pinning him in place with even more strength than before. "Listen to me! This necklace has always been mine! It is mine and always will be!"

"You're a liar! A liar and a thief! Let me go I tell you!"

"Enough!" she shrieked at him, her anger growing like thundering clouds gathering for the storm. "Not another word from you, we have no time!" She placed the necklace on the door, and it swung open as if by magic. She shoved Phevos inside and he stumbled, falling on his knees.

With one hand, she lifted him up like a toy from the collar of his shirt, dragging him all the way to the altar. He remained on his knees there, astounded, yet fully alert. There was ample light in there, coming from strange-looking torches on the surrounding walls. Looking around him frantically, he started to shout for help. What was this place? It wasn't a gardening storeroom!

"You see? Your father is the liar after all!" Athena shrieked at him cackling with glee. She lifted her arms in a triumphant stance that didn't befit the weak, hunched figure that she chose as her disguise.

Phevos realized for the first time then that her voice had changed. It wasn't croaky as before. She sounded much younger now. How could it be? He lifted his head to look at her, and as she stood before him by the altar, she relished the bewilderment in his eyes. This was her moment to show him where he truly belonged. She placed her necklace on her heart and hit her cane on the ground repeatedly, producing a deafening metallic sound that filled his heart with panic. He started to feel numb and dizzy again as she stared at him once more. He knew then that he was going to faint again, and this time he was terrified.

As his mind sank all the more into the thickening fog, he thought he had started to hallucinate. The old woman before him had disappeared and now he could clearly see a young woman, unrealistically tall, standing in her place. She had an astonishing beauty. She looked resplendent in a white robe and a shiny suit of armor on top of it, which included a radiant battle helmet. Its long metal strip that ran the length of her nose, made her eyes look even more fearsome, and he shivered under her stare.

From what he could see, she was holding a long spear that glowed with a blinding light. He could not look at it any more than he could face the sun on a summer's day. All of a sudden, she smiled at him as he cowered before her, but there was no kindness in her eyes, only contentment. Phevos managed to whisper a single call for help, and then his mind sank deeper into the cloud that was to steal away all his memories until that moment. He spared his very last thought for his mother. At the core of his fading memories, he saw her precious face one last time as he sank away, and then he was gone, his mind lost in the cloud.

As soon as Phevos fainted, Athena heard commotion outside, and she swept him up effortlessly with one arm as if he weighed no more than a feather. She was so tall that the top of her helmet barely missed the roof of the cave despite the fact that it was around seven feet high.

And here they were now, emerging one by one out of breath, Efimios, Kimon, and then Anna. Unlike the men, she never halted when she saw Athena. Instead, she rushed forward to her in order to redeem her child with a blind yearning that left no place in her heart for fear. Efimios grabbed her and held her back, causing Anna to wail and to scream hateful words at the Goddess.

Athena still held the boy. Being unconscious, he was unable to fight for himself. Efimios continued to restrain Anna in order to protect her, for he knew she would stand no chance if she were to approach Athena. He tried to remain as calm as possible so that he could maintain his capacity to think. If emotion overtook him as in Anna's case, the result could be catastrophic for them all. He was the only one who stood a chance to turn this around. He needed to distract Athena. Perhaps if he tried to talk her out of whatever plan she had... He could imagine what that was. It would satisfy her hurt pride for sure. It would serve her arrogance but not his family's survival.

"How pitiful are you, common mortals!" shrieked Athena. Her voice echoed like the sound of battle that carries the strike of swords and the screaming of men. She stood before them, lifting Phevos high with one arm, making him look like a rag doll. She was mocking them now, finding the sight of Anna, who kept trying to break free, quite ridiculous. What was she hoping for if Efimios were to let her go? "Do you really believe you stand a chance against me you pathetic human?" she said, laughing. The thundering noise filled the cave like the sound of a thousand spears in the air about to hit their target.

Anna seemed undeterred still. She kept on wailing and begging her husband to let go.

"I am Athena! The daughter of Zeus, born from his wisdom! No one can stand before me and hope to win!" The Goddess took a single step forward. As soon as her sandal hit the ground, it lifted a cloud of dirt, and the earth started to shake.

The three mortals before her stumbled uncontrollably as the ground continued to shake for a few more seconds. When the earthquake was finally over, Anna spat on the ground and turned a fiery stare at Athena. "You may command the earth, but you don't command *me*! Give me back my son! " she shouted, wriggling to free herself from her husband's grasp in order to reach her.

"I am begging you Athena..." pleaded Efimios. He could understand his wife, but what she was doing was suicide. They needed to appease her, not to aggravate her further.

"Please forgive me! I am ready to come with you and serve you once more. But please, have mercy! Let my son stay here with his mother, I beg of you!"

"It is too late now Efimios!" came Athena's swift answer, as she fixed him with a stony stare. "You are no longer welcome to serve under my command! I have changed my mind. All I need is your son now!" She held the boy against her chest, against the cold steel of her armour. His arms and legs were swaying limply in midair.

Once again, Anna began to wail, mad with rage and longing and then, Eleni appeared through the entrance. As soon as she saw Athena, she froze in shock. Her knees buckled, and she collapsed into a heap next to Anna.

"Enough! This travesty ends here!" yelled Athena with renewed fury. "You!" she shrieked pointing to Anna. "You took my servant once and so, I will now take your child! He belongs to me because if it hadn't been for me, you would never have known his father *or* him!"

Anna went berserk in response, and it took Efimios all his strength this time to keep her from rushing forward like a lioness, all teeth and claws.

Unaffected, Athena rested Phevos on the edge of the altar supporting him with one hand. With the other, she placed the necklace in the center of the altar. Within the few seconds that it took her to do this, all four of them rushed to her, led by Efimios, who now knew what was to come.

In a desperate attempt, they reached her in a flash, trying to grab the child before it was too late. As soon as the necklace was placed in the recess, the three crystal candles on the altar lit up. A loud murmur rose from the earth, and then there was a tremendous roar as the cave started to shake. A blinding light surrounded the mortals, who froze in astonishment, except for Efimios. He had experienced the Passage through Time before and knew what was coming.

Athena was holding the child in her steel grasp. Anna had reached her first. She had placed one hand on Athena's arm and the other on Phevos, trying to pull him away. Kimon and Eleni held the boy by his back and shoulders with the same purpose and the same futile result.

Efimios, having a single hope left, knelt before Athena placing his hands on her knees in a silent plea for mercy. The blinding light had dazed them all, and the deafening sound hindered any attempt for communication amongst them, but each one still hoped and tried to save Phevos.

In the midst of this storm of overwhelming light and sound, Efimios turned to look at them all. They were still trying to save the boy but Athena stood before them with resolve. She didn't seem to regard them as a threat any more than a mountain would fear a mouse to bring it down. It was almost like she didn't even mind them being there, except perhaps for Anna, whom she kept staring at with wild rage in her eyes.

Efimios kept his hands on the Goddess's knees, waiting for her to respond to his silent plea. He was ready to offer anything in exchange for his son, even his own life if he had to. And then, Athena finally took her eyes from Anna and turned to him. There was only anger in her eyes, and Efimios lost all hope for her mercy.

"Efimios, I waited for ten years. It is too late for negotiations. Now, I will take your son and to punish you, I will also take you and your friends!" she yelled and his heart sank knowing well that there was no point in trying any more.

"You!" said Athena turning to Anna scornfully. "You have no place here! I condemn you to stay behind without your family and friends! I curse you to live on your own!" she spat out, lifting Anna with one hand as if she weighed no more than a pebble.

Efimios started to wail begging her to reconsider, but of course, she wouldn't listen. Anna was clawing at her neck now, but Athena pulled her hands away effortlessly as you would remove mere pieces of fluff from your shirt. With hate, she lifted Anna even higher, and threw her forcefully a few feet away from the altar.

A few seconds later, Anna opened her eyes and tried to sit up. She was in pain after having suffered this mighty fall, but that was nothing in comparison to the angst of her discovery. An eerie semidarkness surrounded her now. She was alone from what she could see, thanks to the moonlight that crept through the entrance. She collapsed onto the dirt again at the frightful realization of what had just happened, crying inconsolably.

When she finally found the strength to stand up, her body felt bruised all over. Aching, she stumbled in the dark all the way to the exit. When she emerged into the night, she filled her lungs with fresh air lifting her head up high. Spent, she stood there gazing at the moon. It seemed to her that it was casting its silvery light down at her with clemency and purpose, as if it were trying to speak to her.

No one else was there to talk to, and so she stood there and offered a prayer to God for the return of her loved ones. She spent the rest of the night there, outside that hateful cave, in case they returned. At dawn, she awoke reluctantly, fighting off the early sunlight behind her eyelids, finding herself unwilling to face life without them.

But then she thought of Ksenia and Manos, who would soon wake up alone. Driven by a strong sense of purpose, she stood up and started to make her way toward the house. She didn't know how she was going to explain to them that their parents were gone. She didn't know how to cope with her own loss either. But she had to try. She would have to survive somehow until they all returned.

Anna was a fighter. She had fought many battles in her life and already knew this one was going to be the hardest of them all. This one wasn't over. It had only just begun.

Chapter 23

That morning, Anna got out of bed earlier than normal. It had been ten days already since that fateful evening. The police had concluded their investigation without any helpful findings, just as Anna had expected.

Ksenia was much calmer now. During the first couple of days she had refused to eat, play or even watch TV. School had been out of the question in her state, and all she had seemed to do all day is cry for her parents.

Anna had had to exhaust all her patience to get her to lie in bed at night. The little girl would wail and cry for hours before finally falling asleep, exhausted. For some reason, she had feared Anna would disappear too if she were to go to bed and so, she had refused to fall asleep without holding Anna's hand. She had also refused to sleep in her room any more, and only slept on her parent's bed with her now, next to her brother's cot so that she could watch over him as her mother had asked her.

Anna had had no choice but to accept this new sleeping arrangement that gave Ksenia a sense of security. She had also taken to singing to her the lullaby that Eleni used to sing. It had stayed in their family thanks to Eleni's grandmother, who had been a refugee from Asia Minor. Anna had heard Eleni sing it to her children so many times that she knew it well enough now to sing it to them too. It had an almost magical effect on them, calming them down and lulling them to sleep. Ksenia had taken to singing it to her brother too as she held him in her arms. It seemed to Anna as if the little girl was trying to take her mother's place for him.

Anna hadn't had much sleep the night before. She had kept tossing and turning with the irresistible urge to go upstairs. The only thing that didn't stop her from going there and then in the middle of the night was the fear that by getting up, she'd wake up Ksenia. So she stayed with her and slept only a little.

Shortly after dawn, she put on her robe and ever so lightly, tiptoed out of the room. She reached the bottom of the staircase and looked up. It felt to her like months since she was last up there and yet, it had only been about ten days since she'd brought down a few clothes. Ksenia and Manos had required constant attention from that very first morning and Anna had had to put her own pain aside in order to relieve theirs. But now, as she grasped the wooden banister until her knuckles turned white, she felt desperate to steal sometime for herself.

She needed to go upstairs and to pickup the pieces of her own life, to sit alone with her thoughts and meet her pain headfirst. Anna had never shied away from pain. She had never sought it of course but when it came, she'd bare her chest to it, ready for it. But other than needing to deal with her loss that day, there was also a practical reason for her to go up there. She had decided early on that she had to put the children's welfare first. That meant she had to move in with them downstairs in order to provide them with her undivided attention and constant care in the long run.

The apartment upstairs could be put up for rent so that she could earn an extra income for their upbringing, other than what she could help make with the business in Pallada. She was ready to do anything she could with the help of Mrs. Sofia as to make sure the children would be safe and provided for. That morning she was going to start packing her things away. They would all go to storage. She would put her past in a box, her own life on hold, for the sake of the children until her loved ones returned.

Slowly, she began to go up the stairs, knowing she would find evidence of her husband's and child's past presence up there, and she tried to brace herself for it. Efimios's shirt and trousers would be hung on the hook behind the door with his bag, ready for work, and Phevos's pajamas would be neatly folded on his bed. Everything would still be where she had left it that Sunday morning, when she was still oblivious to the fact that an hourglass was being flipped over somewhere to count the seconds toward the end of life as she knew it, with every grain of sand rapidly falling, falling, until there was nothing left but reminders of the happy life she once had.

The steps creaked under her feet until she reached the tiny landing. She stood before the wide open door and lingered at the threshold looking in. It seemed untouched by time, just as she had expected. Her bed was made with lavender sheets and large pillows. The kitchenette in the corner was perfectly tidy as she seldom cooked in it. They used to share the expenses with their friends, cooking and having most of their meals together downstairs.

Off to the left, the tiny hallway led to the bathroom and Phevos's room. It was a small dwelling, and it suddenly looked like an empty shell in her eyes although her mind was still full of happy memories within its walls. But after all, it is the people that make the dwelling and not the other way round.

Numbly, Anna walked up to a chair and picked a shirt of her husband's that she had left draped over its back. It still smelt of him and that made her knees weak. She collapsed onto the chair and burried her face in the smooth, cotton fabric. As if the shirt were alive, its sleeves caressed her arms as she held it against her, breathing in deeply, with her eyes tightly shut.

She stood again, never leaving it from her hands and sat on the bed before the mirror on her dresser. The woman who looked back at her startled her. She looked different, defeated. Deep inside, she knew she hadn't given up, but the stranger before her looked like she thought otherwise, and Anna felt angry with herself for her doubts.

She wiped the sudden tears that streamed down her face and picked up her brush from the dresser. She recalled the multitude of evenings where Efimios offered to comb her hair before bedtime, knowing how much she enjoyed it. He would stand behind her as she sat on the very same spot, combing away the long strands of brown hair, as she smiled at him tenderly from the mirror.

The echo of their laughter died away, as his reflection disappeared from the mirror taking away with it her own image too as she remembered it. Anna looked at the silent stranger before her again and lowered her gaze.

There were a couple of vases of cosmetic cream on the dresser, a bottle of perfume, and a square jewellery box made of onyx. Anna opened it. It contained very few items of gold, just a few bracelets, earrings and golden chains that her family had given to her as presents on her engagement day. Her only surviving relatives these days were her aunt and uncle, who lived in Macedonia in a village near Thessalonica. She hadn't seen them in years, and they rarely phoned each other. Anna's parents had both passed away since her wedding. Her father had died first of a heart attack and then her mother too, after only one year. The doctor had said it was due to a stroke, but they all believed that she'd died of grief, having given up on life after losing her husband. Anna's parents had been childhood friends brought up in that same Macedonian village, and they had never been apart before.

Anna wished her mother had been stronger because she needed her now, more than ever. But sadly, when some people give up, they forget that the world is not only about them, but that it's about the others too, who count on them also for their own survival.

Anna sighed. It seemed that all she had to draw strength from were the two children downstairs, who desperately needed her. There was also Mrs. Sofia of course. Anna knew she could count on her too. She couldn't wait for her to come back from Corfu. It had been about a month since she had left. Who knew what she was going through herself, taking care of her sister on her last days?

Anna closed the jewellery box and absentmindedly, opened the top drawer of her dresser. On the left side, there were brightly colored scarves in naval motifs and flowery patterns. All of them were neatly stacked and folded. On the right side of the drawer, there were large envelopes that contained records of bills and important documents as well as a large photo album on the very top. The front cover was a picture frame that displayed a photograph of her family. Efimios, Phevos and herself on a beach last summer, smiling as they held each other close. She couldn't see the picture now as strangely enough, it was hidden under a handful of odd items.

Anna was bewildered because they didn't belong there. Both she and Efimios were very tidy, and she knew Phevos wouldn't have placed anything in the drawer either. Who could have put these items there and why? They were a whistle, a box of matches and a few buttons. If she were to exclude her son and herself, then the only person who could have put them there was her husband. She knew he never did anything without a good reason though and that intrigued her. Then, it dawned on her that perhaps these odd items had been left there purposely as a clue. It wouldn't be the first time as Efimios enjoyed posing all sorts of riddles for his family's entertainment. His ability to think new ones up seemed inexhaustible. Could it be that he knew what was to come?

With her heart beginning to race, she started thinking back to that Sunday. He'd had that dream about Athena. And then she remembered she'd opened the drawer that morning to take a scarf. She'd worn it all day at the seaside and when they returned she had put it back.

Anna looked in the drawer and indeed, that scarf was neatly folded on the very top. And then, she gasped. These odd items hadn't been there when she put the scarf back in its place that Sunday evening. This proved her husband had placed them there afterwards. Efimios had been up there alone during the upheaval before they all rushed to the cave. Yes, that was the only logical explanation!

But what was her husband trying to tell her? What message had he left behind? It had to be important! She pushed herself to understand as she picked them up one by one. What if they were representations of her family members? She could easily interpret that message. The whistle was her son's. He kept it in his toy box and often used it to sound the beginning of battle when he played with his toy soldiers. The box of matches would represent her husband because he'd recently been trying to quit smoking and he had limited it considerably, smoking only on his lunch break at work and perhaps during the odd day out. He insisted on using matches instead of lighters, refusing to flick a switch and make his life easier. Everyone teased him for it.

As for the buttons, these were clearly Anna's. She had a small tin box in her closet, which she called 'my sea treasure'. It contained hundreds of buttons of various colors, types and sizes. When she was young she had received tailor training and enjoyed making new clothes and mending old ones. Each time she decided to throw away an item of clothing that couldn't be mended further, she'd throw the fabric away but would store any buttons in her box. This way, at a later time, if she had something else to mend, she'd go back to it and find all the buttons she would need.

As Anna looked at the objects in her hands, her face suddenly lit up. She stood up and paced to the middle of the room with purpose. If her husband had left her this message then there was only one thing he was asking her to do. Being as tidy as her, he expected her to simply put them all back where they belonged!

She strode to the door and got his workbag that hung from a hook behind it. There were no matches in it and nothing else of significance. Undeterred, she threw the box

The Necklace of Goddess Athena

of matches in the bag and put it away, then rushed past the kitchenette and into Phevos's bedroom, now clutching in her hand her last two chances; the whistle and her buttons.

The bed was made and the pajamas were folded in the usual place just as she had expected. Fighting back the lump in her throat, she turned her gaze to the shelves on the wall by the door. They were full of books and model cars. On the floor underneath, there was a stack of board games. Her son loved them; they all did as a matter of fact. Just looking at them now, she easily remembered dozens of summer nights out on their balcony, the three of them playing monopoly or snakes and ladders, as the blaring sounds of stereo music or television echoed from the neighboring windows.

Anna approached the toy box that stood forlorn in the far corner of the room and tipped it over, emptying its contents onto the rug. She knelt down gazing for a few minutes at the heap of toy soldiers, space robots, warrior figures and plastic 3D-puzzle pieces. This is where her son's whistle belonged. He never played with his soldiers without it and had often sounded it with his father playing on the very same rug.

Anna dropped the whistle in the empty box with a sigh and then proceeded to pick up every single object in her hand, putting them all in the box one by one. The last one was a toy soldier with a colorful uniform. He held a sword and returned to her a wistful stare before she threw him in the box too, completing that part of her mission.

Without losing her nerve, she stood up, still determined to do as her husband had expected her to. In her hands, she held the buttons that belonged to her 'sea treasure'. She returned to her bedroom with haste and opened the closet, then took out the tin box from the bottom.

With trembling hands, she knelt on the thick carpet, placing the box before her. Her heart thumped against her chest then, and she willed herself to calm down. This was the moment of truth and she knew it. She opened the box and took it in her hands again.

It was a colorful collection of hundreds of buttons. Ever so slowly, she tilted it from side to side in order to listen to the soft rustle of the buttons, as they tumbled sideways every time. It was indeed, a sea of buttons. The sound they made was like the eternal murmur of the sea, like the rustle of the pebbles, as the wave retreats back into the water from the shore. Efimios often teased her for sitting with that box, doing that very same thing in order to produce that sound and to lose herself in it.

Anna smiled then, for the first time in many days. There was something about this rustling that pleased her psyche like a sweet lullaby. She dipped her hand inside the box as she often did, just to feel the tickle of the buttons on her fingers, and then, her eyes lit up. Something else was in there.

She lifted it out of the box and found herself holding a penned letter, folded into four. Astonished and delighted, as this was far more than she had hoped for, she opened it with trembling hands to recognize her husband's handwriting.

My dearest Anna,

If you're reading this, then both Phevos and I are no longer there with you. I'm truly sorry for that my love, for I can only imagine the pain this is causing you. Believe me when I tell you there was nothing I could have done to avoid this. I promise that I'm going to take care of our son every single minute until we are together again.

Today, I told you about my dream of Athena and saw the fear in your eyes. I had stopped talking about these dreams for that very same reason. Her anger and threats are truly frightening. Judging from them, I'm sure by now we will not be able to avoid her wrath. I believe she intends to break our family apart, taking away our son, if not me too.

I've been fearing for him especially since his ninth birthday last autumn for that was the age I was when she had recruited me. It had been easier for me though, living in antiquity, believing in the Olympian Gods and honoring her already. But our boy is a Christian, and he belongs in this modern world. He would never accept her and I couldn't imagine what she would do then.

Although I can't stop Athena, I thought I'd try to change things in the future, so that we may have a hope of reuniting again. For that purpose, I have secretly visited Poseidon's temple, asking for protection. I'm sorry I've hidden this from you until now, but I didn't want you to worry.

Remember when I told you last month that I wanted to visit a colleague who was off sick? That's when I went to Sounio and I've done this three times if you remember. I knew this ancient ritual from my old world that fishermen participated in inside the temple to ask Poseidon for protection during their voyages. My father had taken me many times along there as he also did this ritual for the protection of his own vessels that fared far across the seas.

The first two times I visited the ruined temple on my own, nothing happened. But the third time, Poseidon appeared before me in a vision where the temple itself also transformed into its old self during its glory days. It suddenly gleamed full of gold under the light of thousands of oil lamps, with its marble pillars, walls and roof erect and magnificent once more. Poseidon stood before me and listened to me. It doesn't matter if he truly cared. Perhaps he only saw an opportunity to spite his niece, Athena. What matters is that he accepted to help us. I left the temple that day with three wands that I found before me when the vision disappeared before my eyes, proving it had all been true. Poseidon has given me full instructions on what to do with these wands in order to reunite our family in the future.

I promise you that when Athena tries to take our son, I will not leave him on his own. I will stay with him to protect him and I know this is what you'd prefer too, despite losing us both. It is Sunday afternoon when I'm writing you this letter. We've just come back from the seaside and you're downstairs with the others. I said I would lie in bed and read my newspaper for a while, if you remember. I'm deeply sorry for all the secrecy, but as I said, I didn't want you to worry without cause.

Deep down I'm still hoping none of this will ever be necessary. But if you wind up reading this letter, it will mean there was nothing else I could have done. I will also need to give you instructions, should this happen. This is why I've placed these odd items in the drawer. I know that when you find them, you'll realize who put them there and why.

Your regard for tidiness will surely lead you to your 'sea treasure' and funnily enough, the name now bears a far greater significance for our family. I've placed this letter there in secrecy because the things I'm about to tell you are the secrets of Poseidon and you must swear to keep them safe just like I have.

As I said, he gave me three wands sculpted by his own hand. They are wondrous artifacts that carry in them grains of sand and shards of seashells from the great oceans of the world. The water inside them has been taken from the darkest depths that never see the light of day. There is one wand for each of us. They will only illuminate when at least two of us are together, holding one each. When all three of us manage to hold one each simultaneously for the first time, that will be the day when Poseidon will reunite us no matter how far apart we'll have scattered by then in terms of distance or time.

There are strict instructions we must adhere to, and I ask you to follow to the letter the ones I leave with you. One of these wands is destined to return to the sea for safekeeping by Poseidon himself, but the other two are right now in Pallada. I handed them to Mrs. Sofia before she left for Corfu. They are in a sealed box. I asked her to mind it for me, saying it was a special present I had for you that I didn't want you to find accidentally at home until I was ready to give it to you. Come to think of it, technically I never lied to her.

When she returns from Corfu, ask her to give it to you, saying I had mentioned she was keeping it for you. Poseidon's *instructions for these two wands are as follows: you are to keep one for yourself and to never part with it, no matter what. The other one must be placed in the cave on the altar. Make sure to remove from there all three candleholders made of gold with their crystal candles.*

Do with them whatever you wish. All that Poseidon wishes is that you remove them from the cave, and that you place one wand on the altar. After you've done that, talk to our friends Kimon and Eleni and arrange for the cave to be buried under tons of earth until no trace of its existence remains. Beware to ask for their permission seeing that the cave is on their land but don't offer them any justification.

I trust our friendship is strong enough for them to honor your wish without needing to know the reasons. You must then find the strength to leave our home and friends behind and move to Sounio. Poseidon wishes to keep you safe there until the right time comes to move again. He wants us to look out for signs all the time. Never forget that. Also remember we've been sworn to secrecy about all this. You mustn't disclose any of this to Kimon and Eleni or Mrs. Sofia.

This is a burden for you, I know, but think that across Time, we are sharing it together. You shouldn't even return to Athens until the right time comes. Only the signs will show you when! Have faith and remember that no matter what wicked plans Athena has in store for us, we have Poseidon on our side to make amends. Although he hasn't revealed his full plan to me, I know it will unravel through a series of signs for all three of us, and therefore, we must all keep our eyes open. I want you to know that thanks to Poseidon, we won't ever need to worry about Athena again. I love you and think of you as I draw each breath. One day, we will both be back to you. I promise.

With eternal love, Efimios.

Anna read the last few words of her husband's letter with difficulty. Her vision had become blurred. Hot tears streamed down her face now, smudging words here and there on the paper. She brought her hands together to say an impulsive prayer, never letting go of the letter. She called out to God, and for the first time wondered if Poseidon was listening too. She welcomed him to, as odd as it felt to her. She would call God any name now as long as he could help her. She hoped her husband and her son were safe, and of course, her friends too. Who could have expected that?

Her husband had urged her to keep secrets from Kimon and Eleni. Of course, he hadn't imagined they would have vanished as well. Hopefully, Efimios was taking care of them too back in his ancient world where no doubt, Athena had taken them. Anna needed to believe that what her husband had written was true, and that one day, her family would be reunited again.

She prayed this would include her lost friends as well. This was unfair to them. Anna felt guilty to have ever involved them. It had brought their lives to disastrous results. They should have stayed with their children that night. Heavy with remorse and sorrow, her body tilted like a wounded tree.

Her robe caught the tin box, tipping it sideways, the hundreds of buttons spilling out onto the carpet before her. Anna lay there crying, her body shaking with every sob before the colorful contents of her sea treasure. As she clutched the letter against her chest, her husband's smudged words on the tear-stained paper became a lifesaver in the sea of despair that she floundered in.

Chapter 24

Olga sat behind reception opening the mail. She'd been working in Pallada for around a month, substituting for Mrs. Sofia while she was away. She was deep in thought, as she opened bills and customer letters absentmindedly. The recent events had overwhelmed and upset her, like everyone else in the neighborhood. What a tragedy! Both her employers had disappeared mysteriously as well as their tenant with his son.

Olga couldn't believe the inner strength that Anna had shown. She had lost her husband and child overnight. Anyone in her place would have shut down mentally. Yet, she had proven capable to function on her own from the very first day and what's more, to take care of her friends' children.

Anna managed only short visits to Pallada nowadays to supervise and help with what little she could, and Olga didn't complain to her for the double shifts she now had to do since Eleni was no longer there to relieve her of her duties. She didn't ask for extra pay either. It shamed her to even think to do that, seeing the sacrifices Anna was making.

She did hope though Mrs. Sofia would come back soon. She had spoken to her on the phone last week. Her sister had been rushed to hospital again and this time, it sounded like the end was drawing near. The news had upset her but she had agreed with Mrs. Sofia that when someone suffers so much, it's best to let them go.

Like Mrs. Sofia, Olga was very kind and compassionate. In the last ten days, she had visited the house to see the children every evening for a while, at the end of her long day. She brought them little treats like chocolate bars, sweets, strawberries from Mr. Giorgis's store, or a souvlaki from the corner shop, anything to make them smile. She felt good to know she could contribute to the care of the children somehow, even if it only involved something so trivial.

It was easy to cheer up Manos. She didn't always succeed with Ksenia though. She had changed a lot overnight, and was now often melancholic. Sometimes, Olga resorted to singing to her silly songs or telling her jokes, managing to get the odd smile out of her. That was a great reward to Olga. She couldn't handle seeing people unhappy, especially little girls.

She was in her early thirties and had been working in hotels all her life. As a child, she loved to help her mother, who worked at the family hotel back home, on the island of Sifnos. Many years ago, she had come to Athens for University studies and had got a job in a nearby guesthouse after her graduation.

Kimon knew the owner, who was a friend, and that is how he had met Olga. When the hotelier sold his business, Olga had found herself hating working there, as the new owner was dishonest and a bad businessman. Just over a month ago, Olga ran into Kimon in the street one day and wound up confessing to him her woes. Things had got so bad for her at work, and she had got so fed up that she was thinking of packing her bags and heading back home to Sifnos, despite the fact that she preferred life in the city.

At the time, Kimon was looking to find a substitute for Mrs. Sofia, who was preparing to leave for her long stay in Corfu. Kimon offered her the job on the spot adding also that he'd like her to consider long-term employment in Pallada as well. In her old age, Mrs. Sofia couldn't man the guesthouse by herself alone any longer. The business was going well. They could afford a second member of staff easily, and someone experienced and honest like her would be welcome. Olga had accepted the offer on the spot and had marched back to the hotel to resign at once.

The sound of screeching tires brought her abruptly out of her reverie. A yellow taxi had just stopped outside and seconds later, Olga saw to her surprise that the passenger getting out was none other than Mrs. Sofia. The taxi driver took her luggage from the trunk and carried it for her to the top of the stairs. As he was leaving, Olga rushed to welcome her.

She hugged and kissed her and then noticed she looked different. Her smile was not genuine, and she looked drawn, exhausted. Olga didn't say anything but instead invited her to sit on the sofa while she brought her a glass of water.

As soon as Mrs. Sofia had a couple of grateful sips, she told her the bad news. Her sister had passed away. After the funeral the day before, and having completed her family obligations, she had rushed back to her life in Athens, ready to face the routine again as she put it, in order to look to better days.

Yet, to her surprise, when she asked for the news, instead of the expected trivial issues about guests or neighbors, she heard of the terrible tragedy that had taken place during her absence. Of course, Olga had been reluctant to talk about it at first, but when Mrs. Sofia had asked after her employers' health, Olga's discomfort and upset had been too obvious to conceal. She was honest after all and honest people have honest faces. They don't know how to lie.

Mrs. Sofia grew very distressed. She never expected the grief she'd been suffering for the past month would be crowned by this tragedy upon her return to normal life. Her eyes welled up with tears that found familiar, well-beaten paths as they rolled down her face.

***

"My darling girl!" Mrs. Sofia cried out with emotion when Anna opened the door. The two women embraced in silence feeling each other's pain. Once in the sitting room, they allowed their tears to flow this time, away from prying eyes. When Anna asked Mrs. Sofia about her sister, she heard about her loss too and expressed her sympathy. They both said how odd it was they were both grieving all of a sudden, how events can turn your life around sometimes, from one day to the next.

It was a cloudy day. The dim, natural light was coming in through the window with solemnity, like another comforting friend. Mrs. Sofia had no words to express her sorrow to Anna for her terrible, personal loss. She only held her hand and squeezed it with feeling. She told her she had arrived just half an hour earlier, and that upon hearing the news, she had felt she had to visit her immediately.

Anna felt moved by her compassion. Also, she couldn't help thinking the timing was amazing. She had only found her husband's letter upstairs that very same morning, and now Mrs. Sofia had returned. There was going to be no delay. She was going to get the wands soon after all. Despite her grief, she didn't help feeling comforted now, aware she had a mission to complete, knowing she could do something instead of going from day to day through the motions with a vague hope for a miracle.

Mrs. Sofia asked her questions about that night. How did they disappear? Was any evidence found? What had the police said? Anna started feeling guilty as she replied to her questions, in the same vague manner she had answered the police. Inevitably, she told her the same lies she told everyone else.

Her story was that she had a headache that night and went to bed early, leaving everyone else downstairs to watch TV. She fell asleep and in the morning found only the children downstairs. Due to the state of shock that Ksenia was in during the first days, the little girl was in no condition to offer anyone any information either.

Anna felt guilty again when she saw the despair on Mrs. Sofia's face. She had hoped the police had found some evidence that could help move the investigation forward. But what could Anna have told her? She couldn't tell her the truth. Instead, as she sat with her old friend, she started to form a plan in her head.

Her husband had asked her to bury the cave and she would have to justify this to Mrs. Sofia somehow. She had to think quickly. What could explain her intended action to bury the cave, and what would also keep Mrs. Sofia away from there? Anna had left the door of the cave open. She had placed a boulder in front of it to make sure it wouldn't shut by the wind. The door had no lock on it. Only her husband could open it with the use of his necklace, but that was gone now too. She had to keep Mrs. Sofia away from that place. She couldn't allow her to venture in it, alone or otherwise, driven by her mystification.

Feeling already ashamed of herself for the load of lies she intended to tell the kindly woman that sat beside her, Anna then started to speak, expressing an obsession with the cave and an inexplicable fear of it. She fabricated stories that her husband had allegedly told her once, about how it was haunted by evil spirits.

Mrs. Sofia became so horrified that Anna had to stop the conversation for the time being. She intended to return to the same subject again at a later time though. She would have to convince her that the cave was somehow connected to the disappearance of her loved ones, despite the fact that the police had searched it and had found nothing there. This had been true.

The police had looked all over the orchard and when they had got to the cave, they had found it very odd with its decorations, thrones, elaborate wall torches and central altar. But that had not been the object of their investigation, and Anna had no information to give, saying she was only the tenant and not the owner of the property. She had commented however, that the owners were eccentrics, and that they had created this space in order to host theme parties for friends and family. The police had seemed to believe it and thought no more of it. Everyone in the neighborhood had talked to them about Anna's integrity, kindness, and loving nature. Her own grief was so obvious that they had no reason to doubt what she had said or to think she was connected to the disappearance somehow.

The two women fell silent eventually and sipped their coffee together on the sofa for a while, each one lost in their own thoughts. Anna's guilt subsided somewhat during that time, and then she felt ready to address the old lady again, this time with the most important issue on her mind.

"Mrs. Sofia, I believe my husband had left a box with you for me, is that right?"

"Yes *psyche mou*, that's right! But how did you know that?" she replied, astonished.

"Well, he had mentioned he'd bought me something special for our anniversary..." Anna faltered when she felt the prick of guilt inside again, yet she knew she had no choice but to lie. "He mentioned he was going to give it to you for safe keeping until then, in case I found it accidentally in the house. I'm afraid there aren't any good hiding places in our living quarters upstairs..." she continued, smiling bitterly. "He probably wanted to avoid the downstairs rooms too because of the children. You know how inquisitive they can be when they're small," she added, getting more fluent on the lying game as she egged herself on.

"Oh, now I understand, *kyra mou*!" she smiled kindly and then her smile turned into a frown. "Aye poor soul, he didn't even get to give you your present! What happened to them? *Agie Spyridona,* this is crazy!" she burst out lamenting again, causing Anna's eyes to well up with fresh tears. As soon as she realized how she had affected her, Mrs. Sofia forced herself to calm down, for her sake.

"I'm so sorry, Anna! Come on, calm down now. Have faith in God! We'll find them, you'll see!" she comforted her patting her on the back, as Anna dried her eyes with a tissue from her pocket.

"I know Mrs. Sofia.... I know... thank you."

"Good girl! Here's a thought! Why don't you and I go to church this afternoon to light a candle? Don't underestimate the power of prayer," she pointed out with a shaky finger, "and I'll ask my niece in Corfu town to do the same for you in St Spyridon's church. And that's a saint who performs miracles!" Her pale brown eyes lit up then, as if illuminated by hundreds of candles offered in prayer. The old lady had lit that many candles in her past, always with the same unwavering faith.

"Bless you Mrs. Sofia, thank you!"

"Anna, if you want my advice, I say pray! Pray... and then pray some more. That is the only thing that brings on miracles!"

After a few moments, Anna excused herself to check on Manos, and Mrs. Sofia followed her in order to see him. He was happy, playing in his pen in Ksenia's bedroom. They stood at the entrance of the room for a while just watching him and envying him for the blissful ignorance of his age. He was the only one left in the house who was incapable of conceiving the tragedy that had befallen them.

But that is the beauty of being a toddler. There's no emotional pain and no sense of loss. It's a blessing that is only temporary in the life of Man. That is why, during tragic events in people's lives, you may witness people who are grieving or suffering in any way, manage a smile again upon spending a few moments in the company of a toddler.

It's as if they help them to remember back to the time when they were little too, when they had no worry or regard in the whole world. In that same way, Anna and Mrs. Sofia forgot their woes for a while, as they picked up little Manos from the pen to cuddle and play with him on their knees.

They laughed as they watched his face light up with joy and excitement at every word they said and every smile they gave him. They marveled at the chopped up words he managed to say, and the awkward steps he made as they held his hands. There's nothing more comforting to Man than the thought that despite the pain in the world, life goes on.

People draw courage from the safe knowledge that for every loved one who draws their last breath, there's a little baby emerging into the world somewhere else, full of vibrant energy and inconceivable capacity and will for life; a new person, who claims his own place in the world with every incoherent word and baby step.

Ksenia was going to be in school for another couple of hours, and Anna offered to escort Mrs. Sofia to Pallada in order to get the package from her. They got out to the street with Anna holding Manos in her arms. Mr. Giorgis was outside his store at the time, and they stopped to greet him.

He expressed his condolences to Mrs. Sofia for her sister's passing and was obliging to Anna, who asked if she could have a few empty cardboard boxes. He was tactful not to ask what they were for and only offered to drop them by the house in the evening after he closed the store.

Mrs. Sofia didn't ask her either and Anna was thankful for that. She would have the time to explain to her all about the boxes in a few minutes in privacy. She was going to Pallada to pick up the package, but also to have a talk with her that was going to be a very difficult one, as it involved a tremendous amount of guilt on her part.

She held little Manos a little tighter in her arms now, willing the guilt to subside. Mr. Giorgis asked them to wait returning quickly with two bags of fresh fruit for both of them. They declined at first but he was adamant. Like Olga's little treats to the children in return for a smile, that was Mr. Giorgis's instinctive contribution to the purpose of comfort. As often applies to all gestures of kindness, it's not what you give, but the fact you're giving that matters. A loving heart is always a giving heart. Just as the opposite of love is not hate, but indifference.

The two women thanked Mr. Giorgis and went on their way. Anna had given Manos to Mrs. Sofia in order to carry the two bags. She didn't want her to carry weight, and it was easy to convince her as she welcomed the chance to hold

Manos in her arms for a while. When they reached the entrance of Pallada, Mrs. Sofia went straight in to meet Olga. The young girl had seen them coming and had rushed to hold the little boy, squealing with joy.

Anna watched them from the threshold, her features pinched. She had stopped there, her body rigid, frozen by an overwhelming feeling. Today, there was no reason for her to turn her face away from the hateful sign above her head. Today, she felt triumphant enough to face it. She lifted her head, and when she looked at Athena on the painting, the hairs raised on the back of her neck.

The feeling of abhorrence coursed through her body like a jolt of electricity. Her husband deserved praise for painting such a vivid picture of Athena. The sight made her gut clench with revulsion. Anna took a deep breath and dug her nails into the palms of her hands as she held the bags.

"It's my turn now, Athena. *My* move," she whispered behind gritted teeth. She looked at the hateful image for one more second and then, fully composed, entered Pallada. Nothing was going to stop her from carrying out her husband's instructions, not even the guilt she felt for the lies she'd have to tell, and the people she'd have to leave behind. But the cause justifies the means and her cause was sacred.

Her cause involved her family's survival, and Anna held nothing more sacred than that. Her main regard was not to give Mrs. Sofia the wrong impression. She could never tell her the truth. She'd have to be vague, yet she hoped the kind old lady would accept to do the great favor she was about to ask her.

Chapter 25

Mrs. Sofia stepped into her room in Pallada still holding Manos in her arms. Anna followed her inside and asked if she could speak to her about a serious matter. Mrs. Sofia was taken aback. Her smile faded from her lips. She'd had more than a fair share of distress recently and hoped not to hear any more bad news.

She sat down by her small table and asked Anna to join her. Holding Manos on her lap, she looked at her with a worried expression on her face. When her heart started to race, she wasn't too surprised. She'd had to change her medication while in Corfu in order to protect her heart from increased palpitations. Since the heart attack that she suffered shortly after her husband's passing many years ago, doctors had advised her to avoid upset, but somehow, life kept creeping up on her having other plans. Instinctively, she placed a hand on her chest.

The gesture alarmed Anna. "Mrs. Sofia, are you okay? Shall I get you some water? Let me have Manos! Was he heavy to carry?" she offered, standing up.

"Don't worry, *kyra mou*. I'm fine. Just say what you have to say," she replied motioning to Anna to sit back down. She was used to her heart problems by now. They never seemed to worry her, unlike the others, who panicked every time she even hinted on her heart playing up. She hadn't even realized she had placed her hand on her chest. She took it away, placing it on Manos's tummy. The child gave a little giggle then that made her smile, before fixing Anna with a benevolent, expectant gaze.

Anna gave a soft sigh before speaking. "Mrs. Sofia, I've made a decision. It may sound strange after what's happened I know... but I have to do it." She tipped her chin with resolve.

"What decision is that?"

"I have to leave. I have to go away...." she hesitated as she looked at the elderly woman, knowing she was unable to justify her decision.

"Go away? Where would you go and why?"

"I..." Anna faltered again. She was tempted to tell another lie but then thought that Mrs. Sofia deserved better. She was sitting before her, an earthly angel of kindness holding Manos in her arms. They were the picture of innocence, and they *both* deserved better. In the next few days, she would allow herself to lie in order to justify burying the cave but not for the great favor she needed to ask today. No. She had to remain honest for that. She couldn't tell the truth to her old friend, but she could beg her to understand anyway.

"I have to leave Athens and move to Sounio," Anna finally said, collecting her thoughts.

"To Sounio? What for?"

"Please don't ask me why. I cannot tell you..." She gave a deep sigh. "But believe me, I have a very serious reason! Can you just take my word for it? Can you do that?" Her eyes were pleading.

"Anna, you're a good woman and a good person. Of course I believe you! I don't understand, yet I won't ask you again about your reasons if that's what you want. But have you given this enough thought? Do you seek to leave us so that you can forget? Because trust me, if that's what you're doing, it's wrong! You can't run away from pain. Pain will find you as long as you carry it. The best way to beat it is to will yourself to heal. Time helps! But running away is the wrong thing to do...."

"Thank you for your advice and your trust, but this is not the reason." She gave a wistful smile. "Actually, I had decided to move downstairs with the children and to put up the upstairs apartment for rent, but something has come up... something I can't possibly ignore. I need to leave the soonest possible. It's not up to me. I have no choice, believe me!"

"Are you sure about this?"

"Yes! I have no other option but to leave. I assure you that this is an obligation toward my husband and child. Please take it as a given if you can believe me, and don't ask me to justify it." Her voice wavered, and she willed herself not to break into sobs.

Mrs Sofia leaned forward and patted Anna's hand that rested on the table. "I do believe you, *psyche mou*! I can see that what you're saying is coming from the heart. But what about the children? As you know, there's no next of kin. I won't allow Social Services to get a sniff of them and take them to some ghastly institution! *We* are their family now. We can't let them down!"

"I know Mrs. Sofia. I know but—"

"Do you intend to take them with you? I don't think you should take them away from everyone and everything they hold familiar. They've lost enough already. And what about Pallada? I'm getting too old! I cannot run it on my own. Please reconsider, you can't leave now!"

Anna sighed. She felt done in, spent from her efforts to convince her with her vague justifications. But she had thought this through since early morning, since reading the letter that had changed everything, bringing her unexpected and solid hope.

"Mrs. Sofia, of course I don't intend to take the children away from their home and the familiar faces they have left. And how could I deprive them of you? I mean to go away on my own! I'm so sorry to let you down Mrs. Sofia but I have no choice." Her voice broke, and finally, the tears she'd been holding back began to stream down her face.

"Don't cry Anna, please! We will think of something. We will work it out—"

"Please don't try to sway me, it's futile!"

"But what about the children? And what about Pallada?"

"I have the perfect solution for Pallada." Anna took a deep breath and wiped the tears away with her fingertips. "Olga can run it! She's more than capable. She has run bigger guesthouses than Pallada on her own in the past. Kimon himself had told me."

"Yes I know that. He had mentioned it to me too. He had said a lot of good things about her, and indeed she is a lovely girl. But does she even wish to stay?"

"Yes she does. I asked her the other day if she'd like to work here on a permanent basis, and she said she'd love to!"

"Really?"

"Yes Mrs Sofia! You see? You don't need to worry about running Pallada on your own."

"Thank you Anna, thank you for arranging that. But what am I going to do without you? And what about the children?"

"Well, about the children, I was hoping..." Anna's voice trailed off. This was far too big a favor to ask of a woman at the threshold of her seventies. Somehow, she didn't dare put it in words.

"You mean for me to..." asked Mrs. Sofia, pointing a finger to herself.

"Yes..." came the monosyllabic answer from Anna, who stared back at her now, hopeful and full of guilt.

Mrs. Sofia gazed at her for a little longer and then smiled. It was a genuine smile of acceptance. Despite her years she had just taken on the most demanding challenge: to raise two children that weren't even her own by blood. But they felt like her own by love, and somehow that made them even more precious to her. Instinctively, she squeezed the child in her arms with affection.

In response to the cuddle, Manos started to giggle. Mrs. Sofia watched as the expression on Anna's face turned from worry to relief and from sorrow to joy. She still thought she would miss her but felt ready to let her go. With Olga running Pallada, she could stay with the children in their house to take care of them and still help around the guesthouse when she could. If the business continued to flourish, they could still use additional staff for busy periods, even for a day or a few hours at a time, like they had often done in the past.

In her heart, Mrs. Sofia let Anna go without resentment. She wasn't abandoning these children. After all, they weren't her own to abandon. And although she didn't understand, she trusted her friend had her reasons to go. And if her reasons as she said, were an obligation to her loved ones, then by all means, she had no right to stop her.

***

Anna left Pallada and walked to the house with haste. She was holding Manos in her arms and was also carrying one of the two bags Mr. Giorgis had given her earlier. Mrs. Sofia had transferred most of the fruit of her equal share into that bag saying she only needed very little for herself.

Anna had put in the same bag, the oblong package that her friend had given her. She couldn't wait to open it. As soon as she got through the front door, she took Manos to Ksenia's bedroom and put him back in his pen. She kissed his fragrant hair and hurried to the kitchen.

Her casserole meal for lunch was ready in the pan since morning. In half an hour, she'd have to leave to pick Ksenia up from school. She put the plastic bag on the kitchen table and took the paper box out. It was sealed with duct tape. Using a knife to open it, she lifted the lid slowly, just as you would open a door to a room where someone is sleeping.

She looked inside to find the wands just as her husband had mentioned. When she lifted them with reverence together out of the box, they looked wondrous indeed. She held them up in the faint sunlight that came through the window and marveled at the iridescent contents that floated in the water inside them.

Anna didn't waste any time. Two minutes later, she was outside the cave. Efimios had written that thanks to Poseidon, they didn't need to worry about Athena any more, so she entered the hateful place without fear. The familiar interior brought back the raw, devastating memories.

Inevitably, they filled her with an overwhelming feeling of unease.

She hurried to the altar, eager to carry out the instructions she'd been trusted with and then leave as soon as possible. She yanked the three candleholders with their crystal candles out of the carved recesses, dropping them carelessly to the ground. She didn't care if they were made of solid gold. If Efimios hadn't asked her to remove them, she would never have opted to take them with her, but she knew she had to. She didn't have to treat them with respect though.

She had already hidden one wand among her things back home and now had brought the other one with her. Solemnly, she placed it on one of the three carved recesses, choosing one at random. The wand fit perfectly there, and she watched it for a few moments, mesmerized at the sight of its tiny contents that began to sink softly to the bottom until they fully settled.

Satisfied with the result, she picked up the candleholders and paced out of the cave. Once out in the fresh air, she finally relaxed and smiled to herself. She removed the boulder and slammed the door shut, happy to oblige Poseidon for that particular task.

The loud metallic noise echoed in the air. From the nearby cypress trees, two wild pigeons took to the sky startled, seeking refuge in the pines that stood high above, on the side of the Acropolis hill.

Chapter 26
Present Day

Anna finished the storytelling by turning to her son and giving him a wide, hopeful smile.

Phevos gazed back at her speechless. He had hardly made a sound for the past hour or so, as he listened to his mother speak.

She had been shuddering and sobbing in his arms, as she relayed the story of her separation from her loved ones. Phevos opened his arms to hug her with compassion, and his eyes welled up with tears at the thought of what she had been through, all alone.

Anna held him a moment longer and kissed the top of his head.

"I'm so sorry you had to go through all this pain, Mother," he whispered.

"Well, my son, that was then and this is now," she replied, squeezing his hand on her lap. "Besides, I'm not the only one who's suffered; we all have. And we all still do."

"But we can put an end to it, Mother. We can bring Father, Kimon and Eleni back to us."

"Yes, Phevos. Hopefully Poseidon will make amends for us all. Every day, I pray that he'll also allow Kimon and Elleni to reunite with their children."

"You said that Father mentioned we no longer need to worry about Athena. How's that, do you think?"

Anna shook her head. "I don't know, Son."

"You know, I've been wondering why she's not trying to get in our way. If she knew what's going on, she'd be furious, wouldn't she?"

"I'm sure she would be! But maybe Poseidon has managed to keep it all secret from her. Who knows? In any case, don't worry. I'm sure we'll find out in the end why she's no longer a threat to us!"

"Can I ask you something about the cave? Did Father make that door?"

"Yes! I was there when he made it. In the old days, when the land became privatized, and your dad helped Kimon's grandfather to fence it, the opening of the cave was still naturally hidden behind bushes and rocks. Yet, at the sight of the necklace, they all yielded for your father to pass."

"Father had mentioned that to me, about the rocks and the bushes I mean. He didn't mention Kimon's grandfather of course."

"No, I guess he wouldn't have. Anyway, once your father told me, and also Kimon and Eleni, about the cave and Athena, he had no reason to hide it from us any more, so he decided to make a proper door. He used the crescent on the back of the necklace to come up with a secret way to open the door, as you obviously know."

"Yes, it was quite exciting when that worked out!" Phevos chuckled as he recalled the day he had entered the cave with Ksenia.

Anna gave a slow, easy smile. "Your father is very inventive as you know."

"Yes, he truly is. And you had to bury the cave in the end..."

"Yes, that's how Poseidon wanted it. But in order to do that, I had to tell Mrs. Sofia so many lies... I still feel guilty about that." She frowned and shook her head.

"But you had to, Mother. Don't feel bad."

Anna gave a little wave and smiled again. "Anyway, tell me all about the signs that led you to the cave. How did you discover it? And you must tell me more about Mrs. Sofia. How's she doing these days?" Anna gazed at Phevos, the excitement coloring her face as she waited for the answers.

And so, Phevos took his turn to fill her in on his part of the story and also, on the news of the neighborhood in Plaka that she had missed so much.

***

An hour later, mother and son joined the others downstairs. Anna took Phevos to the kitchen where she introduced him to Mr. Fanis the cook. Ksenia and Daphne were helping Mrs. Gregoria in the sitting areas now, arranging flowers in vases and placing miniature oil lamps on the tables for the evening.

Manos had spent the past two hours helping in the kitchen with the others and now he was taking a break outside, feeding the fish again with some stale bread, courtesy of Mr. Fanis.

By the evening, they had all contributed to the preparation of the food. They chopped and grated a great number of various vegetables, stirred sauces and stews, cut potatoes for roasts, decanted wine from barrels into demijohns and jugs. They were all going to attend the opening that evening, delaying their return to Athens till the next morning.

Of course, they made sure to phone Mrs. Sofia in order to announce to her the big news. She knew they were going to Anavisos and Ksenia told her the truth only in part: that they had run into Anna and recognized her. Mrs. Sofia was thrilled to hear that and to have news from her old friend after so long. Ksenia even put her on the phone and they had a little chat. Anna promised her to visit soon and by the time she hung up, her eyes had pooled with tears of joy and nostalgia. Phevos made her promise to visit in the coming week, and his mother accepted to do so on Tuesday.

When the big night finally came, they all had a lovely time, although they found it quite tiring too. Lots of people came, and it was a great success. Anna was beaming at everyone, the perfect hostess, the happiest she had ever been.

Around three a.m., they shut the restaurant and slept on the terrace floor upstairs, seeing that there was not enough room indoors for everyone. Anna slept outside too, despite not having to, as she felt unwilling to part with the others overnight. It was cool and pleasant up there with the murmur of the sea and a light breeze that blew from the mountains.

They managed to sleep for a couple of hours only as they had to rise early in order to take the first bus into Athens. They had to, seeing that Daphne and Ksenia had to go to Pallada, and Phevos had to get to work too. Luckily, they managed to be only slightly late.

When Mr. Giorgis saw Phevos's radiant face that Monday morning, he knew at once that something was different. In the end, he was so intrigued that he had to ask him. Of course, Phevos didn't tell him he had reunited with his mother. Yet, when he mentioned they had run into Anna in Anavisos and that she was coming to visit the following day, Mr. Giorgis was agog with the news.

It was a rare sight indeed for Phevos, to witness him laughing and crying at the same time. The stories he told him that same morning about Anna during her last days in the neighborhood, were only a validation of what his impression of his mother had been so far. It seemed that the people there remembered her as a tower of strength. She had been an inspiration and an example to all of them and they couldn't wait to embrace her, welcoming her back into their lives.

***

Anna stepped out of the taxi and lingered outside the front gate. She cast a glance at the familiar surroundings, looking to find any differences to how she remembered the street and found very little. She was pleased about that. It's comforting, as you grow older to find that a place is still as you remembered it. She opened the gate and raised her eyes to the top balcony, willing herself to stay strong. She knew this was a day for joy and yet, she couldn't help fighting back tears.

With a deep breath, she composed herself and walked up to the front door, swallowing hard to dissolve a sudden lump in her throat. This house carried so many memories! She rang the doorbell and immediately heard commotion on the other side of the door. It opened quickly and the shrieks of excitement from the youngsters before her overwhelmed her. Her precious son came out first to hug her and then the others followed suit.

Her beautiful daughter Daphne, her darling Ksenia, and little Manos of course. She knew she'd have to stop herself from calling him 'little' though, but it was hard when she still remembered him playing in his pen as if it were only yesterday.

As soon as she stepped into the tiny hallway, she couldn't help raising her eyes to the top of the staircase. Ever since the taxi stopped outside, the old memories had started to sneak out of all sorts of dark, long-forgotten recesses and flood her mind anew. She tried to focus on her happiness now, but the banister kept calling to her like an old friend. She turned away from it, trying to ignore it. Her expression revealed how hard she had been trying to fight back the tears. Ksenia approached her to give her an encouraging cuddle.

They went to the sitting room, and everyone sat around her, their faces bright and expectant. They all looked like pupils around a teacher on a field day. After a few minutes, Ksenia and Daphne excused themselves to return a while later with coffee, tea, and biscuits.

Later on, unable to control herself any longer, Anna asked if she could see the house. Phevos guessed she needed her privacy for that and beckoned to Ksenia to do this with her alone. Ksenia led her out of the sitting room and up the staircase first. They returned downstairs several minutes later, moving toward the bedrooms. Anna was still emotional when they returned. "I'm sorry... but this proved harder than I had expected," she whispered, managing a faint smile.

Phevos put a protective arm around her shoulders. "No need to apologize, Mother."

"Come now, Mother," piped up Daphne then, her cheeks tainted pink with her excitement. "Let's finish our coffee, and then I'll take you to Pallada. Mrs. Sofia is bursting at the seams to see you!"

Chapter 27

Anna couldn't believe she was in Pallada in Mrs. Sofia's room again. It hadn't changed at all through the years. After escorting her there to meet her old friend, Daphne had gone upstairs to resume her duties, leaving the two women alone to reminisce about the past. Mrs. Sofia sat with Anna around the little table having served homemade cake for them both.

"My dear Anna, long time no speak!" Mrs. Sofia gave a sweet smile, her face alight with joy.

"Ah, Mrs. Sofia! It's been eleven years," replied Anna shaking her head, still amazed at the thought. The last time she had sat around this table with her, it had been a difficult time. The conversation they had that day had remained unforgettable to her. Their faces were full of sorrow and worry back then. But now, there was only happiness.

"Eleven years! Really? You haven't changed a bit you know, *kyra mou*!" The old lady reached out across the table to pat her friend's hand.

"And you Mrs. Sofia, you look great! Same as always." Anna thought she had aged visibly, but her eyes had the same tenderness, her smile the same sweetness.

"Bah! I'm eighty now you know." Mrs. Sofia laughed and gave a little wave, but it was evident from the sparkle in her eyes that she appreciated the compliment.

"You know Mrs. Sofia, I still feel guilty about the past."

"Whatever for, *psyche mou*?"

"You know! For letting you down back then. For leaving you alone to raise Eleni's children."

"What are you talking about? You never had to stay. The children were not your responsibility. You had to go for your own reasons!"

"I just wish I had a choice. I would have stayed if I could."

"Of course Anna, I know that! And you had your own loss to deal with…. you did what you thought was best for you at the time. Don't feel guilty!"

"Thank you, although I can't help it. I abandoned you all without even checking up on you by phone. I drifted away from you, and we lost touch so soon."

"What did I just tell you about guilt? Let go Anna! Just look at us! Aren't we happy? Didn't we come out of this alive and well?"

"I guess," Anna nodded, startled.

"Well then! If our choices have led us to this moment in time where we're sitting happily at this table, then why torture yourself, *agape mou*?"

"You amaze me, Mrs. Sofia! Of course, you're so right… Oh, how I've missed you!" She gave a chuckle and felt her heart lift somewhat. The guilt that tormented her, involved also the lies she had told her about the cave. What's more, she wished she could tell her she had finally found again her precious son. Perhaps when everyone had returned, they could all sit her down and tell her, explain to her why they had to protect her from the truth that might shock her to a possibly frightening effect. They all still worried about her weak heart and didn't dare imagine how she would take the news that Athena and Poseidon are real entities.

Mrs. Sofia chuckled. "There you go, you finally saw sense! I did just fine when you left and besides, I wasn't alone. I had Olga in Pallada, remember?"

"Yes of course! How is Olga? Is she still around?"

"She's doing okay! We speak on the phone from time to time. This girl has proven to us all that you can't escape your destiny!" She grinned from ear to ear.

Anna knitted her brows. "What do you mean? What's happened to her?" If Mrs. Sofia weren't smiling like that, she would be very worried.

The old woman gave a little laugh. "She got married. That's what's happened to her!"

"Oh, that's great! But why is it funny?"

"Well, do you remember for how many years her mother had been begging her to go back to Sifnos?"

"Forever I think. But Olga was always cringing at the thought!"

"That's right! She loved her homeland but loved Athens too. But once she met that man from Sifnos, all the hounds of hell couldn't keep her from leaving the city!"

"You're joking!" said Anna, her eyes growing huge.

"Would you believe it? She met him right here, in Pallada! He had come to attend an exhibition in order to find new suppliers. He has a large souvenir shop back on the island you see. It's in Kamares, her hometown! They fell so madly in love that within six months she was back in Sifnos getting married!"

"That's amazing! How strange to fall in love here with a man from her hometown! But how come she didn't know him already? Isn't Kamares a small community?"

"It is! But he's not from Sifnos. He was born and raised on the island of Folegandros."

"How did he wind up in Sifnos then?"

"Well apparently, there's a shortage of single women on the island and so, he went to Sifnos that's close by, hoping to meet someone and settle down."

"Except in the end, he had to get all the way to Athens to fetch his Sifnos bride!" Anna exploded with laughter and her friend joined her.

"That's why I said you can't escape your destiny," commented Mrs. Sofia when she managed to catch her breath.

"Well, I'm not sure if I agree with that," replied Anna, her face turning serious again. "People make their own destiny, Mrs. Sofia! We always have a choice... that's what I think."

"What about the difficulties of life, Anna? What about the grief? What choice do we have then?"

"Although we can't avoid them, even then we can still choose how to react to them... this is the only thing that separates the strong from the weak, don't you think?"

"Maybe it is so, *psyche mou*... but thankfully, I don't have to worry about the storms of life any more. Life seems to be more behind me than ahead of me these days. I've grown too old to even worry about tomorrow," answered the old lady, avoiding her friend's eyes.

"What's wrong, Mrs Sofia? Why do you talk like that?" asked Anna, disquieted by her answer.

"It's nothing really... Just the mumblings of an old woman! Anyway..." She waved dismissively then, and tried to look amused. She never spoke aloud about the thoughts that kept coming back in her head, more and more often these days. "So, that's the story with our Olga! Aren't happy endings great?" she added to change the subject.

"I bet her mother is happy these days!"

"Would you blame her? Her only child had been away for so long."

"It's hard for parents when their children are far away..."

"Oh, I know that only too well," answered Mrs. Sofia, nodding in agreement.

"Of course! How's your daughter in England?"

"She's fine, thank you. Haven't seen her in about fifteen years mind you! But she's well and happy and for a mother that's enough. Well, at least I have my son close by."

"Does he live in Athens?"

"He lives everywhere! He is an engineer for the Merchant Navy, but he visits me often. I'm expecting him again today. He'll be here in the late afternoon. You should come back then and meet him!"

"Oh, I'm afraid I'll have left by then. But not to worry, I'm sure I'll meet him another time soon. I'll be visiting often from now on, I promise."

"I hope you will, *agape mou*..."

"Mrs. Sofia, isn't it strange how I've known you for so long and yet, I've never met either of your children?" Anna seemed incredulous at the sudden realization.

"Ah! You couldn't have possibly met my daughter, that's for sure! She met her husband in Corfu where he holidayed one year. They've lived in England ever since. That's over twenty years ago. As for my boy, he lived in Corfu most of his life. I had to send both my children there when they were still little as you know."

"Couldn't you have kept them with you in Athens?"

"I wish I could have, but we had no choice then. Both my late husband and I worked all day for long hours at the time. My mother had to leave Corfu and stay with us in Athens in order to mind them. But she missed the island terribly. She had the farm there and longed to return. So in the end, we decided she should take the children with her there. What were we to do? If she hadn't gone back, the farm would have deteriorated and wind up derelict, and then all my parents' hard work would have been wasted. If we had kept the children here, I would have had to stop working but then, we wouldn't have been able to make ends meet.

This is why they had to go to Corfu with their grandmother. And they were happy there among the chickens, the sheep, the goats and the pigs! They had plenty of food and lots of love from my mother. We visited them as often as we could and sent them money regularly. I'm grateful that my children have had such a blissful upbringing even if I missed them over here. God rest my mother's soul for what she did for them! She wasn't young at the time either."

"You chose well Mrs. Sofia. And you know? Perhaps it was your mother's sacrifice back then that made you who you are."

"What do you mean, Anna?"

"Well, when the time came to take on someone else's children under your wing, you didn't hesitate either!"

"Oh yes! Ksenia and Manos! My darlings... it all worked out so well too. I'm truly grateful!"

"Were there no big problems along the way at all?"

"Not really! It all worked out just fine with God's help. Olga stayed with us and has been a wonderful help for many years. By the time she left, Ksenia was a teenager and already very sensible for her age. I was able to trust her on her own at home with Manos if I had to work in Pallada. Business has been good all through, and I was able to hire temporary staff anytime I needed it."

"It's such a relief to hear that!" Anna felt the guilt subside in her heart, the sting easing, as she gazed back at the elderly woman's blissful face. A strange light had ignited in her eyes as she spoke of Ksenia and Manos, the same one as when she had spoken of her own children earlier. Anna realized then that far from being a problem to Mrs. Sofia, raising Eleni's children had been a breath of life to her. It had been an opportunity to avoid loneliness, a chance to fill her heart with even more love and contentment. Somehow, these gifts from life had kept her strong and agile, despite her years.

"It's truly a remarkable thing, what you've done for these children."

"I haven't done anything different to what any other decent person would have done. I knew their parents, I owed it to them."

"Mrs. Sofia, it's been wonderful to sit and talk with you again," said Anna after a small pause. With a sweet smile, she stood up.

"Are you off already?"

Anna pointed to the clock on the wall. "Well, it's getting late. The children expect me back home for lunch. They asked me to take you along, you know. Will you join us?"

"Oh! Thank you Anna but I can't! Please thank the children for me, but I'm too busy to stop for lunch today. I had a bite earlier and—"

"Oh Mrs. Sofia, please come!"

"I'm sorry, *kyra mou*, I really can't! You know how it is. My Aris is coming this afternoon, and I haven't had time to prepare everything yet. There was a lot to do in Pallada this morning. I need to carry on with the dinner preparations, you understand."

"Oh come on, there's plenty of time to prepare for dinner!"

"Not really. His favorite meal is quite fussy to make! Not that I mind, it just takes time. And besides, I haven't even shopped yet for the dessert I'm making!"

"Ah Mrs. Sofia, as always you're bending backward to please your guests, aren't you?" observed Anna. She had sampled her cooking a few times and knew how much she loved treating dinner guests with delicacies. "Aren't you tiring yourself a bit too much though, if I may say so?"

"*Kyra mou*, if I don't treat my own child, then whom am I going to treat?" she answered with a dismissive wave. Preparing anything other than a hearty meal for her son's homecoming was out of the question.

"All right, I won't insist any more. I'll drop in to say goodbye before going back home, okay?" said Anna and turned to go.

Mrs. Sofia nodded and opened the door for her. "You do that! Hopefully, Aris will come a bit sooner and then you can meet him. You'll see what a fine lad I've got! And he's so tall! All the way up there, bless him!" she said with a beaming smile, extending her arm with exaggeration as high as she could over her snow-white hair.

"I'm sure he is! I also hope to meet him soon," said Anna, as Mrs. Sofia followed her outside her door. "It was so great to see you again. I'd missed you so much!" Anna flung her arms open wide and gave her old friend a cuddle.

"I'd missed you too, *psyche mou*... And I'm sorry too we drifted apart. Life does that to people. But it only takes to meet again to realize how much you've missed an old friend..." Her eyes welled up.

Anna gave her a gentle pat on the back. "Isn't it strange how life works? You missed your own children growing up, and then you raised someone else's... you're an angel, Mrs. Sofia!" Anna squeezed her in her arms one more time before turning to go.

Mrs. Sofia smiled as she watched Anna walk away. The old woman thought that indeed it was strange she had raised someone else's children instead of her own. But then, it dawned on her that all children are the same in God's eyes. If we were to see them as God does, they would all have the same little hands that seek to touch you, the same eyes that thirst for your attention, the same lips that say 'I love you'.

Slowly, she closed her door again and returned to her little kitchen. She had preparations to do and was running late.

Chapter 28

Lunch was a success. Ksenia had cooked roast lamb and lasagna and had received repetitive congratulations from everyone as they ate, for her mastery in the kitchen.

Anna had looked radiant sitting next to her son. Her expression had changed only for a moment or two when she spared a thought for their loved ones, who were absent. She had regained her cheerfulness soon enough though, aided by the beaming faces all around the table.

When Ksenia served coffee and cake in the sitting room, Anna surprised them by taking an old photo album out of her shoulder bag. They all huddled around her immediately, thirsty for a glimpse of the blissful past when their loved ones were still with them. She started to leaf through the pages, and the youngsters listened to the stories behind the pictures, gasping and laughing.

Most of them had been taken in the early years of her courtship with Efimios and the beginning of their friendship with Kimon and Eleni. Others were from their later years of married life and parenthood. Everyone gasped when Anna turned a page and revealed the identity of a small boy with curly, blond hair. No one could believe this was Phevos, least of all him. He had never seen a picture of himself as a child before and neither had the others.

Ksenia approached to study the picture closely and couldn't believe that the boy with the ruddy cheeks was the man she loved. He was photographed playing a board game with a little girl whom she easily identified as herself. They were sitting on the carpet in Manos's bedroom, which at the time had been her own room. Ksenia marveled at the picture. It looked like such an everyday scene in a child's life. They knew now that Athena had caused Phevos to forget his earlier life here. But how could *she* have forgotten him? She didn't understand but could only guess that Athena was behind this too.

Phevos placed an arm around her, and she turned to face him, their mirthful eyes locking together. It felt wonderful to have shared a glimpse of their past together as children despite the fact that they both had no recollection of it. Now, they had solid proof they had never been strangers after all. The night that they met at the orchard, they were actually reuniting instead of meeting for the first time. That realization gave them a strong sense of destiny that made them feel powerful inside and full of love for each other, more than ever before.

Anna moved on, turning the pages and telling stories of the past. Many pictures had been taken outdoors, mostly on the seashore. As she spoke, she came to the realization that she, her husband and their friends, had always been drawn to the sea. She wondered then if they had always known instinctively that it would play an integral part in their lives one day. Perhaps, all they did every time they visited the seashore in the past was pay homage to Poseidon for what was to come.

***

Daphne had left the house straight after lunch as time was pressing. She needed to return to Pallada at once. Mrs. Sofia had been busy during her absence preparing the special dinner for her son's arrival. They were both still running behind with their duties for the day.

In the last two hours, Daphne had done all the remaining chores upstairs, and Mrs. Sofia was just finishing up the last room after a departure. Daphne was now dusting the bookshelf at reception. It had been done again recently and didn't need any attention, but she had tried sitting behind reception and the idleness had turned her into a bag of nerves.

Aris was due to arrive any minute now, and she felt she had to keep occupied otherwise she'd go nuts with the anticipation. She sprayed some more detergent on the cloth and kept dusting the same shelves over and over, singing a tune she had heard on the radio earlier. She would have carried on forever if it weren't for Mrs. Sofia's hurried footsteps that made her turn around. She was coming down the staircase with a bunch of sheets in her hands and she looked vexed.

"It's a good thing those girls left today! I was at the end of my tether, I tell you. So glad I won't have to clean after them again!" With a heavy sigh, Mrs. Sofia threw the last batch of dirty linen on top of the pile in the corridor.

"Was it that bad?" Daphne hurried to leave the dust cloth and the spray bottle behind the desk. "You rest Mrs. Sofia. I'll take these for you," she said picking up half the linen from the pile to take them away.

Mrs. Sofia gave an exasperated sigh as she watched Daphne enter the laundry room. "Why would they be any different on their last day, huh?"

"Oh, come now Mrs. Sofia! I did their room a few times too, it wasn't so dirty," answered Daphne when she came back to get the rest of the sheets.

"I'm not talking about dirt. There's nothing my broom and detergents can't fix, don't you worry," she replied as Daphne disappeared into the laundry room again. "But there's something about having to work in an untidy room that really gets me!"

"Oh, is that it? I'd have thought you'd be immune to untidiness by now after all these years. They weren't the first ones who spread their belongings all over the place." Daphne had just returned to reception to find the old lady still standing on the same spot, looking all hot and bothered. "Come on, you must be accustomed to it by now!"

"You can't get accustomed to untidiness, *psyche mou*! It either bothers you or it does not. And these girls were by far the worst I've ever seen. They didn't even leave both their shoes in the same place, for goodness sake! I'd find one sandal in the room and one in the bathroom. I mean, who does that? They left their underwear anywhere you can imagine! Coins under the bed, wet towels on the floor... whatever they dropped, they just left it there! And that includes empty cans of lager and souvlaki wrappers!"

Daphne returned to her a gaze full of sympathy. "Well Mrs. Sofia, you don't have to worry about them any more, they've gone now."

"Yes, thank goodness for that! Dear me, just imagine the state of their houses! *O popo, Agie mou Spyridona!*" Mrs. Sofia crossed herself and shuddered.

Daphne found this hilarious and burst out laughing.

Still wincing at the thought, Mrs. Sofia walked to the sofa and sat down with a heavy sigh. She had been standing for hours and her back was playing up. When the sound of Daphne's laughter stopped abruptly, she turned to face her, puzzled.

The girl's face was all lit up now but not with merriment. It had the glow of the sky at dawn, and she was smiling broadly, facing the entrance.

Mrs. Sofia darted her eyes there and suddenly there was no back pain any more, no tiredness and not a hint of bother for little things like messy rooms. Glowing, she sprang up and strode all the way to her son's open arms.

"My boy, *levendi mou!*" she cried out when he embraced her. He bent his head to kiss her as his body followed softly the swaying motion of her cradling hug.

Daphne stood close by, the way one stands near an open fire to warm up on a cold day. Scenes like these continued to remind her of her own mother. Their joy radiated toward her, covering her too like a large, comforting blanket.

When his mother finally let him go, Aris walked up to the young girl with a beaming smile on his face. "Hello, Daphne!"

"Hello Aris, welcome back!" She gave him a sweet little smile and offered her hand for the customary handshake. Except this time, as well as holding her hand, Aris also leant in closer to kiss her on both cheeks. Daphne was startled and bowed her head when she felt herself blush.

"So, how are you?" he asked, pretending he hadn't noticed her reaction.

"Great! And you?" Daphne looked up again and flashed him an easy smile. She didn't care for the burning sensation on her cheeks any more. She felt thirsty for the look in his eyes more than she felt embarrassed.

Mrs. Sofia was standing beside them and noticed they still held each other's hand after their brief handshake. She guessed they hadn't even noticed as they seemed to be so busy gazing into each other's eyes. He was now asking her after everyone's health. Mrs. Sofia smiled to herself, wondering if they had even realized they were doing this. Perhaps they did and were just unwilling to let go.

She brought a hand over her mouth and smirked, then turned to go and give them some privacy. As she was about to disappear down the corridor, she saw a classy-looking woman in her forties coming down the staircase with a little boy in tow. They had arrived to Pallada earlier that morning.

Both of them were dressed rather formally. The woman wore a long, blue dress with a sunhat in the same color, high heels, and a long string of pearls around her neck. The boy wore a white shirt, blue cotton trousers and a baseball hat that made him look quite cheeky. Mrs. Sofia approached and met them at the bottom of the stairs. She never missed a chance to say hello and strike up a conversation with a stranger. She believed that strangers are like gifts. They come with a mystery but once revealed, some of them can prove to be delightful, useful, and even miraculous. A stranger has the potential to be a brand new friend, a life companion or a major transformer of our lives.

"Oh, hello again!" said Mrs. Sofia when they came down the last step. "Hello little one!" she added, pinching the boy's cheek when they both greeted her back.

He was very cute, no more than six or seven years old. She took a bowl of candy from the coffee table by the sofa and offered them one. The lady declined politely, but the boy took one, smiling and saying 'thank you'. He removed the wrapper and popped the candy into his mouth.

Mrs. Sofia marveled at his long eyelashes, as she watched him blink and nod appreciatively at the velvety feel of the buttermilk candy against his tongue. She was about to speak and compliment him for his brilliant blue eyes, when she gasped instead. The boy had just scrunched up the wrapper between his little fingers and walked to the coffee table to leave it in the ashtray.

"Oh, my goodness! What a good boy you are!" she exclaimed with delight. "Madam, congratulations! I can't believe a boy so small would do something like that. What manners, I'm impressed, I must say!"

The lady arched her brows with astonishment. "Thank you but... I don't think he did anything out of the ordinary."

Mrs Sofia shook her head. "Oh, I disagree! Not every parent is like you, Madam. They let them run wild, I'll have you know. Some of these kids are like monkeys! Others are like garbage-producing machines; they leave a trail behind them wherever they go. Believe me, I've seen a lot. Good for you for raising your boy like this!"

The lady accepted the compliment gracefully. She introduced herself and offered her hand to Mrs. Sofia, who was only too happy to return the courtesy to her. She turned around to introduce her son and Daphne, only to find them still engaged in conversation. She noticed they weren't holding hands any more, but the body language was still loud enough to tell her she hadn't been proven wrong yet. They stopped talking to each other in order to nod at the lady guest as Mrs. Sofia recited their names, and then lost themselves in each other's eyes again.

"And what is your name my little darling?" Mrs. Sofia asked the boy patting his baseball hat with her wrinkled hand.

The boy gave a sweet smile. He was beaming with pride still after hearing her compliments. "Spyros."

"Spyros? Your christian name is Spyridon? *Oh, psyche mou*, what a beautiful name you have!" she replied, enthusiastic to hear that the boy was named after her protector saint. It was a name that had followed her all her life, like every other Corfiot.

Everyone on the island has a bunch of family members called Spyridon or the female equivalent, Spyridoula. As baby names in Greece are carried from grandparents to grandchildren, they're always reminiscent of precious members of one's family, some of them—as in the case of Mrs. Sofia—no longer living. In Athens, the name is not as common, so it was a special treat for her to hear it, and to be able to savor its sound again, so far away from home.

She didn't let the chance go wasted. She loved to talk about her favorite saint, and when she offered the boy information about him, both he and his mother stood eagerly to listen. Soon, she was telling them about the two miracles he's mostly revered for on the island: the one where he saved the city from the plague, and the other where he turned his cane into a snake. He had worked these miracles when he was alive, but she told them he still appeared through apparitions to cripples and other patients who prayed to him, curing them beyond logical explanation. She looked into their eyes, saw wonder, and so she carried on, telling them this time about the miracles she had witnessed herself in the town of Corfu.

She relayed the story of the worker who had lost his balance while on the steeple of Spyridon's church. He fell down to the ground and stood again, unharmed. Then, she recounted the story of that terrible night during the bombarding of the city by enemy planes in the 40's. She and lots of other people had rushed to Spyridon's church for refuge, praying to him to save their lives, their eyes pinned to the ceiling, brimming over with terror. For one terrible moment, they all saw the roof of the church open up. They saw the dark sky and lights from the explosions and then miraculously, the roof closed in again within split seconds. Shocked, they asked each other and to their amazement, they had all seen the same thing.

The little boy's mouth was now gaping open in wonder, and his mother seemed equally fascinated, her eyes huge and glazed over. Mrs. Sofia had a melodic voice and the unique talent of storytelling. It charmed her listeners and her two new guests couldn't have been an exception.

A few paces away, Daphne and Aris were still talking, standing by the reception desk.

"Oh, I almost forgot! I have a present for you," he said bending over to open his backpack. It rested on the floor by his feet. He took out a duty-free shopping bag and offered it to her.

"But why? It's not my birthday," answered Daphne, perplexed but quite enthused.

"I know. But I saw it in the shops in a few ports and I couldn't resist. It reminded me of you," he said, his voice trailing off.

"Thank you," she said, taking the bag. There was a perfume bottle in it. She took it out and stood looking at it for a few moments, her eyes twinkling. "I've never had perfume before."

Her smile, albeit awkward, gave Aris the encouragement to take it from her hands and help her. She seemed rather flustered. He opened the box and sprayed some perfume on her wrists. A couple of squirts were enough for them to be enveloped in a delicate fusion of flower and herbal scents. Aris put the bottle back in its box, placing it in her hands again.

"Thank you Aris, this is beautiful!" she said. The sweet fragrance was exquisite. Her enthusiasm made her heart beat frantically. Beside herself with elation, she leant in and kissed him on the cheek. Her hands trembled somewhat as she held the box and he noticed. Smiling, he placed his hands over hers and gazed into her eyes. This was the moment he'd been waiting for, except now he felt as embarrassed as she was.

"It's nothing Daphne. As I said, it reminded me of you..." He faltered, despite his best intentions not to.

"What do you mean?" she asked tilting her head. For the first time, she noticed the picture on the box. "I don't have such long ears, do I?" She gave a giggle. The way he looked at her and held her hands made her feel buoyant. She felt so happy she could grow wings on her back, just like the model in the picture who had diaphanous wings, and her face sparkled with glitter.

"No silly," he replied with a titter. He bit his lower lip immediately, regretting what he had said, in case it had offended her. He was still very cautious around her, but she was smiling still and her face was glowing. She was waiting for him to explain, and he had planned this a million times as he thought of her night and day on board ship. He couldn't bear any longer her not knowing how he saw her in his mind. "That's a fairy, you see? This is how I see you. Incredibly beautiful, I mean!" He chewed his lip, and studied her face for warning signs, surprised at how badly he was doing.

He could remember other women in his past with whom he was far more eloquent than that. But then, his chest was not burning with this kind of love at the time. He wanted to tell her more but he faltered. There was a lump in his throat, and as he gazed into her eyes still, he felt lost for words despite the fact that he had a lot to say.

For example, how he had been running across the advertising posters of this perfume on every port he had visited, and how he had associated her in his head with the fairy on the box. Many times, as he stared out to sea on the deck, he had got frustrated when he couldn't remember her face, and his mind could only produce the image from the poster instead. In the end, he had felt he should get her the perfume as a present. He wished now that he could confess the tricks his mind had been playing on him but he couldn't. All he could do is hold her hands and hope she wouldn't spread her wings and go.

As if guessing his insecurities, Daphne smiled at him then. She wasn't going anywhere. Instead, she slipped one hand out of the cradle of his own two hands and caressed his fingers tenderly.

Chapter 29

The next few weeks had passed in the blink of an eye. It was now early August. Since reuniting with Anna, every Saturday afternoon all four would take the bus and head back to Anavisos. There, mother and son tried to catch up on lost time. Anna spoke to Phevos extensively about his childhood. Sometimes, they chatted for hours on her veranda looking out to sea or they took long strolls along the beach.

Ksenia often volunteered to take Anna's place in the kitchen assisting Mr. Fanis so that she could have this quality time with her son. Manos loved to be in the kitchen too, learning the secrets of food preparation from Mr. Fanis. They had formed a friendship since the day he placed a chef's hat on the boy's head after asking him to slice lemons for garnish.

Since that day, Manos had taken it upon himself to be his helper. By now, he knew off by heart all the secret ingredients for a delicious lamb roast and Mr. Fanis's famous tomato sauce. On Saturday nights, all four assisted in the restaurant and of course, they had their meals there too.

At night they'd sleep on the veranda floor with Anna amongst them, as she remained unwilling to retire to her bedroom and not share every possible moment with them all. That was their favorite time together, and they always took ages to fall asleep. They talked under the stars, joked and even sang till their eyelids got heavy and they had to say goodnight.

And as they fell asleep with the sigh of the sea for lullaby, they all felt blessed for the amazing changes in their lives. Each one of them had been blessed with so much since the day Phevos and Daphne came to Plaka. Anna had redeemed her son, Ksenia had found love and Manos had gained confidence in himself. Phevos had Ksenia now and also his mother back into his life. As for Daphne, she had found confidence in herself through her work but that was not all. The last few weeks had changed her life again in a major way.

On the day Aris gave her the perfume, that same evening he finally confessed his feelings to her. They had their first date that night with a meal on a taverna terrace. On their way home, as they walked along a quiet cobble-stoned lane, Aris pulled her gently to him and kissed her. When they walked into Pallada, their faces still glowed with the warmth of their hearts.

Everyone was thrilled to receive their news and especially Mrs. Sofia, who loved Daphne and couldn't imagine a better bride for her son. She knew her son too well and could see it was heading that way.

Daphne was walking on clouds these days just like Aris. The only difference was that among the clouds she walked on, there was still a dark one too, called Zoe. Despite Aris's love, she still couldn't help feeling uneasy when she thought of her.

That Saturday afternoon in early August, Aris was back in Pallada and now that Daphne was finally his girl, his daily routine was different. This time, he didn't have to miss her while having solitary strolls or meeting colleagues in the city or reading in his mother's room for hours. This time he followed her like a shadow all day around Pallada, helping her with her chores, eager for her to finish sooner so that they could go out afterwards.

He had just carried all the dirty linen downstairs to the laundry room and he had returned upstairs with a bucket. He put it over his head behind Daphne's back and startled her when she turned around to see the ludicrous sight. She laughed uproariously and he growled like a beast, chasing her up and down the corridor upstairs, bumping his knees against the odd chair and the walls as he couldn't really see where he was going.

Their laughter echoed everywhere, filling the air with vibrations of happiness. Mrs. Sofia heard the noise in her room and came out in a rush. She'd spent all morning in there. Aris had volunteered to do all her chores for the day with Daphne, as long as she made for lunch a meal he had really come to miss: *papoutsakia*, stuffed aubergines with mince and bechamel sauce. The elderly lady came out startled, holding a ladle in her hand.

She looked up and when she spotted them on the landing, she told them off for the racket while shaking the ladle in her hand. Deep down though, she thought it was the sweetest thing to find her son acting like a teenager. As she walked back to her room, she couldn't help chuckling to herself.

A couple of minutes later, Zoe entered Pallada accompanied by Ksenia. Zoe had phoned her friend earlier that day asking her to meet her for coffee in the afternoon because she had some pressing news. They had met in Syntagma Square after the end of Zoe's shift at the travel agency where she worked during the summer months.

Ksenia had been thrilled with Zoe's news, and the two girls had come to share it with all the others. By the time they stepped in, Aris had taken the bucket off his head and was now kissing Daphne at the top of the stairs.

Zoe was taken aback at the sight because Ksenia had purposely not told her anything about them. She knew Daphne was quite private about her life, and so she felt it was up to her to decide if she wanted to talk about Aris or not. Obviously, the kiss Zoe witnessed didn't leave Ksenia with much choice, and when Zoe threw her a puzzled look, all she could do is give her a nod of confirmation.

Then, looking up again, Zoe took a step sideways and stumbled rather clumsily over a little coffee table by the door. The noise startled the couple upstairs. They drew back from each other and turned around, looking rather embarrassed. Still, that didn't stop them from holding hands as they came down the stairs.

Aris greeted Zoe in a friendly manner as always, shaking hands with her and asking her for her news. Since the day they were introduced, they had met briefly a couple of times again, as Zoe often visited the guesthouse during the summer to see Ksenia. By then, they knew enough about each other to strike up a conversation for a while without awkward pauses.

Daphne still found it unbearable to watch them talk. She felt uneasy again although she noticed for the first time that day that Zoe seemed different. She had the same air of confidence about her, but her eyes seemed confused, dark somehow. Daphne thought that perhaps she'd had a bad day at work, but this notion was soon abandoned.

The pressing news that Zoe had already told Ksenia and had come to share with them all was anything but distressing. Apparently, her boss had offered her the chance to bring her friends along on a coach excursion. It was to take place the following day. Daphne was annoyed at first, as they had all planned to go to Anavisos again for the weekend. This time was special to her as she was taking Aris along to meet Anna. Being Phevos's mother, she had started to feel like a mother to her too. This was her chance to introduce to her the man she loved, and she didn't want to postpone it just because Zoe had decided to come along in the last minute with an alternative plan.

Daphne listened on with her anger brewing in silence, feeling her dislike for Zoe grow inside her. However, when she heard that the excursion was to Anavisos for a swim and then the temple of Poseidon for the famous sunset, her face lit up. This was exactly what they had been waiting for! Phevos had said they had to wait for a sign in order to visit the temple. That had to be it.

When Daphne turned to look at Ksenia, it was obvious on her face that she felt the same. Daphne tried to hide her enthusiasm but even for someone as contained as her, it was difficult not to shriek with joy. In the end she gave in, jumping up and down in Aris's embrace. Zoe had invited everyone else to join her too: Aris, Phevos and Manos, and even Anna. Zoe had heard a lot about her from Ksenia and she couldn't wait to meet her.

The unexpected offer from her boss had been possible thanks to a major cancellation from a large group of German tourists the day before. They had tried to sell more seats in the last minute to cover the lost revenue, but they had been unsuccessful. A great number of passengers had been booked, including the driver and the guide for the day. Zoe's boss then had the idea to offer two of his best salesgirls the opportunity to go along with their friends.

It had been an ingenious idea that would offer his staff the chance to sell this excursion in future, having the benefit of first-hand experience. Furthermore, it would be an incentive to keep striving to reach their sales targets. Zoe was one of the best in the office. She was sociable, confident and chatty and never lost a sale. So was her friend Maria, who had also been invited to come with her own little group.

When Zoe left a few minutes later, Ksenia rushed next door to the fruit store to tell Phevos the news. He was thrilled of course, and they hugged laughing and cheering beside themselves outside the shop.

Mr. Giorgis heard and flung outside to see what the excitement was all about, but all he found was Phevos and Ksenia cradling each other in silence. He hovered there for a while, gazing at the two young lovers that stood on the pavement. He felt envious then and tried to think back to the time when he had their youth and their zest, when young love burnt like fire in his heart, when every touch felt like electricity, and explosions of such excitement were still possible.

Noticing him then, Ksenia and Phevos turned to him and wondered why he stood so quiet all of a sudden, with his eyes gazing into space. Normally, he'd be teasing them and cracking jokes by now.

Phevos opened his mouth to ask him if he was all right, but then Mr. Giorgis shook his head of graying hair, still staring into space. With a melancholic smile on his face, he turned around and went back into his store.

Chapter 30

The coach had arrived on time at Syntagma Square to pick up the group. On its way to the south Attica coast, it had stopped again briefly to pick up more passengers from a couple of hotels. It had just reached Poseidon Avenue and was now cruising through medium traffic, heading east.

Many among the cars that followed the same route were laden on the back with beach umbrellas, bags and foldable chairs. The faces of their passengers were radiant with the anticipation of a full day out on the beach. The suburban beaches outside the window were already crowded despite it being early morning.

In the coach, the enthusiasm among the four was even greater. Yet, they felt guilty too for having to keep their secrets from Aris and Zoe. For them, this wasn't just a day out on the beach. This was the blessed day they had all been waiting for. It seemed to them the sun had risen just for them that morning, to make it all possible. Even the colors of the world around them seemed more vivid that day. They pulsated with energy. It felt like someone had removed a veil from before their eyes revealing to them a world of resplendent clarity.

Aris sat with Daphne, and behind them, sat Zoe and Manos. Across the gangway, Ksenia and Phevos sat together having behind them Zoe's colleague Maria with her eleven-year-old son, her husband and her sister.

Manos hadn't exchanged a single word yet with Maria's son, who sat across from him. It wasn't due to shyness though. He had no problem striking up conversation and making new friends these days. But he still had a soft spot for Zoe, and as she sat next to him, he had eyes only for her. He kept looking at her every now and then as she gazed out of the window, wishing he were a bit older so he could ask her out.

He had just spoken to her again, telling her how he couldn't wait to introduce her to Anna and Mr. Fanis. Zoe had smiled but had hardly said anything and Manos had thought that was strange. Zoe was a chatterbox but that day she just looked aloof. It was almost like she didn't want to be there. Being observant as always yet tactful, he turned to his magazine and thought no more of it. He trusted that by the time they got to Anavisos, she would be back to her normal, jovial self again.

Oblivious to Manos's frustration, Zoe gazed out of the window and into space. Every now and then, she glimpsed at Aris and Daphne before her and every time, the stab in her heart returned. She watched through the gap between the seats as they kissed, as they held hands, as she put her head on his shoulder and her hair fell in thick auburn curls on his back.

She watched as they turned to look at each other, their eyes electrified, oblivious to everything else in the world, least of all her. Every time she looked, Zoe's feelings of pain and guilt stirred inside her. She would then turn her gaze to the coast again, the way you come up for air after you've dived underwater. But even when she looked away for relief, in her mind, she still saw Aris's eyes full of love and adoration. It was such a wonderful sight, but it devastated her because he reserved that look for someone else, not her.

The previous day she had got to Pallada full of hope as she had heard from Ksenia he was there again. She wanted to ask him to come along today, hoping... hoping.... it didn't matter. Whatever she had hoped for, she couldn't even bear think about any more. What she had witnessed when she entered Pallada had shattered her hopes.

It had taken more than her usual reserve to hide her feelings. Of course, she'd had boyfriends in the past. Her parents were liberal enough to even encourage it, but she had never felt this way before. No one knew how she felt about Aris. Not even Ksenia. It is easy to talk about boys with your girlfriends when you still hold your heart in your own hands, intact and safe. But when you lose it to someone like that, you don't dare talk about it. You pretend it never happened or perhaps hope to finally confess it once your love has been requited; when you can feel somewhat safe again but clearly, that would never be the case with Aris.

The coach arrived in Anavisos around ten a.m. and parked on the side of the main road across from the aero-modelers' wasteland. Manos squealed with excitement when he saw where they had stopped. The sound startled the boy sitting across from him. With a start, he looked up from his electronic game that had kept him occupied in the last hour.

"Hey, would you like to see model airplanes fly?" asked Manos reaching out to touch the boy's arm.

The boy nodded eagerly, and Manos urged him to follow as the passengers started to alight. By the time they were all out on the roadside, Ksenia had talked to Maria, confirming that Manos had been to the wasteland many times before. Anna's restaurant was closeby, and the boys could join them there soon. Maria was happy to let her son go, and the boys went off, blabbering excitedly.

Manos had revisited the aero-modelers on every weekend since that first time. A couple of them were happy by then to let him take the controls for a while. That day, he managed to impress his new friend with his abilities.

After an hour or so, the boys returned to the restaurant to join the others. A few of the German tourists from the coach group had followed the Greeks there. The restaurant was busy. Some of its patrons were enjoying a drink on the balcony while others were on the beach nearby, swimming or sunbathing.

Manos grew excited showing his friend around and forgot to introduce Zoe to Anna and Mr. Fanis after all. Of course, Ksenia and Phevos had already done that for him. Daphne had also introduced Aris by then to the woman she could now call mother. The notion had felt unnatural to her at first but with every kiss and hug, Anna had soon become a maternal figure to her. Considering how much she still missed her own mother, she had welcomed this new blessing in her life with gratitude.

Following a long stay on the beach, everyone had returned to Anna's restaurant for lunch. After the intense heat, they relished the cool breeze on the balcony outside. It felt welcoming like a dive into river waters. Their sun-kissed faces glowed with happiness as they tinkled their glasses, enjoying fine barrel wine and delicious meals.

Anna stole some time from her serving duties to join them for a while. She sat between Daphne and Aris, patting his hand every now and then.

At the agreed departure time, Anna joined the group to board the coach. Mrs. Gregoria had arrived earlier on at the restaurant to relieve her so that she may enjoy the rest of the day with her children. Phevos had gone up to her apartment to fetch her wand, and it was now safely put away in the company of his own inside his backpack.

This time, when they boarded the coach, Phevos sat with his mother. Little did they know that as she held his hand, the wands in his bag were glowing now in unison. The time was drawing near, and their power had been amplified. As they all headed to Sounio in a pilgrimage of hope, Poseidon awaited them for the final part of his ingenious plan.

***

The temple stood proud on top of the hill despite its devastating demise over the centuries. The German tourists had gathered around the female guide like chicks around the mother hen. She was informing them now about the history of the temple, and they hung on her every word in reverent silence.

The small group of Greeks stood on another side of the temple, and Manos saw an opportunity to impress everyone with his newly acquired knowledge. The night before, he had read a lot on the Internet about the temple and was now eager to share a few interesting facts about it.

"This magnificent Doric temple was built circa 440 B.C. by the Athenians during Pericles's rule" he piped up, flinging an arm out to point at the impressive ruins with a theatrical gesture. Everyone listened with interest as he spoke of its destruction by the Persians and later on by slaves, who looted it during a revolt.

At the end of his presentation, he added the Athenians had also built in Sounio a temple dedicated to Athena. However, he commented with glee that it was situated at a lower level on the hill and that it was nowhere near as glorious as Poseidon's. The majority of Manos's audience received this last piece of information with appreciation but without grasping the secret meaning behind his words.

Of course, those among them in the know i.e. Phevos, Ksenia, Anna and Daphne responded with gaiety and cheer. They already knew about Athena's temple closeby but felt obliged to show him they had understood well what he was trying to say. This was clearly Poseidon's kingdom, not hers. It was their sanctuary; a place where Athena had never ruled over him, not even in antiquity. This was the perfect place for him to orchestrate his plan, being the ruler of these sacred grounds through the ages.

The air was getting cooler as the sun crept toward the horizon, all the more filling the sky with colors. The guide finished her presentation to receive an outburst of cheer and applause from the appreciative tourists. As they still had ample time till the sunset, she invited them to follow her to the nearby café for refreshments. When she passed by the Greek group she offered them to join her. Maria went along with her own party and Manos followed eagerly to get an ice cream, but the others lingered behind, drawn by the imposing temple and the idyllic sea view.

Anna, Phevos and Ksenia sat on some marble blocks by the temple while Zoe stood further away with Aris and

Daphne gazing out to the shimmering sea. Phevos called his sister over as they had started to wonder what they were to do next, and he wanted her input. So far, there had been no sign, and Phevos had grown restless.

Daphne was aware her brother needed her opinion too, yet she felt unwilling to leave Aris alone with Zoe. Phevos kept beckoning to her and of course she couldn't refuse him, so she excused herself reluctantly in the end and went to join them. Phevos proposed to go with his mother into the temple in case Poseidon were to appear before them in a vision just like he had with his father. There was no guard in sight, and he thought if they went then, no one would stop them.

Anna didn't oppose his suggestion but didn't feel restless like him either. She was equally happy to wait, having the faith that Poseidon wouldn't leave them guessing but rather, would make his move unprompted. She was certain he would come to them when he was ready. She voiced her opinion and for a while, they mulled over things.

All the while, Daphne watched in silence, feeling the unease grow inside her, pricking at her insides like needles. She hoped Phevos's anxiety would subside soon so that she could run back to Aris. He had walked on further and was now out of sight with Zoe. She couldn't see them behind the dense foliage in the distance. She watched as Phevos and the others discussed the matter some more, considering all possibilities while she remained silent, the irresistible urge to seek Aris screaming inside her head.

***

Aris had proposed to Zoe to walk a bit further together. He was thankful Daphne had left them for a while, as this was perhaps his only opportunity to speak in private to Zoe. Out of sight from the others, they stood together near the precipice, impressed by the beauty of the scenery unfolding before them. Like a live painting, the sky changed every second with brushstrokes of ingenious artistry. All they could hear was the soft break of the waves on the rocks underneath. Aris dared a few careful steps toward the edge of the precipice and looked down. It was a sheer drop.

"Aris, do you mind stepping away from there please? You're making me nervous," said Zoe.

"I'm sorry," he replied, following her a safe distance away. They both looked up when they heard squawking. A flock of seagulls passed low over their heads flying leisurely toward the sea. Enchanted by the serenity of the scene, they stood watching them disappear into the distance.

"Can I ask you something?" said Aris after a few moments.

"Of course," she stammered, taken aback. Ever since they arrived at the sight, she'd been having these mad thoughts that perhaps, there was still hope. He had been acting strangely. Of course, he had been very attentive and tender to Daphne as always, but he had looked somewhat preoccupied too. While Manos spoke about the temple earlier, she had noticed how he kept looking around nervously, as if scanning the place, expecting something. She had also caught him giving her some odd looks, while looking pensive and anxious. Could it be possible that he was interested in her after all? She turned to meet his gaze. He looked hesitant. "Is everything all right, Aris?" she asked breathlessly.

"Well, as you know, Daphne and I..." His voice trailed off, and instead of carrying on, he let out a deep sigh.

"Yes I know," she interrupted him. She didn't want to hear it. Secretly, she scolded herself for her stupid thinking earlier. To conceal her upset, she forced a smile. There was no way she would ever allow him to know.

"Okay..." he replied, oblivious to the distress he was causing her. He was still too preoccupied with his own thoughts and worries to even notice the lingering frown on her face.

"Well? What was your question?" she asked trying to appear nonchalant. She desperately needed to be distracted by striking up a conversation. That awful silence had given vent to the feelings she was trying hard to suppress. He seemed anxious again, scratching his head and giving nervous chuckles. She watched as he stood against the overwhelming palette of colors in the sky and felt grateful for the safe sanctuary of her mind that shielded her thoughts.

She was so close to him that it stole her breath away. She was close enough to see the soft movement of his thick eyelashes as he blinked while gazing down at the ground. The tiny hairs on the back of his neck trembled softly in the breeze inside his shirt collar. A strand of hair danced in a hypnotic way before his eyes stirring in her a mighty urge to reach out and touch it.

"Ok, here goes...." he said at last, producing a small jewellery box from his trouser pocket. Then, he opened it to reveal an engagement ring with a single diamond.

Zoe's eyes widened and stared at the ring with disbelief, as she strove to ignore her wishful thinking. She wasn't going to jump to any stupid conclusions again. "I'm guessing this is for Daphne," she managed to say without avoiding the gleam of frigidity in her voice.

Once again, Aris was too distracted to notice. "Yes! I intend to ask her to marry me tonight when we go back home. What do you think of the ring? Do you think she'll like it?"

"Well I don't know! Tastes vary—"

"Ah! Just tell me what you think! I bought it from the States on my last journey. It was an impulsive buy. I've shown it to all my mates on board, but I can't really count on them, can I? What would a bunch of guys like me know? But you're a woman, and you're French too, with such finesse! I value your opinion, Zoe. You're the perfect woman for the task! Go on, say it, I can take it!" He was smiling now, but his worry was still quite evident.

"Well," she mumbled. His last words had cut her like a knife. Fancy him saying to her he thought she was the perfect woman! How ironic... Zoe felt stupid. The sadness in her eyes returned, but this time she couldn't conceal it. As she looked at the ring wistfully, she felt lost for words and tired of the charade of indifference she had to play.

"Oh, my God! I knew it! I knew you wouldn't like it! I should have got one in Athens with your help. Go on tell me Zoe! This ring is all wrong, isn't it? What an idiot I am!" Aris waved his arms about, and kept touching his face, and running his fingers through his hair. He was indeed a bag of nerves.

Zoe met his eyes and saw the full extent of his anguish. Suddenly, she didn't care for her own distress. She opened her mouth to speak but Aris was faster.

"Oh, it doesn't matter!" he said, misinterpreting her silence for hesitation to voice her disapproval. "Who cares about this stupid ring? I'll get her another one! I so want Daphne to love it! Zoe, will you please go with me around the shops tomorrow after work? I need to buy one you'll approve! I trust no one better than you. Please?"

"Aris, don't be silly!" she finally said. Her pain was gone now, or rather, if it was still there inside her, now she was willing to let it go. All that mattered to her was his happiness now. She had just witnessed his devastation at the prospect of disappointing the woman he loved. He had just bared his soul before her, and it had made her see he was worthy of absolute happiness, regardless of what she wanted for herself. This thought had finally delivered her from the ache of unrequited love, deep inside her heart.

"What do you mean?" he asked confused.

"The ring is beautiful, Aris. It's perfect! Daphne will love it, trust me!"

"Really?" His eyes turned huge, and he opened his arms to embrace her, beside himself with relief.

"Congratulations!" she said when he hugged her, and they kissed on both cheeks as is customary in Greece between friends in such circumstances. She knew there was no harm in it but couldn't help feeling guilty all the same, hugging him in a secluded place, hidden from view. Because of her secret feelings, it felt wrong, as innocent as it was.

Smiling nervously, she stepped away from his arms muttering something about going back to join the others. She was about to hand the ring in its open box back to him when a tiny, uncertain voice echoed from behind her.

"What... what are you doing?" stammered Daphne. She had just emerged through the bushes, startled at the sight of Zoe in Aris's arms. She stood a few paces away trembling from the shock, tears streaming from her eyes.

"Why are you crying, my love?" replied Aris, stunned. At once, he took a few steps toward her putting out his arms, eager to hold her.

"Don't come near me!" she yelled, sobbing. "I saw what you were doing with her! And you know something? I knew it! I could tell!"

"What are you talking about, my darling? You know I love you! Only you!" he responded, chuckling with disbelief at the ridiculous accusation.

"Don't lie to me! How could you Aris?"

"Daphne, please listen," intervened Zoe, "Aris is telling you the truth!" She felt guiltier than ever now although she hadn't done anything to cause this awful misunderstanding.

"Don't you speak to me, you devious snake! Aren't there enough men in your life? You had to get my Aris from me?" Daphne burst out, furious.

"Please my love, please don't cry and listen to me! I'm not lying! There's *nothing* going on between me and Zoe!" he insisted, attempting once again to approach her. This caused Daphne to start retreating, but the direction she was taking was dangerous.

"Daphne, be careful!" warned Zoe.

"Please, don't go that way! That's a sheer drop for God's sake! Will you please stop and listen to me?" pleaded Aris, frozen with fear.

"I saw you! He gave you that ring! How long has this been going on behind my back?"

"No Daphne, you misunderstood! I was just handing it back to him," replied Zoe.

"Stop lying! How dare you insult me with this nonsense? I saw you kissing!" Daphne put her hands over her ears and with her eyes tightly shut, retreated further away from them.

"We weren't kissing Daphne! Not the way you think anyway! Please listen," Zoe begged daring a step forward along with Aris.

"Don't come close to me! I'm warning you both, I don't care any more!" she shrieked, her pain rising in her like a roaring fire.

"Please!" shouted Aris, freezing on the spot again.

"Listen, Daphne! Aris showed me the ring, but it's for you, not for me! He asked for my opinion, you see?"

"I told you not to speak to me! You're a liar!" cried Daphne edging further back.

"Please don't take another step, for the love of God!" Aris stretched out both his arms toward her as if he could reach her. "Please come to me! You're making a big mistake!"

"You said you loved me…"

"Oh I do… I do… more than you can ever imagine! Please believe me, my sweetheart!"

"From what I saw, you love *her*, not me…"

"Please listen!" Aris pleaded, taking the ring from the box in Zoe's hand. "You see this ring? It's for you! I only showed it to Zoe! I wanted her opinion, that's all! Tonight, I was planning to ask you to be my wife! I swear, please believe me!" he added, his voice trembling, his eyes glazed with the promise of tears, his mind numb by sheer terror.

"What?" Daphne muttered incredulous. "Is this the truth?" Shaking all over, she searched their faces.

"Yes, this is the truth!" confirmed Zoe. "I congratulated him, and we kissed on the cheeks like friends do. This is the only truth! I'm so sorry!" Zoe felt spent by her feelings of remorse. If anything happened to Daphne she'd never forgive herself.

Daphne had stopped one breath away from the edge. "Aris? Do you swear this is true?"

"Of course it's true! I love you more than anything in the world! Please come away from there!" he begged and started to walk slowly toward her, still afraid she might step back again. He couldn't risk it. He couldn't even dare imagine it in his head.

"You love me? And you want to marry me?" Daphne managed to say in a broken voice. She was still cautious. The unbelievable joy that knocked on the doorstep of her heart found it hard to gain passage. The fear of pain and loss still stood guard at the threshold. She was standing at the very edge of the precipice. If she tried to take a single step back, she would fall into the sea for certain.

"Yes, my love! I know it's early still but I already know! If you'll have me, I will spend the rest of my life telling you how much I love you. Please come to me!" Aris beckoned to her with two eager hands. All he needed was for her to take a single step forward and then he'd rush to take her away, into the safety of his arms.

He watched as she weighed his words in her mind. He saw the glimmer of hope in her eyes, the relief, the sudden realization of this unbelievable misunderstanding. But she stood frozen still, and he found himself praying now, praying she would believe the truth of his confession. If he were to lose her like this, before his very eyes, he would surely jump to his death from there too, no question about it.

At the dreadful thought his knees buckled, and he collapsed to the ground, kneeling now before her just a few steps away from her. He looked up, peering at her through his tears. Against the backdrop of the sky that kept filling up with warm colors, he thought then she'd never looked more beautiful than she did at that moment. Her cotton dress flowed in the breeze like the open sail of a ship. The fabric stuck to her lithe body, and she seemed like an elusive fairy more than ever before, about to fly away after all, just as he'd always feared.

Long strands of hair swirled before her face taking away her tears to mix them with the salty air. Aris felt his love for her overflow from his heart. When he saw a hesitant smile slowly form on her face, he jolted upright like a coiled spring. He advanced hurriedly toward her but right then, the earth started to shake.

"Oh my God, it's an earthquake! Daphne be careful!" shouted out Zoe.

"NO!" Aris yelled as he watched Daphne falter on her feet. He froze on the spot, just two steps from her now, stumbling away uncontrollably. He reached his hand out to her and she did the same but it was too late. Unable to control her footing, she stepped back one last time too many. Her eyes were full of terror as he watched her fall in stunned silence.

"DAPHNE!" he burst out in a bloodcurdling scream. The earthquake stopped then, and he rushed to the edge just in time to see the splash in the deep waters below.

Zoe rushed by him and they looked down together, mad with worry, waiting for Daphne to emerge. They started to shout for help but they didn't move from the edge nor take their eyes from the water, waiting breathlessly for a sign of her.

"Tell the others! I'm diving too!" said Aris grabbing Zoe by the shoulders. She didn't even try to sway him. She'd have jumped too in his place. He took off his shirt and scanned the water surface one last time, but then, an incredible thing happened. A flash of light appeared before his eyes, and he screamed with pain, collapsing to the ground.

"What is it? What's wrong?" asked Zoe kneeling before him. Aris had both hands over his eyes now and was wailing with pain. "Aris talk to me! What's happened?"

"I can't see! Oh, my God! I can't see!" he yelled when the pain subsided, and he removed his hands. All he saw was darkness.

"What?"

"I can't see Zoe! Can you see in the water? Can you see Daphne?"

"No…. no sign of her…" Zoe mumbled checking on the water below. She knelt before him again and put a hand on his shoulder. "I don't understand! How come you don't see? What's happened?"

"A flash of light! It was too bright! Didn't you see it?" he muttered.

"Where?"

"In the water just now! Where Daphne fell—"

"But there was no light! I was looking down there all the time too! How's that possible?"

"It doesn't matter! Tell me, can you see her? Oh, my God Daphne…" Aris lamented, rocking himself in despair. "Please get the others, please hurry! We need to help her. Please! NOW!"

Zoe squeezed his hand in silent response and then sprang up, running through the bushes.

Chapter 31

Manos returned from the café to find the others debating still whether or not they should enter the temple. Anna had remained adamant that all they had to do was wait, trusting Poseidon would make his move when the time was right.

However, Phevos was still restless, insisting on entering the temple just in case. The others sided with Anna, but even then, Phevos wouldn't change his mind so they gave up trying to convince him. They watched as he started to walk away on his own, eager to get inside as soon as possible while there was still no guard present to stop him.

Suddenly, the earth began to shake and Phevos stumbled over the rocky ground, falling down. The duration of the quake had only been a few seconds long. As soon as it ended, everyone hurried to Phevos to find he was all right. Within seconds from reaching him, they heard frantic screaming and calls for help.

Alarmed, they turned their gaze to the distant bushes across the empty space. Without a word spoken among them, they all rushed in that direction. As they approached the bushes, they saw Zoe running toward them.

She beckoned and urged them to follow, mumbling things that made no sense. When they reached the edge of the precipice, they found Aris crouched on the ground in a frenzy of despair, wild with panic and what's more, blind.

Amongst his incoherent mutterings, they finally made some sense; Daphne had fallen over the edge. Horrified, they all scanned the water surface below, but there was still no sign of her. Anna grabbed her son by the shoulders and took him to the side. The intense expression on her face made him understand, even before she opened her mouth to share her thoughts. Poseidon had caused the earthquake, but he wouldn't hurt Daphne. He was attempting to lure a specific person into the water. What's more, he had blinded Aris in order to stop him from diving in. He wasn't supposed to do that, Phevos was! It had to be him, the leader among them. Phevos nodded. This was it!

"Go my boy! God be with you!" she said, putting her arms around him.

Ksenia heard and rushed over to them. Phevos explained to her their theory, and she nodded her assent.

"What is it? What's going on? Have you seen her?" asked Aris upon hearing their whispers. Manos and Zoe had helped him up, and he kept turning around, facing all ways but seeing only darkness. Yet, he didn't care about his predicament, and how it had happened. All he cared was to know Daphne was alive and well.

"Don't worry, Aris! I'm going to get her," said Phevos patting his shoulder. Next, he turned to Ksenia, who gave him a hug, and then started to pray as soon as he walked away.

Anna stood with her, holding her hand.

A few steps away, Manos was cheering Phevos on, his eyes twinkling away.

Zoe sat on the rocks nearby, looking lost, worried about both Daphne and Aris, and wondering what madness had possessed the rest of them.

Phevos stood at the edge of the precipice, secured the straps of his backpack over his shoulders and then dived headfirst into the water.

***

The sea swallowed him into its dark depths making him lose his sense of direction. It seemed to him he had been tumbling in a cobalt blue wash for a while and now, he couldn't tell any more which way was the seabed and which the surface.

Breathing out, he let some air bubbles escape, watching to see where they would go but to his surprise, they scattered in all possible directions. He barely had the time to think how strange that was because then, he started to tumble again due to forceful underwater currents. He felt dizziness overpower him and closed his eyes shut, willing himself not to lose consciousness.

And then, he realized he was breathing normally again. How was this possible? His eyelids felt heavy and next thing he knew, he was out of the water. The first thing he felt was the warm caress of the sea breeze on his face. He was lying down and could feel the coolness of wet sand underneath him.

***

"What is that?" Aris muttered to himself. He was sitting on a rock near the edge with his back to the others. They were all standing at the precipice watching the water, looking out for signs of Daphne and Phevos. They never heard Aris speak, and he was too preoccupied by what was happening to him to repeat it.

Before him, where up till now he saw only darkness, he started to see swirls of light. Gradually, this turned into a haze, then a blur and now, it was clearing up quickly. His eyes seemed to be trying to focus. Stunned to silence, he started blinking repeatedly and rubbing his eyes. They felt stingy now, the way your eyes feel sometimes when you've had one dive in the sea too many.

He didn't mind the discomfort. He welcomed it because it meant his eyes had started to work again. The blur kept clearing up and he kept blinking, willing his eyes to focus. He could see movement. Something was approaching behind the blur. A silhouette. It cleared up some more. Was that the temple behind the person? Who was that? And then in a flash, his sight was fully restored.

"Daphne! Oh my God, Daphne!" he shouted springing to his feet, but the shock was so enormous that he was now frozen. Too many bizarre things had happened in the last few minutes. Was this a dream? The girl who was approaching looked just like Daphne, but she had fallen in the water! The girl was smiling, approaching fast. Was that her spirit? Was she dead?

In those moments, as he stood staring in shock, Aris thought he had lost his mind. But then, he saw the others rush from behind him toward the girl. They shouted out her name too. It was Daphne and she was perfectly all right. Aris watched as the others hugged and kissed her. When she came up to him, he was still in shock, standing like a pillar of salt.

"Daphne?" he said in a faint whisper. "Are you alive? Is this a dream?"

"Oh, Aris!" she said putting her arms around him. "I'm here. Everything is all right, my love!"

"I'm really sorry, Daphne," interrupted Zoe, offering her hand in reconciliation.

"No, Zoe," replied Daphne, pulling her close to her in a warm embrace. "It is I who should be apologizing. I've been unfair to you. Forgive me!"

Zoe and Aris then started to shower Daphne with questions. What had happened to her? How had she got out of the water and on top of the hill again? Did she just come out of the temple? And how come she was dry? She had fallen into the sea just a few minutes ago.

Daphne was overwhelmed. She had so much to say, but it was difficult to explain it to Aris and Zoe. She was going to have to tell them everything. They would think she's crazy, but the others would back her up.

"Is Phevos all right?" Ksenia asked her then, before she could open her mouth.

"Have you seen him, my darling?" enquired Anna.

"I haven't seen him, but I'm sure he's all right too. It felt like a split second in the water only. And just before I found myself in the temple, I saw a wand flash before my eyes. Poseidon is down there right now with Phevos, I'm sure of it!" she told them and Anna, Ksenia and Manos cheered, hugging each other with delight.

"Poseidon? What are you talking about?" asked Aris with a puzzled look.

"Maybe you should sit down for a bit Daphne.... I think we should call an ambulance..." suggested Zoe to the others looking alarmed. Her logical mind could only interpret her words as the mumblings of someone with a severe concussion.

"Zoe... Aris.... I assure you I'm all right. But I think you'd better sit down. We all have something important to tell you," said Daphne.

Anna, Ksenia and Manos nodded in agreement. Everyone who had the privilege of knowing what was going on could guess that the amazing developments of the last few minutes had only been the beginning. Poseidon was going to fulfill his promise and they had to inform the last two among them what to expect. Lesser things could drive someone crazy unless you gave them a logical explanation or even the chance to leave before things got even more surreal.

***

Phevos placed the palms of his hands on the wet sand and helped himself up. He knew this place! It was the beach from his dream. The waves were enormous but like in the dream, they never came to shore and rather hovered foaming, high above the surface.

He turned around and gazed at the hill that towered over the beach. The temple stood magnificent on the top in all its former glory, resplendent under the strong rays of the sun. Phevos reached his arms behind him and was relieved to find his backpack was still there. He pulled the straps off his shoulders and opened it. The two wands were still there, and they were now glowing side by side.

"Welcome to my kingdom!" Poseidon's voice echoed like thunder. Phevos looked up and saw him then, towering over him, dressed in fine deep blue robes. In his big hands, he was holding the third wand. It was glowing just like the other two. At the awesome sight, the young man knelt down with reverence.

"Almighty Poseidon, Ruler of the seas! We meet at last! I receive this honor with all the joy that my mortal heart can possibly contain!"

"So, now you know who I am!" Poseidon laughed out loud scaring away a flock of seabirds that had been circling his head like a wreath of beaks and feathers. With a single flap from their wings, they fled toward the angry sea.

"Yes of course, my lord! It's impossible not to tell after all the fine signs you've been sending me! Forgive me for not recognizing you when you had first appeared in my dream."

"There is no need for apologies, Phevos! After all, it was I who confused you at first with those signs; seemingly from Athena. Whether I like it or not, it is easier to find references to her in Athens as opposed to me. Besides, I expected you would think she was guiding you just because your father used to serve her."

"Do you mean it was you who sent me the signs from Athena in the beginning?"

"Yes, Phevos!"

"Is she oblivious to it all then?"

Poseidon gave a hearty laugh. "Indeed! She knows nothing, and she doesn't even suspect. You see, I had instructed your father to instill in you respect for her as he raised you. That was on purpose, so that she could put the past behind her and forget about you all. This way I could work on my plan to bring your family together again without her apprehension standing in my way! I cannot believe what she has done to you all! She is a menace! She is the selfish, spoiled daughter of an indulgent father!"

"You don't seem to like her much, my lord..." Phevos smirked, his spirits heightened by the presence of his powerful ally.

Poseidon pulled a face of distaste. "Like her? What's to like? My brother Zeus has entertained all her whims! He never interfered when she stole the patronship of Athens from me! It was mine until she came along, misguiding the Athenians with lies. He didn't control his daughter even when she kept favoring Odysseus, that scoundrel! Despite my efforts to kill him by leading him to treacherous lands on his way home to Ithaca after the Trojan War, she kept helping him over and over again, as he fared at sea in his wretched vessel. He didn't deserve to live! He dared blind my son, the Cyclops Polyphemus! And there was my own niece, protecting him until he safely reached Ithaca in the end, despite my will to drown him at sea!"

"I can understand how all this may have angered you Poseidon... but tell me something! How is it possible that Athena doesn't know anything about your plan and my being here at this very moment?"

"Phevos, you underestimate me! You see, the sea is my kingdom, my element! I have absolute control over it and everything that derives from it. When I returned the necklace to your father in the gut of that dogfish, her necklace was mine by then! The sea had permeated through it, lulled it to sleep for thousands of nights on its bed. The moment it was placed on your neck, and as your father threw salt in that fountain, you and Daphne became totally invisible in Athena's eyes! That was my will!"

"But I'm not wearing the necklace any more! I exchanged it for your wand that my mother had placed on the altar in the cave... wait a minute! Does the wand have the same effect?"

"You have guessed right! It is the wand that now renders you invisible in her eyes just like your mother has been while keeping hers all these years. As long as my will remains the same, Athena cannot see what is going on."

"And what about the third wand? How is Father going to get it?"

"Patience, Phevos! I will reveal everything in good time."

"I'm sorry, Poseidon! It's just that I worry too much! I haven't seen my father in a long time…"

"Time…" Poseidon shook his head. "You mortals! You're bound to it and keep forgetting it is only an illusion! I tell you, do not worry! I have made a promise to your father and I will keep it. Have faith in me!" To emphasize his last command, Poseidon stamped his foot on the sand. The earth shook violently, and clouds of sand rose off the dunes as far as the eye could see.

Phevos put out his hands, palms facing upwards. "I know, I'm sorry. But it's hard to be human. We're so helpless compared to the Gods…"

Poseidon nodded, a smile playing on his lips. "I can appreciate that. But you mortals have the power of faith. Use it!"

"You're right, my lord! I should have more faith after all the amazing things that have happened so far because of you. By the way, was it you who caused the earthquake on top of the hill? Did you cause Daphne to fall into the sea?"

Poseidon winked. "I would think you are quite capable to answer that for yourself, my lad!"

"Is she all right? Where is she now?" He looked around him but without anxiety. He trusted their mighty protector wouldn't cause her harm.

"You are guessing correctly. She is fine and she is now back on the hill with the others! You wouldn't think I would let anything happen to her now that you are preparing for such joy, would you? The remaining three of your loved ones are about to return!"

"Thank you, Poseidon! I knew you wouldn't forget Kimon and Eleni! Their children are missing them so much!"

"I know, Phevos! There is no child in this world that doesn't miss their parents; and likewise, no parent who doesn't ache, when away from their children. Sometimes the mortal heart may harden and may not allow the mind to grasp the pain, but it remains deep inside even then, whether you can feel it or not. And that wretched Athena has torn apart not one but two loving families! She has caused you all so much pain, even you, despite the fact that she tried to protect you by stealing your memories. The fool! She thought that by erasing the memories of your mother from your mind, she could also uproot the yearning from your heart for her! How could the Athenians ever be so blind, choosing her instead of me to protect their city?"

Poseidon's anger about Athena was boiling again inside him. His facial features had hardened, and his crimson beard foamed like the angry waves in the water, as he spat out his words. He turned to gaze at Phevos and suddenly, his eyes lit up. "Oh, I just remembered! Come closer to me, my lad! Don't be afraid now!"

Phevos hesitated for a few moments. Poseidon towered over him at the height of eight feet at least. His voice was deafening. He was the most fearful sight he had ever seen. And yet, he knew he was his protector.

As awesome as he looked standing just a few steps away, he had no reason to fear him. He approached him determinedly, stopping in front of his enormous sandals. They were made of gold and pearl. Bits of dark seaweed and anemones with glistening tentacles had been trapped between the shimmering straps. Phevos fixed his gaze there, filled with too much awe to look up and face Poseidon at such close proximity.

He was startled at first when he felt the palm of his enormous hand on top of his head, but he relaxed quickly. It was a tender touch that filled him with a sense of warmth. As soon as he closed his eyes, he saw a series of lightning bolts flash behind his closed eyelids. Scattered images flashed in his mind in between. They seemed familiar. They were images from his own life. An old woman with a chilling cackle. A dark kitchen and a frightening sound. A game of monopoly with little Ksenia. And then, there were no lightning bolts any more but only memories flashing one after the other at a tremendous speed.

Somehow, his mind acknowledged them all or rather retrieved them. There were thousands, millions of them and he could identify them all! His mother tucking him in bed with a kiss. His father teaching him how to ride his first bike. His school. His classmates. The yard where they played hide-and-seek. The little girl who had kissed him that summer. The ginger kitten he'd saved from the street.

"I remember... I remember...." that was all he could mutter and then, ecstatic still, he looked up to face Poseidon.

"Indeed, my boy! That 'cloud' as you called it, is finally gone! Now you may live a normal life as the Gods intended. Man, especially when young, is supposed to have the privilege of his memories! When you have your whole life ahead of you, your memories are your compass! They show you where you have come from and where you are going. They define who you are, based on who has touched your heart and what impressions you have formed about yourself already."

"Thank you, Poseidon! You are truly merciful!"

"It is my duty to right the wrong. That scheming niece of mine had deprived you of all this until now. Although I must admit, for someone lost in life without a compass you have done remarkably well!"

"I've never felt lost, my lord, and I can never be! Not with the father that I have been blessed with!"

"That's right, my lad! Your father has raised you well. I had to be sure that you were capable of the task so I tested you first, but you have solved all my riddles. Well done!"

"Thank you, Poseidon! And now, for the final part! I'm ready, my lord!"

"Oh, I can believe that, lad!" chuckled Poseidon. "Now you must listen to me carefully and then you can go back in time to fetch your loved ones. But before I give you my instructions..." Poseidon paused and then threw the wand he was holding into the sea. It rested for a few seconds on top of one of the gigantic waves and then sank under it. Its brilliant glow faded gradually in the wash until there was no trace of it left.

Phevos watched startled, but he didn't speak. He had hoped Poseidon would hand it to him instead but obviously this was not the right time. He opened his bag and put the two wands back inside. They were still glowing. He turned his gaze back to Poseidon and awaited his instructions, his expression solemn. As he had hoped, the instructions were thorough, but he had very little time left. He had to hurry.

***

"Phevos!" shouted Anna. She saw him first. He was coming out of the temple, and they were all sitting outside at the time. Ecstatic, Phevos ran to them, and they huddled around him hugging and kissing him and patting his back. He was bone dry just like Daphne had been when she had emerged from the temple a few minutes earlier.

At once, they informed him that Aris had proposed to Daphne and also that they had just told the whole truth to Aris and Zoe. They both looked quite pale from the shock of the revelation. Still, Aris responded with warmth of sentiment when he received congratulations from his future brother-in-law.

"So tell us, Phevos! What happened?" piped up Ksenia.

"Did you see Poseidon?" enquired Anna.

"Do you have the third wand?" asked Manos.

"I saw Poseidon! He hasn't given me the wand, but I now know how to get it!"

"Tell us! How?" demanded Daphne.

"I'm sorry, I can't tell you now, there is no time!" answered Phevos looking at the sun. It was very low on the horizon, dipping into the sea at the far end of a shimmering path of gold across the water. Alarmed, he turned to Anna. "We must hurry! Mother, please come with me!" He meant to ask her to follow him into the temple, but when he turned to it, he noticed for the first time the rest of the coach group standing together a few meters away, waiting for the sunset. He had forgotten all about them.

"Oh no! How can we do this with them being here?" he wondered aloud as he panicked, bringing both hands to his head. He couldn't understand how Poseidon could have missed this. Surely the guide, if not anyone else, would immediately call the guard if he saw him enter the temple.

"What is it, Phevos?" asked Daphne and Ksenia in unison.

"What do we need to do, my son?" asked Anna.

"Mother, Poseidon said that you and I must go with our wands inside the temple. He will then do the rest! But I don't see how we can get in there with these people present," he answered, agitated as he pointed vaguely at the tourists.

"Don't worry about them!" piped up Manos before anyone else could speak.

"What do you mean, don't worry?" Phevos darted his eyes toward the distant horizon again. He had better think fast.

Manos gave a huge smirk. "It means I can solve your problem for you. Just watch me!" A couple of German tourists had just come to sit on the rocks a few paces away from them. They were busy in conversation and one of them had just taken out a guidebook. They had their cameras in hand as well, eager to capture the magnificent sunset that would soon be underway.

"Excuse me? Can I have your attention please?" Manos shouted over to them.

"Manos, what are you doing?" asked Phevos astonished. He turned to look at the sky again, trying to think. Actually, if these people were to join all the others perhaps they could get away with it. Maybe they would all look at the sky and never see what's going on in the temple.

"Hello?" continued Manos, undeterred. He skipped in a comical way, stopping right in front of the tourists. "It's nicer over there. Why don't you go join the others? Shoo!"

"Manos, that's rude!" Phevos was vexed now. As if being pressed for time wasn't enough, the boy had to choose this moment to act out of character. He was annoyed with the others as well. Why wasn't anyone else protesting? Why were they chuckling?

"Phevos, I'm only trying to show you!" replied Manos shrugging his shoulders. He bent over the tourists, who were now leafing through the pages of their guidebook, ignoring him completely.

"Hello!" he shouted to them but they never replied or looked up.

"That's enough! What's the matter with—" Phevos's eyes lit up and his features froze.

Manos rolled his eyes. "Finally!" With a cheeky grin, he rushed back to him in a flash.

"What? How?" mumbled Phevos.

"Do you need ask? Poseidon did this, for sure," answered Ksenia.

"What happened?"

"Zoe will tell you," answered Manos.

"Yes, I'm the one who realized it first," said Zoe rolling her eyes, "when they all returned here from the café, I beckoned to my friend Maria and her family to come over to us, but she never responded! I thought they didn't notice me so I went up to them. That's when I heard her ask the guide if she had seen me or anyone else among the Greeks, but we were only paces away! And I was standing right in front of them! If I hadn't stepped aside in the last minute, they would have bumped into me!"

"Poseidon has thought of everything," interrupted Anna. "You know, I don't think they even experienced the earthquake!"

"Well, it looks like we're good to go then. Time is almost up!" said Phevos. He turned to Ksenia and gave her a hug. "Soon, you'll see your parents again my love... have faith," he said, kissing her lips.

"Are you going back in time to get them?"

"Only for a while. It will all be over within a few minutes for you. Poseidon told me Time is an illusion, and after hearing his instructions, now I believe it too."

"Be careful," she whispered as she let him go. Her eyes were full of worry, yet she managed a brave little smile.

"Hurry back, Brother," said Daphne when Phevos squeezed her in his arms. He patted Manos's head and then stood for another moment in their midst with a solemn look on his face.

Zoe and Aris returned his gaze looking as if they were lost in a dream. He couldn't blame them or make it easier for them. All he could do was offer them a sympathetic smile.

"Whatever you see, please don't come in," he asked them all. "Poseidon instructed that only my mother and I should enter the temple."

"Can't we do anything to help?" asked Ksenia.

"Don't worry. I'll be back soon, I promise," replied Phevos.

"You can pray, Ksenia," answered Anna and then mother and son turned to go.

They entered the temple in a hurry and stood in its midst facing the west. Phevos took the wands out of his backpack. They were glowing still. Anna took one from his hands, and they stood side by side looking at the sunset that was now fast in progress.

Soon, the wands took the color of the sun with shades and swirls of light that matched those of the sky. Orange, violet, turquoise, mauve... The sea breeze picked up, and the soothing light of the setting sun came in the temple like an honored guest entering with reverence, bringing tears of ecstasy to their eyes.

"Mother, Poseidon wishes that you stay here! I am to go fetch them alone. But that does not mean you are not a part of this. Far from it, you are the lighthouse that will lead us all back here to you. The light in your wand is the beacon! Do not move from here. Whatever happens, hold that wand before you and keep looking at the setting sun. Do not take your eyes away from it until it disappears behind the horizon. The rest is up to Poseidon!"

"I will my son, I promise!"

"This is the last day that we've spent scattered apart!" he said squeezing her hand, and they both faced the west again.

Half of the sun was sunk in the horizon now, a dark red semicircle surrounded by an orgy of pastel colors. The wands were still alternating colors accordingly. The others stood outside watching the sunset too, happy to be standing further away from the tourists and the repetitive flashes of their cameras.

Ksenia had an arm around her brother as she looked at the sun. She lost herself in that view, freeing her mind from worry. She no longer even felt the need to turn around and watch the others in the temple. It was as if she knew instinctively that watching the sun in full faith was the most effective prayer she could choose at the time. This was the most beautiful sunset that anyone had ever seen.

Anna kept watching the sun like she had been instructed. Tears streamed from her eyes as she marveled at the fire of reds and yellows in the sky. The light in her wand reddened more deeply by the second. The sun was almost gone. Just as the last trace vanished behind the horizon, she noticed that the light of the wand had turned a solid red, the color of hot iron. It looked as if it could burn her hands, but she didn't fear it. Her son had asked her to keep holding it, no matter what.

Suddenly, its color changed back to the original white and it glowed the way it normally did when in the company of another. She guessed Phevos's wand had changed in the same way too. Now that the sun had set, she could take her eyes from the sky. She looked next to her and smiled. Her son was gone. Anna stood and waited.

Chapter 32

Phevos opened his eyes and gasped in astonishment. He was in the public square outside his estate. Then he felt the coolness of water surround him and realized he was once again inside the same fountain. He stepped out of it and looked at his wand. It glowed with a white light. He put it in his backpack and looked ahead. He could see the tall walls of his estate. He saw someone walking along the tree-lined path toward its gates. Was that his father? His robes were wet. He had gone into the fountain too. Had it only been minutes since he left? His father was walking slowly among the shadows that the tall cypress trees cast on the dirt path.

"Father!" cried out Phevos running toward him.

Startled, Efimios turned around and his eyes opened wide.

"My son! You're back already?" he managed to say as Phevos embraced him. "Where is Daphne?" he asked looking around.

"Don't worry, Father! Daphne is fine and so is Mother, Anna!"

"Oh my son, you have found her! Glory to Poseidon! He has done it all as he promised!" replied Efimios crying now with joy in his son's arms.

"Yes, Father! I found Ksenia and Manos too!"

"Phevos," Efimios answered in a trembling voice, grabbing his son by the shoulders, "how long has it been for you? It has only been a couple of minutes since I left you!"

"It's been five months for me, Father! But come now, there's no time!" He said, urging his father to walk toward the gates.

"Is it time, my son?" asked Efimios as he started to walk, hurriedly now.

"Yes, Father! We must find Kimon and Eleni at once! They'll be so happy with the news!"

"We can not take them with us, Son! Poseidon never mentioned them. I guess he could not have foreseen Athena would take them too. Oh, the guilt I have had to live with for all these years..." His voice trailed off, and fresh tears streamed down his face.

"Father, don't worry! The time has come for them too! Poseidon has said so! Let's go find them!"

Efimios's joy was indescribable. He followed his son running through the gates and despite being an old man, he could no longer feel the discomfort in his knee joints. The elation in his heart had given him wings.

Within seconds, they found Kimon and Eleni still sitting in the kitchen quietly together. When they saw Phevos wearing totally different clothes to the ones he had on when he had left just minutes earlier, they knew instantly.

Crying with joy, they rushed to him with many questions, but there was no time to talk. Phevos promised to explain soon and asked them all to follow him to the stables. They got the servants to prepare the horse cart immediately and within a few minutes they were all on it, with Phevos at the rains.

The cart emerged through the gates as fast as the two fine horses could run, leaving behind a cloud of dust. As they sped along, Kimon and Eleni held each other crying as Phevos told them news of their children. They watched as the estate grew smaller and smaller behind them until it disappeared behind cypress trees and centennial olive groves.

When they arrived at the port, Efimios led them to the sailboat of his captain friend. Poseidon's instructions had called for them all to go to Sounio by sunset, and they had to hurry. As Efimios had expected, the captain obliged them at once although he wasn't offered any information about the purpose or the urgency of the request.

Soon, they were on their way on the fine vessel with the captain at the helm. The sea was calm that sunny afternoon, and a flock of seagulls soon appeared. From the moment they came, they followed the boat, flying in circles overhead.

"Tell me, Father," asked Phevos as the four of them sat at the bow, "when did you throw the wand in the sea?"

"It was on the following day after we were all brought here by Athena. That fateful evening," Efimios paused to frown at the devastating memory, "I went upstairs... I hid the letter to your mother in the box, left a handful of her buttons, my box of matches and your whistle in the drawer and then, before returning downstairs, I hid the wand inside my clothes. The other two were at Mrs. Sofia's. When we came back here, I threw it in the sea with the necklace."

"But hadn't Athena got the necklace that night? How did you get it back from her?" asked Phevos.

"It was easy! She didn't even care about it once her deed was done," said Eleni, a bitter smile playing at her lips.

"She forgot it in the cave," Kimon explained, "she left it on the altar on her way out. I noticed it and gave it to your father."

"Which wasn't a surprise!" added Efimios. "You see, Poseidon had instructed me to throw the necklace with the wand into the sea in Sounio! Therefore I knew it would wind up with me somehow!"

"This is amazing," said Phevos incredulous, "so what did she do once she brought us all back here? What did she say?"

"She was furious," said Kimon.

"She was ruthless, that's what she was!" said Eleni.

"Ruthless indeed!" confirmed Efimios, "When it was all over, I begged her in the cave to take us back, but she wouldn't listen. She was too angry. Then I pleaded with her to help *you* at least. You were lying in my arms still unconscious, and we couldn't bring you around."

"We feared you were dead," said Eleni with a shudder.

"And in the end, she gave in. She touched you on the head and just like that, you opened your eyes. She smiled haughtily to herself and went without another word. We never saw her again," said Efimios.

"What did you do when she left?" Phevos's face had grown pale from horror to hear their side of that dreadful story.

"We went to the estate," answered Kimon.

"I will never forget the look on your grandparents faces!" said Eleni.

"Of course," replied Phevos.

"Imagine their joy to find a grandchild on their doorstep. And of course to see me again! I hadn't seen them since I decided to marry your mother and live away from them."

"Oh Father, I hadn't thought of that until now! It must have been hard for them to part with you."

"I remember the last time I went back to announce to them my decision. It was difficult but I told them how much I loved your mother and they understood. Of course, they had known everything about my service to Athena over the years, the decades, that is! My mother wanted me to settle down, so she accepted with delight the prospect of any kind of normal life for me, even if it meant she would never see me again." He shook his head forlornly. "It was hard to say goodbye to them..."

"But I expect they were ecstatic to see you again," said Phevos.

"To see us all! It was strange, such a mixture of emotions... We were all distraught to be there away from our loved ones, worried sick about you, who seemed lost for days, and on the other hand, my parents were overjoyed. Bless their souls... they welcomed Kimon and Eleni with so much kindness!"

"They were really nice people, your grandparents...." said Eleni.

"Yes, they were. I remember them quite well. So does Daphne..." replied Phevos.

"Shame we lost them so soon," added Kimon.

"And the cave? When did you destroy it, Father?"

"Again, on the same day I threw the necklace in the sea with the wand. I woke up that morning determined to set Poseidon's plan in motion."

"How come Athena didn't seek vengeance for that?"

"I honestly don't know, Son! Poseidon instructed me to destroy the interior of the cave and to seal its entrance. He assured me she wouldn't punish me for that, and indeed she never did. Perhaps he knows her well. Maybe she was so pleased with herself after what she had done to us that she didn't even mind. Who knows? Maybe she never intended to use you or anyone else as her servant. I am guessing this is why she didn't even care to pick up the necklace on her way out."

"Strange," answered Phevos.

"Indeed! But then, who can fathom the thinking of the Gods?"

"Were you sworn to secrecy by Poseidon? Is this why none of you ever told me or Daphne anything all these years?"

"Yes, that's right. And believe me my son, it was hard to do." Efimios patted Phevos's hand. "Especially during those first few restless nights... you were just a little boy and you cried for hours in your bed asking for your mother although you couldn't even remember what she looked like any more. Oh, I was shattered! All I could do is be there for you, but I couldn't tell you a thing."

"It's been hard not to be able to speak about my children to anyone all these years," said Eleni. Her voice wavered, and fresh tears escaped from her eyes. Kimon put his arms around her. He had been her tower of strength over the years.

"Don't worry, Mrs. Eleni! Soon it'll all be over," said Phevos.

Eleni slid a hand inside her robe and produced a small key. "You see this?"

"What's that?"

"That's the key to the back door of my house." Eleni wiped a lingering tear from her cheek. "I locked it that night after tucking my children in bed for the last time."

"She's been carrying it about her person all these years," explained Kimon as he held her close to him still.

"This key has been giving me strength all along. It's been the only thing from home I had left. I'm going to give it to my children today when I see them... just to show them I never forgot them."

Phevos gave her an encouraging smile. "I'm sure you'll find they never forgot you either."

"Can I ask you something too, Son?" interrupted Efimios. "From what you have seen in the last five months, has Daphne been an integral part of Poseidon's scheme? Do you think it would have made a difference had she not been with you?"

"Why do you ask that, Father?"

"You see, I had to make a difficult decision earlier today. Poseidon had instructed me to send you to the future world when I see the necklace again, but he hadn't said anything about Daphne, of course. When I sought his protection I only had one child: you! Only once we got back here, I became blessed to have her as my daughter. So I didn't know what to do when she started crying and begging to stay with you. In the end, I thought I had nothing to lose if I let her stay in the fountain with you. I thought that if Poseidon opposed, he wouldn't let her leave with you anyway. I was still unsure when you both disappeared together before my eyes, and it has been playing on my mind ever since. Have I chosen well? I haven't put her in any danger, have I, Son?"

"No, Father! Rest assured that this experience has only benefited her. She has a job in Pallada helping out Mrs. Sofia now! And what's more, she's engaged to be married!"

"Oh! What wonderful news!" exclaimed Efimios.

"And guess who the lucky man is!"

"Who?" all three asked in unison.

"Aris! Mrs. Sofia's son! You probably don't know him.... he was raised in Corfu and is now traveling all the time. He's in the Merchant Navy—"

"Yes, we know of him!" Efimios interrupted excitedly.

"He's a very nice guy!" said Phevos.

"Does he love her?" asked his father.

"He loves her enough for Poseidon to have to blind him today!"

"What?" answered all three in one voice.

"Don't worry! It only lasted for a few minutes. He can see fine now!" chuckled Phevos and then carried on telling them all about the surreal events that had taken place around Poseidon's temple. Soon, they were all chuckling away, amazed at Poseidon's ingenuity and the wonderful way that everything had panned out. Their loved ones were still on that hill waiting for them to return.

***

The sailboat had finally arrived at the cape of Sounio. Efimios had been the first one to make out the temple in the distance.

Exhilarated at the sight, they were all now standing at the bow as the boat sailed to shore, bringing closer and closer to view the temple that had become the symbol of their eternal prayer. Discussing their plan of action in hushed tones, they all marveled at the idea that Anna was waiting in the temple, being the one chosen by Poseidon to bring them all back. Of course, she wasn't expecting them in the magnificent one before their eyes, but in its derelict self in the far future. Only Poseidon could have had the brilliant notion to bring them back together inside his sanctum with a wondrous leap across the centuries.

At a close distance from the port, yet still far enough to avoid prying eyes, Efimios called out to the captain to lower the sail and drop anchor. He also made him promise not to disclose to anyone what he was about to witness.

When his father prompted him, Phevos threw his wand into the sea. They were all still standing together at the bow. In the first few moments that followed, the tranquillity of their surroundings was broken only by the odd squawking from the seagulls that still circled the boat overhead. Small waves made a soft splashing sound against the keel. The afternoon sun shone softly as it crept toward the horizon.

Suddenly, a single wave rose high from the sea, far away from them. Making a mighty roar, it started to approach rapidly, in a very peculiar way. Instead of being followed by other waves, it advanced on its own, surrounded by calmness. All the while, an eerie, white light followed it underwater as it moved ahead.

Finally, it stopped at the bow right in front of them, rising even higher until it was at eye level. This is when they saw for the first time two wands glowing on the very top. Phevos's wand had attracted the other just as Poseidon had promised. Efimios reached out to take them and as soon as he did so, the wave sank into the stillness of the water, as if it had never existed.

Under the unbelieving stare of the captain, Efimios handed the two wondrous objects to his son for safe-keeping in his backpack. The captain had approached the others for a closer look at the strange, approaching wave. Having seen the wands too by then, he stood rigid with astonishment, despite the fact that after a whole life at sea he had quite a few amazing stories to tell. Yet, he had never seen anything as wondrous as this.

Still confident his friend would never betray their secret, Efimios patted him on the shoulder asking him to weigh anchor again and make sail for the port.

When they reached the docks, they jumped out in a hurry, aware that the sun would soon be setting. Efimios spared a few moments to say goodbye to his old friend. The captain cried as he embraced him but still didn't pose any questions.

He was laconic with words as always but didn't fail to assure Efimios that what he had witnessed would go no further.

Without further ado, they took the uphill path, stopping briefly at a spring to drink water. Halfway through to the top, they reached a busy marketplace. An inn and a line of workshops stood by a small square. Loud-speaking voices echoed in the air from the open market a few feet away. Rich-looking merchants stood behind their stalls, chattering with their customers and negotiating.

Although Phevos and the others never approached the busy market but carried on ahead past the square, they still managed to attract attention to themselves. Inevitably, Phevos raised a few eyebrows among the passers by, who stared at his strange clothes, shoes and backpack. In response, he cowered somewhat, picked up his pace and avoided their eyes. He felt glad that both the wands were out of sight in his bag.

Leaving the square behind, they carried on along the road that continued uphill, and after another few minutes, they took a moment to acknowledge the temple of Athena that stood before them. Although they knew they had nothing to fear, they still felt uneasy to be near holy ground dedicated to her at a time like this. Just in case, they picked up their pace again and moved on.

However, as they passed by the entrance of the temple, they never noticed the old woman lurking in the shadows that the setting sun cast behind the marble pillars. The gnarly figure watched them go for a few moments, frozen on the spot with disbelief, her dark, sunken-in eyes ablaze with malice.

When a young priestess came out from behind her, she swore under her breath and stepped aside. Then, with a low, guttural sound, retreated further back into the darkness.

Instinctively, Phevos turned his gaze in that direction, but all he saw was the priestess standing outside the temple, marveling at the beauty of the sky.

Chapter 33

By the time they arrived at the temple of Poseidon, the sun was a bright semicircle sunk in the horizon, sprinkling gold on the surface of the sea. The temple stood magnificent, bathed in warm colors, as if reflecting the heat of a roaring fire.

Ignoring the aches and pains in their legs after the steep uphill climb, they rushed inside where they found the head priest. Efimios didn't lose any time for pleasantries. He took a satchel of gold coins from inside his cloak offering it to the man in return for time alone with his companions to pray before the altar. He said it was a matter of life and death and that time was pressing.

Seeing the handsome offering, the priest was more than happy to oblige them. Immediately, he called out to all bystanders, urging them to follow him outside at once.

Moments later, when everyone else had left, Phevos took the wands out and handed one to his father. They looked at them mutely for a few moments, moved at the thought that Anna was standing at the same time right there across the centuries, holding the third one. No doubt, at the time, her wand had the same white light that theirs had.

Phevos explained again to his father that their wands would soon start changing colors repeatedly to match those in the sky. The last color would be solid red, but he wasn't to fear it. Then, he directed everyone to keep their eyes on the sun and to not look away for a single moment. He had no specific instructions for Kimon and Eleni to follow but knew that just like Ksenia, they would be praying all the while.

The sun was about to set now and suddenly the wands changed color at the same time. As expected, the colors changed again and again, matching always the hues of the sky. Violet, indigo, yellow... And then, just as the sun disappeared altogether, the wands turned bright red but of course, they didn't let go.

Golden light surrounded them all, as the temple started to shake, but all four of them planted their feet on the floor and stood fearless, unwavering. The light grew stronger and stronger until they couldn't see anything before them any more. Soon, it became blinding, causing them to shut their eyes. Yet, none of them let go of the wands or moved an inch.

Efimios opened his eyes first. It was twilight now. The first thing he noticed was the change in the temple. The roof and the walls were gone. The marble pillars had lost their luster; the gold and the fine sculptures had vanished. He noticed all these things in a split second and when realization hit him, he turned to look at Phevos, who gazed back at him speechless.

By that time, streams of tears were flowing from his eyes, and when he turned the other way, the vision of Anna was blurred, as she fell into his embrace with a heart-wrenching cry. As they held each other, their wands illuminated in their hands with a soft, pure white glow and then disappeared from their grasp.

Phevos rushed to hold them and as soon as he did, his wand simply perished from his hand as well, having completed its purpose. That's when they realized in panic that Kimon and Eleni weren't in sight. But then, they heard commotion outside. Rushing out, they found Kimon and Eleni holding their children again, shrieking with joy.

Ksenia and Manos were basking in their affection, relieved and elated like wanderers coming out of the desert into the oasis.

Daphne couldn't get enough of holding her father and his two old friends again. Her face was alight with joy when she introduced Aris to them.

Zoe was the only one who stood rather awkwardly among them, but of course, she was among friends and when they all huddled together to rejoice, she found herself cheering along, as if she were also part of the family.

They lingered outside the temple for quite a while. Time being an illusion, it was seemingly flying now, an element of no importance.

Darkness slowly fell upon them, and the moon shimmered through, shining high on a canvas of twinkling stars. It was a full moon; crimson as if on fire. Sitting down on the ground, they admired the site, still reluctant to move. They all expected it would be impossible to find transportation to Athens at that hour but were too excited to even care.

Suddenly, the full moon grew even bigger against the dark velvet of the heavens. And then, a thunderous voice pierced the stillness that surrounded them. Startled, they turned to look in the direction it had come from. To their absolute horror, they saw Athena then, standing at the entrance of the archaeological site.

She didn't dare approach without permission from Poseidon, but she stood there, roaring at them like a wild animal, mad with fury. Her radiant suit of armour reflected the moonlight to a terrifying effect. Her hair fell on her shoulders in waves of dark silk.

In her hands, she held a shield and a long spear ready to charge but of course, she couldn't yet. She had to wait until the mortals, driven by their human needs, finally grew too restless to stay on Poseidon's sacred ground. Sooner or later, she knew, they would have to wander around, desperate to find shelter, food or water. Unlike them, she had all the time in the world to wait. Once they tried foolishly to escape in any direction, she planned to pounce on them in an instant and tear them to pieces.

However, as she watched them, she grew restless herself. Everyone had grown rigid with fear except for Phevos and his parents, who had started to call out to Poseidon. This angered her even more and she began to shake her spear. It made a fearful sound that this time, raised terror among them all without exception.

"How dare you deceive me, mortals?" she shrieked at them exasperated, her voice a tremendous roar that sent their hearts racing with panic. "Didn't you think you would perish like twigs in the face of a roaring forest fire? I am Athena!" she hissed. She took one step forward and stamped her foot, bringing forth her spear. She knew she could not advance further, yet it gave her pleasure to see the terror in their faces as they huddled together in response, helpless before her.

All at once, a blinding light emerged from the temple ruins. It exploded in all directions and when it subsided again moments later, the temple stood there in all its magnificence once more, a stunning vision of marble and gold. It was illuminated by thousands of oil lamps, to a spectacular effect.

Further to this instant transformation of the site, the people found themselves standing in the courtyard of a fortress. Walls had been raised all around them. The top of the hill now looked just like it used to in antiquity.

Athena cringed as she guessed what was to come. On the contrary, cries of excitement rose among the humans. Most of them had never seen the temple in its former glory before and even the ones who had, were awestruck by the splendor of the sight. And then, with a loud, whooshing sound, Poseidon appeared behind them standing on a massive wave.

It had just risen from the sea below. As soon as he stepped onto land with a single hop of several feet, it dropped without form again into the sea with a thunderous roar. Poseidon looked resplendent in a crimson robe of fine embroidery. On his wavy hair he wore a wreath that gave off lightning flashes. It made his eyes look as if they sparked like flint.

Across the distance, he squinted at Athena gritting his teeth. For a moment she recoiled but didn't move. The humans knelt with awe before the mighty god, but he seemed too preoccupied to notice. He strode past and stood in front of them facing Athena, his nostrils flaring.

The trident in his hand glinted in the eerie lights from the temple to a mesmerizing effect. Athena didn't dare take a single step forward, yet her anger was too great. She scowled back at him, determined to make a stand.

"Just as I thought, Athena! I see you didn't waste time," he burst out, his voice the sound of avalanche rolling down the mountain.

"Poseidon! As always you are warmongering. My father, the almighty Zeus, will not be happy to hear you have been plotting behind my back."

"You are a spoiled daughter, indeed! But your father is my brother. He will side with me this time. I have not been plotting! I only assisted these families that you have broken apart for a whim!"

"Why can you not ever leave me alone? Why must you always spoil my plans?"

"Plans? Is that what you call the devastation you have caused these people? Am I not supposed to empathize and alleviate their suffering? You expect me to watch and do nothing?"

"You knew well this was my wish for them! How long have you been scheming to help them?"

"Eleven years, my darling niece!"

Athena's face dropped. "Eleven years?"

"Yes! And I expect you have just found out, have you not?" He was taunting her. He knew precisely when she had found out. He had willed it so.

"You! You and your pathetic little tricks!" she replied, avoiding to admit before everyone that she had been oblivious to it all until the last minute. "Efimios was my servant! You had no right to intervene!"

"He chose to live a normal life and that is his birthright! Man was made on purpose of flesh and bone! Time is his prison but also his best friend. He cannot make sense of his feelings, his accomplishments or his losses without it. Efimios had to belong somewhere, and to make a family for himself. It is not natural for Man to deceive Time! What gives you the right to upset the natural course of human life?"

"That is my business, not yours!"

"Athena, do not try my patience! Let these people live their lives in peace, or you will hear from me! And now leave! This is my sanctum and you are not welcome here. Go downhill, go and crawl into that little temple the Athenians built for you here!"

"Oh I see, here we go again! That same old story. Why will you not let it go, Poseidon?"

"I will never let it go!" Poseidon stamped his foot down, raising a cloud of dust into the air.

Athena smirked. "How typical of you!" She was pleased to see she had managed to vex him so. "Is it such a sore for you that the city is called Athens and not Poseidonia, like you might have hoped?"

"I never understood how the Athenians could be so fooled!" he shook his head, frowning.

"Fooled? What do you mean? I won fairly!"

"There was nothing fair about it, Athena! You know well I had been the first to visit Athens and present my offering. I struck the ground on the Acropolis hill with this very same trident! The Athenians marveled to see the spring of Erechtheus appear before their very eyes."

"That appalling salt spring?" She grimaced with distaste. "What benefit could the Athenians ever have from salty water? Besides, the sea is not too far from the city. King Cecrops himself told everyone that your gift was useless to them. Was that really the best you could have offered the glorious city of Athens, oh great Poseidon?"

"You are mistaken. My gift of salty water represented the sea, which holds an infinite value! And have you forgotten? I did not give them only the spring. I also offered them the horse to use for transportation and war."

"Of course! I am not surprised why only the men among the bystanders voted for you. What is it with you men? Why can you not be like women and wish for peace instead? It is no surprise to me that I won the contest. For I struck the rock with this very spear to give them the olive tree. For nourishment, healing, beauty and light!"

"And yet, you did not offer them light! Instead, you dragged them all to the darkness of your deception! You visited the city after me, and yet you lied you had got there first. You and King Cecrops, who sided with you! If you had been honest, you would have let them name the city after me!"

"Poseidon, do you even recall what you did when you heard that you lost? Let me remind you! You stormed to the west of the city and flooded the Thriasian Plain in wrath! I may have told a small lie, but my intentions were pure. My main concern was to protect the city. As I said, I offered them light, nourishment and all other things that can sustain life in times of peace. If you had won, you would have caused them similar disasters just like that flood, each time you threw another one of your childish tantrums or pushed them to war!"

"Childish tantrums? Huh! You should talk! What do you call the devastation you have caused these people? Just because this man wanted to live a normal life, you scattered away two families to please your hurt pride! Has it not occurred to you that these people are Athenians too? Did they not deserve the famous protection you vowed to provide to everyone in the city?" As Poseidon said these words, he stepped back a few paces carefully, allowing the group of mortals to surround him. He opened his arms to point at them, and they all looked at Athena mutely, exhausted by the emotional intensity of the last few minutes.

Athena gazed back at them in silence, and for the first time she seemed astounded. Her facial features had softened, and she was holding her spear and shield limply now. If she were to loosen her grip even a fraction more, they would both fall to the ground. Her eyes reflected the lights from the temple and seemed both bigger and brighter now. As she gazed at the mortals still, she grew pensive.

Finally, she turned to face Poseidon, and when he nodded, she paced toward the people slowly. Poseidon let her come quite close, but his body remained rigid, ready to intervene if she were to attack the humans.

The youngest among them had cowered somewhat and were holding each other nervously, but Anna hadn't flinched in the least. She stood out from all of them, even the men, for she was holding her head high, standing closely by her husband, and fixing Athena with a defiant stare. She knew she had been a winner and not a loser in the last battle against her.

Athena studied everyone's face intently, and when she turned to Anna again, she held her gaze for quite a while. And then, the expression on her face became quizzical. Her eyes lit up, as if by a sudden realization. With a quiet little laugh, she turned around to face Poseidon. "All right! I do admit I may have been rather cruel to these people, driven by anger. I confess I do not find it easy to be disregarded, but I can see now that from a human point of view, they have done nothing wrong. Indeed, they are Athenians too, and I was supposed to protect them. I must admit I forgot that for a while..."

"Athena, acknowledging your mistake is to your credit. In return, I am willing to forget that old story that took place on the Acropolis hill, and I promise not to mention it again! What do you say we start anew?" With a throaty laugh, he offered her his hand.

"I agree," she said, shaking his hand. "Let the Athenians judge us through the ages, and let us not seek to spite each other any more."

Efimios took a step forward. He was holding Anna by the hand. The relief was evident on his face. He had feared the worst while watching the two great Gods fight and was now ecstatic it was finally over.

"Athena, regardless of the past, I will always feel honored that you have chosen me to be your servant!" he cried out. "Indeed, your fury had made you forget we are Athenians too. Yet, you have proven your greatness to us all here today, on this sacred ground where the Athenians once honored both Poseidon and you. Truly, no Olympian Gods have ever been loved by our people more than the two of you!"

Athena moved toward Efimios and Anna, causing Phevos to approach as well in order to stand beside them. Ksenia followed suit with Daphne and Aris. Behind them, Kimon, Eleni, Manos and Zoe huddled in silence, impatient for Athena to go away.

"Anna, tell me something!" said Athena turning to stare into her eyes again as she towered over her. "What have you done with my candleholders? They were made of solid gold!" she added, her expression stern.

The criticizing look on Athena's face distressed almost everyone again, including Poseidon. He had relaxed in her presence in the last few minutes, but now he took a hurried step closer to her again, just in case. Strangely enough, the only one who had remained perfectly calm was Anna.

"Athena, you condemned me to live alone without family or friends!" she replied fixing her with a bold and rather impertinent stare. "I'll have you know I sold them! I had to do what I could to survive. I easily found a satisfactory price in one of the many antique shops around Plaka. I don't regret it! The money helped me buy my restaurant. Without it, I wouldn't be here now with my family. So don't you look at me expecting an apology!"

Before Athena could respond, Phevos came to stand in front of his mother.

"Almighty Athena, the candleholders are indeed gone! But your necklace is still safe. It is in the cave on the altar this very moment! I left it there myself. Take it! And if it's gold you want for what you have lost, we can give it to you!"

"Indeed," interrupted Efimios putting an arm around his son, "Take whatever you want among our possessions in exchange for the candleholders that you have lost. We only care that you do not hurt any of us. Our family is what we hold most valuable!"

"Athena..." interrupted Poseidon putting a hand on her shoulder, "what is this now about gold?" He was confused. Why did Athena care about a few pounds of gold? But when she turned to look at him, her eyes were smiling.

"Do not worry," said Athena chuckling, as she turned to face the humans again. "I do not care about the candleholders. I was only trying to grasp the magnitude of this woman's courage!" she added pointing to Anna. "I had never imagined that a human is capable of so much defiance in the knowledge that they are innocent and that their purpose is just. Rest assured I do not want anything from you. As for the necklace, I do not need it any more! You see, I do not intend to appoint another servant.

I have been watching Athens grow and mature over the centuries despite consistent war, poverty and exploitation from outside and inner sources. But now, I believe Athens is able to stand on its feet again, unaided. The whole world can now see that more can be accomplished with peace than with war. Of course, the world will never be perfect. But people's minds are open now. They can find their own way out of difficulty. I have taught the people of my city well. Now, you can continue on your own, my beloved Athenians! I will always protect Athens of course, the way a parent still watches over an adult child. But now you are mature enough to make your own interventions and your own choices!"

"Well said, Athena!" replied Poseidon patting her on the shoulder. "I must confess though, you had me going for a while back there!" He gave a thunderous laugh and Athena joined him.

The group of mortals watched speechless, as the sound of the gods' gaiety filled the air. Finally, they relaxed around them, feeling safe.

"I am offering you my necklace as a present," Athena announced with regal formality, when she turned to the humans again, taking them by surprise. "You can have my cave too!" she added with a dismissive wave. "You will need it. I can see your family has grown!" Athena chuckled and turned to Poseidon with a raised eyebrow to which he responded with a nod and a knowing smile.

All this puzzled everyone, but they never got the chance to ask her to explain because she swiftly disappeared from their eyes. Her magnificent form turned into a swirl of rose petals that released their sweet fragrance into the air, as they fell softly on the ground. The echo of her laughter lingered for a second or two longer after she was gone.

Mystified, the mortals started to chatter excitedly.

"Listen to me now!" commanded Poseidon and silence spread among them at once. They felt grateful to him for protecting them from Athena, and what's more, for turning the whole situation around to a peaceful end.

"You are safe now," said Poseidon and everyone cheered. He raised a hand and they stopped, allowing him to continue. "Now you may go and lead your lives in peace. Every mortal has a right to both love and happiness! Your prayers to acquire these things have now been answered. It was your unwavering faith that made it possible, as is the case with all answered prayers! And now go, go to your homes!" he urged them motioning to them to go through an arched passage inside the fortress walls.

As the site they were on was still the one from antiquity, they were unsure as to what they would find beyond the walls. The temple was still illuminated by the soft light of oil lamps, and Efimios didn't fail to make the connection. It seemed that deep down, even Poseidon agreed that the olive tree was a true blessing. In his temple, Athena's valuable present to the Athenians had been acknowledged as such.

"Do not be afraid! Go through the passage, trust me now!" said Poseidon as he watched the humans stare at its dark entrance, hesitant to take another step.

Efimios thanked Poseidon on behalf of them all and urged them to obey. He walked ahead with his wife and everyone followed behind. It was pitch black inside the passage, but once their eyes got accustomed to the darkness, they were able to make out the exit at the other end.

Relieved, they came out into the night and walked along a narrow dirt path lined by pine trees. After a few minutes, they found a paved path that, surprisingly enough, carried on uphill. When they reached the top, they stood amazed.

Even then, after all the miracles they had witnessed that day, they were dumbstruck at the realization of the distance they had covered within minutes. Before them, stood none other than the Parthenon in the center of Athens. Somehow, Poseidon had transported them there to help them get home without delay or adversity.

Everyone thought the Parthenon had never looked more beautiful than it did that night despite the destruction it has suffered over the centuries. They stood there quietly for a few moments, enchanted by the sight, each of them gathering their own thoughts after the shocking events of the past few hours.

Afterwards, they took the familiar route that led them downhill and back to Plaka. Once they got to the house, they all went to the sitting room, and even Zoe stayed around, sharing in everyone's joy. As for Aris, he was over the moon sitting next to Daphne and getting to know his extended new family. Besides, if he were to return to Pallada in the middle of the night he would only disturb his mother. Thankfully, they had told her they were probably going to spend the night at Anna's.

The sitting room that had witnessed so much anguish and sorrow in the past was now full of merriment again. Laughter and cries of joy reverberated from its walls, when Odysseus joined them, busy smelling all the strangers among them. He guessed from the commotion that this was no ordinary occasion and continued to bark excitedly as he received affectionate pats and cuddles.

***

At first light, they all came out to the orchard. Efimios had suggested that they should mark the dawn of the new day with closure, as far as the cave was concerned. Athena's last words had been quite enigmatic, but she had made it clear she wasn't interested in it or her necklace any more.

Efimios and Anna led the way to the cave, and everyone else followed. They were going there to shut its door forever, leaving the necklace right where it rested on the altar. Of course, they didn't intend to bury the door again. Instead, it would serve them as a precious reminder of what their love for each other and their faith had accomplished. Once they passed the last clump of trees, they came out to the clearing, but what they saw then, left them speechless.

A magnificent three-storied building stood against the rockface where the entrance of the cave used to be. The building seemed to emerge from the rock, as if it were part of the Acropolis hill. Its sidewalls were cliffs of pure white stone. The façade was decked in pentelic marble. On the large balconies, solid gold lanterns hung above the windows. Ceramic owls perched on the tiled roof across the front.

The main door was made of iron. In its midst, the figure of an owl stood on an olive branch. It looked similar to the one Efimios had made for the door to the cave except this one was made of solid gold. It caught the early morning sun, glinting in a mesmerising way. On either side of the owl, two golden shapes, a spear and a battle helmet, were studded with brilliant, yellow gemstones. A key had been placed in the lock, a long golden chain hanging from it.

The key was the calling card of the maker behind this fine edifice. It had a brilliant moonstone on it and was studded with sparkling quartz crystals. Above the door, a rectangular sign made of olive wood bore a carved message in ancient Greek.

Everyone stood mutely at the entrance. They were all mystified as to what the sign said, but the lump in their throats didn't allow them to speak. Instead, they all turned their gaze to Efimios. Astounded still and deeply moved, he cleared his throat before translating the message for everyone.

"I am guessing you have no use for the cave or the necklace so I have taken the liberty to transform them into something useful to you. Do not refuse my offer for it comes with no obligation on your part. Think of it as my atonement for the devastation I have caused. Allow me, the patron of this great city to leave my last offering here, on the same sacred hill, where my very first one had been presented."

There was no signature but of course it wasn't needed. Gods do not take pleasure in stating the obvious. They give mortals much more credit than that.

They all entered the building to find incredible beauty and luxury in its interior. Everything they touched, every doorknob, every switch, and every tap was made of solid gold. All light fixtures and even some of the furniture were studded with diamonds and other precious gems. Exquisite works of art hung from the walls, and throws of pure silk were draped over the living room furniture. The beds were made with sheets of luxurious satin, and the wardrobes brimmed with fashionable clothes for everyone and for every occasion.

The abundance of wealth that exuded from every nook in

this house was of such magnitude that not even the palaces of the greatest kings of the world could ever match it. Despite all that, Kimon and Eleni opted not to live in that building. They had come to miss their home so much that nothing could keep them away, so they stayed with Manos there.

On the other hand, Efimios and Anna moved in immediately, accepting Athena's offer and apology, eager to put the past behind them once and for all. Ksenia and Phevos lived there too and so did Daphne.

Before Aris returned to Pallada that morning, Efimios raised the question how they were going to explain their long absence to everyone in the neighborhood. They were particularly worried about Mrs. Sofia because of her weak heart. Therefore, they thought it best to give it a bit of time in order to think of the best way, before presenting themselves to her. Aris was to return to Pallada but not to mention anything at all.

That same evening, Mrs. Sofia retired to her room for the night smiling. Her son and Daphne had gone out to dinner but before leaving, they had all had some tea and cake together. She was still over the moon with the news of their engagement. She put on her nightdress and slippers and before getting into bed, as she did every night, she stood on the corner before the mounted icons.

As always, the overhanging oil lamp was burning. She made sure to light it every night before bedtime. It was her way to honor the memory of her late husband. The sight of its delicate flame that flickered in the slighest breeze comforted her somehow. It made her feel like her husband was there with her again.

Mrs. Sofia rested her gaze at the tiny flame. For a moment it spat and twitched, then softly bent over as if beckoning to her. She gave a soft sigh, and her eyes welled up. Then, as she did every night before she went to bed, she turned her gaze to the icon of St Spyridon and crossed herself.

"*Agie mou Spyridona!*" she said, lacing her fingers in prayer. "Thank you for the joy you have brought me today! I love Daphne like a daughter. I know she'll make my boy happy. Give them health and joy! Protect my daughter also, who is far away but never forgotten. And please mind my other children too: Ksenia and Manos. They lost their parents too young, but I am glad I could be there for them to raise them safely. I wish that all the children in the world could be safe, but sadly, this is not the case. Why is it that some people have enough love to give and others have none? There are times that I feel like my heart is about to burst! It is the love that overflows from it, and I'm thankful God has made me like this. Why do so many people see darkness when there is only light? Evil never made sense to me, and I don't even think it exists. I think all there is, is love and light... Darkness only creeps in when you let the light fade in your heart! Throughout my life I've been trying to keep the light on.... I've known so much love but sadly, so many of my loved ones have long departed from this world. My husband, my parents, my siblings... and it's getting so lonely without them! People my age don't have a lot to live for. I find myself wishing to see them again these days more than I wish to get up in the morning... Life befits the people who keep their minds on the living. Unlike them, I spend my evenings making conversation with age-stained pictures... From this world, I don't need anything any more and only have one wish: for all the children to know love! There's no other way for goodness to survive in this world. I'm contented that I can look back on my life and see that I've done my bit. This is all I care for and my work is done. Nothing else binds me here. If I could, I would grow wings on my back tonight and fly up to heaven to see my loved ones again. I have nothing to fear and all to look forward to..."

***

The next morning, Aris was startled when he rose from his bed to find his mother still lying in hers. This wasn't like her. Concerned, he rushed to her side to find her lying on her back with her hands resting over her heart. Her eyes were closed, her face serene with a hint of a smile. She was finally where she wanted to be.

Chapter 34

It was two years to the day after their reunion. To commemorate the occasion, everyone went to the Acropolis that evening to marvel at the sight of the August full moon. They had done the same the previous year. Already, this had started to feel like a favorite annual ritual. Dressed in their finest, they walked along the paved path to the top of the hill under the enchanting moonlight.

Efimios led the way with Anna, who was holding a baby girl in her arms. It was her granddaughter. She was only a few months old. Her parents, Daphne and Aris were walking right behind them. They had named their baby Sofia even before she was born to honor the memory of Aris's mother, whom everybody still missed beyond words. They still spoke of her as if she were still alive and were all excited that the baby would soon be baptized in her name. It meant it would live on in the family, never to be forgotten.

Phevos and Ksenia were walking behind them. He was holding her hand looking rather nervous. She was five months pregnant, and he was being overprotective, too worried she might slip and fall on the cobblestones. She relished his attention as always and smiled at him tenderly each time he pointed out a stone that looked threatening in her path.

Kimon followed with Eleni and Manos. Two years later, the boy still couldn't get enough of his parents' attention. He kept close to his mother, who spoke to him gently, touching his arm and smiling to him while his father listened with interest to everything he said.

Zoe had been present the year before for the occasion, but that day she hadn't joined them. Still a valued friend to them all, her heartache over Aris had long faded away. On the day he got married to Daphne, Zoe was introduced to one of his old colleagues and they fell madly in love. She was now married to him and at the time was accompanying him onboard ship for a few days. He often took her along on short trips, and she enjoyed seeing the world by his side.

When they reached the top of the hill, little Sofia got startled by the hustle and bustle of the crowd—not to mention the strong floodlights— and started to cry.

Daphne took her in her arms to soothe her while Anna helped by making cooing sounds and pulling funny faces the way all grandmothers do.

Efimios walked up ahead on his own and stood before the Parthenon to marvel at its beauty. The combination of the illumination effects and the full moon made it an enthralling sight to look forward to every year. Captivated by the magic of the moment, he then proceeded to walk leisurely toward the precipice on the far end, still on his own, this time to admire the view of Plaka down below. At this hour it looked magical, its lanes lit by old-style lanterns and quaint lamp posts. Nostalgic bouzouki chords from the tavernas in the lanes underneath reached his ears, putting a wistful smile on his face. The air carried the aromas of honeysuckle and basil from the whitewashed yards. He took a deep breath, half-closing his eyes, grateful he was home at last, his troubles finally over.

"Mr. Efimios... can I ask you a question?" The young voice came from behind him. Efimios turned around to see Manos's earnest face. He was already fourteen, an intelligent and promising youngster. He had the whole world in his hands because he had already acquired a lot of knowledge that normally is not gained even throughout a lifetime. He had learnt a lot from Efimios in the past two years and followed him around often, thirsty for more.

"Of course, my boy," answered Efimios.

"It occurred to me the other day, and I've been meaning to ask you... how do you think Athena found out that day in Sounio what was going on?"

Efimios grinned. "Yes, the truth is, she did find out quite mysteriously, didn't she?"

"Well? What do you think happened? You had the wands with you and Mrs. Anna had hers. That made you invisible in her eyes! How did she find out?"

"I think Poseidon allowed it. Maybe as we passed her temple on our way to the top—"

"But why?"

"I'm guessing because he wanted to make sure this ended there and then. He had to have his say and also to make sure she would never hurt us."

"Of course! He couldn't leave it to chance! She would have found out sooner or later."

"Yes... yes she would!"

"I'm so glad Poseidon thought of everything!"

"So am I, Manos! Thanks to him we're all here together today. I am the happiest man in the world because of that."

"You must be missing what you left behind in the old world though..."

"What would that be, Manos? I must say, I can't think of anything!"

"Well, your massive estate for one! Surely you miss your home and your friends there?"

"My home?" Efimios gave a little laugh and then bit his lip. He didn't want to discourage Manos, to give him the wrong idea that he found his impressions ridiculous.

"Forgive me for my reaction, Manos. I guess your thinking would make sense to a lot of people but not to me. First of all, my life had been split between two different worlds for many years. Therefore, to say that my estate in the old world was my home sounds one-sided to me. I could be there right now and have someone ask me if I miss my home here in Plaka! Do you understand what I mean?"

Manos looked puzzled and Efimios continued, "You see Manos, home is where one is happy. And to me, home is where my family is. So I'm home *here* and *now*! And as for missing my estate, you should know that the bricks and mortar have no value, no matter how large or impressive the house may be. For these things help make a house but are never enough to make a home. Only family makes a home! I could be living equally happy anywhere and anytime in the world, as long as we were all together like this."

Manos finally understood and smiled with a nod. They turned around then to look at the others. They were still gathered around Daphne cooing at the baby in her arms and talking.

"Would you like to know a little secret about my house in ancient times?" continued Efimios in a hushed voice causing Manos to nod eagerly. "In a way I never left it, Manos! Geographically speaking, it was a stone's throw from the Acropolis hill, just like the house that we all call home today. If you think about it, it is the Acropolis hill that is our home! It is everyone's home in this city. It is the point of reference of our people; what we hold most sacred among all places in our hearts..."

Manos said nothing as he nodded again, but it was evident to Efimios that he had been really impressed by their conversation. Truth is, it had reminded the boy of his yearning for his parents in his earlier life. He had known early on, the hard way, the value of family. He was also enchanted by the idea of time travel and the notion that places undergo incredible changes in the passage of time.

It impressed him to think how every corner of the world changes gradually, sometimes beyond recognition, through progress or devastation. Buildings become derelict and then replaced by brand new ones. Land is built upon; rivers overflow and then go dry again. Grass shoots up from the earth and flowers bloom in the spring even after the cruelest of winters. People age and die while others are born. Everything follows the never-ending cycle of life and death. Everything is always moving, changing. Every day is lost at sunset, never to be retrieved again. Thoughts like these made Manos feel like every moment in life is precious. Thanks to Efimios, he had been given a legacy that's most advantageous to someone so young.

"Look at the sea shimmering in the distance!" Manos cried out after a few moments of silence, still deep in thought. He had been sauntering alongside Efimios around the site to admire the rest of the view.

"Indeed Manos, it looks spectacular under the light of the full moon! You know, the sea has always charmed people and you know why? Because it's one of few things on this earth that does not follow the cycle of life and death. It follows no rules. The sea is unchanging through the ages! It only exists, infinitely. It cannot be tamed and this is why Man fears and respects it!" Efimios paused as he noticed Manos's enthusiasm grow in his eyes. He looked fascinated by that notion. He opened his mouth to continue but Manos was faster.

"Do you think... do you think this is why Poseidon gave the spring of Erechtheus to the Athenians on top of this hill? Perhaps by offering them a pool of seawater he was aiming to grant them its unique power to remain unaffected by time!"

Efimios was stunned and thought about it for a few moments before speaking. "Perhaps you're right! I must say, I had never thought of that and we can only speculate. Yes... indeed, why not? Maybe he did choose to give the Athenians the gift of the sea's timeless freedom and power."

"Surely, it must be so! You said the sea never changes and that's true! I bet the Athenians used to come up here in ancient times too to enjoy the sea view under the full moon, just like we are now! I'm sure it looked just as enchanting then..." replied Manos.

"Oh, yes it did!" replied Efimios with a wink. He knew it for a fact after all.

"Hey! You two look engrossed in conversation. I wonder what this is about," piped up Anna from behind them.

Efimios put an arm around her, planting a soft kiss on her cheek. The rest of the family joined them soon, and they all marveled at the sea view.

"Mother, what would you say if I told you I'm considering joining the Merchant Navy, just like Aris?" asked Manos, even more thrilled now at the idea of life at sea. It had been brewing in his mind for the past two years, and Efimios's words had just made him certain.

"I would say that you can do anything as long as you put your mind to it," answered Eleni, her face animated with mirth.

They all stood there for quite a while, staring out to sea under the crimson moon. They were surrounded by ancient marbles and wandering groups of strangers, who didn't know anything about their unusual story. Across the distance, the Acropolis museum cradled within its protective walls its legendary treasures, lulling them to a peaceful sleep under the eerie light from the heavens. Yet, through the large window, the five Caryatids stood alert on their strong platform. The ageless maidens, with the long braided hair down their backs, remained awake even at this hour gazing across to the Acropolis, full of nostalgia for their sacred home. Inside their marble chests, they nurtured as always, precious hope for the return of their long lost sister.

All at once, high in the sky, the full moon increased in size but in the magic of the hour, standing among the timeless marbles, no one amongst the humans noticed. The only creature that did was a lonely owl that was perched on the branch of an olive tree at the top of the hill. Drawn irresistibly to the moon, it stretched its wings and flew toward it, sweeping through the air in a leisurely flight until it disappeared from view inside the radiant, crimson circle.

And I, Efimios, who has responded to your call to tell you this strange story, can assure you that it's absolutely true. Should you doubt me, spare a moment to reflect upon the magic of fairy tales. They are so fascinating to listen to because our souls take pleasure in hearing the timeless truths of life. Every child quickly learns what these are, from all the stories their loving guardians ever told them at bedtime. Sometimes, all you need to do is think back to the fairy tales of your childhood in order to be reminded what is most important in life and what is really true.

THE END

Thank you for taking time to read The Necklace of Goddess Athena. If you enjoyed it, please consider posting a short review. Even one or two lines would make a world of difference. Word of mouth is an author's best friend and much appreciated.

Find it now on **Amazon US** or copy and paste this universal link in your browser, to visit your local Amazon store: myBook.to/GdssAthena

Acknowledgements

Heartfelt thanks to my husband Andy for his ongoing editing assistance and moral support. Also I offer my gratitude to Deborah Mansfield for the fabulous cover she has created for me, and to Adrian Leach for letting me use his stunning photograph of the Parthenon.

About the author

Effrosyni Moschoudi was born and raised in Athens, Greece. As a child, she often sat alone in her granny's garden scribbling rhymes about flowers, butterflies and ants. Through adolescence, she wrote dark poetry that suited her melancholic, romantic nature. She's passionate about books and movies and simply couldn't live without them. She lives in a quaint seaside town near Athens with her husband Andy and a naughty cat called Felix.

Her debut novel, The Necklace of Goddess Athena, is an urban fantasy of Greek myths and time travel that's suitable for all ages. The book is a #1 Amazon bestseller in Greek & Roman literature. In 2014, it made the shortlist for the "50 Best Self-Published Books Worth Reading" from Indie Author Land.

Her historical romance, The Lady of the Pier – The Ebb, is an ABNA Quarter-Finalist. Set in England in the 1930's and in Greece in the 1980's, it follows the lives and loves of two young girls who've never met but are connected in a mysterious way. The book is the first part of a trilogy. Effrosyni is currently penning the remaining two volumes.

Her books are available in kindle and print format.

What others say about her writing:

"Effrosyni layers her words on the page like music"
~Jackie Weger, National Best-selling Author

"Effrosyni's descriptions create a live sensation i.e. you easily see, hear, and smell. I truly fell under the spell of her apt writing."
~Amazon customer

A note from Effrosyni

To breathe life into 'Pallada', I've drawn on my experiences as a young girl helping out my grandmother to run a small family guesthouse on the island of Corfu. I've modelled my character Mrs Sofia after her, and she resembles her in many ways; particularly in her melodic vocal expression, tenderness and fiery temperament.

To find out more about my real-life guesthouse experiences, checkout this humorous guest post on Effrosyni's Blog: http://bit.ly/1KEYS9t

The book includes tiny tributes to two special people:

My husband Andy is an avid aero-modeler as well as a bookworm, and he often wishes there were more references to his hobby in literature. In order to put a smile on his face, I've included in this book a scene in the seaside town of Anavissos where Manos gets to meet some aeromodelers. This is a real place, where hobbyists come together to enjoy their passion. The camaraderie among them is truly amazing, just like in the book.

In another chapter, Ksenia quotes a schoolteacher who preached that if life were easy it would be a cookie with sugar on top. I've included this to honor my beloved English teacher, Mr Fraggoulis from Athens. He'd often say something similar, using the Greek word 'Zaxarokoulouro' (sugar cookie) that sounded amusing to us youngsters back then and made us laugh.

Mr Fraggoulis taught me English from the tender age of ten. He'd often push me to get over my shyness and engage in conversation with British tourists in Corfu during the summer break. Back then I was around twelve and still made too many mistakes to dare it unprompted.

Mr Fraggoulis, this mention is to say thank you, for being an eager and earnest teacher, both of English and of life in general.

I'm always delighted to hear from my readers, and highly value any comments. I'd love to hear from you!

**Email me at ladyofthepier@gmail.com

**Visit my website to send me a direct email, to download FREE excerpts, to watch book trailers and to read the latest news about my works in progress:
http://www.effrosyniwrites.com

**Sign up to my newsletter to be notified first about my new releases and book promotions ($0.00-$0.99):
http://effrosyniwrites.com/newsletter/

**Like me on Facebook:
https://www.facebook.com/authoreffrosyni

**Follow me on Twitter:
https://twitter.com/frostiemoss

**Find me on Goodreads:
https://www.goodreads.com/author/show/7362780.Effrosyni_Moschoudi

**Follow my blogs by email or RSS feed to find your next favorite read. I mostly post author interviews and book reviews, but you'll also find travel articles and the odd Greek recipe!
http://www.effrosyniwrites.com (*NEW*)
http://www.effrosinimoss.wordpress.com

More from this author

Effrosyni Moschoudi

THE LADY OF THE PIER
The Ebb

Love will go on forever, seeking a second chance

Amazon Breakthrough Novel Award — QUARTER FINALIST

LOVE WILL GO ON FOREVER, SEEKING A SECOND CHANCE.

BRIGHTON, 1937

Dreaming of wealth and happiness, Laura Mayfield arrives in Brighton to pursue a new life. She falls for Christian Searle, a happy-go-lucky stagehand at the West Pier theater, but when she's offered a chance to perform there, her love for him is put to the test. Charles Willard, a wealthy aristocrat, is fascinated by her and pursues her relentlessly. Will Laura choose love…or money?

CORFU, 1987

On a long holiday with her grandparents, Sofia Aspioti meets Danny Markson, a charming flirt who makes her laugh. Although she tries to keep him at arm's length, worried that village gossip will get back to her strict family, she falls desperately in love. That's when strange dreams about Brighton's West Pier and a woman dressed in black begin to haunt her. Who is this grieving woman? And how is her lament related to Sofia's feelings for Danny?

What other readers said about the book:
(Excerpts from posted reviews on Amazon.com)

"Addictively mesmerizing"
"I defy you to put this book down after the first chapter"
"I got withdrawal symptoms when I ended it"
"The writer has an undisputed talent for creating vivid imagery"
"An inner glow, an inherent purity emanates from the pages to create a sense of completeness, like a dream you don't want to wake up from"

Excerpt from The Lady of the Pier

Outside the tearoom, Meg said goodbye quickly to rush back to her post, leaving Laura behind to have a look around. Feeling the most carefree she'd felt in a long time, the young girl sauntered to the eastern landing stage in order to enjoy the sea view.

She sat on a bench and watched the world go by for a while. Generous views of the Hove and the open sea that stretched toward an indigo horizon made it a pleasure to be there, even though it was late afternoon. The remaining sunlight was fading fast. She stood up and walked to the railing, dreamily watching the sea horses breaking on the shore. The breeze had picked up in the past few minutes, and she was almost shivering now in her dress and woollen cardigan. She looked up to see clouds travelling to the west, growing darker and darker by the second as the feeble sunlight continued to be engulfed by the growing darkness.

"Excuse me," she heard a voice from behind her. She turned around to face a young man around her age. He didn't look older than twenty-two, twenty-four at most. He had short dark hair and sparkling blue eyes. He wore a rather shabby-looking jacket, dark trousers, and a pair of worn out shoes that had seen better days. His choice of clothes would have been unworthy of notice had it not been for a thick, rusty-brown scarf that was tied snugly around his neck.

He stood smiling at her rather awkwardly, his thin lips twitching and all the while, his eyes seemed to speak to her through their amazing sparkle.

She felt drawn to them as if they were sending out signals she was meant to interpret. He was nervous; she was sure of that. It was evident in the way he had dug both his hands in his pockets, looking a bit lost for words. And yet, the look in his eyes seemed quite confident.

"Yes?" she asked, mystified by his body language.

"Hello Miss, sorry to disturb," he finally said, rather unsurely.

"Yes?" She asked again after another awkward pause.

"Um, I was wondering if you could do me a favour..." His voice trailed off as he scratched his head.

Laura gave him an encouraging nod. "How can I help you?"

He still looked hesitant as he stood before her, shifting his weight from foot to foot but then, he finally spoke. "Well, I was wondering if you could pretend that we're friends."

Laura knitted her brows. "I don't understand."

"Could you offer me a handshake please? Or smile and give me a hug or something?" The half-smile he flashed her then, could also be perceived as a rather cheeky smirk.

"What?" she protested. "What on earth for?"

"You see that chap behind me, sitting on the bench?" He motioned with a slight movement of his head, shifting his eyes to one side. "No! Please don't stare! He mustn't suspect anything!" he pleaded, his blue eyes huge.

"Why not? Who is he?" she asked even more intrigued now, as she darted her eyes surreptitiously to the young man on the bench once more. He wasn't even looking, and she wondered what the fuss was all about. Silently, she thought the whole thing was rather amusing, but she wasn't going to show that to the dashing lad before her. Instead, she fixed him with a stern stare that demanded an instant explanation.

"Look, I'm sorry, all right? It's just that I made a bet with him that I could prove that we're friends. He sort of said you're too beautiful for the likes of me, and I wanted to prove him wrong; that's all!"

"So you told him a lie about me and now you want me to help you confirm it?" she asked, trying to sound stern despite aching to dissolve into laughter by then.

"In essence, yes!" he answered, giving her a smile that this time, could definitely pass for a cheeky smirk.

"But how does this benefit me?" she retorted with a naughty look in her eyes.

He cocked his eye at her, startled. "Excuse me?"

"What is there for me to gain from helping you out?"

"I'll buy you a drink if you like!" he offered immediately, and she wondered if that had been his goal from the start.

"No thanks!" she answered sternly.

Instead of speaking again, the boy regarded her silently in response with sorrowful eyes. It was a sad look of such intensity that the thought that crossed her mind then was that he was doing it on purpose. In the end, she gave in anyway. He surely was heaven. She had to admit it. And he seemed harmless enough.

She took a step toward him and offered her hand to him. He took it gratefully and to his surprise, totally unprompted, she reached up then and left a kiss on his cheek.

"Thanks! It's more than I hoped for," he whispered.

Laura chucked. "Now what?"

Without moving his head, the boy darted his eyes sideways in a comical way and spoke behind his teeth. "Is he still there?"

Laura tittered, but when she cast a glance at the bench behind him again, the smile on her face froze. The lad was no longer alone there. A young girl, barely older than sixteen, was sitting next to him now. They seemed lost in conversation together, oblivious to what was going on around them.

"You never spoke to that young man, did you? There is no bet, is there?" she put to him when realisation hit her. With her green eyes squinting at him, she placed a hand on her hip defensively, waiting, demanding the truth.

The boy smirked and gave a wink. "My dad always said, 'never lie to a beautiful girl, unless you're after her heart.' So I took my dad's advice. Is that so bad?" he asked mischievously, tilting his head, amused by the stunned expression on her face.

"Oh I see! So you were pretending to be nervous all this time. What an act! And for what?" she asked when she finally found her voice again.

He shrugged his shoulders. "I got a kiss on the cheek, didn't I?"

"And?"

"You make it sound so trivial."

"It is, isn't it?"

"Oh, I beg to differ Miss... Miss.... Sorry, I didn't quite catch your name."

"Huh! As if I'm going to tell you that! I'm not falling for another one of your tricks!" Laura turned around and started to walk away, but the spring in her step revealed that she was light-hearted.

"You're wrong though." His voice trailed behind her, and she turned to face him again.

"Wrong about what?" she demanded, her chin jutted out, her emerald eyes twinkling at him, her red hair flowing in the breeze, rendering him speechless for a few moments.

"That the kiss you gave me was trivial. A kiss from a pretty girl like you will keep me warm after you go, all through the night," he said with a grin and a hand over his heart.

"Why don't you get under a blanket to be sure," she teased him and turned away.

The echo of his laughter hung in the air between them as she strode off along the deck, her hand over her luscious, red lips, stifling her giggle.

Find it now on **Amazon US** or copy and paste this universal link in your browser to visit your local Amazon store: myBook.to/ladyofpier

Available in kindle and paperback format

Effrosyni Moschoudi

Table of Contents

Prologue 4
Chapter 1 6
Chapter 2 16
Chapter 3 35
Chapter 4 52
Chapter 5 62
Chapter 6 70
Chapter 7 80
Chapter 8 89
Chapter 9 103
Chapter 10 115
Chapter 11 131
Chapter 12 141
Chapter 13 153
Chapter 14 165
Chapter 15 171
Chapter 16 185
Chapter 17 189
Chapter 18 202
Chapter 19 220
Chapter 20 233
Chapter 21 244
Chapter 22 255
Chapter 23 262

Chapter 24	274
Chapter 25	283
Chapter 26	289
Chapter 27	295
Chapter 28	303
Chapter 29	313
Chapter 30	319
Chapter 31	333
Chapter 32	348
Chapter 33	357
Chapter 34	374
Acknowledgements	381
About the author	382
A note from Effrosyni	384
More from this author	386
Excerpt from The Lady of the Pier	389

Printed in Great Britain
by Amazon.co.uk, Ltd.,
Marston Gate.